Brevonni Man From Bama

Dena Eskridge & Cindy Eskridge

ACKNOWLEDGEMENTS

Dena Eskridge:

Thanks to my sister, Cindy, who encouraged and pulled me through all my doubts and fears to the completion of a dream, a real dream. Thanks to my husband for enjoying my sense of travel. Thanks to my mom for the love of reading. Thanks to my dad, who encouraged me to 'go'. Thanks to my children, and their families who continuously fill me with love and joy, and have tolerated my dragging them all over the world. I love you. Thank you, Ann, for being my dear friend and my first reader and for all the adventures that we have shared. I treasure all the friends and experiences of travel throughout my life. Finally, thank you Christopher Moyer for your endless talent and advice.

Cindy Eskridge:

Thanks to my sister, Dena, who has picked me up throughout my life. She has always been there. I love you, sister. Thanks to Mom and Dad who taught me how to work and live successfully. Mom, you kept me sensible. Dad, you taught me to go for it. All that is good in me is because of the two of you. Thanks to my family and extended family, you know who you are, I love you. To Chris Moyer, our editor, a special thank you for putting up with my Sister! You are a great person to work with! Thanks to the soldiers who deployed with me to Afghanistan. Your willingness to follow me is humbling beyond measure. It was an honor to be your Commander. To all, I love you, gotta go now, bye.

TABLE OF CONTENTS

Chapter One
TWO SISTERS TRAVEL, INC.

"Damn it, Daphne, I know that man is going to leave our antique shop and go to the beach, but I'll just have to deal with Mr. Magnus Bruce later. I wasn't going to miss this for his escapades at Pensacola. Not only did we need the family gathering, me and you have got to sit down and do our two year plan for the travel business. We've got to finalize this upcoming Italy trip and decide on our next destinations. And this is not going to take me long, and then I've got kids to play with. And maybe we can find some time to work on your yard. What is all this crap?"

"You're right, we do have work to do, a lot of work, and I am glad that you sacrificed your big weekend to come and help, but it's really the only time that we could find. So, just get off your high horse and let's get to it."

"Oh, sister, Mama-n-nem always said you were the bossy one, and you are. How your family puts up with you, heaven only knows. So, just to let you in on something, I've been practicing my bossing on Magnus and I'm getting pretty good at it myself, so you settle yourself down too and we'll get some work done. What comes first, the business or your trashy yard?"

"Business first," Daphne says, with meanness in her eyes. "You know we've always had a tendency to play before work, and right now we can't put it off any longer. All the travelers for the October Italy trip are confirmed with deposits, and we have to work out our usual details. We've got to book the rooms, reserve the rental van, and get Nino to work on the dining options. We have to finalize the itinerary and on and on, probably about a thousand other details."

"Okay Daphne, it sounds like you've got it done. Next. Can we go get in that redneck pool yet?"

"You've always been a lazy, good for nothing sister. Don't you get in that above ground, biodegradable pool right now. We still have more work to do."

I can barely hear her as I'm walking toward the pool with my around-the-waist duck float, flippers, mask, and snorkel. As I reach the top of the paint ladder, I am stopped in my flipper tracks. "Sister, were the kids here yesterday, because I see what is possibly a Recreational Water Incident (RWI) in the pool, or is that just a Baby Ruth that the kids didn't finish? I think we need to shock the shit out of this pool."

"Andi, how do you think I know if that is candy or a formed incident? You go on and get it out, and I'll get the shock. You know the drill." We have done our fair share of shit shocking around here. Everyone in town is always asking us how we keep those dark haired children so blonde, but it's our own little secret.

"That shit did not come out of me and I ain't touching it. They're your grandkids. No, fine, I'll get it. You know I love those kids to be handling their shit like this. You just go get the shock," Andi says as she starts removing her gear.

Pool thoroughly shocked and my snorkeling plans postponed, I think I'll go and mix up my Andi's Allligator-Ass-Whippin'-Obliteration Cocktail that has been my rock during troubled times such as this. It's a good thing that I remembered to bring my conglomeration of tropical rums and peach schnapps.

Shortly into my second round, here comes Sophie, my niece, in Pop's passed down '57 Chevy pick-up, in a cloud of dust. Her radio is blasting Colt Ford's "Chillin on a Dirt Road." It's a truck bed loaded down with four white-haired children yelling and screaming, "Let's go swimming." "Is my Aunt Andi here?" "Move outta my way, Chase, I'm getting out." "No, you move, I was getting out first because I called shotgun."

"Yeah, I'm here, but y'all better behave or I'll go get that fly-swatter. All you kids get in that pool and stir that shock up. Y'all go on and swim a bit while I finish my orange juice and then I'll be right in behind ya. I gotta get my battle rattle on again," Andi says with a sly grin, looking at Daphne.

High pitched squeals, fussing, and belly-flopping instantaneously transform a calm, over-chlorinated 24 foot by 12 foot by 52 inch pool into a boiling fury of storm erupting swells. Three boys are tormenting their little sister by splashing her face and not being still despite her urgent commands to do so. Welcome to summer!

"Darn, it if ain't hot as hades already," complains Sophie as she reaches for my full glass of orange concoction on the patio table.

"Whoa, hold up little girl," objects Andi, "that little glass of juice may be more than you're bargaining for."

"Hey, mama, where are you buying that juice? That's my brand from now on. Juice with a little kick, I like it," she says with a wink and knowing grin. "It must be yours, Aunt Andi."

"You know it. Now you be careful when the kids want some, make sure you pour theirs straight out of that labeled container in the fridge. But, if you prefer mine, I've got it mixed up in the half gallon pitcher with the black sharpie picture of a skull and crossbones," replies Andi.

"That's good to know, you two lushes, now I really need for us to get some work done, sister," shouts Daphne. "Now, can everyone just sit down and help me." With that said, she puts her nose to the grind and frantically starts typing little details into her laptop. With multiple windows open, the screen is flashing from hotels to history to Word documents. Fingers are flying and her brow is starting to sweat.

I stealthily tap Sophie's thigh under the table and motion with a slight nod toward the pool, and we quietly sneak away from Daphne as she is furiously at work. We lean on the pool, sipping my Triple A WO (Andi's Alligator Ass-Whippin' Obliteration). Daphne doesn't even know that we have left, she's so dedicated to her work.

My sister and I have different philosophies concerning our work ethic. I tend to allow things to happen and slowly respond to the direction which fate seems to send me. But not so for Daphne, nope, she needs to have all things plotted and planned and will drive herself crazy trying to control fate.

Oh, yeah, at this point, a few details are in order. Two sisters, living in Alabama, named Daphne and Andalusia might require just a small amount of explanation. You see, before we were born, our parents liked to travel in a van, although they deny being hippies or vagabonds. So, before we were born, they drove all over the state of Alabama. They decided that as they had children, they would name them after their favorite towns in this fine state. My sister Daphne Fairhope, the first-born, was labeled after the coastal communities – Daphne and Fairhope. Then I came along, Andalusia Eufala, aka 'Andi', for these historic Southern towns.

Though these names are a bit on the fringe, they are way better than our little brother's names. Warrior Tuscaloosa, aka 'Tusk', and Winston Demopolis complete our Alabama destinations. Of course Tusk, was destined to play football at 'Bama', and he did, not quite so successfully, but he'll always have that claim to fame; and in Alabama, believe me, that goes a long way. Winston D., as he goes by, is a high speed lawyer in Montgomery.

Now, back to the party. So, while she's hard at work, me and Sophie and the kids are hard at play in the pool. With boy bodies being tossed around in the pool, Chase jumps up and starts accusing his brothers of eating his candy bar yesterday. "I know you did, Robert. You ate it when I got out of the pool to pee. You owe me a candy bar." At that he starts toward Robert with menacing threat.

"Wait just a minute, boys," I yell. "Are you saying there was a candy bar near this pool yesterday?"

"Yeah, and somebody ate the rest of it," Chase complains.

"I didn't eat it," little Erich quietly responds. "I didn't think you wanted it anymore, you left it on the table. So when mom made us get in the truck yesterday, I threw it in the pool. I thought it would be funny for Gran to think we pooped in the pool. Did she find it this morning?" With that said, all the kids and their mama burst into hysterical laughter.

"Well, I'll be darned. Boys, your gran made me skim that chunk out of here while she put enough chlorine in this pool to turn my highlights green. We went through all that for a candy bar? Are you kidding me? I'm getting you now." I re-gear with the duck floatie, snorkel, mask, and fins and climb that ladder and go after me some boys. "It's on, assume your battle lines." I tell them. Uproarious laughter and a splashing frenzy erupt.

After I've given more than I can take, I shed the gear and hobble out of the pool, leaving them at a game of dodgeball with beanbags. Ouch, they can put a little sting on you. Sophie stays in the pool, offering some protection for little Jessica. A flurry of synchronized swimming moves off to the side of the pool.

With Daphne doing our work, I take the golf cart for a spin around her property. Daphne and Nino have about twenty acres here in Rock Holler, mostly pasture and weeds. A few years ago, the neighbor to her east passed on, leaving his forty acres to the local Botanical Group. Together with the Boy Scout and Girl Scout troops they transformed the property into gardens that can compete with Bellingrath in beauty and awe. It has become a popular site for weddings and other party events.

My casual golf cart tour takes me down toward The Gardens. Knowing that my sister's property is a stark demarcation line between beauty and ugly, they've foreseen a need for foliage blockade. The problem is that it hasn't grown quite tall enough to block the view just yet. The two-foot high privets don't impede my view of the gorgeous park, so I decide to sit awhile and appreciate the vista while I sip my juice.

A huge white tent is being raised, and tables, chairs, and linens are awaiting their placement. People are running to and fro, carrying flowers, small trees, and flapping lace fabric. Ladders support women attaching lights to the trees. Caterers are unloading lots and lots of stainless steel cookery from trucks.

I pull out the binoculars that my sister keeps here in the cart for bird watching. Oh, Lordy, I think the screaming little woman frantically running back and forth, correcting everyone's mistakes must be a bride. Poor little thing, she reminds me of Daphne. Look at her go. There is no way in hell that she can get control of all that chaos. Maybe I should take her some Triple A WO.

Just as I'm thinking of how I might offer assistance to her near nervous breakdown, she pulls out her own binoculars and focuses them in my direction. As our gazes meet, I flash her a little two-fingered wave and hold up my glass as an invitation to a much needed break. The gesture must have been too much for her because she slaps her forehead pretty hard, probably a skeeter, and then throws that left hand onto her hip and her binoculars move left and right as I swear I can see her exhale in disgust. I'm pretty sure I can hear her shout, "shit," "damn it," and "hell fire" as she turns in a tizzy. She almost runs to the nearest flunkie and starts pointing toward me.

No, it's not quite toward me. I think she's pointing to the three toilets sitting in the yard to my left. The man nods, and then she points to Nino's shed with all those red plastic oil and gas containers and the six big plastic trash bins that my sister can't seem to part with. I'm also certain that that plastic red, now faded to Tiddie Pink ten year old plastic swing and slide set is responsible for its share of her current pain. The man shakes his head in wonder, and he then points out all my sister's beautiful flower pots with a variety of weeds and trees growing out of them. I turn to give the yard a look over and can quickly understand their frustration. This property is a damn mess. I give them an understanding wave and leave them with their worries.

I ride back to the pool and deck, grateful that this portion of the redneck yard is out of their sight. I believe that bride would swoon here and now if she could see our above-the-ground pool party. I run to the kitchen for a juice refill and sit at the table with Daphne. "Are we done yet? I think we've worked long enough today," I exclaim as I lean back and put my feet up on an empty chair. She must have found this comment offensive, as she starts fussing at me.

"We? Are we done? You have some nerve. You haven't helped me do anything. You've just played. That's all you ever do. I think that I'm going to fire you. I'll change this business's name to The Only Sister That Ever Really Works Travel, Inc."

"Sister, don't get all riled up. I was just asking because I've been busy helping take care of your grandkids and solving all kinds of problems. The poop in the pool with Chase's left-over candy bar. I've discovered that there's apparently a big shindig at The Gardens today. I believe it's a wedding, and the bride appears none too happy that your porcelain cemetery is a backdrop to her event."

"Oh, My, God, Andi, we've got to get that mess cleaned up or we're in big trouble. Do you know who that is? It can only be Georgette and Theodore! Theodore Bankhead, one of Tallulah's relatives, I guess. Oh my word, Andi, they have booked our Italy trip for their delayed honeymoon. If they find out that their fancy, smancy travel agents live like this, it will be all over Facebook. Help me, hurry. Get the kids out of that pool. I'll get trash bags and we'll get everyone over there cleaning up. "

After three hitches, she obtains the necessary momentum to elevate herself from the chair. Then, at lightning speed, she rushes into her house, screen door slamming. With Daphne gathering bags, I laugh my way to the pool and insist that Sophie and the kids are urgently needed to clean up the yard. We make our way garden-side, with kids shouting and yelling and laughing like a bunch of banshees. Billowing, floppy, huge white garbage bags suddenly crest the hill. Daphne is running full force without realizing that the five air-filled trash bags are working as a parachute to slow her progress as she runs into the wind.

Breathing erratically, having run all the way from the house, she makes her way to a crowd of laughing, pointing kids. The two oldest boys are on the ground screaming and rolling like they've never seen a more hilarious spectacle. They don't know my sister like I do. They've got many more years to come having fun at their Gran's expense.

She finally catches her breath and yells at them, "Hush, boys, this is a quiet adventure. We have to pick all of this mess up, but no one can hear us. Now, stop laughing, stop it. Big boys, take your bags and throw everything you see in them. Chase, will you and Rob go and clean up that crazy bike ramp that you built with your Aunt Andi? How did she manage to build a ramp out of a bright pink plastic Barbie doll RV camper? Oh Lord, wait until your sister sees that mud all over her camper. Pick it up and put it in your bag, take all those sticks and that lumber and just dump it in the edge of the woods, OUR woods, don't go anywhere near that park, do you hear me?"

"Yeah Gran, we got it, what's wrong, why do we have to be quiet? You always tell us to go outside to be loud. We're out here and now we can't even talk," says Chase.

"No, you cannot talk, not now, I'll tell you later why this is a secret stealth mission."

"Erich, you come with me, bring your bag, and try to keep it from waving like that. No, hurry, just give me that bag," my sister says with that on the edge of a breakdown quiver in her voice. I can't believe the wind has got hold of that huge, innocent bag. It is now above his head, white and flapping.

With our five white, thirteen-gallon wind socks in perfect horizontal positions, indicating a strong gust from the west, the wedding tent itself is suddenly transformed into its own gigantic wind sock without an opening to ventilate the crosswinds. That tent is rocking and rolling over there, swaying in the rhythm of a polka. Gratefully, they're occupied with their own problems and don't notice our shenanigans up on this hill or that white bag that just blew out of Erich's hand going straight toward them.

Relieving poor little Erich of his crazed Granma, I take his hand and we quietly make our way to the shed. We move all the oilcans and the six huge garbage containers to the other side, out of sight. Together we pick up all sorts of scattered debris. Hell, it looks as if a tornado targeted the inside of her house and threw all kinds of shit in this yard. We've now got our bags weighed down with enough junk that at least they're not flapping so noisily anymore. I'm glad the big boys are out of sight with Daphne so that Erich and I can be quieter here alone.

We even picked up our Daddy's entire collection of rainbow, windmill blowing things that he has put all over the yard, having bought about fifty of them at the dollar store. He said he loved watching the rainbows twirl, and he has stuck them all over this hillside to get rid of Daphne's mole problem. Of course, he has no clue that the international symbol of gayness is the rainbow. The wedding planners down in The Gardens probably think this is the Lower Alabama Gay Headquarters.

It almost looks like a miniature mole-type obstacle course. Quiet, little distant cheering moles in the heat of competition come to mind. Erich has now got most of them in the bag. Now that I think about it, maybe it worked; I'm not sinking in mole holes. But then again, maybe he just got rid of the all the straight moles. After the wedding, I'll have to put them back or there will be hell to pay.

Having removed all the naked dolls, windmills, Barbie campers, teapots, oilcans and trash containers, it now looks pretty good. Daphne and Sophie loaded the toilets onto the golf cart, and they are gone. I finally had the chance to ask my sister why three toilets were in her yard.

Once she was able to breathe again following our frantic workout, she explained. "A few weeks ago, we had a toilet mishap and decided that we would change out those twenty-year-old toilets for newer, more energy efficient models. But, after two overweight, fifty-something year olds hauled and installed three toilets, the most we could do in cleanup was to carry the heavy commodes to the back yard. And there they have set. We thought about hauling them to the dump, but were waiting to pass that job on to Sophie and Roger.

"I knew last week that we had left them in the yard too long when I looked out the window and saw Chase relieving himself in one; thankfully he was just doing the pee pee part. Then later the same day, little Jessica mentioned that maybe we should plant some flowers in them. I just haven't had the time to get them out of here yet."

"That sounds like a perfectly good explanation to me," I tell my sister. "I think we're okay since only this hillside is in view of the wedding party. They shouldn't have a reason to walk up to the other side of the property." There is no way we have time to rid Daphne's entire property of all of her junk.

We all jump back in the pool, leaving the anxiety and worry to the stressed out little bride. Daphne has gone to fix us some lunch. It's about time, too; it's one-thirty and I'm starving. Pool play is in full force between me and the kids. Sophie is lounging in the lawn chaise, music cranked up and sipping her some more Triple A WO.

Suddenly the music stops, and Daphne is about to have her another damn fit. Apparently no one helped her make lunch, but with her ranting we know that it's time to eat. The pool spews out kids and an aunt as if it is vomiting. Running right past her, we head to the table. Man, can my sister make a spread. We have tomato sandwiches, banana and peanut butter sandwiches, and banana and mayonnaise sandwiches. There are peanut butter and jelly and bologna sandwiches too. A variety of chips and slices of watermelon await our consumption.

Grandma Lola's old washtub is filled with ice and interlaced with all types of colas.

Within three minutes, the table is near empty of that wonderful feast. Daphne approaches, in search of her bologna sandwich, which is now in the hands of Robert, half-consumed. Having settled for the last banana and peanut butter sandwich, she loads her plate with the last of the potato chip crumbs and grabs the last generic soda before she sits next to me on the deck steps.

"Thanks, sister, for all the help and for keeping everyone calm. You know how excited I get. At least it's all done. We've got the Italy trip finalized and the unplanned yard clean up went well. Now, we can just enjoy the weekend."

Pranks, play, and laughter filled the following two days. I'm really spent. Every fifty-year-old muscle that I have hurts. Those kids have stretched my physical limits, and they knew it too. My nephew and his family arrived after the clean-up, of course. He and his wife have two children, which added to the fun.

It's great to be able to enjoy all the excitement, knowing that I get to load up and leave it, retreating to my own peace and quiet. However, this family time is vital to me. As I've never married, I consider my sister's family as my own. Her kids are mine and her grandkids are mine, too. Nino – he's all hers.

However, throughout the entire weekend, there is a dark gray cloud of doubt and unformed concern far back in the crinkly folds deep in my brain. I quite prefer it remaining unformed, because as visions flicker, gloomy shadows of a huge man in danger and/or disaster flash through the optical centers of said brain. Right there between folds of gray matter, there is always a fear for that man.

Magnus Bruce, the magnificent brute, my longtime business partner and friend. He, my sister, and I own an upscale junk/antique store in Birmingham, aptly named, Chik Picks. My sister does most of the pickin' and we do the selling. After much argument, debate, and pouting, Magnus finally assured me that he would 'man' the shop while I visited my family. So, why do I feel so uneasy?

Chapter Two

MAGNUS BRUCE

What in the hell am I doing in this store? Its Memorial Day weekend, and I'm here working while Andi is living it up in the country. Her family outing, she says. Fine for her, but for me, this is a sacrifice that I'm not sure I can make. I need my outing, too. She shouldn't have put me in the position of playing hooky when I'm supposed to be working. Anybody in their right damn mind, especially her, knows that there was about a one hundred percent chance that I would at some point close the shop, lock that door, and leave for the beach. Sitting here in Chik Picks alone, babysitting this antique shop while all my friends are at Pensacola Pride, is not what I'd call fair. Damn her, she knew that.

Me and Andi go back a long way. I was in the same year group at the University with her brother, Tusk. We both played for 'the Bear' in his last national championship, 1979. We were rough and tough, big and bad, having some great times on and off the field. Back then, I was trying everything possible to deny who I really was. About ten years ago, I had to admit to myself that I am gay. It's been a journey; I've lost some of my closest relatives and friends. Some people just can't accept it. Many of my old teammates must have thought it contagious as they've forgotten ever knowing me. But, I was there. I know their secrets, too.

I have always known that I had a lot of style and class and could decorate better than anyone in my family, even if I am 6 foot five inches and weigh two hundred and forty pounds with nine percent body fat. My team locker was a testament to this fact. If there had been a 'Most

Beautiful Locker of the Month' contest, I would have kept that title for four years straight (or not)—or was it five years? Until then, I had always tried to be the big football star, dating the prettiest girls in school, living the expected life of a jock. However, through it all I have emerged a happy, secure man.

Andi and I are very close, in fact, she's my best friend and I'm sure that I am hers. I get along great with her crazy sister Daphne as well. She's been like my big sister for as long as I've known the family. She's more serious than Andi, but I know I can count on her for anything and consider her a trusted friend.

Now again, I have to ask myself: why am I sitting here at the cash register of an empty store on the Thursday before Memorial Day? Memorial Day weekend is the annual gathering of the hottest, gayest community in the world. The Redneck Riviera is quickly filling with thousands of men and women out to enjoy the beach, each other, and a universal acceptance.

So, who will know if I just flip the sign on the door to CLOSED, turn out the lights, lock the front door, and slip out the back? It feels right to me. I'm doing it. Oh, yeah, I'd better empty the cash drawer; I can lock it up in the glove compartment and drop it off at the bank on my way home.

Andi is not due back in town until Tuesday morning. She probably won't even call. When she's with her sister nothing in the world matters to them. They're like dynamite together. She will not give me or this shop a second thought. No one will ever know. After much thought, or maybe a full sixty seconds, I've decided what to do. I'm outta here. I'm certain that Andi will be clueless.

Oh, yeah, before I bolt, let me study that picture once more. I am really feeling that that book is right. If you picture it as though it has already happened, it will happen. And I know right now, I feel it, it's mine.

My rash decision quickly takes me on my fifteen minute drive home. Packing is a thoughtful detail, every possible scenario must be considered. I almost forgot my picnic basket of china, cutlery, and serving dishes. These travel with me everywhere, as I can't abide using rental property dishes. An hour has ticked along since my fateful decision as I lock up my home, secure for a few days. I toss a thoughtful kiss to Mrs. Carmichael, my friend and ghost, wishing her a peaceful few days without me, and then I'm out the door.

I stand fixed like a statute, admiring my new Infiniti IPL G convertible, Moonlight White, with stone leather interior. This purchase was the sole reason I succumbed to the pressure to model for that Bar-B-Que place in Tidal Town (oh contraire to many people's disappointment—I refused to model the pork sausage). Top down, shades up, this year it's solo for me. Rodney was so last year, on to better and brighter things. I do feel a bit—just a teeny, weeny bit—bad about deceiving Andi and closing up the shop, but hell, she'd do the same to me if given half a chance.

The gang and I have already reserved the condo. Everyone is planning on arriving tomorrow afternoon. I'd better call Henri at his real estate office and negotiate my way into arriving a day early. Dreading the call I'm about to make, I can't put it off any longer. The car is loaded, and I'm on the road already. Here goes; one ringy-dingy, two ringy-dingies.

"Henri here, is this my beautiful Brucie calling me?"

"Yeah Henri, it's Magnus, how the heck are ya?"

"I'm good, dear friend. I've got a surprise, and I hope you can help me," I tell him.

16

"How about that? You are asking for my help. You know that I would do anything, anything for you Magnus. What do you need?" He asks.

"Well, you know the crew is arriving tomorrow, and I was supposed to work all weekend. But, I've decided to skip work and come along, only a day early. I was wondering if I could check into the place late this afternoon. I'm already on the road, just passing through Calera. What do you say, Henri? Can you help me?"

"Hmmm, let me see. You are asking me to get you into the condo a day early. I know you are aware that everything within fifty miles is booked. I wonder what it is worth to you, Brucie?"

"Henri, don't you start making innuendos to me. You know that I consider you a friend, but nothing more. I'll tell you what. Get me in the condo this afternoon and I'll make you a nice dinner and we can go out for the night. How's that?" I ask.

"Well, if that is all I get, I guess that I'll gladly accept. I'll have your condo ready. The key will be in our regular hiding place. I'll see you around nine. Oh, yeah, and dinner had better be great!" Henri insists.

I can't believe that I had to promise that no-good, pretend queenie that I'd prepare dinner for him tonight. The weasel, I hope he chokes on the meal, but of course, he won't. Everyone knows what a great gourmet chef I am. I trained two years after my football days, and then worked for three years in one of finest Italian restaurants in Atlanta. I'd better stop in Montgomery where I can find a good market grocery, or else I'll never find all the ingredients I need in Pensacola.

I'll also plan a great meal for the arrival of our 'Greek Goddess Club' tomorrow. I'll make lots of appetizers that will stay fresh for hours. As they enter the door of the condo, no, even walking up the steps, they'll know that I'm there and in the kitchen. The aroma of fresh simmering vegetables and hot spicy sauces will greet them as they approach the walkway. Oh, my goodness, I'd better pick up a case or two of Italian wines. Okay, now I have to figure out how to load all of this in my hot little already-overloaded little sports car. Oh, forget it, once I unload the car in Pensacola, I'll just have to go shopping for food and wine.

Full of self-deserving righteousness, I try to convince myself that I need a day alone. I'll pay the piper by feeding Henri, and then we'll hit the town for a quick reconnaissance. Just as long as I'm home before four in the morning, everything will be fine. That will give me time for six hours sleep, up by ten, and then I'll start cooking for my friends. I haven't indulged myself for such a long time. What a surprise, the guys think that I'm stuck in Birmingham working all weekend.

Gee, probably the last spontaneous fun I had was when I went to Scotland with the girls. Wow, what memories. Andi and Daphne dabble with their little tour business, and they're planning trips all the time. And mind you, these are not the everyday, run of the mill type tour groups. It is always more than you bargain for.

Oh yeah, Scotland, hmmm. Men were everywhere wearing kilts. Gorgeous legs on every corner. That was a good trip. I'd always wanted to investigate my roots, and I did. One of my Bruce cousins went with us. She had done all the background research, and so once we arrived she had our fact-finding mission planned. *And* I bought a Bruce tartan kilt, made to fit, I might add. I was measured from head to toe so that everything was perfect. I'm still impressed with my awesome Highlander looks every time I put it on.

Once I got back, I joined the local Scottish Society and haven't missed a meeting yet. I go to a few clan gatherings a year and lots of Scottish events. My cousin, Kenna, has been a long time member and is wonderful networking me into the organization. She has even talked me into being her partner and taking Scottish Country Dance lessons. We've been at it for about a year, and I secretly love it. And I get to wear my kilt outfit, and I always look so damn good, the club can't even handle me.

This drive is long and can be boring, but as I know this lonesome two lane road like I know the back of my hand, I know the end is near. Finally, I can stop riding my clutch in this bumper to bumper traffic. It did seem faster than usual though, no doubt thanks to the great playlist Andi made for me. Little does she know how much enjoyment she added to my skipping work from her shop? She would just die, she would.

The key is right here where Henri said he'd leave it, under this beautiful palm. I'll unload the car and get to the market. It's six thirty and I don't care what Henri thinks he's having for dinner—he's getting what I have time to prepare. I'll just pick up some onions, tomatoes, salad greens, olive oil and bread, some pasta, and since Local Market has good tiramisu—he's having store bought dessert. He won't care by then; he'll have enough wine in him that he'll think I made it all. He's supposed to be here at nine-ish, we'll eat, and then we're outta here. He says he'll show me the best event planning party of the week. It's at eleven at The Trieste. I'll be ready!

Just as I am placing the Local Market tiramisu on the Victorian glass plate serving dish that I brought from the shop, Henri is gently knocking on the door. Why does he have to be such a girly man? Just knock, damn it. If I weren't expecting him, I'd think there was a baby kitten paw knocking on the door. Oh, I hope I get through dinner without offending him. He's not so bad really, but I like my men just a bit more virile than Henri. However, there is no one more in the know of the Pensacola scene than him. The evening will be fine, I'm sure.

"Henri, please come in." Kiss cheek, kiss other cheek. "I can't thank you enough for arranging the extra night for me. I hope you arrived ravenous; I've been cooking for a few hours. Let me pour you some wine."

"Let me feast my eyes on you, Magnus," said Henri. "The good Lord don't make 'em better than you. Mmm. Honey, why haven't you ever agreed to move down here and let me take care of you? I would set you up in whatever enterprise you want. Just as long as you let me look at you all day, I would take good care of you. And once all the other kids know you're here, they will have no illusions about winning the Wet T-Shirt contest or the Best Buns contest. There is no contest. I guess only the newbies will assume ignorant illusions until they see you."

"Henri, stop it. I love you dearly, but you know that I just consider you my sweet ole Troll. Heck, I could never belong to anyone but Andi. You know how she is. As far back as I can remember, regardless of the serious relationship at the time, she insists on my heart."

"All right then, let's feast on this delicious food you've been slaving over. What a slave you'd make. I've got to stop thinking like this. What have you made us?"

"Just some Spaghetti Carbonara, a salad, and Tiramisu. How's your wine? Sit, let's eat."

"This is terrific. I love it when you're here and I can get a home cooked meal," Henri sighed with a large mouthful of pasta. "What about these plates? Were these in the condo?"

"Ha," I said, "You know you don't furnish your rentals with this kind of elegance. I brought these from the store. My food can't be served on your cheap, truly made in China, china. I always insist that the presentation is as important as the food. Andi and I found this Victorian antique set at an Estate Sale. This basket just fits into my new car, so there you have it. I always bring my own dishes."

"I noticed that nice car with Birmingham tags," Henri said eyeing me in his Lady Di way. "Are you sure that you don't have another troll in tow?"

"No Henri, I finally agreed to do the BarBQue ad."

"Haven't they been after you for the last two years to do that full billboard ad?" muttered Henri.

"Yep, but only after I saw this new Infiniti model did I decide that I must have it, and the only way to get that kind of cash quick was to sign the contract for the ad."

"Nope, that's not the only way," he says with a sly grin.

I explained to Henri that I only agreed to a single one hour photo shoot and that I had complete authority over the finished ad. I am a good looking man, but I am not a slut, and will not allow my image to be portrayed in any possible light that is demeaning to me or my community. "It's a tasteful ad, Henri, so don't start with all the innuendos. I am shirtless, but hell, who wouldn't want to see this? And they paid me enough to put a huge chunk down on my new car."

"Well, Magnut—can I call you that?—how about you walk your shirtless self over to that coffee machine, make me a cappuccino, and let's dive into this tiramisu. Then, we'll get into that fine new ride and head—I mean drive—on over to The Trieste for the party?"

"No, you may not call me nut, nor touch mine. I reserve the endearments for those that are allowed to be touchy-touchy with me and my nuts. Now Henri, you've just got to know that I love you, but you will never be in that club. Go on and drink your coffee. How's the dessert?"

"It's good; I honestly don't think it's your best effort though. It's probably because you didn't have the time that you usually have for cooking, or perhaps our little local ingredients were not up to your standards. In, fact, it tastes a little familiar. I could be mistaken, but don't you worry, it's good enough for me. I'll wolf it right down, and then let's get this party started. I hear The Trieste will have the ice slide tonight; they've kept the sculpture a secret. I do have my suspicions, but we'll wait to see."

I make Henri drink wine while I clean up the dishes. I never, ever leave a dirty kitchen. Most cooks hate to clean, but once I got into buying and using wonderful dishes, I enjoy cleaning them and gently drying and returning them to their rightful place in the pantry. I love their feel; I turn them and hold them into the light while I dry them, admiring their translucency and reflection. I've always enjoyed cooking, but I enjoy my food best when it is placed with love on plates that have been cherished for years by people who valued them as I do. I am certain that my food tastes better on them. Even Local Market tiramisu is improved on my treasured plates.

Chapter Three

RECEPTION

We stroll out to the parking lot, just as the sun is setting on the beach behind my new car. What a beauty. I call her Irene! She is worth the pork jokes from my friends. Sunset with the roof down, listening to her purr, is a joy. Henri is quietly in awe, the result of the ambience and the wine, no less. He's not a bad guy, just about twenty years too old for me, and he will never be monogamous. He'll be a player till his last day on this earth. And frankly, as much as I enjoy the field, I feel that I am winding down and hope that I can find my one and only.

Before going to the resort, I insist on driving to the beach and staking our claim to the piece of sand that will be our domain during the next few days. Groups of people start arriving from all over the country and probably a few from abroad as well. They all head for the beach to proclaim a pristine twenty-foot by twenty-foot piece of sand. Tents go up and coolers and grills go down. Parties and events are non-stop for days. If you don't arrive early, you're left to the sands of suburbia and can only walk the beaches without your own homestead.

Even when you do arrive early, the beach fills up, and it can be difficult to locate your space among the many others. As there are hundreds of tents from waterfront to sea grass, unless you make your own tent stand out, you may never see it again. So, I decided to fly my Scottish standard high enough to spot it from half a mile away. Having accomplished the task, we drive over to the planning party.

Look at that resort, an island, surrounded by turquoise water! Golly, what I'd give to stay there for a month. I'm glad Henri wanted me to come with him tonight. What fun. "Henri, wow, I'm shocked. That is the most gorgeous resort I've ever seen. Look how the sun is so low, it looks like it is sitting on top of the water. The turquoise blue of the water looks almost like the Mediterranean Sea spectacularly reflecting the white sands. How can anything be this beautiful? Thanks so much for bringing me along tonight. I think I owe you another homemade meal or two. You're a great friend, really, thanks."

"Forget it, Magnus, it's my pride and pleasure to make an entrance by your side. I'll be the envy of them all. Let's start down by the pool, then we can work our way up to the balls room, as we call it. I've got to see the ice slide; it's been the talk of our town for months. Jacque (Jock ee, in costume) said it would blow me away."

I insist we take the path along the beach. There are glorious tents scattered like some nomadic clan reunion all around the island. There's coral and sea foam colored gauze fabric tent flaps billowing in the breeze. Simple and unstated elegance, these tents make a summer statement, for sure. There are two tiki lamps which softly silhouette the entrance. I grab my phone and start taking pictures as Henri pulls my sleeve.

"Give me just a few minutes, Henri, these are great ideas that I must incorporate in my store. I can just see it as a backdrop for my outdoor wrought iron furniture display."

We continue along the path, me delaying him long enough. He insists on getting to the pool. The soft night is soothing as he hurries me along. I'd much rather take my time and enjoy this wonderful landscaping. There are too many fine details for me to take in while hurried.

"Oh my Lord," Henri gasps, as we round the last corner before arriving at the pool. "I can't believe it! Who had the balls to order that? It's great. Furthermore, who had the balls to sculpt that?" Henri is glowing.

So much for our entrance together, he has hauled ass and left me standing here. In my day, I could sprint 40 meters in five seconds. Who would have thought that Henri at sixty something years old would blow, yeah blow, right past me? He is headed for the ice sculpture faster than lightning.

For the past several years, each Memorial Day is an effort to outdo and up do last year's events. The ice luge is an ingenious way to get a shot of booze. It is a large piece of ice with a small trench. The upper end is where someone pours a shot of liquor, while you wait at the lower end of the shoot with your mouth wide open, excitedly ready to receive your shot of ice cold wonder.

Now, in the past few years, I have seen this sculpture worked in the shape of a high heeled shoe and a wavy super slide, but I can't even imagine what Henri has seen to be running and squealing like he is right now. As I round the corner, nothing could have prepared me for this. Oh, my God, leave it up to a bunch of crazy gay men to have contracted this piece of work.

Before my eyes, raised high on a platform of white foamy plaster, is an enormous expanded lipstick tube. Unbelievably, it appears to slant at the angle used to apply lipstick. The tube is painted a luminous gold with a perhaps one foot length of the brightest, reddest lipstick that I've ever seen. This iced lipstick case is about five feet long—is that big enough for a bunch of queens? And, just look at Henri, pushing his way through a crowd of men to line up for the first shot. Good thing everyone here knows him and caters to his money. There it goes, he gets the first shot. What a sight that is.

Before I get wild and crazy myself, my mind drifts back to my plan for Florence. As soon as I get back to

Birmingham, I must confirm my plans with Jackson Bergman. He's a guy that I went to high school with, and we're working on a project. I've got to have that project complete by the end of September for our trip to Italy in October.

Chapter Four
AT THE BEACH

Whew, last night was just a little blurry. Henri, a huge frozen lipstick, laughter and disco music: it seems like those crazy puzzle pieces that don't fit. Glimpses of memories flit around in my achy head. I can't connect a coherent sequence. Surely, I didn't do anything more foolish that anyone else. My phone is screaming at me, probably just my alarm, let it be. I'll just relax a bit longer. No one is set to arrive until around one. I'm sure it's just nine or ten. A little more sleep, then I'll get up and cook for the guys.

The phone is now ringing, not the alarm. What in the hell is going on? Who would be calling me now? In Bama country, there are universal rules of etiquette. One doesn't call to chat during the game or when one is at the Redneck Riviera. I'm turning it off, not even looking at the caller ID. I need just a little more snoozing, please.

What? Is that someone beating on my head or the wall next to my head? Really, what is wrong with the world? That isn't a voice; that is screaming. Is the building on fire? WTF? I'm up and moving now, running through the condo in my briefs, God, are these my briefs? I don't recall ever seeing grown-up men's Incredible Hulk underwear in my chest at home. Who cares, the fire and my pending demise are much more important than underwear. I sniff, but I don't think I smell smoke.

The pounding and yelling is not stopping. I run from room to room with a big green monster on my precious package. Frantic, out the door I go. Now I am screaming too, but I don't know why. I just know that something terrible must be happening to the world around me.

God, it's so bright, a giant fire, obviously, just in front of me. Oh, no, I feel the earth falling beneath me. Damn, it's an earthquake, with an erupting inferno obviously as a result of a seismic cracking. Gas lines I quickly guess. Oh, no, I never wanted to die like this, and certainly not in these undies. I feel myself tumbling, tumbling, with deafening screams and shouts all around me. The whole world is ending.

As my momentum slows and all becomes still, I realize that the sky must be falling. That, or else it is a large, dooming shadow over me. The building must be falling on me. I must not have, certainly I fell clear of it, here it comes. Someone is screaming like they're dying. It must be a woman or child near me. Oh, no, I'm filled with a tremendous foreshadowing of sorrow for the poor thing, helpless as it must be and so filled with terror at the moment of death.

But wait, there's noise coming out of my mouth, it sounds a bit like a girl—oh, it is me screaming like a little girl. I hope no one knows that this high-pitched scream of death is coming from a six foot, five inch, two hundred and forty pound man.

The shadow is nearing me. I'm doomed as it's just in front of my face. Then, I hear laughter, giggling, yelling, and I think I see pointing fingers and hear phone cameras clicking. What is going on? I hear my friend Kevin's voice. Is that what they mean when you see your friends just before you're dying? But no, I don't quite feel like I'm dying. In fact, I feel like I'm coming back to life after sleeping for a hundred years.

Kevin, yeah, it's Kevin, and he's laughing hard and saying things like, "Is everybody seeing this? Giant Magnus, crying like a girl. He is a crying little girl wearing the biggest, ugliest Incredible Hulk underwear that I've ever seen. I bet during special circumstances, that Hulk becomes pretty incredible, busting right out of that little tiny underwear. Did you guys get that on video? Did you see him fly out of that condo and fall down those stairs in the full noon sun, landing here on the grass at our feet? That is the funniest thing I've ever seen in my life. We'd better have this recorded guys, I hope to God one of you got this, no one will ever believe it!"

I hear an echo of Sammy laughing and saying that he got every bit of it. "In fact, it's on You Tube right now."

Oh God, what have I done? It's all coming back to me now. The bright fire must have been the sun. The phone wasn't alarming; hell, I didn't even set the alarm. It must have been the guys calling me. The pounding and screaming must have been the guys banging on the wall at my bedroom. They must have arrived early. No, it's noon or after. I've overslept.

As I try to stand, without help or assistance from guys who used to be my friends, I fall to my knees. Really, how can they help when they're laughing like that? I see Randy, running inside and holding his front like he's about to pee. Okay, enough already, it cannot possibly be that funny. If they worked for me, I'd fire them. Once my head stops hurting, I'll decide if they will remain my friends.

We all finally make it back up the three steps and inside the condo. Only three steps. I'm a little stunned. It felt like I tumbled twenty feet. I've got sand all over me, even in these stupid Hulk briefs. Where the hell did I get these and why am I wearing them? At least the guys quit laughing long enough to help me. All right, it might have been a little funny, and I guess I'll keep them as friends.

"Sorry guys, I didn't mean to sleep all day. Henri and I went out to The Trieste party last night. I don't know when or even how I got home and where this awful underwear came from. I meant to be home by three or four AM and sleep for a few hours, then wake up and cook for you guys before you arrived. Hey, where is my car? Did you guys see my new ride out there?"

"Yeah, it's there," said Kevin, "that's how we knew that you were here and that we were locked out. We called Henri, and he said that you arrived yesterday and had the keys. He even told us that you were probably sleeping. He said that he had a couple of his friends bring you home last night, as you were not in any condition to drive. What were you doing? As much fun as you might have had, that's not as important as the fun we've planned for the weekend. We've got the beach bash at two o'clock, so you'd better get yourself awake and ready to go again. I'm planning on cruisin' the beach highway in your new car. Sammy and the Randy will have to drive this damn Camry. I'm making my first impression getting out of your car. So, come on, I'll make you some strong espresso. Step lively, young man, let's get going."

Kevin and I don't leave the condo until three. The others have gone on ahead with plans to find our spot on the beach. I told them that I'd placed the tent and the Scottish standard is flying, so they can more easily locate it. They have all the supplies, as my cargo space is quite limited, especially with the hardtop stowed in the small trunk. So, it's just Kevin and me, with Kevin driving my new car, as the light is still a bit too bright for me to open my eyes fully. So much for making my entrance driving this beautiful machine—it's all Kevin's honor now. And, really, I'm grateful to him, otherwise, I'd have to crawl my big body to the middle of the back seat of a rusty old Camry.

This is horrendous. Cars and cars line both sides of the hot black asphalt with no parking spaces seen for miles. We turn around and head back along the road with the beach to my left. I see tents, white tents, beige tents, more white tents, a crazy rainbow tent, tents ten deep all the way to the waterfront. But, I do not see my chalk white tent with my blue St. Andrews cross waving in the warm gulf breezes. Oh, wait, I think I see it there. Now, let's just park. Oh yeah, we can't.

As we pass our tent, I turn back to keep my eye on it, so we can walk right to it once we park. Kevin just keeps going, slowly, slowly. Eventually, I lose sight of the now tiny blue flag. Onward we drive. And drive. Maybe a mile past our tent, heading back toward the condo, Kevin lets out a "woohoo" as I see a large SUV pulling out. Kevin saw and is patiently riding the clutch, waiting on it.

"We got it," he yells. I'm just grateful to be able to park, but I'm wondering how in the heck he expects me to walk a mile down the beach to our tent. He's phoning the others. They are in the tent and have hot brats and the shrimp boiler ready for sunset, the beers are iced, and they have the bar set up with the mixers and all. The chips and dips are ready. They say they gave up waiting for us and have already met some guys from New York and Idaho. Now, who would think family from Idaho would show up?

Thankfully, we sent all the gear ahead with the other guys and have nothing to carry. I've left nothing in my car that would attract thieves. I make sure that Kevin has the keys, and we now attempt to cross the highway. Here we go again. The endless stream of slow-moving traffic trying to park hinders our crossing. At least they can't go too fast, it's like a parade out here. Every car or truck is full to capacity with guys and dolls. Cars full of guys and trucks full of girls.

There's what I think may be a 1972 silver convertible Impala, with a quilt on the back end, and perched atop is a drag queen wearing a banner reading

"Homecoming Queen" across his chest. He's waving like a professional parade champion. I notice that the tag is Alabama with a 67 county assignment. That is great! I know that county. Probably his sister's real homecoming queen banner. Everyone is yelling and waving at him as he smiles like a teenage girl that just scored a date with the captain of the football team. Yep, it brings back memories for me.

We finally get a break and can cross two lanes of slow moving traffic, all in search of a place to park and hurriedly head to the beach for the real fun. However, I have to admit, after all the years I've been coming down here, I've never had a chance to experience the parade of cars in search of the cherished vacant spot in which to park.

Now we slowly have to work our way between, through and around tents in our one-mile trek, in deep sand, to our own little beach home. At least everyone— and I mean *everyone*—is cordial. We've only managed a hundred yards, and we each have a drink in hand. Kevin's got a Coors and I have a glass of red wine. We've also had to refuse offers of food three times already. And 'we've miles to go before we sleep,' as Robert Frost might put it.

This is quite an experience. I'm collecting lots of ideas to improve our own tenting arrangement. Some of these folks, probably the New York ones, have quite a set up. They seem to have transported all the swankiness of their home lives in the big city to right here on our Riviera. I've met several groups of good people.

I run into a tent of guys from T-town who recognize me from the new ad on the billboard. They say they've put it up on the corner of Paul Bryant and University. I'll have to find a hat to hide behind; I can't keep explaining that ad to everyone I meet. I need some kind of disguise. Give 'em all a few hours of drink and they won't know me from Sam. I wonder if Sam is coming.

Onward we march. It's been forty-five minutes and I can just see Old Scotland flapping atop a tent about a hundred feet ahead. We must first master the gauntlet ahead of us. There are still about five rows of tents between here and home base. I think it will be easier to go right to the water and wade our way ahead for the last leg of this endeavor. We finally make it. As I approach our humble tent, my skin feels a little tight and warm. It's probably all that drinking last night. I need water. No more booze for me for six hours. Water and rest, that's what the doctor ordered.

The guys don't notice us approaching. They're talking to the girls in the tent next door, and they are all talking to the guys in the tent behind us. Kevin walks towards them, asking for another brewsky, and I stumble to the nearest lounge reclining in the shadows at the edge of the tent. I grab a bottle of water and decide that I must lie down for a while. I hear their voices behind me and to the left. I hear laughter and yelling, hooting and hollering, something about You Tube and the Hulk, voices softly fading as I fall off to sleep.

I awaken with more cell camera clicking and video cameras in my face. Everyone is laughing and pointing, and even strangers, probably from Nebraska, are bent double as they laugh at me. I rise up, looking at my watch. It's eight o'clock in the evening. I feel much better, at least. Maybe I can figure out why I'm the butt and bollocks of their jokes again.

I notice that my left wrist is a little tender as I look at my watch. The skin feels tighter and redder than I remember. I don't think it was that red when I went to sleep in this lounge chair. I notice my left leg is quite red as well. I glance to my right leg; it looks fine, as does my right arm. I check out my great well-muscled chest. It appears to have a distinctive line between red and white. And there appears to be a little drawing of a twig and berries on my left pectoral muscle.

What the hell? Did those guys draw on me? What is this, a fifth grade camp out? The shadow of the tent must have faded into bright sunlight as it passed over my left side. The sun must have fully set before it could reach my right side. So, now I look like a half fried crispy big hunk of a hillbilly. Oh, well, maybe everyone will be too drunk to notice. I'll get a hat and some stupid looking clothes and no will recognize me.

Sammy now runs up to me, wanting to show me the new video of the half lobster, half he-man sleeping in the lounge chair. He says of course it's also posted on You Tube. "You've made our tent famous," he says as he falls down laughing. "You are a hit. Everyone has connected this snippet to your Hulky condo exit. And then, there are some local T-town guys down the beach that followed you here. They are telling everyone that the Hulk is also the Hunky Pork Sausage on the billboard in Tuscaloosa. They forwarded me the picture of the BarBQue ad. I'm working on making a full production of how a gorgeous man like you can be such a fun loving redneck. It will be great, you will see." He is now laughing and running to the tent revival behind us, caressing his phone like it's a jewel.

"I am going to kill that sum-bitch." Just as soon as I can get my blistered-ass left leg to move fast enough. But, now that I think about it, I'd better go find somewhere to buy some stupid looking clothes and hats/caps to hide behind. A good disguise is essential at this point.

Let me just wash off this stupid ten-year-old drawing from my chest. As much as I dread putting this alcohol-based sanitizer to my burnt skin, I'd rather be rid of another identifying marker. So, alone in my tent, I endure the pain of the ink removal. As I didn't wear a shirt to the tent, I must go find one. I'll just grab one of Randy's t-shirts until I can buy one. I'll take his faded green one that he left on the chair. It's on, but man, is it tight. Come to think of it, none of my friends are my size. This shirt must be four sizes too small. But what the hell choice do I have? I can't be walking around with my chest half burned and half white.

With my wallet still secure in my shorts, I slip into my flops for the hike to buy some things. Damn, if that left foot don't hurt with those straps rubbing on the burned skin. I should buy some aloe gel while I'm out shopping.

Fortunately, I make my way down the half-mile of sand to the nearest surf shop. Thankfully, no one glances at me twice. I get some amazing offers through my hike out of tent city. I have to say no to all of them, thanks to my 'fried like a lobster' condition. I do accept about three bottles of water. Now, I've got to piss like my bladder-impaired grandma. This must be how Daphne feels; she's always having a continence kind of problem. I'll have to hold it until I get to the water.

I find an ugly t-shirt, as the most attractive styles are very limited in my size. I buy a large straw hat and a baseball cap with an extra-large visor to shield my face. I wanted some more sandals or flip-flops but they don't have my size.

About twenty feet back into the tents, I notice some stares. No one says anything, so I really don't think they recognize me. Then, I hear someone say "he does look like the Hulk, and he's even wearing that tight green t-shirt. I hope he busts right out of it in front of us." Hell, they must be talking about me.

Picking up my pace, I realize that I have to change shirts right here, right now. This green Hulk shirt has to go. It's drawing attention to me. I open the bag to find the shirt, which is light blue, not green, thank goodness. I never thought about how important color choice can be while on the beach as a Hulk impostor. As I'm looking in the bag for my new shirt, I almost trip on a crowd of people along a staged up boardwalk. I hear a man on the loudspeaker shout, "look at that, would you? Hit him, Tommy."

Before I can blink, I am hit with a water cannon directly on my chest. I wonder what in the hell is going on. Just then the megaphoned man starts up again with his excited yell of "now that, my boys, is our winner." Sudden reality dawns on me like the rising sun. I've meandered right into the Fifth Annual Wet T-shirt Contest. Damn it, damn it, damn it. I really did want to enter this contest, but not in this fashion. After all the crazy fodder I've given my friends to malign my character on YouTube, the last thing I need is more crazy publicity. Right now, all I want is anonymity, not attention.

Now I am in full retreat, nearly encircled by a mob of full-grown boys in hot pursuit. On any other day in my life, I could easily outrun them and cherish the chase. But I realize that never before in my life have I been half fried with a left foot rubbed to a nub by some cheap ass flip-flop and inner thighs chafing holes in my skin thanks to the wetting down I just received. Now, right now, I've got to lose them and change this damned shirt.

I quickly whip out the blue one while simultaneously removing the green one. Oh, the shirt was *way* too little when I put it on, but sopping wet, it is not coming off with one hand. I stick my shopping bag and my new t-shirt between my legs and try with both hands to get the shirt off. At this very moment, near the shoreline, my flip-flop has busted the blister on my foot, and I stumble due to the instant stabbing pain on the top of my left foot.

I had just managed to get the shirt off of my chest, and it is now stuck on my face. The neck hole is not big enough for my huge head. Down to the sand I fall, and with the tight green shirt covering my face I can't see a thing. The blue shirt and my purchases fall to the water just in front of me. I know that it's in the water because my fall has splashed salty water onto my sunburned skin. I yell in pain, unable to see a thing with this shirt stuck on my face and head. I'm exposed from the neck down. At least nobody can see who I am. As I'm flopping around like a beached whale or possibly a giant squid, I again hear cameras clicking. Shit, I want to go home. I just want to disappear. How could anyone know it's me? I know I have a nice torso, but so do a lot of guys here. How can I be recognized by a torso?

"It's him, it's him, it is Magnus Bruce." I hear the chatter all around me as I'm still trying to get upright to remove the shirt. Impossible, I think, this is not happening to me. "Look," I hear someone say, "he's got the twig and berries and half-sunburned body. It's him, just like the video on YouTube."

Twig and berries? I endured severe—okay, not severe but mild—pain to remove that ink. I saw the ink on the cloth. It's not on me. Just then a hand reaches to help me stand. I reach up with both hands and pull on the shirt that is squeezing my head like a vise. The unknown hands grab the shirt, and someone advises me to pull my head out while he pulls the shirt forward.

This is working, I think, because as I'm backing out with all the power that my massive legs and back can muster I feel my head breaking free. Suddenly my huge head pops free of that tiny shirt. Losing my momentum, I stumble backward again. I am on my way down when more hands catch me. At this point, I'm feeling a little dizzy and disoriented from obvious oxygen deprivation with a shirt squeezing my head like a boa constrictor.

When my eyes finally adjust from the lack of oxygen to my brain, I notice a crowd of people. Girls, guys, young and old, black, white, yellow and red skin surrounds me. A lot of red skin, I might add. At least I'm not alone with the lobster appearance. Once recovered to my full height, I'm looking down on the balding, blistered head of a man standing approximately five foot two. He takes my hand and introduces himself.

"Hello, I'm Brad Armstrong. You must be Magnus," the short little stranger says.

"Good to meet you Mr. Armstrong, but might I ask how you know me?" I inquire.

"I'm glad to say that your physique is quite recognizable, even without your gorgeous face and smile," he continues. "You are instantaneously famous, lucky for me. A fortunate confirmation that it was you is your now signature tanning tattoo on your chest."

I look down, not quite sure what he is talking about. I'd removed that drawing before I left my tent. To my surprise, I now see a pink twig and berries on a bright red background. The black sharpie must have blocked the sun. Great, now I have a semi-permanent child's drawing of male genitalia on my chest. It's a good thing that I already did the shoot for the BarBQue ad.

"I was planning on coming by your tent and talking with you later on. Lucky for me you stumbled near my tent," he says with an amicable smile.

"How do you know me and how could you have found my tent among these several hundred? And who are you and why would you be interested in hunting me down?" I ask with a bit of concern.

"Don't worry, he quickly adds, "you're safe. I'm not interested in hunting you, I'm interested in a business opportunity for both of us. And, thanks to the uploaded post, everyone here knows how to find you. Let me show you."

Mr. Armstrong walks me a few feet to his tent and offers me a chair and some sparkling champagne. This is a really plush chair and expensive champagne. All we have at my tent are white plastic stackable chairs that you buy from Fred's or Walmart. He pulls out his iPad and pulls up the post.

It starts out pretty good, though I don't understand the title, 'Kraken the Brute,' then a still shot of me on the billboard. I have to admit, that is a damn good picture. But then it goes south real quick. Sure enough, there I am, a near naked disheveled heap opening the door and falling down the stairs of our condo. I'm whimpering and crying like a baby, then let out squeals of little girl type terror. As I fall, rolling in the sand and grass, I suddenly go still and he zooms onto my cock area with full focus on the Incredible Hulk underwear, with the Hulk doing his best angry Mr. Universe pose. The character is on the verge of going berserk, with his shirt ripping to shreds as his body is erupting from his regular man size clothes. Then the camera fades back to my full frame as I lie there looking scared and talking about a fire and earthquake. The shot pans around, proving there is no natural catastrophe occurring, then back to me whimpering. It continues through my recognition of friends and cussing them as they have to help me up. It closes with three guys assisting me up the steps into the condo. Then another quick shot of the BarBQue ad. "Damn those guys," I quietly say. Well, at least they chose a powerful reference to the titan, Kraken, as my call sign.

"Hold on, Mr. Bruce, there's more," he says. The shot then fades to soft white sand, then a plastic lounge chair with a huge long body lying on it. The chair is not long enough for the body, as the zoom is starting at the lower part of the body, and one can see the knees flexed at the end of the chair and feet resting on the sand. The shot starts at the feet, where you can see a red left foot and white right foot. It continues in that color scheme up the legs, past khaki shorts to the torso, again half red, half white, to the chest and the obscene drawing, and then the camera focuses on my face. I'm asleep, with only my left ear fried crispy. There is drool running a haphazard stream from the left side of my mouth, down my neck, then just hitting the drawing and anatomically coming out of the twig. How could they be so juvenile?

Yep, I realize these are now my ex-friends. Then the person filming, I know it must be Sammy, backs out of the tent, still filming, and focuses on the flagpole in the sand, and carries the view to the top of the pole focusing on the waving St. Andrews flag. He then pans around to the tents right and left, then to the shoreline. Finally, the video closes again with the ad shot. Damn, I'm doomed. I'll not be strutting around this weekend. I'll have to hide the entire time. I close my eyes in shame, suddenly overcome by the comfort of this relaxing, cushy, soft lounge chair and bubbly. Oh, God, I'm falling asleep again.

A few hours later, I awaken in his heavenly lounge chair. As I stir, Mr. Armleg—no, it was Armstrong—walks over. "You're not much of a drinker, are you, Mr. Bruce? You only had one glass of champagne and you were out. I made the crowd leave, knowing you must need the rest the way you fell asleep so easily. I've got your purchases here. Everything is fine, don't worry, you are safe here. It's to my advantage at this point to protect you from yourself and this crowd.

"Let me explain an idea that I've had since the guys in the tent next door from New Jersey showed me the video that is on fire around here. You see, I work in New York as an advertising executive. My largest client is a leading men's fashion magazine. When I saw the picture of you modeling the sausage, so they say, I knew you had star quality.

I currently have a contract with the famous Italian menswear designer, Riccardo Brevonni. We are preparing his fall line campaign featuring a mature, handsome man in the peak of his career, with all the confidence that age acquires. I have been searching for the perfect model to launch as the next Brevonni man, and I think he will approve of you. You have just enough gray and yet are still in top shape. Time is of the essence; I've waited for as long as possible, refusing to settle for less than perfect. I've decided you are my Brevonni man. Do you have an agent?"

"Whoa, what? Are you shittin' me, Brevonni? I own one of his dress shirts. That's all I could afford. His suits are the best. *So* nice. I'd love to own one of his classic suits, but now you are asking me if I'd like to *be* the Brevonni man? I can't imagine that. Do I get to keep the clothes? This is too much, unbelievable. Give me the clothes, I'm ready."

"Hold on, Mr. Bruce, we have several details to work through. But as I said, I do need to hurry things along. Let me ask you some questions. Would you be free in about two weeks?" Mr. Armstrong asks.

"I think that I can be. I'll have to clear it with my associate," I say, trying not to sound so damn happy.

"OK," he says, "then what about an agent? Are you under contract with someone?"

"No sir, I handled the BarBQue work myself," I tell him. He then asks if I have a compensation plan. I tell him, "No, I don't have a lot of experience modeling; I'm not sure what the going rate is."

"We'll work that out," he says, "I would love to be your agent if you would like. You're welcome to shop around. You will need to find a lawyer with publicity experience, and then just send me his info. I'll prepare a contract and send it for his review. What do you think of that?" he offers with a knowing smile.

He assures me that he will treat me fairly and encourages me to check his clients and fellow agents to be certain that I am confident with the package that he prepares. He says I'll have to report to his offices in New York for the photo shoot. He gives me his card and encourages me to quickly find an attorney to represent me before I sign the contract.

We agree to try to meet up again while here at the beach for just a social visit. He says he will find my tent by looking for the Scottish Flag. He also mentions that if the Italian design job works out, he is going to check with some Scottish designers as well as the Scotland Tourism Board about some kilt and sweater shoots for me. He says that he sees me in formal and informal kilt poses with some Scottish cattle on a heather filled burn. I might really like this job, if it is not all just a dream.

Fully disguised in a XX Large blue t-shirt and straw hat, and carrying the dat-burned flip-flops, I finally find my way back to our little patch of ground. The guys are scattered throughout the area, and there is a large group of people with Randy at our tent. The party seems in full force now.

The evening and activities seem endless. We eat and drink from tent to tent for the next several hours. I meet a lot of new people, as I have become the most famous idiot at the beach thanks to Sammy, but hey, it might have landed me the biggest job of my life.

By two AM, I've finally had all I can take. I am totally exhausted and ready to retreat to the condo and get some sleep. I locate the guys one by one to see if they are ready to ride back with me. Everyone but Kevin is still partying and not interested in turning in. I stopped drinking after my champagne with Mr. Armstrong. Kevin is not a big drinker either. I like to think that maybe we are just wiser than the rest of them, but probably not. We're just old and tired. We grab two bottles of water and start the walk back to the car.

As we walk along, I notice small crowds clustered around several parked cars. I don't think a lot about it, assuming that they are at their own vehicles. After walking for about fifteen minutes we approach my car, and I notice three guys standing by my passenger door. When we are about twenty feet from the car, they see us and run. At first I wasn't alarmed, knowing that I had left nothing in the car of any value. I figure they were just admiring my great car.

As we arrive at the car, I give it a quick look over. Nothing seems out of place. Kevin asks if he can drive again, and I tell him sure. I am a little relieved that I don't have to shift gears with crispy fried legs and chaffed thighs. I'm content to sit in the passenger seat and be thankful that someone is driving me home.

As soon as we start down the highway, I recline the seat and close my eyes. No sooner have they closed than I remember the shop's cash bag which I've left in the glove compartment. I jump up and open the box. Insurance papers, owner manual, an ink pen, and of course some personal essentials are all in place, untouched. But there's no cash bag.

Oh, shit, what have I done? Andi is going to kill me. Did I even count it? Let me think, there was a twenty-five hundred dollar check, three hundred dollar bills, about eight twenties and maybe a hundred dollars in miscellaneous bills. I've just lost about thirty-two hundred dollars of Chik Pik's money.

I check everything in there again. I pull everything out and look again. No cash bag. I look under the seat, no cash bag. How could I have forgotten that I put it there? I didn't even lock it. What will I do? I can't tell Andi. She thinks I'm working all weekend. If I tell her what happened, not only will she think I'm irresponsible, she will know that I played hooky. I can replace the money with my own. I'd hate to part with thirty-two hundred dollars, but I'd rather give her my money than her know that I left work about four days earlier than we planned. That's what I'll do. Damn it, I have to start thinking better about my work and thinking less about my play.

With that problem settled, Kevin and I arrive at the condo and go our separate ways. I'm glad the others are not here. It's nice and quiet as we head to our rooms. I throw off my clothes and gently try to find comfort in my bed. With my skin so sensitive, it is hard to relax. I am nearly asleep as my day's mishaps and YouTube postings flash before me over and over. Be still my brain and just sleep. Let it go, I can't change a single moment, it's over, I must live with it.

What a wonderful morning. I feel rested and alive again. Today is a new day. The house is quiet, probably because it is only six o'clock. Kevin is still sleeping, and I haven't heard from the other guys. I take my coffee to the porch and enjoy the solitude. Waves rise with crescendo and then crash heavily onto the crystal white sand. The seagulls squawk as they compete for early morning finds.

I intend to have a very low-key day today. I'll call my bank and check on getting cash transferred to replace the lost money from the shop. I've got to think about the proposed contract by Mr. Armstrong. I've agreed to meet with him for brunch at eleven at The Triese. I'll make some calls and ask our shop's attorney in Birmingham for his advice. Then I'll go by the beach for a few hours, watching the madness, though I refuse to partake. I'm meeting Henri for dinner at a hole in the wall place that only locals frequent.

Tomorrow is another story. I plan to party hard until about four in the afternoon, and then I'll come back here to the condo to recover. With a restful night's sleep tomorrow night, I'll pack up and get back to Birmingham Monday morning.

I don't know when Andi is coming back home from her sister's house, but I want to surprise her with a nice dinner and tell her about my surprise modeling proposal. I'm really psyched about the chance to work in New York and wear those fabulous clothes. Mr. Armstrong said that the clothes would be mine to keep as they will be altered to fit. I'm as excited about the clothes as I am the modeling work.

I devote the next several hours to business. I've made my calls, and the bank has agreed to transfer my money into the store account. I feel better now that I've replaced Andi's money which I lost through my irresponsibility. My financial cost is painful because I try to be careful with my money. But, at least I've got a possibility of making a lot of money with the modeling contract. My friends will just die, they won't believe it. Heck, I don't believe it. I think I've got the legal details worked out too. I've talked to my attorney and have an appointment on Wednesday.

After a refreshing shower I feel alert and ready to meet Mr. Armstrong for brunch. It's a good thing that I brought a more formal outfit along. Like I always say, you just never know what event will present itself on a whim. I'm in my car, cruising in the early morning coastal heat. How nice. I really love this car. This car make could make anyone look like a model. I pull up alongside Mr. Armstrong as he exits his rental. It's nice, but not like my little baby.

We shake hands and head inside. We are seated at a corner alcove table. I order shrimp and grits, scrambled eggs with cheese, French toast, and bacon. Mr. Armstrong orders granola with yogurt and black coffee. We start eating and chatting.

"Magnus, may I call you that?" Mr. Armstrong starts the business conversation.

"Yes, please, I'm much more comfortable with that. Few people call me Mr. Bruce. In fact, I'm called all kinds of things and I answer to most of them, though some are not so polite," I tell him.

"Alright, then, Magnus, I also prefer that you call me Brad. Now, I'm a businessman, and I usually always try to get the most and pay the least. But your wholesomeness and boyishness make me want to treat you fairly and kindly. So, for once in my life, I'm going into this arrangement with both our best interests. I'm going to offer you a lot of money for a two-day photo shoot. However, you will need to commit four to five days for this contract. You will have to travel to New York and possibly to other locations. You will have to make plans to stay in New York as long as it takes to complete the shoot. We will provide transportation and your housing, but you will be responsible for your meals, which is a good thing for me considering how much breakfast you eat."

We both laugh at this reality, noticing the differences in our meals. I try to offer excuses for my appetite, but he holds up a small hand and continues with details.

"There will be fittings and more fittings. There will be hours of you standing in different locations to determine lighting effects. You will have to agree to possible hairstyle changes, and there will be makeup and wardrobe changes. There are many details and unexpected changes necessary before the final shoot. But, for this four-day period, I think an offer of forty thousand dollars is fair. You have to keep in mind that you are a relatively unknown, inexperienced face and I'm taking a chance that you will produce good work. Now, what do you think?"

"Mr. Armstrong, I mean Brad, I'm thrilled. I think you are being more than fair. Hell, I'm just a good 'ol boy and I don't know anything about big city ways, but I'd crawl through hog shit for ten thousand dollars a day. The money is great, the trip to New York is great and the clothes are a terrific bonus. What's not to like about this deal? Hell, yeah, if you want me, I will promise you that I'll do the best that I can to make this successful."

Another handshake as we agree to the deal. He will overnight me a contract which I get approved from my attorney, then I will mail it back. He will set up the details and call me with as much notice as he can. He'll then arrange travel, and I will report to his office in New York. We have another cup of coffee and leave the restaurant. In the parking lot, we talk a bit about the beach activities for the day and agree to try to visit later at some of the events.

I drive back to the condo feeling like the luckiest man in the world. I don't care at all about the modeling or the publicity, in fact, that's the part I like the least. The clothes are a great perk to me. I'm thrilled about that. I wonder what pieces I'll wear, casual or formal, I don't care, I'll take anything. And the money is astonishing. I don't have any illusions about making a career in modeling. I like what I do, working with Andi, I'd never leave that. But, forty-thousand dollars for a week's work is great. I'll save the money for something special; I just don't know what that might be yet. Or maybe I should just pay down the mortgage.

After quickly changing, I leave for the beach. When I arrive at the tent, there are people everywhere. They all want to party at our tent. I'm the famous squid they say. Squid, what do they mean? Someone shows me the definition of Kraken—that explains it. I'm trying to be a good host and partier, but for once in many, many years, I'm just more excited about something else than I am being here. I must be growing up. Andi would be proud.

I stay with the guys at the tent enjoying our new friends. We laugh and drink, though I stick with water, and have a good time. I leave at six o'clock to meet up with Henri. We agreed to an early dinner so that we can make it to the beach dance tonight. I was going to turn in early, but everyone changed my mind. I'll dance the night away with the rest of them. I told Henri about the stupid video, but of course, he already had seen it. I hope this video is only a local virus. Please God, don't let it leave this area. Don't let my friends and family see it.

"I've got something that belongs to you," says Henri, leaving me a bit concerned. What in the world is he talking about? I don't know if I want to pursue this. Out of respect I agree to play along for just a little while.

"What could you possibly have that belongs to me?" I ask him.

"Oh, just a little blue zippered bag with the word 'CASH' stamped across the front," he states proudly.

"What? You have our cash bag? How did you get that? I thought that it was stolen or that I lost it. The last I knew, I put that bag in the glove compartment of my car as I was leaving Birmingham. I meant to drop it by the bank as I left town but forgot all about it until yesterday. I checked the glove box, and it was not there. Why do you have my cash bag? Does it still have money and checks in it?" I ask.

"I just glanced in and saw some money and a check or two. I zipped it up and took it with me," he says as he is smiling. "Your first night here, remember, when you got wasted after one drink at The Trieste party? I had to get some friends to drive you home. After I put you in the car, I checked around for valuables and found the bag. I decided it would be safer with me than you, so I held onto it. Here it is, but count it, as I don't know what you started with," Henri says.

What a friend. Nothing is missing. I've got the money back. Damn, I already transferred my money into our business account. Now after the holidays I'll have to find a way to get my money out of the store account and back into my personal account. How will I do that without Andi seeing all this on the bank statement? Getting out of this mess with my balls intact will be challenging. Transferring money in and out of accounts sounds a little like embezzling to me. I don't know if hiding my hooky time from Andi is worth messing with her money. Even though it all balances out, on paper it is not going to look right. Hmm, I'll have to worry about that later.

"Thanks, Henri, you are a caring friend. I appreciate you taking care of me that night."

"Honey Mag, I've told you that I will take care of you anytime. Just give me the word," Henri pleads.

"Oh, yeah, Henri, do you know anything about me wearing stupid Incredible Hulk underwear?" I ask.

Henri emphatically declares, "I've promised to never tell that secret, but don't worry, you were never in danger, I was looking out for you the whole time. I know you can't hold your drink. And no, you didn't do anything with anyone."

We finish our delicious seafood meal and I ask Henri if he would like to ride back to the beach with me. "Sure," he said. We settle into the fine leather seats and enjoy the luxurious seaside highway drive. Soft amber sky and cooler breezes delight us during our slow ride. A good meal with a good friend on a good night after a pretty good conclusion to a sucky yesterday—I can't ask for more.

The dance party is *wild*, as usual. Somehow I don't participate as fully as years past. I've just got too much on my mind. After a few hours, I decide to leave and go back to the condo. I leave Henri in good hands—lots of hands, I should add. Brad was there, and it seems that he and

Henri have known each other for years and years. They are both having fun reliving past times. The other guys will never leave this place tonight. I might not even see them before I hit the road back home tomorrow. I'll see them when I see them. They are all big boys.

The morning comes quickly. I settle on the sofa with my large Dark Roast coffee. As I sit alone, about twenty thoughts are running through my mind. The modeling job, my work at the shop, talking to Andi about lots of stuff, the trip to Florence with the sisters, which necessitates my partnership with Jackson, so much to do and so many details. Now that the weekend is over for me, I've really got to prioritize and get to work. I'm anxious to get home and work through all of these many projects. I am going to be a very, very busy boy.

Chapter Five

BACK TO BIRMINGHAM

I really, really love my new car. It is worth every cent, and I'm so happy with it. This car sits nicely on the road, hugs the curves, and has the most comfortable seating that I've ever had in a car. The weather is great with the top down, not too hot this time of year. That will quickly change to a sweltering, sweaty, stinky heat.

My house temperature is mild, and I've opened some windows where a soft breeze is crossing through the living room. Everyone loves my house. It is in the revised retro area of Crestwood. I bought the house from my dear little old friend, Mrs. Carmichael, just as the neighborhood was early in its rise. Her husband had passed on years before, and she stayed here alone for fifteen years. Once she reached ninety, her daughter persuaded her to sell it and move in with her at Hoover.

I have known Mrs. Carmichael for the past ten years; we volunteered together at the zoo and became fast friends. We would go to Bingo and have coffee together every Monday night. So, when she was ready to sell, she asked me if I was interested. She said she knew that the neighborhood had a lot of 'my kind' and she was happy that they were investing in the area and bringing it back to life. She wanted me to have the chance to get it if I wanted it. She said that if I did, she wouldn't even list it and would sell it to me for eighty thousand dollars.

Eighty thousand was a steal here five years ago. I argued that I would pay a fair market price, but she refused. I even insisted on meeting with her, her daughter, and their attorney. I told them that I realize that my dear ninety-year-old friend didn't know what she was doing and I refused to take advantage of her.

Mrs. Carmichael quickly took control of the conversation and, turning to me, said the most endearing thing that I have ever heard. Holding my hand, with a trembling, tearful voice she said, "My dear Magnus, in just a few years you have become one of the truest friends that I have had in all my life. You are an honest, genuine man. You are always true to your word. You have a deep-seated kindness, and most important, you have kept these qualities while God has gifted you with handsomeness equaled by few. Your gorgeous black hair and sparkling crystal blue eyes are magnetic. Those dark curls are so youthful. I'm sure they are the same as they were when you were three years old. You have remained a man of character through your many highs and lows. You fill my life with joy, and the only sad part is that I didn't know you longer. You have been as loving and loyal to me as a son. Hell, Magnus, I'd give you the house if I could make you take it. I love you dearly, my boy. I do not need more money. I want you to love and cherish my house. I want you to keep my house a home of laughter and joy; that is all I want." At that, her daughter and attorney smiled and hugged her, saying they agreed with her decision. That was it, the deal was set, and my faith that goodness and kindness were still strong in this world was confirmed.

I bought the house, added another seventy thousand in remodeling, and now have one of the finest houses in the neighborhood for one hundred and fifty thousand dollars. Mrs. Carmichael and I continued our friendship until she passed away two years ago. She taught me a lot about compassion and strength and courage. I miss her a lot. Even now, on Monday nights, I still sit and visit with her in my mind. She knew more than I that I would need her spirit and could feel her love for me here better than anywhere else. I'll even ask her opinion on things, and I swear I can hear her voice telling me what I should do. I have never failed to follow her advice when she speaks to me in the quiet of our house.

Now, I need to soak up her love in this peaceful place and talk to her about my plans. I would say I wish she was here with me now, but I feel her so strongly, I know without a doubt that she is here. My ritual is to walk through the house, room by room, talk to her about her my dilemmas and wait to hear her recommendations. We laugh a lot. I'll say something crazy or inappropriate, and I can hear her giggle, and in a few short words or phrases she explains what I should do. So, here we go, Mrs. Carmichael, talk to me.

I sit in the living room on my gray HD sofa set by Italy Design. I really wanted the sofa and chair from the Tonino Lamborghini line but couldn't afford it. The entertainment center is shiny with tones of light gray to dark gray. The walls are covered with modern décor; the floors are sleek with the original oak. The Mrs. and I decided that the house should be vibrant and modern and light. She wanted the house to be young again, not dark and old. I wanted the house to be reflective of my favorite place in the world, Italy. The exterior of Italy homes and buildings are classically old, but the interiors of those old buildings are ultra-modern and sleek. So, as we shopped together, yep, we talked it through and agreed with what we have.

The kitchen has a retro look. My stovetop, warming drawer, and oven are Viking. I have a Thermador refrigerator. I love the matte silver surfacing of these appliances. My countertops are light and dark gray marble. The kitchen is small, but is very functional. Cooking is one of my pleasures and I'm quite good at it. Everything in my kitchen serves a purpose. This is the one room that I do not allow waste or fluff. I need and use everything in this room. Nothing is decorative. This is my workspace and in here I work. Mrs. Carmichael is always with me, advising, helping or fussing at the way I cook, saying that I'm too fancy with my food. She doesn't understand Italian cooking—she thinks foreign food is a waste of good ingredients. Often, my guests come in here and ask who I am talking to; I just smile and tell them 'the Mrs.'

My dining room is from the Saarinen collection. The dining table is glass, and the chairs are white with black cushions, and to me they look like little champagne glasses. They have a round white base with a narrow stand that rises up to the cup-shaped seat. I *love* them. Mrs. Carmichael chose the chandelier. It is a white drop-down with over 100 star lights cascading over the table. Actually, it is beautiful, like stars falling from the sky, but I thought it was a bit over the top. It is the one she wanted though, and its selection gave me a glimpse of how straight married men must feel. Her voice kept insisting on it even as I argued against it. After fighting in my head about it for two days, I cussed and told her fine, get it, and we did. I don't hate to admit that she was right. It is probably the masterpiece of the house. I'm glad she is so strongly insistent with me. I only pray that she never leaves and is waiting for me as I give up this life and enter her world on the other side.

Now, she didn't say a word when I was choosing my bedroom pieces. I am not sure why she didn't have opinions on that, but she never gave me any feelings. I could hear her giggle fleetingly off and on but I never sensed her presence in my bedroom. Anyway, I have the best bed in the world. It's the Silhouette bed in Bianco. I was torn about the color for days. I finally went with the white. It's a low curved wood design; I've never seen anything like it. I have the nightstand from the collection as well. I went with the Arco dresser. It's white with curved edges and sleek, flat drawers. No hardware, just clean and crisp throughout.

The polished oak floors are highlighted with flat white rugs. The walls throughout the house are painted in Benjamin Moore 'Heaven' to keep my connection with Mrs. Carmichael close. Really, I think of it like that, but it was the first color card I went to. It is listed as the palest of lavender, but it is in the color block with light to dark grays. It was just serendipity that the name is 'Heaven'. So, I prefer to consider it another of Mrs. Carmichael's ways of making me smile. Anyway, on my bedroom walls, I've displayed black and white and some sepia prints of pictures that Andi took. She's really good at photography, and her lens has a way of zooming and angling buildings in a way that I love. So, over the years she has given me enlarged prints as gifts. They now cover my walls.

When I remodeled, I converted the small guest room adjoining my bedroom into a master bath. I have a huge Jacuzzi tub and a walk in shower with a waterfall showerhead and wall mounted water spray nozzles. The entryways are arched and have a Venetian feel. This bathroom is my dreamy sense of masculinity and softness combined.

I can't say the same for the guest bath. The walls are tiled in small, mixed neutral tiles from the base to forty-eight inches from the floor. This is topped with a two-inch dark stained trim. I have a dark framed flat mirror flanked with dark wood sconces. The sconces hold white marbled light fixtures that have the appearance of thick heavy candles with light filtering through the white marbled glass. The sink is a raised white bowl fitted onto a flat white base. The base is floated on four tall dark wood legs with a lower glass shelf eight inches off the floor. I installed soft subdued lighting just under the sink to showcase the lower shelf. The faucet and handles have a nickel finish and come out of the wall above the sink. It is a small room with a simple small shower finished in the same tiles with a glass door.

The toilet is a different story; it is out of this world. It has a unique square design. It is a Numi with a built in ejecting bidet with drying capability. It has a motion-activated lid; it is self-cleaning and has a heated seat. There is even a little heater in the bottom that warms your feet. The back is illuminated, *and* it plays music. Yep, it has all that. I paid a fortune for it, but I saved and decided this was my splurge item.

The self-ejecting bidet with built-in blow dryer was a great surprise to many a guest. In the beginning, people came running out as soon as the water hit them unexpectedly. Once, a friend whom will remain nameless came out with his pants around his ankles yelling, "Lordy Mighty, Cheese and Crackers, what in the hell just happened to me?" We all laughed and had to explain the ways of the big wide world to him. Now everyone knows to sit back and enjoy the ride.

I hate to say it, but in our world here in Crestview, competition is rampant. The gay community prides itself with looking better than the house next door. We keep the home design places in the black, so they cater to us and our money. This is one of my flaws, I know it. Combine my inborn competitiveness with my gayness and you have a one-up-manship that is hard to equal.

I have topped them all with my Numi. Nobody has this. When I have parties, you wouldn't believe the traffic that my guest bath gets. Of course at parties there is drinking, so the toilet is always the most used item in the house. When the guest bath is occupied, I tell my friends to feel free to use the master bath. They used to, but now word is out about my Numi, and no one ever goes to the master bath anymore. They will wait and wait for the experience of my toilet. I've seen some hopping and dancing in an attempt to keep their urine retained in order to have a chance to use my Numi. All my friends have toilet envy.

But here is where I have a serious problem. Once you are seated on this fine device, you are forced to look at a small wall. The wall is not the problem; the blank wall is the problem. I have decorated it with dark wood abstract art that matches the wood accents, but it didn't work. I have put up some of the wonderful prints that Andi gave me. Again, it didn't speak to me, nor did Mrs. Carmichael. At first we had the most fun in this room. She loved it all and we were always in total agreement. But since I got to this wall, we're both silent. Nothing works for us. In this, she is silent, she doesn't speak to me, and she appears to be shaking her head at me without a voice. I think she is as exasperated as I am. We didn't like the clock that I put on that wall either. I had decided that people should realize how much time they were sitting on my toilet and *not* visiting with me.

All of this ended about three months ago while I was at the store. Behind our cash register is a picture that has been there for about five years. It is a picture of Andi and Daphne standing on a corner in Florence, Italy. Nino took the picture years ago, during their first trip to Florence. Andi and Daphne are no models, mind you, but they are good, happy people. So, the picture doesn't have great appeal. It is just a picture of two little middle-aged ladies standing on an ancient corner in a foreign city, nothing special.

That is until one of our newest clients, Filippo Russo, noticed the picture. We were alone in the store at the time. I was sitting on the stool behind our desk that serves as our cash register. Mr. Russo was talking to me about the Italian cabinet that we have. He immediately noticed the picture and said that the picture was of an obscure area of Florence near the Duomo called Piazza del

Giglio. He recognized Andi, and I explained that she and her sister have a travel company and the picture was taken on their first tour of Florence. He pointed out the plaque on the wall of the building just behind the girls. I had never noticed it, as it was dark and blended right into the stone building.

He went on to explain that in Florence plaques are placed on buildings that denote homes of famous people or other interesting historic detail. He said that some plaques are in place to enforce ordinances established by the local government of the time. There are plaques that tell one that food items cannot be sold here. A plaque in another location admonishes one to behave decently. A plaque at Via dei Peppi forbids a prostitute from living in this area. The plaque in the picture, he said, is at Piazza del Giglio, and it tells those in the piazza that "one is not to play ball or other games." What? At that location, you cannot play ball or other games.

I imagine a time in the Renaissance when the area was a favorite of the local boys for their daily street ball games. I can see them running and kicking soccer type balls and being yelled at by the local magistrates as this particular piazza may have been in the path of their walk to the Duomo and Baptistry. They were probably hit in the head and kicked in the legs as boys competitively practiced their play. There were probably many mishaps with high ranking officials that culminated in such an ordinance. Poor kids, I guess they had to find another place to play ball.

Play ball. One cannot play with balls here. One cannot play other games here. An old, aged plaque in Latin, telling you that one cannot play ball or other games here. Wow! A greater epiphany was never known. My blank, unloved bathroom wall had just met its masterpiece. I want that plaque. That old, weather-stained plaque will be on my wall, facing the toilet. My Numi toilet deserves this. Now, my gay friends and foes can sit on my toilet and read that they cannot play with balls or other games here. Damn, no plaque has ever needed a more perfect exhibition than my bathroom.

I must find a way to get that plaque. Well, not that plaque—it's attached to an old building in Florence, Italy, and I am here in Birmingham, Alabama. I mean a plaque like it. Hmm, why can't I have that plaque? No one in Florence even cares now, I bet. Most of the people in Florence probably don't even know that it is there. Doubt grips me. I don't know if this is possible. I don't think I have ever stolen anything. Okay, maybe that candy bar when I was six years old, but I am not a thief. I do not have any experience in theft. But, I really, really want that plaque, the original.

It really won't be like stealing. It is only a sign, not a work of art. Heck, in high school, my friends were always 'taking' signs to put on their walls. You know like 'One Way' signs, or 'Yield', or 'Johnson Ave'. They were just street signs and were quickly replaced with new ones. No one really cared; it was all an appreciation of street art. So, isn't this the same? It is just a street sign, they replace them all the time, and I'm sure it is not a big deal. It is not like I want the 'The Birth of Venus' or something.

Chapter Six

DINNER WITH ANDI

I've been sitting on my Numi toilet for the past twenty minutes. What a study, this wall in front of me. The plaque belongs here; without it my wall will remain blasé. However, I feel some resistance from Mrs. Carmichael on the 'heist'. I'm not sure she's convinced that taking a sign is not theft. I keep telling her that I'm replacing it with a newer, better one. I think she will come around. She just needs some more time. Right now, time is what I don't have.

I have to start dinner for Andi. I know she is coming back from Daphne's late this afternoon. I want to surprise her with dinner. She moved into the house next door as soon as it went on the market last year. We've done a lot of work on it, but it has a long way to go. Anyway, I have missed her; I want to hear about her time with Daphne. I would love to tell her about my time at the beach, but I can't.

She thinks I stayed in town and worked. She has no idea that I went to Pensacola. I have to tell her about my opportunity with Brad Armstrong, because I'll have to be away from the shop. I just don't know how to tell her it came about. She can't know the truth, but I am not good at lying, either. I hope it will just come to me during our dinner.

I'm making her favorite dinner, meat loaf, green beans, buttered carrots, a tossed salad, and yeast rolls. I'll make her a chocolate cake, too. I will cook it here and then take it to her house. Her pitiful little kitchen, bless her heart, is just unfit for a cook like me.

I make my meat loaf with grass fed lean ground chuck. Andi and I went in together to buy an organic farm raised cow. This meat has no resemblance to the garbage you buy in the store. It makes all the difference in the prepared meal. I hand mix my beef with finely chopped onions, green bell pepper, panko, cracker crumbs, salt, pepper, and other spices. I add a small amount of ketchup for texture and taste. I bake it for hours and then top it with a special sauce made on the stove top.

The local farmers market has fresh green beans, which I've washed and snapped. I cook them in a frying pan with butter, salt, and pepper. The organic baby carrots are cooked on the stove top with butter and brown sugar. I hand toss some spring greens and mix up dressing with oil, vinegar, sugar, salt, pepper, and a variety of chopped herbs. The yeast rolls are an old recipe from my grandmother.

Now that I've got the main dinner on the stove, I set to work on her cake. I got this recipe from Andi's mom. It is a homemade chocolate cake with lots of cocoa. The icing is a cooked icing that is somewhat like fudge. It gets almost firm, hardening too much if you cook it too long. Just before that point, I have to ice the cake quickly. The icing cracks, which reminds me of 'Kraken the Brute'. It is too bad that Andi cannot hear about my torment while I was at the beach in Pensacola. She would be appalled at my treatment.

The sweet chocolate smell of the cake fills the room as I ice it without cracking and place it on my prettiest raised cake plate. It is really a nice presentation. More antique bowls hold the vegetables. Hot, raised rolls are on a bread plate, atop the hand embroidered, linen bread cover that my grandma gave me years ago. I put the meat loaf on a gorgeous dish that I just got from an estate that the shop purchased.

Earlier, I used my key to Andi's house and let myself in to freshen it up. It needed lots of freshening. She is not the best housekeeper. It wasn't so much a mess though, just a little stale. I fixed it up and opened some windows. I set the table and selected a bottle of wine for our meal. Everything is ready for me to cart the food over.

I load up the cart that we use to transport stuff, usually food stuff, back and forth between our houses. Heading that way, I push my cart along the connecting sidewalks from our back doors. I make my way into the back, which opens directly onto the kitchen. Onward I go with my cart to the table. Everything is set and now I wait.

Oh, how long will she be? It is six-thirty now, and she should be getting here. What could she be doing? What the hell, I'll just have a small glass of wine while I wait. She'll be here soon. I check my phone, but no missed calls or texts. Taking my wine to the living room, I kick back in her recliner. I'd like to turn on some music, but I don't want Andi to hear it and think that someone is in her apartment. She's a nut; she could come in here with her baseball bat. That's okay; I'll just sit and think about my plan while I wait.

Gee, my eyelids are getting heavy. How much wine have I had?

Chapter Seven

ANDI ARRIVES BACK HOME

Good Lord, I'm glad that weekend is over. I don't know how my sister does it, living out there the sticks with all those kids running around everywhere, every day. My sister, heck, how in the world does my niece do it? It's busy, busy, busy. I've lived alone for years; I can only take so much of that madness. I like my quiet, my peace and quiet. I like being able to open the door to my house and find that it is just like I left it. There is no one there and I can do what I want to.

But, it was fun to see them all again. I'm glad the gang voted on doing nothing all weekend. My sister can just wear me out. She would go all the time if she could afford it. Good thing she has all the kids to do stuff with her now. She simply has exhausted the rest of us.

I really should have gotten an earlier start back home. But, there really wasn't any reason to hurry. I'd just sit around being lazy, that's all, and I have just had three days of lazy. It only takes me an hour to get home; what a difference an hour makes. Only an hour and you go from the backwoods to the metropolitan city. It is like time travel. So what, I left at six, and I will be home by seven.

I wonder how the weekend at the shop went. I haven't heard from Magnus. That is unusual; he always calls me every day about one thing or another. I guess he decided that I have been working too hard and that I needed a total break from work and him. He's as good as gold, but at times he can be too much, too needy.

Come to think of it, there is not a lot of difference between his behavior and all those kids I just left. Only, his mishaps and adventures are a bit more elaborate and risqué than theirs. Now that I think about it, all boys are like that. When they are little, they run head first without thinking into situations, which might cause problems. Then when they are big boys, like Magnus, nothing really changes. They still run straight away into big ol' man size trouble.

I am sure that Magnus has had a pretty boring weekend at work. It was Memorial Day weekend. and there shouldn't have been a lot of retail traffic. Here in the South, we all tend to have family weekends during the bumper holidays, Memorial and Labor Day. I do feel a little bad; I know how much he wanted to go to the Beach Gathering at Pensacola. I think he is probably a charter member of that group.

He's been going there for the annual gay weekend for maybe fifteen years. This is probably the first one that he has missed. He should thank me for that. Every year he finds himself in more trouble than the year before. He's not a miscreant, by any means, crazy just seems to be drawn to him like some invisible magnetic force. I don't know how an innocent, sweet guy like him finds so much trouble. I really don't. Well, next year he can go. We'll probably just close up the shop for the holiday weekend.

Now that the holiday is over, Daphne and I have a lot of work to do. We have to get to picking. Our shop is getting a little low on inventory. We have some estate sales contracted in June and July, so that will keep us busy. When it comes to picking and hauling we really depend on Magnus and his muscle. I don't even know why he fanatically goes to the gym every day when we work out all his major muscle groups lifting and moving furniture.

And, we usually have him lifting and moving big heavy stuff from one spot then to another spot, then back to the first spot over and over. He is so sweet; he's never once sounded like a husband and complained. He just puts on that big sweet smile on that tanned face, smiling all the way to his icy blue eyes, and that smile is surrounded by those beautiful black curls cascading to just above his shoulders. You just want to squeeze him, he's so adorable. That sweet, innocent, smile with those looks, is probably how he attracts all the trouble. It's like pouring honey all over you.

And if all this summer picking and selling isn't enough, we have the shop to maintain and we must prepare for the Italy tour. That is okay; I am looking forward to the trip in October. It will be nice to go back to Italy. Who could want more than all that pasta and pizza and wine? Magnus is going with us on this trip. God, I hope it is not like our last trip with Magnus to France. He wandered off one night to all those burlesque shows, and then he went into the 'gay' district. He didn't even know where he was going and it found him. I swear he has some kind of trouble radar.

At least we have that church lady to keep him somewhat shamed into decent behavior. And when he is not battling with her, he will be wrapped up in the hoity-toity fashion girls that will hopefully keep him focused on something other than trouble. Daphne's really got an eclectic mix for this trip. God only knows how all of us will get along.

Oh, the city lights, what a beautiful site after three nights of bonfires and stars. I grew up in the country so I do appreciate so many things about it. But, I have lived in the city for thirty years and I *do* appreciate so many things about it. For me, right now, it far outweighs the country life. There are no huge home improvement stores in the country. If ever you need to repair something or buy something, you have to go out to the barn and strip a part or find a way to make something out of nothing. And whenever you want to cook something, there is not a choice of Winn Dixie or Local Market, again you have to go to the kitchen and make something out of what you've got.

Like this afternoon, my sister was going to make me a cake. I wanted a chocolate cake with that hard cracked icing. She pulls out all kinds of stuff and starts the cake. She sent me to the refrigerator for the eggs. I open the door and don't see any eggs; I look high and low throughout that overflowing fridge, but still no eggs. I tell her that she doesn't have any eggs. She then sends me next door to see if our mother has eggs, which she doesn't. I remember that we used them all this morning for our huge country breakfast. "Don't you have any chickens running around this acreage, laying eggs?" I ask her. She just gives me a look like I'm crazy.

"I tried that," she said, "but the dogs kept eating my free range hens. I gave up chicken raising. We get eggs like everyone else, at the store, or from Mr. White up the road. But I'm not leaving this house today."

She then goes to the cabinet and pulls out the flax seed and tells me to get out the coffee grinder she uses for her flax seed and grind them up. I did and then she added some water to it and gave me the bowl and eggbeater and told me to whip it up. I did and sure 'nuf, it ended up looking like dark egg whites. She said the color wouldn't matter in a chocolate cake and it would have more healthy protein and omega-3s than eggs. I was telling her that it was okay and I didn't really want a cake anyway. I really did and was ready to go to the store, but she wouldn't let me.

She is bossy like that, always telling me what I can and can't do. She never missed a beat, went right on making that flax seed chocolate cake, yuck. I wasn't going to touch that mess. Once she got it done, she cut me a huge piece and gave me a glass of milk. I hope this milk came from the store and she didn't get it straight out of the cow at Mr. White's.

She was sitting straight in front of me at the table, drinking coffee and eating cake like it was perfectly normal to put flax seed instead of eggs in your cake. Talking, talking, talking and eating, she never slowed down. I was just looking at her like she was a crazy person; I was almost gagging every time she took a big ol' bite. She slowed down just long enough to tell me to close my eyes and try a taste. She insisted that I wouldn't know the difference if I hadn't added the flax seed myself. As usual, she finally guilted me into taking a tiny, small bite; as I immediately chased it with what I hoped was homogenized store bought whole milk. It tasted safe, so I took another bite. She was right, I couldn't tell the difference. It was good and I asked if I could have the rest. So, here I am, arriving in Birmingham with that leftover cake in the car with me.

I am hungry now. It's five till seven, and I know that I don't have any food at home. Thank goodness, there is my Olive Garden. It is great to be in the city again. I pull in and reach for my phone and realize that it's in my travel bag. Damn, I forgot. Daphne made me turn it off and put it away. She says that I can't look at her when she's talking while I look at my phone and text all the time. She is like that; she has to have your undivided attention at all times. And she insists that I divide my attention way too much with that phone. So, now, as I arrive at her house, I have learned to turn off my phone and put it out of sight. Usually, I pull it out and catch up once I'm alone in my room, behind closed doors. I can't believe that I have forgotten it all weekend. Those kids and my sister had me so exhausted day and night. I was too tired to think of my phone. Never in my life, since the discovery of the cell phone, has that ever happened to me. I can't believe it. What if someone wanted or needed me? Darn that girl!

I go through my bag and grab my phone. It seems like years since I have seen my little iPhone. "My pretty little phone, mommy is so sorry. I've neglected you for days. It's okay, you're home now, and I'll never let you get lost again." That is, until the next time your Aunt Daphne comes out of the woodwork. It is probably deader than a doornail. I power it up as I'm being seated at my usual table. It has full power. I guess it needed a rest. It usually dies on me several times a day. Wow, maybe I do spend a lot of time on this device.

John, my usual waiter, asks if I want my Four Cheese Ziti. I tell him that I sure do, unless they've got a new item that tastes better. He's already brought my tea. My phone is going crazy, loading message after message— there are about twenty of them. How am I going to read all of these? I start with the most recent one and work my way back. They all are Facebook comments about Magnus. This is crazy. Most of the messages reference the Incredible Hulk, drunken stupors, and twig and berries shaped sunburns. What are they talking about? Magnus? The beach? Sunburns? Incredible Hulk? I'd better back up and start at the beginning.

Okay, on Thursday, there were a few voicemails from some of our upcoming estate sale clients. They gave me some details and don't expect my return call until after the holidays. There is a text from Magnus, saying that he is bored, no one has walked in the door all day, hmm, and it was posted at twelve forty-seven. Then there is another text from Shelia, a friend, asking me to call when I get back to town next week. And now there are comments from Facebook friends about Magnus and the beach again. Now there is a text from Sammy, Magnus's friend. I know all of Magnus's friends were going to the beach, but he didn't plan to go with them because he promised me he would work.

I open Sammy's text, and he has posted the most unbelievable video of what appears to be Magnus wearing only some bikini briefs—with what?—let me zoom in. Yep, it does look like the Incredible Hulk underwear. He's running and falling and screaming. He's yelling about fires and earthquakes. Where is this? When did they take this video? Maybe they didn't go to Pensacola. It was sent Friday afternoon. Magnus must have gone out with them Thursday night in Birmingham. But the steps and that building look familiar. As I continue to watch the entire video, I'm laughing so hard that I am attracting unwanted attention. God, I've got to stop, I'm creating my own scene laughing like this. I get up and start walking out the door. I find John and tell him that I'm coming right back, that I've got to go to the car for something.

I get outside and sit on the bench. I am doubled over laughing so hard that I have to pause this video three times. I laugh right to the end, when I suddenly recognize where this video was made. This is Henri's condo that we always use at Pensacola. What has Magnus done? This better be from a year that I don't know about.

I move on to the next text. It's another one from Sammy. He's attached another video of the beach and Magnus passed out under the tent on a lounge chair. He is half sunburned, just his left side. How in the heck did he do that? The video is moving from his feet. That left foot is going to be sore. How can he wear a shoe on that blistered foot? The camera is moving up his legs and past his shorts. Thank God, he has shorts on. Now the camera is moving up his chest, again showing that he is half fried. I've always known he was half baked, but now I know he is also half fried. He's going to be hurting. I hope he has some Motrin on hand. No, no, look at his poor fried left hand and wrist.

As the camera moves up his chest, my phone is ringing. I check the incoming call. It's from Daphne. I'll call her back later. I go back to the video as the camera proceeds from his waist to his chest. What is that on his blistered left upper chest? I pause the video and look without zooming. It looks like, oh, no they didn't. My God, that is crazy. I continue to watch in horror as the camera moves on up his neck to his face. Passed out, his face turned to the right with a line of drool coming out of the left side of his mouth, running down his face and neck, then onto his chest, streaming right through the drawing of the penis and just dribbling out of the tip.

What have they done to my big ol' Mag? Poor baby, I try real hard to work up some pity, laughing so hard that I am crying. I have to reassure several people going into the restaurant that I am fine. I can't seem to recover. I don't know how I can go back in there and sit quietly and eat. It's not possible. I can't stop this hysterical laughter.

I know exactly what happened. My Magnus can't handle his drink, not at all. It is phenomenal that such a big guy can't ever stay upright for a second drink. He's always down after the first one. We all know that. Seriously, those guys knew that when he fell out asleep that nothing would wake him for several hours. They let him lie there and get blistered, and then once they saw the drool pattern, they wiped it off and strategically drew that penis in the drool path. Those crazy-ass nuts are insane. It is funny as hell, though.

I have to call back in the restaurant and speak to John. I tell him to box up my dinner to go and give him my credit card number. I add a ten dollar tip, apologize to him, and ask if he will bring it outside to me. I tell him that I'm on the bench outside the front door.

As he rounds the corner, he sees me still doubled over crying. His face wearing a concerned expression, he asks, "Are you okay? What can I do? Do I need to call an ambulance?"

I look up with tears rolling down my face. "Really, I'm fine. I'm watching the most hilarious video of my friend. I'm just caught up in uncontrollable laughter, and I can't go back in there and sit quietly. I'll eat at home once I recover my wits." He grins and pats my shoulder, asking if I need anything else. I tell him thanks, I'm good. He goes back inside, and I take my dinner to the car.

As soon as I get seated, I move on to the next message. It is Sammy again with a YouTube post of whom I assume is Magnus. No one else I know is that big. This time I see Magnus with a tiny little green shirt stuck on his head as someone is trying to pull him out of it. I can't see Magnus's face as the shirt is covering it. There is a little tiny bald man pulling the shirt as Magnus is backing up at his full strength. He finally pops out of that shirt like those old cork pistols I played with when I was little. He falls backward and lands in what looks like a hundred hands with some people attached to them. Once he is still, the camera rushes up to his chest and zooms in on the drawing, which is now light, not black. It looks like when you go to the tanning bed and stick on the little stickers to confirm that you did actually tan once you remove them. Oh, no. Again, I am laughing so hard that people are staring at me in my car. God, I've got to get out of here.

I crank the car and pull out into the mall parking lot, when my phone dings another message signal. I am still in no condition to drive. I am laughing so hard that I can't see to drive for the tears, so I park at an empty area of the mall lot. I'm almost afraid to open this post. I see that it is from Sammy.

He now has posted to YouTube and Facebook a full-length production of Magnus and his beach mishaps. Only, now he has interspersed the BarBQue ad picture and he has led off with the title, 'Kraken the Brute'. At least he doesn't come out and list him by name. He has set the sequences to music this time. This is really good. It is funnier than anything that I have ever seen on either YouTube or Facebook. As he opens and closes the video with the hashtag of Kraken, at least Magnus will not be known to the whole world, just us here. And, at least he gave him the great title of Kraken. Magnus is our titan.

Having recovered after an hour of this, I realize that I am still hungry and need to get home. Under any other circumstances I would be furious at that goof off for closing up our shop and going to the beach. But, this is the way Magnus is. Even when you need to be mad at him, you can't. He is too innocent, and situations that are not in his best interest seem to find him. As I drive to the house, finally, I wonder how best to handle him. Will he tell me about this? Will he pretend it never happened? I wonder? Knowing him, he won't say a word, because if he did, he would tell on himself. He is one of the few people I know that is incapable of telling a lie, even a white lie, as we call them down here. A white lie is totally permissible and acceptable as it is said to save someone's feelings. It is still a bold faced lie, but it is said with the intent of protection. Even Magnus can't do this, though. He will let the truth spill out without meaning to.

I have several ideas on how I can crack Kraken. Maybe I'll invite him over to watch a movie and have The Titans playing and talk about that Kraken character. Or maybe I can say that Mrs. Furber called me to say that she came to the shop on Sunday afternoon to buy that $5,000.00 dining room suite. I could say that because I can tell a white lie. I can tell a full out lie and not even miss a lick. Maybe I will just play it by ear and tease it out of him, watching him squirm in his guilt. That would be fun.

I pull into my drive and start unloading my bags. As I walk up to the door, I can smell meat loaf. Its eight o'clock and I must really be hungry, imagining food like that. I can almost taste it, the smell is so real. And yeast rolls, I smell rolls. I need my ziti. I'm starving. No, wait, before I get to the door, I know that the aroma is not my imagination. My Magnus has cooked for me. He was going to surprise me with dinner, I bet. Now would this be because he missed me or is it because he is feeling guilty about his behavior? I bet he is sitting in my kitchen, patiently waiting and not even mad because I am here late. I wish that I knew how long he'd been waiting on me. He is really the sweetest person in the world. I love him!

I quietly turn the key and tiptoe in the kitchen door. My kitchen is empty, not a dish out of place. That is expected—he would never stoop so low as to cook in my kitchen. He says that I never have the right utensils, ingredients, pots and pans, or serving dishes. He, of course, is right. It is usually John and I at Olive Garden, or JoAnne and I at Macaroni Grill. I quietly put down my bags and walk into the dining room.

Look at that, what a perfectly set dining table. All of those bowls of veggies, meat loaf, the rolls, everything is here. And, look at that cake, I bet it has eggs in it, not beat up flax seed. Isn't it beautiful on that pedestal serving dish? Only Magnus sets a table like this. But where is he? He probable gave up on me and went home. The table is set for two, so he didn't even eat before he left. What a gentleman! If I had cooked all this, I wouldn't wait on somebody. I would dig in and eat before it got cold. It is so sweet that he did all this for me. He didn't know what time I would arrive, taking a chance that the timing would be just right. Of course, I messed it up for him. I'll go over to his house and tell him how much I love it. I'll beg him to forgive me for making him miss a great meal and ask him to come back with me and eat.

I grab my key to his house off of the key rack by my back door. We had connecting walkways poured last summer so we didn't have to get our feet in the wet grass when we make our regular visits to each other's house. Magnus has tuned this little concrete connection into the most gorgeous little path. He insisted on the stamped concrete to look like an old stone walkway. He has planted hundreds of little and big and medium size plants to make it look like an English Garden. It is quite breathtaking. He is so creative, and all I contributed was advice.

As I approach his back door, I don't hear any noise. He always has music or movies on, yet all I hear is silence. I let myself in and go through all the rooms calling his name. There is no answer from anywhere. His kitchen is immaculate as ever but still has the fragrant remnants of his cooking here. As I walk down the hall, it hits me that I have to pee like crazy. Oh, goodness, I hope I can make it to his bathroom. I just make it and am enjoying the best piss anyone can have. This toilet is amazing. I wonder how much he paid for it. It is so inviting that I would walk over here from my house in the middle of a midnight snowstorm to just use his bathroom and not have to sit on my ice cold toilet seat.

I wonder why he keeps changing stuff on that wall. Since I usually sit here for five minutes, even though it only takes me about twenty seconds to pee, all I have to do is look at this wall and have a warm butt and warm feet and listen to music and experience a booty rinse and then a booty blow dry. But, every other week, he is hanging something different on that wall. It's crazy. Personally, I liked the clock, that way I could time myself and not just sit here for fifteen minutes. When you're in here for fifteen minutes, people assume that you're taking a dump, when you are not, you're just relaxing. But, even if you did poop in here, that motorized deodorizer works great, really, I guess so, because I would never poop in his toilet. Even though when you were done, hypothetically, that is, it has that self-cleaning mechanism to remove all evidence of streaking. Again, not that I know first-hand.

I finish up and leave his house; his car is in the garage, yet I can't find him. Where could he be? I decide to go back to my house. Maybe he is at my house and was using my bathroom while I was in there. But then again, why would he use my bathroom? It has that hard cold seat and doesn't play music unless you turn on the radio sitting on the back of the toilet.

I go in my back door and start looking quietly and carefully, just in case there is a murderer in my house and I might be the next victim. Darn, I should have gotten the baseball bat out of my back seat. Surely a murderer would have stopped to eat this food after he finished the murdering. The food is still untouched, not even a roll missing. Now I know if I was murdering someone and this was on the table, I would at least grab a roll and that cake on my way out. I have now worked myself up into a little frenzy. As I walk by the coat closet, I open it up to grab the broom, just in case I need to defend myself or beat off someone murdering my Magnus. What am I thinking, who could take down Magnus? Nobody, don't be scared, I tell myself.

I softly creep past the dining room table and into the living room. As I round the corner, the sweeping part of the broom knocks off the stupid porcelain decoration that Magnus made me hang on the wall. It crashes to the floor, and I scream. A huge monster jumps up from the recliner, screaming and attacking simultaneously. He's coming at me and I start screaming and whacking with my broom. Once I recognize this giant in the shadows is Magnus, I start yelling at him as he is wrestling the weapon from my hands.

Once he recognizes that it is me, he grabs me up and hugs me tightly as my feet dangle around his knees.

He is laughing and kissing my forehead. He smells like wine; that's it. As I glance at the wine bottle with a fourth of it missing and I see the empty wine glass, I realize that he must have been sleeping. "Put me down, Magnus, what are you doing scaring me like that?"

"Me scare you? What were you doing coming at me with what looked to me like a big giant club? I would have sworn that some little Tinker Bell was trying to bash my head in with a huge stick."

We both laugh and hug again. By now it's seven forty-five and dark outside. "I wanted to welcome you home with a surprise dinner. I really thought you'd be here by six or six-thirty. So, when you weren't here by six forty-five, I decided to have a small glass of wine while I waited. And, since I haven't eaten since noonish, the alcohol must have went straight to my head and I fell asleep," he says with his boyish grin.

I hug him again and smile, knowing that he could have just eaten half of a horse and a glass of wine would still put him down. He really must have some type of alcohol sensitivity. Poor man, he just can't drink at all.

We walk to the table and look at the cold dinner. "I'll warm it all up in the microwave and we can still enjoy it. I'm starving too," I tell him.

"Hell no, Andi, you are not going to turn my good food into rubber with a microwave. I guess your oven works, doesn't it? If you have some pans, I'll just warm it up in your oven."

"Sure, my oven works, I guess. I've never had a reason to turn it on. If I eat in this neighborhood, it is at your house, not here. But, certainly the oven works. Look." I turn some knobs and we go about looking for pans to put the food in so we can warm it in the oven.

Magnus crawls into the lowest cabinets by the stove. "Andi, how can you live like this? Don't you have any cookware? I don't see anything down here except some recycled frozen metal pie pans. And hey, I don't think I can get out of this cabinet. I feel like I am stuck. Why did I put my shoulders in here, looking for a pan?" He sniffs. "Andi, do I smell something? Is that gas? Andi, get me out of here, that oven might just blow up. Don't light a candle or strike a match, for God's sake! Andi, help me! Where are you?"

"I'm coming Magnus, I was moving my bags to the bedroom. Where are you? Oh, my God, how did you get down there? Can you get out? Hey, do you smell something? Stop screaming at me, I can't understand what you are saying. I think you need to get out of there! I hate to say it, but we may have a gas leak here."

"Andi, just shut up for a minute and be quiet and listen to me. Carefully turn off the oven and do not turn on a burner. Once you have done that, stick your head in the other cabinet door next to me," he says, a bit exasperated but with more control than I think he's feeling.

I try to stay calm while not laughing at this tiny little man butt and long legs sticking out of my bottom cabinet. I crawl into the cabinet door next to him. A giggle slips out as I am going in, but I don't think he hears it as he's taking deep, heavy breaths.

"Did you turn off the oven, Andi? And, please God, Andi, do you have some shortening in this neglected kitchen?"

"Why yes, Magnus I did and I do. Are you planning your next meal down here while you appear to be stuck in my cabinet? What were you doing down here and how did you get your big chest through that little cabinet door?"

"No, I'm not planning a meal. I'm thinking of a way I can get unstuck without busting out your cabinet frame or tearing half of my skin off of a very sore sunburn."

"A very sore sunburn, did you say?" I meekly inquire.

There's a sudden silence in our cabinets. I am sure that he can see my huge shiny teeth in the dark of our cave with the smile that is all over my face. I see his head drop a few inches and he says, "You know, don't you?"

"Yep, I know. I do have a cell phone. And you were all over it." I reach through the space between us, and this time I kiss his forehead. "It's okay, Kraken, I love you. I'm just sorry that I wasn't there to protect you from your fiends, I mean your friends. Now, tell me your plan with the Crisco and let's get you out of here."

I get the Crisco and rub it all over his right arm. Together we rotate his torso as he lies on the floor and squeezes out of the cabinets, moving his arms above his head as soon as he has some extra space. I pull on his right leg, not wanting to touch his tender left side. Once we free him without tearing down the structure, we collapse and start laughing like children. We lie on the floor and talk about his adventures until we realize that we're both still starving.

Magnus decides that we will cart the food back to his house and warm it in the right cookware, as mine is non-existent. He admits that, while in my cabinet, he did finally see some worn out, partially coated Teflon Revel pans way back in the corner. I had forgotten about those pans. I haven't used them for years.

Magnus and I have a great dinner at his house, and we talk until midnight. He tells me how bad he feels that he selfishly closed the shop and played hooky at the beach. He explains about the missing cash—which wasn't really missing. I tell him how bad I feel that I didn't agree with that plan in the first place. We promise that from now on, the shop will close on every Memorial Day weekend. We review the videos on his big screen TV. We laugh so hard we almost throw up our dinner. He shares his proposition from Mr. Armstrong, and I encourage him to go for it, but only if he takes me to New York with him. He agrees and says that he is glad he has been training that cute little girl from the University, and he's sure that she'll be able to handle the shop while we are away. We close the night out with our tentative plans confirmed.

Chapter Eight

MAGNUS AND JACKSON

At my first chance, I call my old high school chum, Jackson. His family owns Bergman Monuments back in Arab, Alabama. He grew up learning how to prepare and engrave marble and granite. He took over the business when his father retired after forty-five years. Since then, Jackson has been running things. He doesn't do a lot of the dirty work anymore, but that doesn't mean he has forgotten how to do it. A few weeks after my enlightenment by Mr. Russo, Jackson agrees to meet with me.

I do some online research about Florence and the plaques throughout the city. I discover the size of the plaque and double-check the translation from Latin to English. The Latin phase is poetic to me now. I print it out so I can take it with me to meet Jackson.

I need an eight-inch by sixteen-inch piece of gray slate colored marble. It will read "Non e quello di giocare a palla o altri giochi", which translates to 'one is not to play ball or other games'. I also print out pictures of the various plaques in Florence that I am intending to copy so that Jackson can see just what effect I'm after. I take one of the prints and zoom in close, and then take a picture of the color. I get the guy at the Benjamin Moore paint store to mix me up a pint of paint the same color. I take it all with me for my meeting.

Jackson and I meet at his monument business on a lazy Saturday afternoon. He wants to show me all the possibilities and has no doubt from the pictures that I emailed him that he can create an exact replica.

Jackson and I are close. We always were. He was my best friend from middle school on through our graduation. After I realized who I really was and came out of my huge closet, he was one of the first old friends to call me up. He said of course he knew that I was gay. He didn't know what gay was when we were in school, but as soon as he did know, he knew that I was homosexual. He told me that knowing me throughout our childhood made him understand that sexual preference wasn't an option. Young children do not know that, but when he thought back, glimpses of our youth flashed through his mind, and he could see it as clearly as he could see that he was heterosexual. We've been closer friends since that acknowledgement than we were in school, and we were best friends then.

After I arrive, he shows me though the workrooms, explaining how they take a plain unfinished piece of stone and turn it into a completed piece to honor a cherished family member. I pull out my pictures and colors, and we go to the back yard area that houses his stone slabs. He says that since my piece needs to have an aged appearance, he will use an old piece that has been outside in the yard for as long as he can remember. His father told him that it had been in the yard when he started working for Mr. Simmons when he was a teenager. Jackson figures the piece of marble is at least eighty years old.

We go out back by the fence in the back corner and have to dig for it. There are piles of leaves and dirt all over it. Once we finally get it out of the ground, I realize that it will be perfect. It is truly aged. It's dark gray and rough. Jackson says that it has never been touched and that marble tends to age quickly, which is the reason that the industry has gone to granite. He explains that this is why when you walk through old cemeteries, you can't even read most of the monuments. Those are marble. The piece that we haul into his workroom was small, which is why he says no one ever used it. It was probably a trimmed off piece and useless for their needs.

"This will be perfect, Magnus. I'll cut it to the dimensions and prepare it like the pictures. I will saw the depth of the piece to about one inch, which will make it stable enough to support the height and width. I've found a font that looks just the picture of the original. Aging the cutwork will be a challenge, but I figure with some chemical staining it will be almost identical. I've accounted for the darkening of the original chiseled cut due to air pollution, and the stain will do the trick."

"That is great! I'm so glad that you've got the experience to make this happen. Are you okay with it, ethically though?"

At that point Jackson confesses to a teenage prank when his dad made him prepare a stone for a relative of our high school nemesis. As this kid had always bullied him, it was his chance to get even. He had prepared the stone with everything the family wanted, but at the bottom he added 'Ralph is a bastard'. His dad didn't preview his work, just ordered him to set it up at the gravesite. As the stone was set a few months after the funeral, it went unnoticed for about three more months. At that time, when Ralph and his parents went to the church cemetery for decoration, it was obvious just what Ralph was.

Let me explain decoration. Decoration is what small communities in Alabama call the Sunday that all the families meet at the oldest, usually wood structured churches and bring flowers to decorate the graves of family members. Decoration is usually in the late spring. Every church has their established dates. Some are the first Sunday in May, some the second or third, and some the last Sunday in May. I never remember a Decoration in

April or June. Anyway, it is a big, festive event. Everyone brings a 'covered dish' for 'dinner on the grounds'. There is usually an all-day singin' in the church. It is a packed celebration without adequate parking room for all the attendees. Family members make this an annual expected journey, driving from Georgia or Texas or wherever they moved to.

I can imagine everyone's surprise to discover that Ralph was a bastard. Some might have suspected it, knowing his mama. I can pretty much say that Ralph has remained a bastard right into middle age. Most of the redneck attendees appreciated the humor and found it to be fitting. Everyone knew where the monument came from, as the Bergman family and the Simmons family before them were the only monument companies in the county. Jackson says his dad was furious and thought it was going to ruin his business. It actually had the opposite effect. Rednecks started ordering monuments with curse words strategically placed in the epithets.

Nonetheless, Jackson was made to bring the monument back to the shop and redo it. He says he had to use solvents to disengage the stone from the base stone. He says he discovered lots of tricks sanding and polishing during the two weeks it took him to correct it.

He says that the many years of experience have taught him how to do just about anything with stone. He emphasizes that most of the time he is cleaning stone up to look new, not messing it up to look old. But he is certain that he can do it.

I then share my secret plan with him. I want the original plaque. I really want to use the one he is making to replace the original in Florence, Italy. I need his help in learning how to quickly remove the marble piece from the building and even more quickly replacing it with the one he will make.

"Wow," he shouts, "now that is a gig I can take part in. It can be done, Magnus, but it will require some expertise. I don't know if you can do it. I know the solvent you will need to loosen the original. That can be done, but you will need someone to help you. I mean, to do it fast you will need an extra pair of hands. You'll have to apply the fixative to the wall, and then you will need someone to pass you the replica to put into place. I know how to do all of this but I don't know if you could do it quickly enough."

"I know, man," I tell him, "but I need you to teach me all these techniques, and then I'll have to practice over and over until I'm fast enough. I've got a lot of details to work out. My early plan is to create a distraction up the street or around the corner, something crazy that will draw everyone there and away from my spot. I then will hopefully remove and replace it and make my getaway."

"How are you going to get the replica and the original into and out of the countries?" Jackson asks.

"Well, I haven't got that detail worked out yet either," I tell him. "This is a heist early in the planning stages. I've got lots of work to do. You are step number one. But, what do you think so far? Have I shocked you? Are you still prepared to help me? You don't have to if you don't want to; I don't want you to do anything that you are uncomfortable with. That is why I am telling you this. But if I go through with this, I will need your help and direction. You will have to be my teacher and me your studious pupil."

"Are you kidding, Magnus? This is the most exciting thing I've had to think about for years. What a challenge, and what mischievous fun. I haven't done anything like this since the Bastard Ralph trick. I would love to help you. When do you go to Italy? Would you be interested in another person going with you? I have never been out of Alabama, except on monument trips to Atlanta and once to Houston. I haven't even done that since my Sally died a few years back. I think I would like to join you. Having the opportunity to see all that stonework there would be terrific. My daughter works for me, and she can run this place as well as I do if I were to leave for a few weeks. What do you say?"

"Well, I'm going with my partner Andi and her sister on their group tour, but I am sure that the more the merrier. Hell, I'd love you to go; I'll even pay your way. You just take a week to think about it and let me know. But, before you decide, just know that there will be about nine or ten other people going and sometimes there can be some crazy ones in the bunch. I don't think that would be a problem for you because you are easy to get along with; I just wanted you to know ahead of time. Gosh, this is a great idea. I'd really love you to come along. We'd have a great time, and you being there will make the job much easier."

I leave Jackson with his promise to think it through and let me know. I will continue to plan the 'heist' as I call it. I've got lots of details to work out.

Chapter Nine

MAGNUS AND ANDI DO NEW YORK OR NOT

A sudden phone call on a boring morning at the shop quickly changes our day.

"Magnus Bruce, this is Stefan Gregg from Mr. Armstrong's office in New York. Mr. Armstrong wanted me to keep you abreast of the photo shoot plans. We have made an appointment for you with a Mr. Jessie Romeo, on the eighth of June at nine o'clock in the morning. He is a local tailor there and has agreed to measure you for the Riccardo Brevonni team. Do you need me to arrange a taxi to pick you up and deliver you to him at the appointed time? They will make your clothing by those measurements, so time is of the essence."

"Upon your arrival to New York on the thirteenth of June, your fitting will be the first stop. If adjustments are needed, they will be performed immediately. That afternoon, you will be driven to the photo studio for some test shots. On the fourteenth of June, we will drive to an upstate New York site for the ad shots. You can expect follow up indoor shoots at the studio on the fifteenth. That should conclude your work. However, you must stay in town on the sixteenth, in case we need any redos. Do you have any questions, Mr. Bruce?" snoots Mr. Gregg.

"Wow, I don't really know anything you just said because you were talking so fast. Slow it down, man—what's your hurry? But I know how to follow instructions. No thank you, I can drive myself to the tailor. We don't have taxis driving us across town down here. So, I should arrange a flight into New York on the morning of the eighth. Will someone from your office meet me at the airport or do I come to your office? I am in your hands after that. Do you arrange a hotel or do I? Mr. Armstrong told me, but I don't remember."

"Sir, Mr. Armstrong asked me to be in charge of all arrangements. He says that he would prefer to leave nothing to chance. All I need from you is a verbal approval of this tentative plan. I will then contact you with flight details. We will meet you at the airport and take you for your fitting. We will deliver you to the hotel and pick you up for every appointment once you are in the city. I understand that your personal secretary is to accompany you, but I will arrange everything."

"Well, Mr. Steve, that sounds fine with me. I will report to the local tailor at the appointed time. I will wait to hear from you after that. Is that good, Steve?"

"It is Stef-Fon, Mr. Bruce. Most people call me Mr. Gregg. You are correct. The tailor will fax us your measurements, and I will call you with details as I confirm them with Mr. Armstrong. Are we clear?"

"Yes sir, Mr. Gregg. Roger That."

"Click."

"Who was that, Magnus?" Andi asked. We were at the shop, moving furniture when my phone rang.

"You won't believe it. It was a Mr. STE-FON Gregg from Mr. Armstrong's office. He called to give me details of the New York trip. Are you *ready*, Andi? I think New York thinks it's ready for us!!"

"Hot Damn, I sure am," shouted Andi. "I am ready. Magnus, Magnus, I can't believe it. Wow. I've never been to New York City. We are going to blow it out! When do we leave? Where do we stay? How long will we be there? Do we need a rental car? I don't know if you can even drive in New York City. All I've ever seen is cabs in New

York City. Wow, wow, wow. We are actually going. Really, I can't believe it. Oh, my, I'm so happy. I can't wait. Do we start packing now? What do we take? I can't wait to call Daphne."

"Andi, slow it down. Let me talk. First of all, I don't know anything. The only thing I know is that I am to report to a local tailor for measurements. From the tone of that conversation, Andi, it's a good thing you are going with me, because people from New York don't like to talk, they just like to tell. And, they don't think you know how to take care of yourself. He treated me like a fugitive flight risk. I think he may come down here to hold my hand while I get on the plane. What do you think is their problem? You know how responsible I am, Andi. I can take care of myself and am dependable to work a job."

"Magnus, who was so responsible that they closed the shop and went to the beach? Just kidding, I would have done that too, and I consider both of us very responsible people. Everyone that knows us knows that we are reliable and dependable and very responsible. Don't worry about them. You've got me. We don't need big city people. We just want the big city. It's going to be great, won't it?"

"I know it, Andi, I am just giggly about this. Whew, can you imagine the clubs they have in New York City? It's just me and you and NYC! Let's tell all our friends."

"I've already done that, Mag, I just put it on Facebook. We already have nine 'Likes'. Listen to your phone, everyone is already responding. Now, we need to start focusing on this trip. I've got to call Daphne and tell her that I can't help with that estate sale on the fifteenth, because I will be out of town. She will have a cow, I tell you. I'll have to think of something to appease her. Maybe I'll tell her that I'll spend all the time in New York, looking through junk stores and will probably find us the greatest piece ever. Just don't let me forget to pick up a little piece of crap somewhere, sometime while we are there. Okay?"

"Sure, but we aren't really shopping there, are we? I mean, not for picks anyway, right?"

"Magnus, Magnus, Magnus, of course we aren't. I am just telling her that, you know like a 'white lie', you know, so it won't hurt her feelings that she has to stay here and work all by herself while I am playing in NYC."

"I will never understand how you know what color a lie is. I think all lies are dark and evil, and I've never seen an innocent white lie. How do you live with yourself, Andi? I love you, but sometimes you are a little bitch. I mean why would you tell her that if you are not going to do it? Oh, well, that is on you and your conscience."

"That's right, Mag, just don't you worry your cute little curly head about it. Let's finish up this work and ask our friends to meet us at the bar for a drink and celebration. You are not drinking though; it is just sparkling water for you. You have to practice not drinking, because you *cannot* drink in New York. You have a contract to honor, and you can't sleep through it."

Chapter Ten
NEW YORK

"Let's go, Magnus, it's time to get to the airport. What is with all that luggage? Are you serious, three suitcases for four days? You cannot possibly need that much stuff. Open 'em up, let's clean it out. You are going to get new clothes from your ad, you'll need room to bring back the new stuff. You need to take near empty suitcases, not packed full ones. You have traveled with us enough to know to travel light. Okay, so your clothes are bigger than mine, but I'm sure that you don't need all of this. What are you, a girl? Okay, I take that back, of course you are, just a big strong one. I've packed one bag, which is the allowable number of checked bags. Don't you know that you will be charged for two extra bags?"

"All right momma, then you pack my bags. Will you forever know what's best for me? Of course you don't need baggage, you wear the same old stuff all the time, and you don't have the same style as me. We're going to New York, my Lord, New York. We can't just wear our country bumpkin clothes in New York City. We have to look good when we go out. Let me open your bag. I bet that you have the same old boring clothes as always. But I agree: I'll remove half of it if you agree that I can take two bags. You are right; I will need more room for new clothes on my flight back."

"Fine, we've got that settled now. Let's get started. I see five pairs of jeans; you don't need them. Take three out please. Three pairs of casual pants—please remove the two that you don't want. Five dress shirts, Magnus, what were you doing? Pick one of those. Do you have any clothes left in your closet? What is this, seven casual shirts.

90

That is it; I'm taking out four of them. What is in this suitcase? Four pairs of shoes? You can keep two of them; all you need is a dress pair and a casual pair. Oh my God, look at all this underwear! Boxers, briefs, bikinis, and thongs! Magnus, my heavens, what did you have in mind? I'm embarrassed. I don't know if I can go out with you in the city. You are scaring me. And, look at all these products. You have stuff for hair, skin, and nails. You are a girl. Magnus, don't you know that you look great all the time. You don't need any products or any fancy clothes; you are perfect."

"Don't you enjoy dressing up and looking pretty, Andi? I do, and I need a lot of pampering. That is what all this stuff is. I must draw the line at my hair and skin stuff. It is all going, okay?"

"Fine, it stays. But we are going to run late if we don't get out of here. And you assured Mr. Stephan that you didn't require assistance. Now, come on. Park your butt into my car. Funny, isn't it, we don't have room in your car, but you're the one with all the luggage."

We load up and drive to the airport. The traffic is a little tight, but we have plenty of time. It would probably have been faster, but we're good if this traffic will just move along. We creep up First Avenue, trying to make it to the airport entrance. I can see the parking entrance just ahead. We're in the parking deck, and I cannot find a place to park. Darn it, if we hadn't needed to repack Magnus, our timing would have been good. I finally see a spot. Man, is it a tight little spot. That's okay, I can do it. It takes me three times up and back, and the car just fits.

I open the door and can just barely squeeze out. I open the trunk and pull out my bag and start running toward the terminal. After twenty feet, I look back for Magnus, expecting his long stride to have caught me in five paces. Magnus is not there. Where is he? I start to yell and I hear a muffled voice from the direction of my car. Damn it, Magnus, why doesn't he get out of that car? I run to the door, yelling at him. He screams out to me that he can't get out, he won't fit. Lordy, I should have known that big man didn't have enough room to open the door and squeeze out in this tight parking spot.

I throw the suitcase down, dig out my keys, and back out the car, almost hitting a car driving through the garage. They blow their horn, deafening any ears. I proceed to back out, more slowly this time. As soon as I clear the car on my right, Magnus jumps out and slams the door. I pull back in and jump out myself. He grabs his two suitcases and slams the trunk. I lock the car and look for my suitcase. It's nowhere. Magnus must have picked it up for me.

We run to the stairwell, and Magnus is already down the two flights and striding across the road. I yell, asking him if he has my suitcase. "Hell no," he yells, "I've got my two, can't you get your own?" I run back, looking for my luggage. I'm back at my car and look on both sides, but I still don't see it. This is impossible. It can't just disappear. I hear Magnus outside below the second deck, which I am on. I run to the front of my car and lean over the rail, looking down at him. "Andi, hurry, what are you doing? We're late, so quit playing around and come on." He then runs across the road in front of the terminal and enters the airport at the departure ticket counter.

I drop to my hands and knees and look under my car. It is not there either. I look under the car to my left— no suitcase. I look under the car to my right, and there is my bright red suitcase. It is dead center under that car. How in the hell did that happen? I am now lying flat on my stomach stretching, and I still can't touch it. I'm going to have to crawl under this Crown Vic and get my bag. This finally works. I've had to go about eighteen inches under this car and spin the suitcase around so that I can reach the handle. However, this maneuver rotates it a bit more beyond my reach.

There is no alternative other than to wiggle further under this monster car, as the suitcase is now under the front tires and resting up against the concrete rail overlooking the road two flights down. I can't get it from the front, so my only option is to keep moving forward under the car. I am now under the motor reaching for my suitcase as I feel something dripping on my head and back. It is probably just air conditioner condensation. No problem. I stretch further, just grasping the bag.

Before I back out, I hear laughter. Two girls are saying that it is Elphaba, with her feet sticking out from under that car. The girls' voices echo as they run off, high heels clicking on the concrete as they head for the stairwell. Those are two little wicked witches, not even offering assistance. As I start backing out, my hand lands in something wet, again, probably just water dripping down from the air conditioner. I finally back all the way out and quickly jump up, wiping my hands on my cargo pants.

I start running as fast as I can with my suitcase. Pushing my damn curly hair out of my eyes, I finally see the stairwell as it is coming at me faster than I am managing the stairs. Just at the end I almost fall but manage to recover. Hurrying down the stairwell with luggage bouncing with each step, I exit the garage and run across the road and into the terminal.

I have only twenty minutes before the flight is scheduled to depart. I pull out my ticket as I wait in line. I am the fifth person back. The line is moving pretty quickly, so I should be fine. My heart rate finally slows to near normal. People are looking at me and my clothes, eyeing me from head to toe. Jerks, what are they looking at? At that moment I drop my ticket, and as I bend over to pick it up, I notice black grease all over my pants and shirt. Oh, well, they are just clothes. I can change as soon as I get to New York.

Finally, I'm face to face with the ticket agent. I hand her my ticket, my ID, and my luggage. Everything goes smoothly; of course my luggage weight is fine. My papers are in perfect order. With my ticket in hand, I head right through the TSA line. For once, I don't get stopped. They do question me about my clothes, but I quickly tell them that I dropped my keys under my car in the parking lot and had to go under my car to get them and crawled into a mess. They believe this crazy story and I'm cleared right through.

Of course, my gate is C-14, the farthest from the ticket area. I start running again, as I've got five minutes before they close the door. I can't breathe. Where is one of those little golf cart drivers when I need one? I see the gate and see the last few people getting on the plane. Where is Magnus? I don't see him anywhere. I keep running and try to yell at the ticket agent that I am coming. I know my mouth is open, but nothing is coming out. The agents are looking around and just about to close the gate when I finally make it. I am again trying to talk, but I have no breath to speak. I just hand them my ticket as I am near collapse. The sweet little girl just smiles and tells me to slow down, that I will board. She says that as soon as they take off and give the signal that we are allowed to move about the cabin, then I can go on into the bathroom and wash my face and try to fix my hair. That is fine for her to say, like she doesn't sweat and get her hair messy when she is running as fast as she can for about a third of a mile.

I get through the gate and slowly walk down the ramp. As I board the plane I start looking for my seat. Gee, these first class people are so snooty. They are looking at me like I'm filthy and beneath them, what we in the South call 'white trash'. So what if there is a little grease on my pants? If one more of them gives me the look, I might just accidently trip and land my greasy pants all over them. They are acting like I alone was about to hold up their plane. I look at passenger 3B and tell him as I hold up my greasy paw that engine three is good now, and maybe some gratitude is in order.

I look at my ticket to find my seat number, 21A, then realizing that I can find it faster by looking for the only empty space on this plane. Another way to quickly locate my seat is just looking for the tallest person on the plane, and then I look to check if there is an empty seat beside him. Yes, that is the quickest way to my seat. At one glance I see Magnus's big tall body and a vacant seat beside him. And of course, the flight is full.

Stumbling down the aisle, I realize this flight must only contain New York people. This assumption is based on the stares with downcast eyes. No, there are some good ol' girls giggling and pointing. Oh, no the witches again! But, wait, I have this backwards. As I now look out at all the people, I realize that the ones looking at me with a 'better than thou' sneer are my fellow southerners. The ones that are reading without noticing me or the ones that meet my eyes and move on without emotion or give a nod without cracking a smile are the New Yorkers. I believe I am right about this, but further observation in the big city is required for confirmation.

I am now even with Magnus, and he is looking at me with this shit eating grin. "Andi, get in here and sit down." He moves out into the aisle and pushes me inside to the seat. "I told them you were here at the airport and had some kind of accident and that you would be here. The stewardess went to the cabin and informed the crew. She came back and told me that the ticket office said you had checked in and that you were on your way. Then there was an announcement that we were prepared to push out early, but that we were awaiting one late passenger. A few minutes later there was another message that the late passenger was en route and would be boarding within the next ten minutes. I think everyone here is holding you personally responsible for a late departure."

"That is just great, Magnus. None of this would have happened if you had stayed and helped me. But, no, you went running off like a ten-year-old, leaving me behind. Then when you knew something was wrong, you didn't even come back to help me."

"I was being responsible. It was your fault that you parked too close for me to get out of the car. You went running off without me."

"Yeah, but I came back for you within two minutes."

"You told me that I have to be on my best behavior and that I wasn't to act silly at all until the studio had released me. So, I was doing what my mommy told me to do. Look at you, what in the Sam Hill happened to you?"

"Well, let me just give you a play by play, dear man. After you went running off moving at four feet per stride I was looking for my luggage that I threw down immediately when I realized that you were trapped in the car. I jumped in the car and, without any care for my luggage, backed up to let you out. When I pulled back into the parking space, you were in the trunk grabbing your suitcases, and then you closed the trunk. Before I squeezed out of the car and got out you were running toward the exit. I didn't see my suitcase, so I went running after you thinking that, as a gentleman, you must have grabbed my suitcase, too. I could never catch you, but when you yelled that you didn't have my luggage I had to go back for it."

"I ran back and still couldn't find my suitcase. Only when I was on all fours did I find it under that old Crown Vic parked beside us. So, I had to crawl under that huge car to get it. But every time I reached for it, it kept sliding deeper toward the front of the car. In order to retrieve my bag, I had to get under the motor where the air conditioner was leaking on the back of my head and shirt. Meanwhile, I was lying in a puddle of oil. When I finally got out, I had to wipe my hands on something, using my pants. No big deal. Heck, these kids wear crazy jeans all the time. I just have a little grease on my pants; it's not really a big deal, is it?"

"Andi, honey, it is not just on your pants. Your shirt is covered in oil and your hair and face look like you've been wrestling in used motor oil. I don't know how you did that. It is a good thing that you have all those expensive highlights in your hair, because that air conditioner dripping is oily black, and it kinda blends in. I can only imagine that when all that unkept hair was flopping around in your face that you pushed it back with those oily hands. Apparently, you didn't wipe it all off on your clothes. Your face has a strong resemblance to a late eighteen hundreds chimney sweep."

"Oh God, Mag, what am I going to do? I can't get off the plane in New York City looking like a mess. At least I don't smell like a mess. I did shower this morning and used my new cologne. So, I smell good, don't I?"

"Hm, sorry girl, I think you are a little out of shape. Those few series of sprints have you smelling like a sweaty towel. Don't worry, though. Look what I've got in my backpack. We will get you freshened up."

Magnus proceeds to pull out everything but the kitchen sink. He has sanitizer and soapy wipes. He starts wiping my face and hair. He cleans my hands. He spins me around and cleans the back of my head and shirt. I feel like a baby kitten being licked clean by its mama cat. He pulls out a bleach stick and spot remover. He puts that to work on my clothes. Then he whips out some hair gel and starts rubbing his hands together and starts massaging my hair and head. He pops out a soapy wash and tells me to wipe my face one last time and then wipe down my neck. He hands me one more and tells me to go under my shirt and wipe down my boobs and arm pits. When he sees the look on my face, he explains that he is an expert on working out and sweating. Even though he doesn't have boobs, he knows they form little pockets that collect drops of sweat, thanks to gravity. Once I've taken my little whore bath, like my grandma used to call it, he starts spraying me down with some kind of deodorizer. All of this activity is serving as entertainment for those seated around us. Onlookers are even offering their own self-cleaning, hygiene tips.

By the time we are flying over Virginia I am almost as clean as a whistle, and we have a communal group of shared knowledge on all things domestic. Magnus now has everyone sharing recipes and gardening discoveries. As our little party continues on, Magnus has made all kinds of notes on his phone and has added several new Facebook friends. He is having a grand time. Now that I'm all clean and fresh, I feel so relaxed that I start to doze off.

I awaken with my big Brute whispering in my ear that we are in New York, but we are the last remaining passengers on the plane and it's time for us to get off. "Last one on and last one off, that's the way my girl rolls. Come on little Andi, let's go." He leads me off the plane and we are directed to the baggage claim. At least I look decent now. I was so upset that I would arrive for my first visit to New York looking like a tramp.

This airport is a far cry from Birmingham or Atlanta. There are so many people here. They are going in every direction as we stand in awe with our mouths agape and our eyes as big as saucers. For just a minute I feel like I am too far from my comfort zone. I feel like I will never be able to navigate this world. We eventually decide to just follow the crowd and hope that they are going to baggage claim. Lucky for us that is exactly what happens. Our baggage is finally located and retrieved. I was so afraid that one of our bags wouldn't make it. And my once red suitcase is now red with smears of black. It looks like a Minnie Mouse suitcase. I would be sad, but I know that Magnus has the cure to degreasing my luggage. He is a good travel companion, even if it is his fault that I am in this condition. I don't know how he does it, but he is always pulling out just the right product at any needed time, and he don't have cargo pants. It's all in his murse.

Magnus is leading us out to the transportation area, where he was told to look for our designated driver. I am behind him, holding on to the back of his shirt. I don't want to lose him or allow him to lose me. I've been in airports all over the world, but this one tops the lists for human congestion. I feel like I am skiing behind a huge boat, only I cannot see anything but the back of this boat.

We are walking along at quite a clip, when he suddenly stops and I run into his back. I bounce off without moving him an inch. He is sticking out his right arm and huge hand to shake the hand of the most petite, well-dressed man that I have ever seen. He is smiling as I walk around and he introduces me to the man. "Mr. Armstrong, please meet Andi my friend and chaperone for this visit. Andi, this is Mr. Armstrong, the man I met on the beach Memorial Day weekend." We shake hands as he welcomes me to New York. He admits that he was worried about Magnus in the city alone and had planned to have someone with him at all times. He was afraid that he might wander around and get lost, and with our tight schedule he had to guard against that possibility.

Mr. Armstrong slightly raises his arm, and within five seconds there are two people gathering our bags and exiting the building. I see a man pulling along my bag with two pinched fingers, like he doesn't want to touch it or something. He directs us to follow them to the ride to his office. Magnus's eyes light up as we exit the building as Mr. Armstrong gentle guides us directly to the waiting limo just in front of us.

We all get into the limo and again, me and Magnus have our mouths open and our eyes wide. We are speechless, which is rare for both of us at the same time. Just opposite our seat is a fully stocked five foot long bar. Magnus looks at me and makes a slight nod toward the bar. My eyes follow the nod and stop at the bottle of Dom Perignon. My eyes look back at him, then my head nods in the negative. His eyes look back at mine and plead. My heads nods negatively, and his eyes look like my granddaddy's blue-tick hound's eyes. We are driving by tall sleek buildings reflecting the longest black limousine that I've ever seen. And we are in it. Oh, I wish Daphne were here to see us. Mr. Armstrong is talking, but we're not listening; I hope that it's not important. After about ten blocks, I come to my senses and realize that he is telling Magnus about a few changes to the schedule.

Mr. Armstrong tells Magnus that instead of shooting here in New York, the Brevonni team insists that the shoot be done in Italy. This was very last minute, or he would have informed him sooner. I glance at Magnus, and his eyes are still viewing the same buildings and people on the sidewalks that had entranced me.

As Mr. Armstrong is talking about our flight to Italy in five hours, I smack Magnus's thigh, and he pulls his view from the limo window and looks at me as if he hadn't remembered me being by his side. I quickly remark, "Magnus, isn't that *fantastico*? Mr. Armstrong says that we are going to Italy in a few hours."

This abruptly awakens him and, turning to Mr. Armstrong, he says, "Say that again, sir, I think I missed something."

Mr. Armstrong replies, "Magnus, please call me Brad. I thought we had settled that at the beach. We are family. Andi, you too, I'm Brad. As I was saying, I received the call from Riccardo this morning. He is so taken with you and the ad pitch that he wants the shots to be from his own estate outside Milan. He sees his Brevonni man adjusting his tie while descending his Tuscan staircase. He sees you, he says, with your jacket casually held over your right or left shoulder, tie undone and shirt unbuttoned, wandering his estate with boulders and green trees and summer blooms as a backdrop. He wants to be right there seeing it all.

"This may require more time than we had anticipated, but Mr. Brevonni wants it this way and is more than happy to compensate you for your time, he says. Your clothes are ready at our office. The tailor is there with an assistant to make any last minute changes. He's sweating it, knowing that Riccardo himself will be seeing his alteration work first-hand. He wants everything perfect. So, I am sorry to disappoint you, but all you will see of New York is your ride from the airport to my office and back to the airport again.

"Stefan has been advised to arrange our travel to include a ticket for him and Ms. Andalusia. We will be in first class; Mr. Brevonni wants us all well rested and ready to go. All is set. It's going to be a fast ride, so just hang on tight, because there will be lots of bumps and snags along the way. I had already worked through most of the details with our shoot here in New York, but with this sudden change of plans, who knows what to expect? But, don't you worry; this is what Riccardo wants, and this is what he gets. Stefan will be with us to sort through the mishaps. He's wonderful at that. You'll see."

As soon as we arrive at this spectacular building with underground parking, Brad takes us to an elevator and up to his personal floor. "This is my apartment. Make yourself at home." Magnus and I share a glance and agree that this must mean we can run through the apartment, jump on the beds, and FaceTime with Daphne. "My office suites are on the floor just above us. I'll make sure the tailor is ready, and I will send for you. Sit back and catch your breath before the ball starts rolling, because once it does, there's no stopping."

The moment we are alone, we both look at each other and squeal. He grabs me up and spins me around. "Andi, we are going to Italy, F-R-E-E. I know you wanted to see New York, me too, but we will have to do it another time. I will be wearing clothes from my favorite designer, *and* I will be in his house and yard and meet him personally. Oh, I have to be good, Andi, can you believe this? I only have one problem."

"What could possibly be a problem, Magnus?"

"Stef-fon," he says. "What an unfriendly, better than everybody, stick in the mud. He thinks we are just a bunch of hillbillies that don't know nothin'," he says with a wink and a grin.

"Oh, Mag, who cares about him? If he thinks we are rednecks, just let it go. Remember, you are the model, and what do we care if we ain't got no class?"

We laugh and can't quite believe our luck. We are looking out the window, seeing the city below us. Giant buildings are spread as far as our eyes can see. We are finally able to sit down, still giggling, and talk non-stop about the city, the changes, Milan, Italy. I suddenly realize that we've got to make some calls to arrange for our changed plans. I tell Magnus to call the little artsy college girl who will be managing the shop, and I'll call Daphne. Oh, Lord, she's going to kill me. I'll probably miss two weekends of estate sales and maybe two weeks of work.

Magnus is busy with Suzanne and the shop arrangements. I call Daphne and she doesn't answer. I leave a quick voicemail, saying that I'm leaving for Italy and am not sure when I will be back, but I'll call her as soon as I arrive back in country. I am happy that she didn't answer her phone. Maybe we can get out of here before she gets the message. I am trying to appear calm, imagining a giant estate near Lake Como in northern Italy. I see myself wandering around with a glass of red wine constantly in my hand. My head is thrown back as I am laughing subtly, trying not to be too impressed by all the staff in awe of my greatness when my phone lets out a 'Hell yeah'. Oh no, it's Daphne.

"What in the heck do you mean that you are going to Italy and don't know when you will be back? Have you forgotten that *you* work here and Magnus works for us, you don't work for Magnus, and you are not free to go off gallivanting around the world with him when we have work to do? What is going on? And by the way, you are fired!"

I explain that it was an unexpected change that we were not aware of. We thought that we would be here for about five days, but now we are just not sure. I tell her about Riccardo Brevonni wanting the pictures of his clothes taken at his villa outside Milan and that we are forced to go along with his plans. He insists that he be there during the entire photography sessions, making sure that it is just what he has imagined. Once she knows that we will be at his house and meet him personally, she calms down a bit.

"Well, you are still fired until I decide to rehire you. Try not to worry about us; Sophie will help me with the sales. We will be fine. We can work from four in the morning till ten at night, it is okay, just don't you worry. Really, you just learn about the Milan we don't know about and maybe it will help us with our tour there in the Fall. Call me when you get back, and I'll see if I can re-hire you."

Just then the door flies open, and the most gorgeous man I've ever seen, after Magnus that is, flies in. He's trying to maintain a sense of order and ease, but I can almost see his heart fluttering. He seems at once, overwhelmed by the sudden change of plans and in shock as he gets his first look at Magnus. Their eyes meet and I can see their brains go into slo-mo. I'm not even in the room. This is quite interesting. I don't know who this golden haired, green eyed man-god is, but I can see that he is stunned by Magnus. Their worlds seem to collide, and they fall in pieces back to earth, hitting the ground at meteorite speed. Thud. Composures are regained and the man extends his hand to Magnus, saying, "Hello, I'm Stefan Gregg. You must be Magnus." Well, shit. It is going to be hard for Magnus to keep on hating him; I can't wait to see how this plays out. I can tell from his rhythmic voice, his gliding gait, and his slightly bent-wrist handshake that there is a strong possibility that he is family.

He directs Magnus out of the apartment, and I'm left standing like an ornamental fern. Hm, I can follow or just sit down and finally relax. I don't think they need me; it appears that Magnus has found a new keeper.

Meanwhile, I spot the bar. I decide that I need to make me a Leaning Bellini, just to set the Italian tone. I'm glad to see they have the individual bottles of champagne; I wouldn't have the nerve to pop a new bottle. Three Bellinis and an hour later, I hope they remember that I am here—what if they get on the flight and leave me? Magnus may never remember me again. I could be here for two weeks, and they will never give me a thought. I could rot here. Not a bad place to rot, though. What do they need me for now? Magnus has golden boy, Stef-Fon.

I continue down this pitiful path of neglect, imagining everything from my stinky dead body found in an uptown apartment to crawling back on a Southwest flight back to Birmingham. I'll have to call Daphne and beg to let me work that dirty, dusty, mildewed estate sale, knowing that she will put me out in the barn with the tools and cow milking equipment.

Suddenly I hear voices approaching the door. In walk Brad, Magnus, and Stefan. Magnus explains that the fitting was perfect. The clothes are wonderful and were made to order. He is thrilled that the sleeves and pants were long enough. He always complains that he thinks his arms have grown in length from being pulled by dress shirt cuffs and continuous stretching and stretching. I've never seen Magnus so at one with the moment. He is usually followed by disastrous mishaps; maybe this will be different with multiple professionals from a variety of disciplines making sure that his contractual obligations proceed without a hitch.

Magnus is excitedly telling me about the fitting, and I just stare happily at his big blue eyes. After I fail to respond, he looks at me and then back to the bar and gives me a little nod and a wink. "Are you just a little bubbly, Andi? How many Bellinis?" he asks.

I hold up 3 fingers as they tell me that the limo is ready, and we are off to the airport for our international flight. Before I know it, we are occupying two Lufthansa Airbus luxury cabins. Without words, Magnus and Stefan are in one cabin, and Brad and I are in the other. This is luxury that I never knew existed. Brad explains that they usually travel first class, but even he has not flown like this. It was arranged by the Brevonni staff so that we have the comfort of a full size bed for a good night's sleep before we arrive. It is like a train cabin. The seat converts to a full size bed, enclosed in its own little chamber.

Dinner and drinks are served, and I enjoy Mr. Armstrong's company. He is very smart, and we talk about everything. He is interested in me and my work. I talk and talk and talk. I tell him about my history with Magnus, football at Bama, and our work in the antique business. I talk about Daphne and our travel business, though not so first class. I tell him about my dreams to be a singer and songwriter, having had one song recorded by that new upcomer Cindy Eskridge. I tell him about our homes in Birmingham and my sister's clan down in the highlands of Rock Holler. He laughs and seems to enjoy it all. He shares that he's never had a lot of family. His parents sent him to private schools so they were never really close. He talks to them a few times a year and tries to visit every couple of years. He is an only child and has few close friends but lots of acquaintances. He seems so enchanted by our family closeness and how we took Magnus in as one of our own.

After several drinks and a five course gourmet dinner, I am fading fast. He helps me with my bed and as I am near collapse, I remember that Magnus is not allowed to drink on this trip and that I insisted that Magnus and I leave most of our clothes at home. We are going to the fashion capital of Europe, and I have three pairs of jeans. Who is taking care of Mag? He can't drink, because he passes out. My brain is slowing, and the little video in my mind is slowing down and fading to black and white and fuzziness, then black.

I am awakened by a refreshed and vibrant Magnus, telling me to wake up and do something with my hair and my face and my breath. What? Where? Oh Lord have mercy, I remember. I'm on a luxury flight to the home of the biggest fashion designer in Italy. I look at my clothes and sigh, and then I get a reflection of my face and hair in my television screen, and I scream. Magnus covers my mouth with his huge hand as he laughs. "It's okay, honey, they've brought you a little toiletry bag with everything you could ever need and a lot of stuff that we don't even know how to use."

"Mag, I didn't remind you not to drink and I drank while on duty. But, worst of all, I made us leave most of our clothes at home. What are we going to do?"

"We're fine. Brad knows from the beach that I can't hold my drink, so he instructed Stefan to see that I don't. I explained our clothing situation while in the office at New York, and Stefan said he would take care of it. He called the fashion buyer at Macy's and told them our sizes and had seven outfits for each of us delivered to the plane. He said that you looked quite a bit larger than the average New Yorker, but he was well trained in calculating sizes. Here's your today bag. Get ready—we land in forty-five minutes. Steffie says just throw your old clothes away. They ain't worth keeping. Not that he said 'ain't'; that was me. Bye, sweetie. Get yourself ready, and I'll be back in a few."

With that he excitedly exits, and I go through this bag like a hobo receiving his first handout. Wow, are you kidding me? All this is mine. I even have undies and shoes in here. How in the hell does 'Steffie' know what size breasts women have? How does he know I prefer granny panties? I didn't even think they had granny panties in New York. I quickly throw myself together.

Chapter Eleven
THE BREVONNI MAN
IN THE MAKING

Stefan expertly guides us through Italian customs. Good thing we have our passports. I bet nobody thought of that bump. Well, of course Stefan would have arranged a backup plan, but good thing we rednecks saved him the trouble. We leave the airport to another awaiting limo and are whisked quickly away and heading out of the city. Oh my God, are we going north? Is it toward Lake Como? It seems to be, but it can't be. Oh, my, I am hitting Magnus's thigh again. It takes him half a minute to finish his conversation with Stefan and give me a glance. "I think we're going to Lake Como. It is the most gorgeous, extravagant acreage in the world, probably. I'm so excited." He just gives my little fat knee a few taps, smiles at me, and turns back to Stefan.

After about two and a half hours we enter a gated property and meander up a long drive to an old imposing classic Italian villa. The two-story residence has a fading yellow exterior that is covered with green leafy vines from the bottom to the top. There is a central curved entry door with a large curving balcony directly above it. Before the car stops there are four men waiting to help us. All the doors to the limo seem to open simultaneously, and hands reach in to assist our exit. This is too much. I don't think that I am supposed to ask about my bags, but I turn to look and retrieve them if it is my responsibility. I am given a smile and a slightly raised index finger from one of the men. He winks, and I understand that I should not speak or even ask if he will take care of my luggage. I turn and follow the others inside. Damn, if I could just keep my mouth closed. It is hanging open in the astonished 'oh' of shocking surprise. It further betrays me by uttering a muffled '*shit*'.

My eyes can't believe what I am seeing. We enter a small foyer with stone walls and floors. It deserves special attention, but my eyes quickly pass it by as they take in the opening of a classic Italian living room. There are Italian tiles on the floor and a timbered ceiling with beams. A massive fireplace covers most of the opposing wall. I imagine it would require half a tree in here for a log. That grate must be ten feet long. The walls are low and stuccoed. The furniture is classic and comfortable. The room is warm and so inviting. It is not pretentious at all. One of the staff explains that Villa Cervidi was built as a hunting lodge in the late eighteenth century. He explains that most was left unchanged, but modernizations were also made where necessary. We continue the tour to our rooms. *What?* We're staying *here?* Am I dead? This must be a dream. I don't think I can ever travel with Daphne again, coach flights and cheap quaint hotels. Never. I fire myself from her business.

We round the corner, leaving this wonderful room that I know cannot be topped, to see the most massive, timbered staircase hugging a natural stone wall. Plants and trees and portraits of animals accent the wood timbers and the stoned wall. Someone better get the smelling salts, 'cause this make-believe southern belle is about to faint for real. No wonder Mr. Brevonni could see Magnus on this staircase: I can too. I pull him back to me as the group continues on the main floor past this impressive staircase. We are so excited and are trying our best not to jump and squeal. I must be dead and I took Magnus with me. We're both dead, and this is a southern country person's idea of heaven. Magnus finally loses it and lets out a pretty loud

'Dayum, ain't this the purdiest thing you ever seen?', while he picks me up, hugging me tight and spinning me around about five times.

At that time, a small, distinguished man, perhaps in his eighties, comes down the staircase with an appreciative smile on his face. With elegant, accented English, he says, "You must be *Magnuss* and this must be your friend, *Andiloocia*. Welcome to my home." At that, Mag-nut drops me to the floor, before I have time to prepare my landing. Instead of my toes touching the floor first, followed by my heels and an upright stand, my right toe gets hung on Magnus' left knee, flexes up while gravity takes me down, and I land on the back of my right heel. My left leg is wrapped around his right knee, trying to knot myself on until I regain my balance. This is not accomplished in the two nanoseconds that something about mass and force has allowed. I land pretty much directly on my upper butt, rolling to my back with my left leg still attached to Magnus as he proceeds to walk toward Mr. Brevonni. After a single stride, I release myself and quickly jump up, hoping no one noticed.

I am still melting from the way he pronounced my name, *An de loo chee ah*—isn't that lovely and romantic? Magnus is doing just great. He is his usual charming self, talking to Mr. Brevonni like he has known him for years. I bet he doesn't even know that the average person cannot just walk up to the man and chit-chat. The rest of our group has continued the house tour without realizing that we have dropped out to admire this part of the house.

Mr. Brevonni asks us to follow him as he tells us about his ideas. He comments on how pleased he is that Magnus agreed to come and take the photographs here. He said that when he saw the pictures of Magnus, he knew that his rugged good looks would best be captured in his villa and the surrounding grounds and maybe even around the lake. He takes us out a side door, and we follow him along a pebbled path through sparse woodlands with large stones and blue skies. Between trees I glimpse the blue of water and the white of reflected sunlight. The dark greens contrast with the blues of the sky and water, creating an inspiring calm. I can easily understand that this setting would be perfect for any type of picture, especially a ruggedly handsome man in well-designed Italian clothing.

He directs us back to the villa, where we meet up with the others. They look a bit shocked to see us walking in with the master himself. I think even Brad wasn't accepted on the personal level that Magnus has just received. After all the introductions, Magnus and I are taken to our rooms while Brad and Stefan follow Mr. Brevonni to what I presume to be his office suite.

Mag and I are thrilled with our adjoining rooms. We sit back on my bed, looking out the window of our upstairs room. We pinch each other to make sure we're not dreaming. I tell him I think we must be dead together and must be in heaven but am astonished at how the hell that would happen. The view from our window is of the grounds and lake. We promise each other that we will be on our best behavior and try to act like we had raisin'. We are surrounded by high-class New York people and European real-classed people. We are going to be good—wine for me and none for him. He says that is okay, because he like that bubbly water with gas as they called it. We are both allowed all the Italian coffee and caffeine that we wanted and Caprese salads and pasta and antipasta and fresh vegetables and fruit and sweets. We agree that we won't ask for anything, only doing what we are told. Of course, I'm hoping I won't be told anything, as my only purpose here is taking care of Magnus, and perhaps others were assigned that job for me.

Magnus says he only wants one thing, and that's to walk around the little town of Bellagio and look at the outside of the buildings. For some reason he is very interested in signs. He explains that in the cities and towns, they don't use street signs like we do. Instead, he says, they are carved in stone blocks and affixed to the buildings. He says he just has a fascination with these and wants to study them while he is here. I think he's crazy but agree to go with him. I plan to eat gelato as we walk and look at stupid signs on buildings. I hope they have a lot of streets with signs, because I need a lot of gelato.

We relax and talk for an hour or so, when Stefan comes to get Magnus. He says that it is time to work. They have planned an afternoon and sunset shoot both inside the villa and outside on the grounds. He says he will stop by for me on their way out, but right now he has to get Magnus dressed and with the stylist and make up staff, so off they go.

I wander around my room and my bath and then investigate Magnus' room and bath. I admire the views from both of our rooms and plan my outside roaming from my heightened view of the garden paths and waterfront. I then leave my room and take a self-guided tour of the upstairs area. I remain good to my word, refusing to open a single closed door. However, if the door is ajar, I consider that an invitation to inspect and admire. Everything upstairs is modernly furnished and tasteful. I prefer the hominess of the downstairs. I like the wood and stone and stucco and tiles. As I head back to my room, one of the female staff asks me to come with her. She says they are ready for shooting, and I am invited to watch if I would like.

We go downstairs through a different staircase. It empties us into the most inviting kitchen that I've ever seen. It has modern sleek appliances set into an old appreciated and worn background. Stone walls, fireplace, and a large wood table with wood benches. She walks to the espresso machine and asks if I would like an espresso or cappuccino. With my mouth watering, I accept a cappuccino. She expertly makes it for me and allows me to sweeten it as I like. She places it on a saucer and adds biscotti. She prepares herself an espresso and we sit at the table and visit. Her name is Guilia, and she tells me about herself. This is just like we would do at home. No formality, just simple enjoyment in time spent with a friend.

After we finish, she takes our cups to an original country sink. It is huge and deep. She explains that it was used here for preparing the large pieces of meat for the fireplace. She said they preferred to cook the carcass as whole as possible on the spit on the fire, rather than cut it in smaller pieces before cooking. She then takes me through a small hallway to the main room again. She says she will leave me here and that if during my visit I am in need of anything, I should just push the little button in my room that is on the wall beside the bed. It will ring in her room down the hall, and she will assist me.

I am left among a beehive of activity. I can see Magnus surrounded by people. He is gorgeous. They have just finished preparing him for the shoot. Lights and equipment are everywhere, with electrical cords running all over the floor. Magnus winks at me and then whispers to Stefan. Stefan runs to me and says that Magnus is glad that I'm here with him. He then explains the details of the shoot. There are several indoor shots, with pictures to be taken on the stairs, by the fireplace, and leaning against the stone wall, gazing out the window. Then they move production outside and take several shots in the wooded area, sitting on the large boulders and walking along the lakeshore. Mr. Brevonni is the director, so to speak.

Stefan explains that Mr. Brevonni knows exactly what he wants. He has communicated his ideas to the photographer and lighting guy, but he wants to make sure the poses and backgrounds are just as he imagined them.

Then they come back to wardrobe and repeat the sequence with a second, more casual suit. Tomorrow's schedule is the same with three more pieces of casual, relaxed, everyday wear. He tells me that I may tag along but to just stay clear of everyone, because it will be chaotic, with people going in every direction. He then rushes back headfirst into the mass of people and equipment.

I am content to watch. This is astonishing. Look at them go. And my big ol' Brute. I am as proud of him as a hen is of her little chick. Nobody deserves this more than him. A few weeks of ago he played hooky and skipped out on our shop just so he could go to the beach. And look at him now, would you?

The afternoon goes just as Stefan explained. As they are finishing up the second shoot, I go outside and enjoy the surroundings. The sunset is beautiful on the lake with the low mountains framing the backdrop. There is a picturesque white dock with a small boat. I would have expected Mr. Brevonni to have a more expensive boat, but this thing looks just a bit more upscale than the old one we used to ski behind at home. Oh well, he looks to be in his eighties, maybe like me, he just don't ski anymore.

I mosey on back in as everyone is about to sit down at that big table. Magnus lops on over with that sweet grin and throws his arm around my shoulder. He's wearing jeans that fit great; I guess Brevonni must have a denim line. He is so darling. There are times that I wish we were both straight. I know that we would be married forever. Well, we will always be each other's soul mate and true love.

We all sit down and enjoy the most relaxed and delicious meal that I've ever had. I have spectacular red wine, and Mag has his gassy water. I eat and eat. Magnus eats and eats and eats and eats some more. Mr. Brevonni is jubilant, saying that the photos are wonderful, just as he planned. He tells Magnus that he wears his clothes like he designed them to be worn. Magnus apologizes for not being a professional and causing them to take a few more shots than were planned. Mr. Brevonni assures him that his southern charm more than makes up for it and is so evident in the photos. It is just the look that he wanted. He said that he didn't want a professional; he wanted Magnus with all his innocence shining through each shot. After coffee, Mr. Brevonni, Brad, and Stefan again go to the office for more business discussion.

Magnus and I decide that we will walk down to the town of Bellagio. It takes us forever to finally get to the central part of the town. I discover that Bellagio is on a little stick-out like my daddy used to call it, with water on both sides. It is very quaint and postcard like. Daphne would want to come here, not that we could afford it. And our little country tourists really don't have that kind of money. My, wouldn't it be wonderful if we could, though?. Little church lady might just say damn herself. If I had the money, I would pay for this excursion, just so she would have the chance to experience this. Hm, maybe good intentions count for something.

Sure to his word, Magnus is staring at the stupid little faded, dirty signs on the buildings. Dummy, what is it about those little stone signs? I don't get it. As I walk out of the gelato shop, licking away at this rich stuff that can't be good for you, he is staring at that sign with his eyes inches away from it. He is even touching it all over. He has his phone camera out and is taking pictures. I interrupt him, asking if he is ready to walk to the waterfront, and he asks me to give him a few more minutes. Walking ahead, I find a bench and sit with the cool breezes on my face, enjoying the moment. It is almost dark, I think, but with this giant full moon just about ten miles from me it is light enough to see everything. I swear if I jumped high enough I could touch that moon. Magnus probably wouldn't even have to jump, that is, if he even sees it. All he sees is that stupid concrete or stone or whatever it is, sign.

He finally arrives and appreciates this magical moment with me. We are still shocked and amazed that we are sitting here, our only expense being our shared gelato. After an hour or so, we meander our way back to the Villa Cervidi. Magnus tells me that during the photo shoot he learned that Cervidi is Italian for 'deer'. This is understandable, since it was originally a hunting lodge. I truly love it—it is not a fancy home at all, and it is so comfortable and welcoming. Even in the dark, or maybe especially in the dark, with a full moon rising on a timeless lake, it is spectacular. We make our way upstairs arm in arm and settle in our separate rooms. Guilia left me a note asking me to ring her if me or Magnus want a coffee or nightcap. I creep in his room to ask him, but he is sound asleep on his bed. I decide against it and return to my room. I crawl in my jammies and curl up in this comfy bed, and I'm soon drifting off to sleep as well.

I awaken to fresh air pouring into a slightly open vertical window. I even love these windows, how nice and different they are. I hear Magnus tiptoeing around in his room with our adjoining door open. I call and he runs in. "I'm so glad that you finally woke up," he said. "Look outside and listen to the birds. Do you smell that air? A soft mountain breeze, rolling across the water and then it picks up the woodsy scent and comes right in this window to welcome you to this day. Andi, isn't it wonderful?"

I tell him that it is one of the best mornings of my life. I agree that I can't remember ever feeling so refreshed and welcomed to a day. He tells me to hurry and get in the shower. He says he's got my clothes laid out and that I need to hurry. He motions me to the door into the hallway. As he opens the door, my nose is now awakened to a different welcome. It is Italian coffee. Oh my word, I don't think I can take much more.

Taking the fastest shower ever, I jump into the clothes he has picked out for me. Damn, if that Stefano, as they call him here, doesn't know how to shop for people. This is just what I would have bought if I were planning on spending eight hundred dollars on a day's worth of clothing. I brush my teeth, wipe on some moisturizer and a quick swipe of makeup, and then notice this frightful hair. Had I known that I was coming to the swankiest place in Italy, I would have got to Leslie's for a new do. Maybe some color touch ups and definitely a stylish cut. As it is, I've been a bit remiss about timely trims and coloring. So, now I am left with this mass of uncontrolled curls in every color possible. There is a black hair base with yellowish/dull highlights with about an inch of grown out salt and pepper roots. What the hell can I do about it now? I grab the gel and activate it with a good rub down. I finger pick the mess and call it a defeat; another win by nature and another loss for me and Leslie. I can never tell her about this. She would just die.

I come out of the bathroom with Magnus in my room looking out the window. When he sees me, he grabs my wrist and says I look great and that we should get coffee and food. Off we go, as he runs to the massive staircase. I pull with all my might, finally getting him to stop. I explain that to our right is a private stairway leading right to the kitchen. We do an about face and run toward the shortcut, letting our noses find the way without our brains. Magnus can barely fit down the stairs, bumping his head twice. We pour out into the kitchen, falling but making a good recovery. We are making more racket than this house has heard in years.

Guilia looks up and smiles while Mr. Brevonni sits at the table alone, enjoying bread and salami. He looks up and greets us endearingly. We sit with him as Guilia brings us coffee. She refills the meat and cheese tray and brings warm bread and butter. Just when I think this place can't get better, it does, every time. It is just meat and cheese and bread and butter and coffee, but this is the best breakfast ever. It must be the magic of this house.

Magnus is talking to Mr. Brevonni about loving his clothes as much as he seems to love all things Italian. He is telling him that when he remodeled his house a few years ago, he furnished it totally from the Italy Design store. He tells him about his living room suite and how much he likes it. He also tells him about how he really loved the Tonino Lamborghini Casa Collection, but that he couldn't afford it. I tell him about how I think this place is magical and so warm and inviting in a cozy, comfortable kind of way. I tell him that his villa reminds me a lot of our friendships in the South. Everyone is taught to be friendly and hospitable and that is how this house feels to me.

We tell him about my sister's travel company and how we are spending a few days in Milan with our small group in October, before we move on to Florence and Rome. He asks about our jobs and how we came to be such friends. We tell him the whole history. He laughs his way through it with us. He asks how Brad discovered Magnus. As Magnus tells him that story, he has to take several breaks for coughing fits caused from the laughter.

He shares some of his past with us, reminiscing about his parents and siblings. He tells us stories of his youth in a small village in Sicily. Sadly, he relates some of the horrors of World War II. At one point, he pulls from his pocket a photo of a long deceased wife, explaining that she died twenty-two years ago in a traffic accident. They could never have children, but didn't feel deprived, he said, because they were anonymously always helping local families during hard times, and they felt like their local community was their children. He said that his family home is in Sicily and that he comes here during the fashion season only.

He tells us how happy he is that we came here. He says he realized that Brad would do a fine job in New York, but that once he saw Magnus's face, he felt drawn to him. He actually dreamed of Magnus wearing his new line of clothing walking around Villa Cervidi. So, he apologizes for the change of plans and says that he is so happy that it is working out just like his dream. He is certain that this will be his best collection yet.

He expresses his gratitude that we are early risers like him and makes it clear that he is enjoying our company. He tells us both that we are fortunate to have such a close and special friendship and that we must keep it well-nourished and maintain it forever. He excuses himself for his daily morning walk.

We are so grateful for the time he spent with us. It was so special and yet comfortably normal. It seemed like we could talk to him like we talk to each other. Okay, well we wouldn't talk foul-mouthed to him like we sometimes talk to each other. But it was very nice. We were both smiling and feeling touched by his company.

Guilia then joins us, and we talk and eat some more. She says that she has been with Mr. Brevonni for about thirty years and that he is like a father to her. She says she loves him dearly and travels everywhere with him. She prepares all his food and looks after him as she always has. Guilia says that we are unusual house guests. Most people who visit Mr. Brevonni are superficial and are always trying to flatter him. She says that before we arrived downstairs with such flare, Mr. Brevonni was just telling her how he was enjoying us.

He said that it was nice to be around people who were open and honest and genuine. He said that he suspected Magnus had those qualities when Brad told him about him. Brad even sent her the link to the YouTube videos and asked her to use her discretion in showing Mr.

Brevonni. Of course, after seeing them and his ad work, she knew Mr. Brevonni, being a worldly man, could handle that. Those videos showed the deep down sweet naïve qualities of Magnus. She says that after meeting me, he told her that he was pleasantly surprised by my open and pleasant personality.

Just then Brad and Stefan appear, and Guilia excuses herself to prepare their coffee and breakfast. For them she brings more meat, cheese, and bread. Yogurt and granola with fresh, local fruit is presented for Brad. They review the plans for the day. It's the same schedule as yesterday, just different clothes. Brad says that I am welcome to watch if I want or that I can have one of the staff drive me around the lake if I prefer.

"Yeah," I said. "You look great in those fine clothes, Magnus, but I'm passing you up for a chauffeured trip in the most spectacular place on God's great earth. Sorry, you come in second to that offer." I tell them to get to work and that I'll see them later. Guilia tells me to take a walk to the lake shore and she'll send Marco for me when he gets the old Alpha Romeo sportster ready.

I run out the door, happier than a schoolgirl. I wish Daphne were here, she would love this. Marco could share the local history with her and she would be in heaven. I stroll to the lake for an early morning walk, and I am rewarded with astounding beauty. Sitting on a beach chair, I put my feet up, soaking in this warm early morning sun. I close my eyes and feel like a lizard or snake must feel. The warmth is a sedative. I am not asleep, but it is almost like meditation. I am not here or there, but suspended in a warm beautiful cocoon of relaxation. My mind is nowhere, it is floating. I don't know how long I am here before I hear a soft voice asking if I am ready for a drive or if I would prefer more time alone. What? I am to decide between this perfect solitude or being driven around paradise in an

Italian sports car. Who can make that decision? No one can decide that.

As I open my eyes, I realize that I shall not be greedy. I will not put Marco out by delaying him of his duty. Duty, ha, what kind of a job is that? I want his job. I slowly pull my heavy and content body out of that chair and tell him that I am ready when he is. I thank him for his services as I follow him back up to the house. As we walk past the window on our way to the garage, I see the same madness that I saw yesterday. People and equipment and wiring are everywhere. Have fun, I think, as I spot a little red sports car backed out, top down and purring like a little hot red kitten. Man, if my friends could see me now. Where is my Wifi spot when I need one? Nope, it's just me here to enjoy this moment. I really prefer it this way. I like my privacy and solitude; this is my idea of a perfect day.

Marco and I spend most of the day driving around Lake Como. He takes me along the little village roads, stopping often to talk to the locals, and lets me have coffee or gelato or shop or use the facilities. He even lets me walk around the little neighborhood chapels. It is splendid. I feel like a Hollywood model with the little red scarf around my neck being driven around in this little car. I think that I saw a movie like that once. We stop for lunch, and he tells me all about the area and interesting facts. He answers all my questions without giving me all that boring information like Daphne does. She drives me nuts sometimes. Nope, I decide that I am glad that she isn't here. We wouldn't have made it to the second village much less all the way around the lake if she were here. I'm sure that Marco would have had to call in a replacement driver if she were here, because she would drive him nuts too.

We arrive back at the villa in the late afternoon. Marco says he tried to get back for a little rest before the evening. Entering the house, all is quiet. The cables, cameras, and equipment are gone. I walk into the kitchen, expecting to find Guilia. Nope, the kitchen is empty too. Where could they all be? I walk outside to the back terrace and listen. Only silence. I walk to the lake, but again no one is found. Back to the house I go, and now I am starting to worry. Did Magnus fall off the balcony and not land on his feet? Are they at the hospital? I run back to the garage, thinking Marco might know what is going on. He's gone. I decide they all went somewhere and will be back soon. I am left to this beautiful place all alone? Oh, my. What shall I do?

I decide that my best choice is to go up to my room and take a little rest, just like Marco suggested. Once inside my room, I hear heavy snoring. I am recalling Goldilocks and the Three Bears: somebody is sleeping in my bed. No, my bed is empty. I carefully open the door to Mag's room and somebody is sleeping in his bed. It's Magnus. I've never known him to take a nap. Has the house been gassed? What has made them all sleep? I walk over to Magnus and sit on his bed. He's usually a light sleeper, but this doesn't awaken him. I have to touch him to wake him up. He startles and opens his mouth to scream when I cover it with both of my hands to silence him. He then relaxes, and his little giant heart slows down to a normal rate. I ask what is up with everyone. The house is totally quiet. Yeah, except you, he says.

He explains that the photo shoot went great and they were finished by two o'clock. Mr. Brevonni was well pleased with all the photos and declared it a job well done. Everyone packed up and left. Mr. Brevonni said that we have plenty of time to enjoy a couple of hours of rest. So, that is what they did. He asks how my day went, and I tell him all about it. I ask what the plans are. He says that Guilia is going to have dinner ready at eight and, other than that, there are no plans.

"Magnus, why don't me and you make dinner for everyone?" I say.

"No way in hell am I going to cook with you, Andi. I might let Nino help me, but you are a disaster in the kitchen, remember?" he says.

"Okay, then, what else can we do?" I ask. "I think we should do something special for Mr. Brevonni. What could it be? I thought it would be nice to extend some southern hospitality to everyone for all they've done for us. And cooking and eating is what we do best."

"You do have a point, Andi. I guess they wouldn't mind us in their kitchen. Let's quietly go down and have a look around and see if they have anything in their cupboards that we know what to do with. I'd like to make them a big southern meal. I don't need to cook Italian; Guilia does a great job at that. They need something different."

We proceed quietly to the kitchen through the back stairway. Magnus is careful with his big head this time. He doesn't bump it once and we don't fall down the stairs. Once in the kitchen, Magnus finds three chickens in the little fridge. At least there are no feathers, but they are whole chickens. I've just bought wings or breasts in the store; I didn't know they came whole, complete with head. There are fresh green beans, potatoes and tomatoes, cheese, onions, and bread. I prowl around and find eggs, sugar, flour, milk, spices and cocoa. Magnus says that's plenty. He can make southern fried chicken, green beans, a salad, biscuits and a cake or maybe even a chess pie. He says he can do it all, but I'll have to stay out of his way and just assist when he asks for help. I promise to do just that.

Just as I hoped, I am allowed to peel and slice and find utensils and cookware. Magnus is wonderful. He does all the hard work. In fifteen minutes he makes three homemade pie crusts and biscuit dough. I convince him that I know how to peel potatoes, so that is my job, even though he complains that I cut off most of the potato with the peel. He then moves on to carving up three headed chickens. I don't mean a chicken with three heads. I mean three chickens with three heads, without feathers. As soon as I get the potatoes prepped, he sets me to work on the beans. I do that to his satisfaction, so he thinks my skills are improving. He has me mix up the breading for the chicken. I am to combine the flour, salt, pepper, and some other spices that he has added to the mix. I proceed under his watchful eye.

He mixes up the custard for the pies. I wash and put green beans and butter in the pan. He lets me chop up the onion, lucky me. I wonder why I am suddenly skilled enough to cut onions. He has me chop up the potatoes. He has me look for some type of fat, shortening, or oil. I find something that he says is lard, and he's thrilled. He starts frying chicken and potatoes.

He has the pies in the oven, and the biscuits are ready to be baked. I am then sent to find the serving dishes. I set the table and find the butter and some honey for the biscuits. I ask Magnus what kind of wine should be served with fried chicken and southern supper. "Do you think they've got some Strawberry Hill downstairs?" He makes some kind of mouthy gesture and refuses to let me make that selection.

He goes to the wine cellar and comes back with three bottles of Coenobium Bianco, exclaiming perfection. He also has a bottle of red for us to drink as we finish cooking. Great! But then I remember that he should be conscious for our dinner and pull it out of his hands before he pops the cork. I go to the cupboard and open a bottle of Pellegrino for us. I pour it in wine glasses, and we resume our work.

We hear people stirring around six-thirty. I am sent as a distraction, good idea. I meet everyone in the living room, their noses leading them toward the kitchen. I go running in and tell them I need them outside. Reluctantly, they agree to follow me. So, Brad, Mr. Brevonni, Stefan, and I slowly follow the path to the waterfront. I'm talking like someone possessed. They keep trying to make sense out of what I am saying. Because they don't want to come with me, I have to break into a creative story.

I'm telling them that earlier, as I was sitting on the chairs of the boat dock, I could swear that I saw a huge serpent-like creature. Have they ever seen anything like that? There must be some kind of Loch Nessie here too. Maybe she's called Lake Comessi or something. If they will sit here and just look off to the left at about eleven o'clock and watch closely, I am sure that they will see it, too. Well, they are all laughing and starting to walk off. As they turn, I scream and say, "There it is! Didn't you see it? Look!" They all stop laughing and quickly turn to the direction of my make-believe monster. We don't see it for the next few minutes, but I convince them to take a chair and help me watch for it. We sit and talk for a bit, while they continue to deny my monster. In the end, I have no choice but to tell them that they are right, that I didn't see a monster, but I did have to tell a white lie to protect a secret.

Now, I have their attention, much to my surprise. They are now all grinning and wanting to know about 'the secret'. I keep them going at this for another twenty minutes. The last they knew Marco had taken me for a drive along the lake. They are guessing that we crashed or maybe I jumped in the car and drove off without Marco. Then they think that I had gone shopping and charged everything to Mr. Brevonni. That is insulting enough that I start stomping off, which gives me even more time, because they beg me to come back, and they all profusely apologize. Then Brad starts guessing that Magnus has had a glass of wine and passed out somewhere. I lead them down that trail for a while, knowing how very close that came to the truth. After about an hour, I lead us back to the house.

During my outside adventure, Guilia has, of course, noticed that someone was cooking in her kitchen. She came down and saw Magnus at work. He insisted that she have a glass of wine and sit at the table and just visit with him while he cooked. She was only allowed to direct him to the location of the serving bowls and platters. She was overjoyed that someone would cook for her. Magnus later told me that he really thought a lot of her. She had told him some interesting stories of her history with the Brevonnis.

As we approach the terrace with the open living room doors, the others are commenting on the smells of dinner. They don't know what Guilia is making. As we walk in, Magnus meets us at the door wearing an apron. He holds four glasses of wine and offers them to us. He asks that we all join him at the table for a surprise dinner. Guilia is already seated. I help Magnus with bringing the remaining platters to the table. After everyone is seated, Magnus begins his toast.

"Andi and I wanted to prepare and serve you dinner as a small token of our gratitude for all that each of you have done for us. I sincerely mean this when I say it; I do not even want to be paid for the pleasure of wearing such fabulous clothes in a setting like this. It is I that should be paying you guys for this experience. I really appreciate the past few days. Never in my life could I have imagined a better time spent with better people. I will remember this forever. Andi described it best to me as we were cooking. She said, 'It is like a dream. I still don't think that I am awake.' We've even pinched each other, and it hurt, so we laughed and decided that we must be not be dreaming, but I don't think we will ever wake up after this. From the better than first class flight, to the clothes, to the stay here and the hospitality that we have received, nothing will ever compare to this. We agree that we literally stumbled into the most wonderful time of our lives and if we saved all of our money for the next ten years, we could never repay you for this experience. We really mean it, from the bottom of our hearts, as we say, Thank You!"

"Well said, Magnus. I can't make a toast like that. But I do want to say that every minute after we landed in New York has been magical. You don't want to know about the minutes before our arrival. We are pretty well traveled for a bunch of Southern hicks. We've been in most European countries and have met lots of wonderful people along the way, but we've never felt more welcomed that this. I talked Magnus into letting me tag along to keep him from getting into trouble in New York. And never did anyone tell me that I wasn't needed or wanted. You treated me just as special as Magnus, even though I contributed nothing to this enterprise. It is I who owe you my sincere thanks. Thank You!"

All the glasses click and we salute the shared appreciation and joy in each other's company. I ask Magnus to tell them what he's prepared for them. "When Andi and I came down, we weren't sure what we would find to work with, but thank you Guilia for such a well-stocked kitchen. I have prepared Southern Fried Chicken with my own blend of your spices. We have Fried Potatoes with onions and basil. There are butter sautéed fresh green beans and a mixed salad. A Caprese Salad was prepared with your delicious tomatoes and mozzarella. In the south, we don't really know how to make good bread like you do, so we have learned to make good biscuits. We usually serve them with or without butter; Andi has to have her butter. Then, if you need to add just a little sweetness, we have found some local honey in your pantry. I've paired the meal with some selections from your wine cellar, Mr. Brevonni. I've chosen Coenobium Bianco, to complement the meal. For dessert, I've prepared what we call a Chess Pie, which is a sweetened custard pie on a slightly salted flakey crust. Please enjoy your meal that we have prepared for you. *And*, when finished, Andi and I have the clean-up detail. Guilia, if Mr. Bevonni agrees, you are off for the night."

Everyone seems to enjoy the meal. Even these three cultured men who have eaten in the best restaurants in the world carry on about how good it is. They say Magnus has changed their opinion of southern cuisine. They all linger at the table after the meal, so I make Magnus enjoy their conversation and I clean up the kitchen myself. As the table is open to the kitchen, I'm included as I clean around the men.

Once the operation has concluded, and having confirmed that the plan is to turn in early, I take a half bottle of wine and two glasses to our room. Magnus and I each have a glass of wine and talk for a few hours about our experience. The next morning, Mr. Brevonni is going to take us to Milan for a quick tour of his clothing factory and warehouse. He wants us to see his line from the sketch to the cutting to the sewing to the shipping. Then we are off to the airport for our flight back home. Magnus and I are flying into Atlanta, then on to Birmingham. Brad and Stefan are on a direct flight to New York.

We enjoy a great night's sleep with the window open to the lake breeze. Guilia's kitchen awakens us, and as usual Mag and I go running down the back way to the kitchen. Mr. Brevonni is there, and our comfortable conversation falls into place. Shortly we are joined by Brad and Stefan. Guilia hustles us along, knowing that our schedule starts early. Each of us completes our packing and arrives in the living room for our departure. I hug Guilia and thank her for being so nice to us. I tell her that I will miss her. In a few short days, she and Mr. Brevonni have touched my heart. They really feel like friends.

We stop by the huge, modern Riccardo Brevonni house of fashion. "Wow," is all I can say. The seamstresses in our family were my Grandma Lola and Daphne, but they would never dream of how amazingly intricate and detailed and exhaustive a huge factory like this could be. If I could give a gift to Daphne, it would be for her to be allowed to float around and observe this operation for a day. She would be in heaven. We wrap up the presidential tour of this facility and head to the airport.

Once our baggage is taken at curbside, Mr. Brevonni gives each of us a hug. I feel that mine was special and lasts a bit longer and does include a quiet whisper. I tell him that I think he is an especially thoughtful and kind person, and I thank him for generously sharing his home with me. I give him a quick and heartfelt kiss on the cheek, and we're off.

Just as I think our processing has gone too smoothly, Magnus is pulled over for a secondary screen. He receives his pat down without complaint, just that crooked little smile. He is then taken into an enclosed room as we are kept waiting outside. After ten minutes or so, he walks out, laughing and talking with the official. They shake hands, and Magnus joins our little group. "What the heck did you do, Magnus? Did you have some type of contraband or something?" I ask.

"No, no, Andi, don't worry. I think he just wanted to feel me up. No, really, he said that once he saw my ID, he recalled a YouTube post that his cousin who lives in New Orleans had sent him. He wanted to know if it was me. I tried to tell him that it wasn't me, but my expression gave it away. I admitted that it was, then we laughed, and he told me how great he thought it was that we could all openly meet together on a beach in Florida once a year. He said that he would like to join us one year. I gave him my card and told him to call me when he planned to make it and he could join us at our tent."

Brad says, "What a small world, huh, Magnus? You never know whom you might meet in Pensacola. It is a great opportunity to meet new friends and new modeling talent. I am very glad that my friends talked me into going to the beach this year. I was very close to backing out, knowing that I had this big Brevonni ad deal closing in. Look at how nicely life works out sometimes. I'll overnight you the shots that we decide to use. Of course, you'll receive emails as we near the launch, and I'll keep you aware of all the sources of exposure that we are planning for your ads. Please call me if you have any questions or concerns. You have been a perfect gentleman, and you have behaved more professionally than any of the professional models that I've worked with. I'd like to keep the lines open between us and maybe call you again with new ideas, if you agree."

Magnus is quick to reply, "Certainly, Brad, you are welcome to call me any time. And I meant it, you owe me nothing. I've got all these sensational clothes. Not to mention the time spent with Mr. Brevonni. I'm as happy as I can be."

Brad laughs and gives Magnus a hug. "Your check will be in the mail, Magnus. You are amazing. I'll never have another model like you, I can promise you that. Call me if I can be of any help to you in the future."

Magnus and Stefan walk away as Brad and I share our goodbyes. They are huddled together for a few minutes, and then they join us. Stefan gives me a tight hug, and then we part ways. Magnus and I walk along to our gate, and Brad and Stefan go the opposite way to theirs.

We are so excited to find out that we are again sitting in first class. This is a different plane, and there are no pullout beds or private compartments for us this time. I guess Atlanta isn't New York. We giggle and talk for hours, sharing the little details over and over. We land in Atlanta without delay and rush to catch our Birmingham flight. We board that flight and again have first class on an even smaller plane, but we don't care— we are still on cloud nine. Our conversation has now slowed and is much quieter. We're a little tired; it's been a long day. We arrive in Birmingham at seven-thirty in the evening.

Our luggage arrives intact. We gather it and roll it to the car. I'm so ready to get home. There is no traffic on our drive. We pull up in my garage and unload the baggage. Magnus helps carry my luggage into the house and gives my house a security check. He always says he can't sleep until he knows that I'm tucked in OK. So, I insist on going to his house and doing the walk-through with him. All's clear. We are safely in our homes. He walks me to my back door and kisses my cheek goodnight. I quickly jump into my cut-off sweat pants and t-shirt, grab me a Diet Mt. Dew, and hop on the couch with my remote control. I've got to catch up on my soaps.

Chapter Twelve
THEY'RE BACK

Since I never called Daphne, she doesn't know that I'm back. I thought about spending two days here before I call her. I take my time when I decide to finally get out of bed. I unpack these fancy clothes that Stefan got for me. I spend some lazy alone time for several hours until I guilt myself into checking in with her. It is not even noon yet. I could kick myself for not being more selfish. Usually, I take a lot of 'me time'. But I do know that she's busy and has quite a bit of work going on.

I hesitantly dial her number, hoping that she doesn't answer, hoping I can leave a message and maybe have a few more hours before I have to be her servant again. After the third ring, I think I'm home free. "Hello, Andi, where are you? Are you all right? Is anyone hurt? Are you in jail? Talk to me, hurry, what is going on? Do I need to call an attorney? Oh, God, I knew it, I knew something terrible would happen. Why are you calling now? I knew you and Magnus would get in trouble in Italy. Andi, Andi, talk to me."

"Daphne, shut up for a minute. I'm fine. Magnus is fine. We are not in jail. We are not in Italy. We are home. It's a long story, and I'll fill you in later. But, Magnus was great; he got everything done in just a few days. We did not get into trouble, and we're back home safe and sound, job complete. I'm calling to see what you need me to do. Magnus has the shop for the rest of the summer, and I'm yours for the picking. What do you have planned? What do you need me to do? Is everything okay on your end?"

"Oh my goodness, I'm so relieved to hear that. I'm glad everything went as planned and yep, we've got some sales lined up and a few picking trips up to north Alabama planned. Let's see, this is Saturday and me and Sophie are working an estate sale in Talladega for the weekend. How about we get together next Tuesday for lunch, and I'll fill you in on the plans for the next few months? You choose a place for lunch and give me a call. I've got to go. I love you, and I'm glad you're home safe and sound. Bye."

A few days later we meet for lunch, and I spend the entire time talking about the trip and Mr. Brevonni. I decide to go on to her house for a few days. While I rework furniture and make little picking trips, I tell her everything. She asks lots of questions—I knew she would do that—and I have to go through every little detail of the trip. I have to tell her about each person and what they said and did. I have to tell her all about Lake Como, the villa, and the clothing factory. After three days, she knows as much as I do. We load a trailer for me to bring back to the shop, and I return with some merchandise for the store. I'm glad to leave that sanding and staining with her. I much prefer the retail end of this.

We talk more about our Fall trip plans and add a few new stops along our tour. That girl is so crazy. She is convinced that she's learned everything there is to know about group travel. She goes on and on about how she is sure all the kinks are worked out. She assures me that nothing has been left to chance and that there will be no bumps or snags this time. If I had a dollar for every time she said that and it didn't go smoothly, I'd be flying first class on this trip too.

I'm not real good at business; I tend to let the mail pile up. I tend to let my bills pile up. I tend to sleep late and open the shop late, but this rarely occurs, I might add. Sometimes, yeah, most of the time, I don't do a daily balance at the shop. I have a drawer full of bank statements. Things always get done, but not always timely. However, a few weeks after we were back home from the photo shoot in Italy, the mailman comes in and we chat for a while. He hands me the shop's mail, and as he is leaving he mentions that he wants to know all about my long distance love in Italy. I ask him what in the world he is talking about. He says with that personal letter from Italy, there must be something special going on. He says he doesn't see many personal letters from Italy.

With that, I start going through my mail, with more interest than when I'm looking for my tax refund, because that's not always a pleasant surprise. Anyway, I start at the top and throw the credit card applications to the side. I toss the electric bill and another darn bank statement. I start a little pile of the sales flyers from Office Max and Walmart. Then, the next to last little letter is a beautiful letter on that special Florentine paper. It is addressed by hand with a return address of Riccardo Brevonni. RICCARDO BREVONNI, are you kidding? Oh my Lord, he is probably sending me a polite little bill for something. I think I left the room clean; I don't remember tearing anything up. I didn't crash the little Alpha. What could I have done? I wonder if Magnus got anything?

I open it very carefully, trying not to ruin this elegant stationary. But probably I'm careful because I don't want to face an unknown transgression. I wish Magnus were here. I need him now. He should be back from lunch within the hour—should I wait? I sit for five minutes, thinking, wondering what this is about. I am almost near tears, thinking that I might have offended this sweet little man with my stupid southerness. Come on Magnus, get back here. Oh, I can't wait. I gently use my letter opener to slice through the envelope with a precision that is preferred for an elegant letter like this. Not so with bills: they deserve ripping. But not this one. I carefully open the envelope and lift out a single sheet of paper. At least. I don't owe him anything.

In a very simple hand-written script, I read, "Dear Andi, It gave me such pleasure to have you visit my home. For the few days that you were here, I found myself smiling and even laughing more than I have in years. You mentioned the small group of travelers that will be visiting Milan in the fall. I extend to you and your group a welcomed stay here for the few days that you are in Milan, should you desire. Please contact Guilia with the dates and we will finalize the details. Again, thank you for restoring my youth for a few days. Riccardo."

What? Oh my goodness, is this for real? I don't know what to think. Have we just been invited to visit the home of the most famous fashion designer in Italy? Wait until I tell Daphne. She won't believe this! Hell, I can't believe this! I'm so excited that I am jumping up and down. Where is Magnus? I glance at the old grandfather clock in the corner of our crowded shop. It's almost 1:30, so he'll be here soon. I'm gonna bust! I've got to tell somebody now. I reach for the phone to call Daphne, and the phone rings. I jump out of my chair. That scared the heck out of me.

Whew, calm down, it is just coincidence that the phone rang as I was reaching to make an exciting call. "Chik Piks, can I help you?" I answer the line.

"This is Daniel calling from Don't Fret We Got Your Freight. I'm trying to reach Magnus Bruce. Is he available?"

"No, I'm sorry. He is not in at this time, may I help you?"

"Maybe so. I tried Mr. Bruce's cell number, and he is not answering. I need to make a delivery to his house. I'm scheduled to arrive by two this afternoon. I'm about twenty minutes from his door, and I need someone to accept the freight."

"Well, give me your number, and I will contact Mr. Bruce and have him call you."

"Alright ma'am, but I don't have a lot of time to waste. I have other deliveries, you know."

"Yes, sir, don't get in a tizzy with me, keep driving and one of us will meet you at his house." Click.

Hm, did he just hang up on me? That was pretty damn rude. What in the world could Magnus have ordered now? I dial his cell phone and he immediately answers as he is walking through the door. "Hello, Andi dear, how can I help you?" he says as he walks up and kisses my forehead.

"Hang up that phone, you dummy. I don't know where to start. I've got great news and crazy news. What did you order that is being delivered to your house today?"

"I didn't order anything. What are you talking about?"

"I just got a call from some stupid-ass name freight company saying they would be at your house in twenty minutes and they needed someone to accept a delivery, and they were busy people and did not want you to keep them waiting. Here's the driver's number. Hurry and call him. I've got amazing news for you."

Magnus dials the number. "This is Magnus Bruce, who are you and what are you delivering?"

"Mister, I don't know, I just pick up the loads and drop them off. Please be at your house. I will wait thirty minutes, then I drive away."

"Wait, who is the delivery from?"

"Some furniture place—I don't know, I think it's furniture. Give me a break buddy; just get to your house." Click.

"Well, Mag, what's it about?"

"I don't know, Andi, I really don't. I haven't ordered anything, I would remember ordering furniture. But, I've got to get to my house right now. Your news will have to wait until I get back."

"No, it's too good to wait. I've got to tell you now. Hold on, let me get the keys. Lock the front door and flip that sign over. I'm coming with you."

"Are you crazy? It's just a mistake that I have to correct before I get billed for something that I didn't order. I have to straighten this out. They're not really delivering anything to me."

"I know, but on the ride over, I can tell you something exciting. You will never guess what I just got in the mail. Come on, we're taking your car."

We quickly close up shop and run to his car. I hold out my hands and demand the key. "What? Andi, you can't drive my car. Stop it."

"No, no, I've got to because you have to read this." He doesn't relinquish his key until I hand him the letter. Once he sees the postmark, he looks at me with his half grin.

"Fine, you drive. What in the heck did you do that you forgot to tell me about, Andi?"

"Nothing. Why do you naturally assume I did something? And, why do you think it must have been something bad?"

"Oh, it is quite natural to assume that if you were involved, it must have gone bad. Remember the time you were going to help Ms. Lenventhal with her Sunday dinner? Remember the time you went to Vermont with Susie? Remember…"

"Oh, shut up and just read. But first tell me how to pull this seat up so I can reach the pedals."

After I finally have control of acceleration and braking, we pull out of the parking lot, and I zoom off toward Crestwood. Magnus has the letter in his hand for about ten seconds when he starts screaming. "I can't believe it. We are invited to go back? All of us? Wow, Yippee, yippee, yippee, I'm going back to see Brevonnee-hee. This is amazing. What kind of nice and sincere were you, Andi? Just kidding—deep down you are a sweetheart. You won my heart, didn't you? Have you told Daphne? She is going to flip out. What about Nino? Even he will be excited about this."

"I know, I know, I can't wait to tell them. In fact, I was reaching for the phone to call her when that delivery guy called the shop. I almost fell off the stool, it startled me so bad. In my head, I was about to scream out to her all about this, and then as soon as I touched the phone, it started ringing. So, no, you are the only one that knows right now. See why I couldn't stay at the shop? I'll call Daphne as soon as we finish with your delivery."

As we arrive onto our street, we see an eighteen-wheeler parked in front of Mag's house. I pull into his drive as Mag is jumping out of the car and heads to the truck. The driver leaps out and is handing some paper to Magnus. Magnus is looking closely at the papers while the guy is opening the side door of the trailer.

Suddenly, Magnus is running toward me and screaming like a little girl. "Andi, oh my God, for real, this is better than your letter. Riccardo Brevonni sent me a present, too. He sent me the Tonino Lamburghini sofa and chair in Racing Red." He continues to scream and jump up and down all over his front yard. I can see the living room curtain at the Jones' house across the street open ever so slightly. With that diesel motor rumbling and Magnus screeching all over the yard like a huge owl, pretty soon all the curtains will be opening to see what is going on.

Magnus opens his door, and the guy proceeds to unload the raciest sofa and chair and tables that I have ever seen. No wonder Magnus has gone nuts. This stuff does look like a racecar. I'll probably never know what it feels like to sit in a Lamborghini, and maybe the chair will be the closest I get. That chair is close enough. Hurry, I think. I can't wait. I hope the neighbors are getting a good look at this. Maybe I should tell the delivery guy to just put it on the grass in the front yard. He can drive away, and I'll go fix us some sweet tea, and we can sit out here and chat for everyone to admire. Let me tell Magnus, he may just go for it.

An hour later, Mag and I are sitting on his great furniture in his perfectly manicured lawn. We have the end table placed between us, holding our two extra-large glasses of sweet tea. I'm sitting in this Racing Red, body-hugging chair, while he is stretched out on his Racing Red sofa. Mr. Jones comes over from across the street, and I offer him a drink. "Do you have any red Italian wine?" he asks.

"Sure." I bring out a bottle and several glasses. We set up the coffee table as our makeshift bar area. We have now attracted more friends. Sebastian and Joel are here from down the street, and Nancy and her new friend Paula have just come over. Here comes my other neighbor, Gladys. I'd better go get more wine and glasses. More friends arrive, thanks to Facebook, and we all enjoy our impromptu lawn party. Everyone has gone back to their houses and brought out cheese, chips and dips and all kinds of canapés. Snacking quickly turns into a full-blown competition and soon it's like a fancy dinner restaurant in the front yard. Some of the guys bring around our collective patio furniture so that everyone has seating.

We tell them all about the visit with Mr. Brevonni in Milan. I pass around the handwritten note from him. Let me tell you, if there is one thing gay men know about, it's fashion and clothing. Now that I think about it, this is the first little block party since our trip to Italy. So it is the first time they all get to hear about Magnus and his ad shoot and our surprise trip to Milan. They were all envious of the story of Mr. Brevonni's generosity in inviting us into his home. Magnus has to go put on his clothes and model for them all. The party carries on until around nine, when the guys help to move Mag's new furniture into the house. We have a pretend auction for his now old Italy Design living room suite. They all want his old stuff, but my big Kraken pulls me aside in the kitchen and says we are moving it to my house. He says he still likes it a lot, and if he gives it to me then he can at least enjoy it when he's at my place. He says Mrs. Carmichael has already told him that she likes his racy new furniture. "It is so *you*," she's told him.

The whole crowd wants to go on our Italy tour with us now. For the chance to stay in the home of Riccardo Brevonni, they say they'll pay us four times the usual price. We laugh that idea around awhile and say maybe we will auction that ticket off at another party. I tell them that if it is all right with Daphne and we have room for one more person, we can do it. We all agree that the extra profit will go to a charity decided by the payee. I think they are actually serious about this plan. Magnus tells me, "Hell yeah, they're serious. A gay man would sell his partner for an opportunity to be a guest in the home of the most famous men's wear designer in the world." What do I know? I think they're all a bit too tipsy to remember a thing about any of this.

The party finally wears itself out, and we're left with a big mess and great furniture. It's not so bad; we clean it up fairly quickly and sit to write out a thank you note to Mr. Brevonni. We graciously tell him we are looking forward to seeing him again in October and agree to email Guilia with our details. We will mail it from work tomorrow. Magnus walks me home and I give him a kiss goodnight.

Chapter Thirteen

THE REST OF THE SUMMER

Daphne was ecstatic to read the letter from Mr. Brevonni. She made me tell her again all about Mr. Brevonni's estate and Lake Como. And somehow she seemed to know if I left something out. I had to tell it and re-tell it a thousand times. She insisted that I had no idea what a magnificent place that is. Like I wasn't there and didn't see the beauty with my own eyes. She said that she would give anything for a ride around Lake Como. And maybe she would even see George Clooney there. And maybe she would have bought a nice scarf at a shop there. And maybe she would have a glass of wine at a bistro there. And maybe…

And maybe she could just shut the you-know-what up. I knew she would have been like that. I was so thankful that Marco was unlucky enough to haul my old, fat butt around in a sporty Italian car and not my sister. Oh, God, I know that is the one thing she is going to want when we get there. I should email Guilia and tell her that when we come, Marco should pull some kind of plug on that car so it doesn't work. He'd save himself an entire afternoon of anguish if he did. She didn't wear that topic out either. Every time we have gotten together this summer, she thinks of other questions to ask me about it. I'd better warn Nino about her, though I'm sure he is hearing more about it than I am.

Everything has been so busy for the past few months. Daphne and I have worked ourselves silly on picking. Daphne's been working hard on restoring and reworking pieces. She's had Sophie and the kids helping her. Nino has been busy with the hobby farming he does.

Magnus has held down the shop. He's very good at his work. He hosts little events every other week to bring in buyers and to socialize. It works, because our sales have been better than ever. He doesn't seem to make just one friend at a time, because that friend brings his friends and before you know it the one friend has become four friends. And, each of them seems to know someone wanting some low cost, reworked antique stuff. He's also got a lot of publicity from the BarBQue ad. So people come in just to meet the pulled pork guy. They seem to have quite a bit of fun with that pun. I think he'll forever more be known as the guy with the pulled pork.

Daphne says we are good with the shop and all our picks. She's now all excited about our trip. I try to tell her to settle down and assure her that everything is arranged. She thinks that the two additional people that Magnus is bringing will put us over the top. Magnus's friend, Jackson Bergman, decided to book in June. He and Magnus seem to have something cooked up. Probably some party they are planning in Rome or something, but frankly, I don't want to know. I'm always worrying about him, especially if I know he has a plan. He has a hard enough time getting through the day without a plan; a plan really puts him at risk.

It seems the front yard party months ago really set off the neighborhood gossip. Gay men and fashion go hand in hand, it seems. There were ideas thrown around about who would go on the trip. They all wanted to claim the fame of meeting Riccardo Brevonni. They were willing to pay any price for the ticket. If we hadn't already had a fully booked trip, we could have charged double or triple for everyone and had a full tour group within the hour. It took weeks for them to develop a plan they were all happy with that would simply allow one of the group to go on the trip.

When Magnus and I first proposed an additional person to join the October tour, Daphne went a little ape-shit. She ranted and raved and talked about how impossible it would be. She said that she didn't know how she could manage another person. She was doing everything but foaming at the mouth when Nino finally told her to settle down. One more person was nothing. Once she was calm and had her near-foamy mouth all cleaned up, I explained the impromptu block party with Magnus's new furniture and how impressed all his friends were with his connection to Riccardo Brevonni. Then, when we showed them the letter that I got the same day, inviting us to stay overnight at his home, they went crazy.

Everyone had ideas on how they could favor themselves in being selected to go on the trip. Leon, he lives in our neighborhood over on Chelsea Street. He even called my cell phone one night, all whispering about how if I choose him, he would pay five times the tour amount, and he would pay me an extra five hundred dollars. I was thinking of how I could pull that off without getting caught when Magnus told me that he had an even better offer than that from Roberto. So, Magnus and I put our heads together and consulted with Nino. Nino said to heck with the raffle or silent auction or whatever we had in mind, he would just decide who could go. Oh no, this would not go well.

Forget them all. I made a command decision and told Magnus that we were having an Italian wine tasting at the shop on Saturday, August seventeenth. We will invite them all and have a silent auction. We'll include a few pieces from the shop and have our neighborhood sommelier bring the wines and attempt to educate us on the fine art of wine drinking while we eat, drink, and get merry. By the end of the night whomever wants to pay the most can get the spot and with the proceeds going to The Birmingham Children's Hospital. That is done and settled.

By the fifteenth of August, our party is set. Roberto is ready with his wines. Magnus and Joe have planned the light menu. We'll use our shop's crystal and serving pieces. The invitations have long been mailed and the RSVPs have been received. We are ready for the party. My only worry is who will be boring me to death on this trip. Please let it be someone that can get along with all kinds of people. I really shouldn't worry; all of these guys are okay. Things will be fine.

The night arrives, and we have fifty-two people in our shop, all wanting to go to Italy to meet Riccardo Bevonni. This was the best plan to raise the most money for our charity. It's turned into a pretty big event. We auction off a few pieces from the store that we'll add to the total donation. Roberto teaches us what he can about Italian red wines. We have a great time, and our shop makes some sales. The silent auction does very well—the winning bid is for $9,700.00. Everything above the cost of the tour fare will go to The Birmingham Children's Hospital. The winner is Sebastian Wainwright. He is the buyer for Ward's Limited, one of the top menswear stores in Birmingham. He says that he had the authority to bid up to ten thousand dollars. Since his store is covering all the expenses, should he win, he goes ahead and offers the ten thousand dollars.

So, now that it's all done, Sebastian will be the last tourist added to our group. He will probably want to obtain the import rights to Alabama for Riccardo Brevonni Menswear. I'll be sure to tell Guilia that a men's fashionista will also be on our tour and have her set up something for him. That will keep him from talking shop with Mr. Brevonni.

Chapter Fourteen
VERONICA 'RONI' ABERNATHA

My, my, I've got too much on my Versace dinner plate. All the society events have kept me so busy this year. There were several golf events and those three New York shopping trips with the girls. My yoga group conducted a few demonstrations at the country club, and the fundraisers for The Children's Hospital have been time-consuming but very successful.

Since my husband died five years ago, I have thrown myself into any activity that keeps my grief at bay. I have been so successful at this that I've barely noticed the change from grief to acceptance, then to warm, comforting memories. Now, the problem is that I do not know how to slow down again. I am determined to discontinue some of my least enjoyable duties and commit more time to living out some of my dreams.

My family is one of the few old money elite left here in town. My great, great, great granddaddy started the first bank here in Birmingham. Our family can be traced back to their 1704 arrival from France in New Orleans. We remaining few families here in Birmingham are a dying breed, I hate to say. Although, there are enough of us left that we do maintain our tight exclusive circle. Of course, I married quite well, so money has never been a concern for me.

I have lived my life as was expected, here in Mountain Brook. I was always a faithful wife to the very end. My older daughter is a marketing executive in Portland, Oregon. My younger daughter is married and living in Atlanta. I'm a young fifty-five year young, vibrant woman. And, after much consideration I've decided to start living just a little on the edge. I've seen it done, but I've never done it. I just have to set my strategy for a planned course of action.

I intend to remain respectful. But there are things in life that I'd like to experience. I've never visited the The Louvre on the arm of a handsome Frenchman. I've never been serenaded on a gondola in Venice. I've never climbed the steps to the top of the Duomo in Florence. I've never visited the Roman ruins during a romantic sunset walk with a charming Italian man. In fact, I've never succumbed to a single lustful, perhaps a little shameful thought. I don't expect to ever love another man like I loved Mark. But probably like most women I have fantasized about having a meaningless short-term relationship. I'm not sure that I know quite how to proceed with this plan, but I intend to try.

Last year, I booked a trip to Ireland with Two Sister's Travel. It was a great trip. Those girls, of course, are not in my upper crust league. They even admitted that to me, so we are all in agreement on that. However, I found that as I flew out of international airspace with these girls, I lost some of my crustiness. I didn't have to impress them or anyone else. None of the other people in the group knew me, nor did they care what I did.

The two sisters didn't care; they just wanted me to enjoy myself. For the first time in my life, my hair was let down, literally. I could continue to dress to the nines, because I will always want to look better than anyone else in the crowd. But, I was not on stage for anyone. I could say and do the things that I would never allow myself to do within my social circles. This was a freedom and empowerment that I've never known. I was incognito, bringing forward only what I wanted to share.

I've decided that another trip with the Two Sisters Travel is what I need. My mission is to really lose my inhibitions and have a fling. Of course, I imagine this man to be tall, dark, and handsome, and for once, breeding is unimportant to me. He doesn't have to be acceptable to my social class. He doesn't need to be important or worthy of me. I will require some social graces and good looks; otherwise his qualities need not be impressive. When I return from my trip, he will be my history, my past. My present and future may continue undisturbed. Neither my daughters nor my friends will have any knowledge of my tryst. So, I must call the girls and see what upcoming trips they have scheduled. Maybe a Paris or London trip will be promising.

Chapter Fifteen
BOBBIE JO

Well, I did it. Praise the Lord! I get to finally take a trip across the pond. I just booked my vacation. I am really doing it. And those girls seemed so nice on the phone. Good Christian girls. God has led me straight to them. I'm so glad my friend Dorothy McKorkle told me about them. They are just like she said. Only the other day, right after our women's quilting meeting, we were talking about the trip she and her granddaughter took with those sister travel agents. She said she didn't have to worry about a thing because those girls are small town people who work hard and understand Christian women like me. She said that Two Sisters Travel is the only company she ever uses.

I'm all by myself now, after my grandson that I've been raising had to go to prison. I'm sure he wasn't doing drugs like they said. They've been after him for a long time, almost as long as his teeth have been bad. Hopefully, they can fix his teeth in that facility. He's in pretty bad health. It seemed like overnight his health went downhill. He's lost so much weight, but I think that's because his teeth are bad and he just can't eat. He started out with good teeth. I told his momma that eventually all those peanut butter and sugar sandwiches and dipping those lemons in sugar would catch up with him. And sure enough, a few years ago, he must have started it again, because now his teeth have started rottenin' right out of his head. That judge was good to little Russ. He assured me that they would rehabilitate him in his preferred field. That's good; he always wanted to cut hair. After that new career training he'll be fine, I'm sure of it.

But now that I'm alone again, I've got to start clearing my bucket list. Oh, Lord, I've got to get a passport. I don't know if mine is good anymore. I got one back in—was that back in 1968?—when I went protesting with that actress. Mmm, I can't even remember her name. Anyway, I was a little wild back then, and we were smoking those MJs. There was this band of four guys singing about some girl in the sky with diamonds. We got ourselves into some real criminal trouble. I said then that if I ever got out of that I would turn my life over to Jesus. Well, Praise God, he did.

I go to our local church now, Blessed Holy Rock. I've been here since 1970. Got my life in order and I've never looked back. I don't miss a service or activity. If that door is open, I'm there and walking through it, Bible in hand. I always have a Bible with me. I keep one in my car, in case I'm in a traffic jam. Russ tried to "hook me up" with some newfangled device so that I could have my Bible read to me. I could never get that dag-nabbit thing to work. I've got two good eyes and I don't even need glasses either, so I sure don't need any new equipment.

Me and Dorothy know all of each other's secrets. That's the way it is with us. We don't judge, each other or anyone else. We do our testifying at the altar every week. We tell most of our stories of sins and redemption. However, there are some things that are best left unvoiced to our congregation. We're a small church in a small town and sometimes our local folk aren't so forgiving. They aren't all like me and Dorothy. Some of them are a little judgmental. And truth be told, my mouth can get a little foul. Now, that doesn't mean that I ain't a good Christian woman, sometimes, the devil really does make me do it. But, like I say, I'm born again and forgiven.

Now, let me get back to my upcoming trip. I'm so excited. I've always wanted to go to Itlee. That's the way we say it in these here parts. I know they spell it like it's got three syllables, It-a-lee, but around here, we say 'It-lee'. That's the way our people said from way back, and we keep calling it that. When I was young, I would look at those pictures of those Itlee men and think how handsome they are. Of course, now I'm older. I'm not looking at those men, I'm just thinking about the food. There will be spaghetti and pizza and pastries and ice cream. Everyone's always talking about that ice cream. They don't call it ice cream over there; they call it something like jello or jellioto. I'm going to enjoy every minute.

That girl Daphne told me that there would be about ten people going on our trip, including her and her husband. I am hoping that they're all good Christians. I might be uncomfortable with a bunch of heathens, but, being that I'm a forgiving, non-judgmental kind of person, I'm sure it will be fine. Who knows, with my good testimony, maybe I can bring some of them sinners to Christ.

Daphne said that her sister Andi would be on our tour. Andi is also Daphne's partner in the travel business. They specialize in European tours. The brochure they sent says that all tours are groups of ten or less. They usually fly into a city, then rent a large van and drive throughout the country or even into different countries. Daphne's husband drives the van and has lots of experience driving in Europe. They each speak different languages and know the history of the places that they travel. There is a general itinerary, but since the groups are small, they can easily adapt plans to satisfy the group. That's good, because I'm sure that I'll want to see all the holy sites where my Jesus and his disciples established their early churches.

I don't know any of the other people who will be traveling with us. Dorothy says that I'll be fine because those girls are friendly and fun. She said that she's never laughed so hard. Laughed every day, that's what she said. She's tried to warn me that sometimes the conversation isn't so Christian-like, but she knows that I don't judge or hate, so I'll have a great time.

Chapter Sixteen

GEORGETTE AND HUDSON

Our wedding was a disaster. I mean, I'm so glad to be married to my Hudson, but the wedding event itself was a total flop. Everyone congratulated us and *oohed* and *aahed* over what a wonderful wedding. They say they've never seen anything so beautiful. My family and friends thought that I was the most beautiful bride in the world. They all thought the outdoor park was fitting for the event. I wonder what in the heck they mean by that?

Fitting! Fitting for a hillbilly, is that what they thought? Do they think all those mishaps were fitting? Hudson's best man was late, so the wedding was delayed by fifteen minutes. The flowers were not the ones that I ordered, *and* they were all in the wrong place. How could I have known that thirty-mile-an-hour winds would roar at exactly ten after three as I was walking down the aisle? The reception tent was whipping and flapping so loudly no one could hear the wedding march. Oh, so disappointing. Really, it was awful.

My entire life, I dreamed of the perfect outdoor wedding. Soft sloping hills of spring green, with the crocus recently bloomed, still fragrant in the air. Birds would be singing sweetly in fresh seventy-degree weather. The azalea blooms completely covering the bush so that it looks like a large ball of flowers. Subtle scents of gardenia softly floating onto my wedding aisle. The guests would be in awe of my perfect wedding. My decorations and planning would set the bar high for all my friends. My wedding would be the standard. So, what the hell happened?

153

Looking everywhere for the perfect location, I had checked out historical houses here in Birmingham, the Talladega forest, wedding chapels from Birmingham to Mobile, and of course, my Hudson's family estate up in Jasper. Nothing, nothing was as my fairy tale dreams of childhood until I saw The Gardens. That was it. Just as I'd always dreamed that it would be. There are rolling hills, paths of gardens, fragrant blooms, and least of all, the price. Free! The Gardens only asked for a donation. No set amount, anything that I felt like giving. That was more like an altar call. Of course I would donate, and probably lots more than those people had ever seen in a single donation. Both Hudson and I come from old Alabama families. Money, quite simply, was not a concern for us. We were happy to provide monetary support for such lovely gardens. They were almost equal to Bellingrath in Mobile.

So on the morning of my wedding, I went with the wedding planners and my binoculars to assure that *everything* was perfect. The background was just as important as the event, as there would be pictures galore by the best photographer in Birmingham. Daddy wrote a handsome check to Elite Weddings for their expertise planning. But no one, and I mean no one, can equal my style and taste, regardless of the amount of money they charge for their services.

So, sharply at 0730, quite early for me, I was there with binoculars, critiquing and reassessing the set up. Of course, there were many things not to my standards, but after several hours of correcting others' mistakes, all was set right. However, there was one disturbing detail. Upon the distant hill, only visible with my binoculars, I could see three porcelain objects that appeared to be some type of obnoxious garden feature. After focusing the binoculars, I could swear they were toilets, but that couldn't be, could it? I had to be wrong, but either way, I made sure that tall, obstructive floral arrangements blocked that view from any eyes eager to find fault with my day.

I also had to keep a sharp eye on that hillside throughout the day, as there appeared to be quite a bit of activity there. At eight o'clock, it looked like there were young boys running around in pajamas, and a little one in only briefs. Redneck parents no less, I am sure.

Around ten AM, there was frantic running and screaming. Kids with bicycles attempted to jump some type of ramp devices. Then, almost simultaneously, a golf cart appeared, wildly accelerated, with two old women and perhaps ten children hanging all over it.

My prayers were answered at around ten-thirty when the two old ladies who lived in that monstrous shoe gathered all those children and cleaned up their messy yard. At least, that is what I hoped was happening as the children seemed to be holding white trash bags, or they might have been kites. With the winds approaching twenty miles an hour, I was fearful that my wedding backdrop would be a redneck kite fiasco complete with beer drinking hoopla from their redneck parents. Only redneck could explain a family with all those children. Thankfully, it was trash bags, as the old women must have realized it was my big day and somewhere in their upbringing they knew that their yard was hideous. How can people even live like that?

All appeared to be going in my favor, until my mother-in-law to be peered over my shoulder with her own binoculars, stating that she did not know why on God's green earth that I would choose such a place for the wedding of her little Hudson. And she thinks he married below his station. I'd better watch my mouth. Two years back in the South and I'm losing some of my own social graces, and it will take them all to be Mrs. Bankhead's daughter-in-law. That is why I told Hudsey that I wanted to book our honeymoon with Two Sister's Travel. I won't have to watch myself at all with them; they're not like his snooty family.

My best friend, Bitsy, told me about this travel company. She says that if you want to get away and have a good time, that's the company I should book with. Now, I have always trusted Bitsy. We've been best friends since the third grade at our private school. We even talked her parents into letting her go to boarding school with me. She's of the same social class with me, however, I do not know if I can ever forgive her cousin, twice removed, from saying my sit down dinner reception "watn't fit to eat." Poor Bitsy, I guess she is not responsible for what her Mississippi people do. So, it is off to Italy that Hudson and I will go in October.

Chapter Seventeen

DAPHNE'S WORRIES BEFORE DEPARTURE

The trip details have all been emailed to our clients. I am confident that this trip, unlike some of our previous ones, will go off without a hitch. We've got a great group of responsible, mature adults. There's no reason for thing to go amiss. October is a great month for visiting Italy. The weather is pleasant, still a bit warm, but not sweating hot. We've got plenty of that in the South; we don't need to endure it on our vacation. And, the best part is that most of the tourists have left the country. There are fewer crowds, so you don't have to put up with hundreds of gaudy tourists like us. There is quainter hotel availability as well. Anyway, ready or not, here we come.

Nino, Andi, and I have used these same stops for many trips. We will land in Milan and spend two days there. Everyone in our groups always wants to see the Last Supper in the refectory, which is a dining hall for us common southern folks, at the Convent of Santa Maria della Grazie. I wonder if they call it Supper in Italy or would they call it the Last Mangia or what. I'll have to ask Nino how to say that in Italian. As exciting as seeing that work of art may be, I think that Georgette, Veronica, and Sebastian will make the most of their time in Milan and shop, shop, shop.

But now that we have this special invitation from Mr. Riccardo Brevonni to visit him at his private villa at Lake Como, we will have to see how things work. It could be that the itinerary may have to change a bit as to accommodate his plans and those of his staff. I'm not certain if we will look at the Last Supper before or after our time with Mr. Brevonni. We are planning one day in Milan, then overnight with Mr. Brevonni, and then the following day in Milan as a free day. Everyone can choose to shop or visit the museums or sit still and do nothing if they want.

Two Sister Travels, Inc. always allows our clients to develop our tour as the events present themselves. They're encouraged to follow us along a flexible schedule, or they are free to wander the cities and countryside as they please. We usually rent a van or bus large enough for our group, allowing us to keep the group informal and cozy. And as firm as our plans are, they always change from hour to hour. The group determines the flow of the trip. The dynamics change with every group we take, depending on the personalities involved. But, come to find out, that is what brings our clients in. Word of mouth, and I mean words of southern mouths, advertise that we run a very loose and easy going tour. So, we don't worry about changing things. Like my grandma always said, "If it ain't broke, don't fix it." Well, we certainly don't.

After Milan, we may try to go to Pisa. Many people want to see the Leaning Tower, feeling that their Italy trip is not complete if they don't visit that mistaken masterpiece. Most trips, the tower has been closed to the public, but once it was open, and we were able to climb its narrow circular stairs to the top. That was the moment that I developed the utmost respect for fashionable Italian women who wear very short, tight skirts and walk in four-inch stilettos. They are so adept at this talent; they manage cobblestones, Vespas, and climbing towers without hesitation. In fact, I've never seen a single slip, stumble, or fall. Mind you, I've fallen, all over Europe, while wearing tennis shoes, sandals, and ugly Army boots. And Andi, my goodness gracious, wearing her desert Army boots, fell all over Europe; up one minute, gone the next. Butt ass on the ground in the blink of an eye. This year the tower is open again, so those wanting to can climb the three hundred stairs to the top for a wonderful view of Pisa.

From Pisa, it is only an hour drive to Florence. We'll spend three nights and four days in Florence. Florence is a great city for art lovers. Little Georgette said she majored in Art, so I expect her to be in the museums from the time they open the doors until they lock up to close. I don't know much about Hudson yet, but I'm sure he'll enjoy anything that his wife does if he is as smart as I think he is. Veronica says she's always wanted to visit the Duomo in Florence. Bobbie Jo told me that she has read all kinds of books about Florence, and she can't wait to walk the narrow streets that she's read about. Andi, Magnus, Sebastian, and Jackson, now they are a different story altogether. Who knows what they will do in Florence. It could be anything from art, to fine dining to drinking the entire time. As for Nino and I, I'll enjoy the architecture and the history, and he'll eat, eat, eat, and then find some more places to eat.

Rome is after Florence, about a four-hour road trip. Sometimes I think the best times of our trips are the times spent on the road. Everyone is forced to be together for several hours without an opportunity to flee and avoid the others. These times are chocked full of conversations. No matter how much you think that a few people from the same area have in common, it is always a surprising diversity of conversations that develop. This is when I really get to know the individuals. They share their pasts, presents and futures with the group. It gives you great insight into the real person, their perceived successes and failures, their dreams, hopes, and disappointments. That is, if they are all conscious. Once, on a tour of Germany, six of our group slept from location to location—the rest of the time, I think they were sampling German beer. The key to our success in traveling is that we prevent the individuals in that van with opposing opinions, religions, and politics from becoming explosive.

Rome, now that is my favorite place. The distant history and architecture is mind boggling to me. I can never get enough. The first time that Nino and I went to Rome, I spent enough time in the Forum to learn it quite well. I had read my history books and went with books in my bag and started at site number one and didn't slow down until I was on site seventy-four. Nino didn't let me finish either. Though I don't think it was possible to complete my two hundred and twenty-three sites in one outing. When some English speaking tourists asked Nino if he knew where the House of the Vestal Virgins was located, he walked them to me, knowing I was well past that location, and I easily pointed it out to them. From that visit on, if we're going to the Forum, he will stop at the local market and buy salami, bread, and cheese for our sit down picnic in the Forum. Now, that is the most romantic thing he could ever do for me, give me a picnic in the Forum. However, that was long before we had smart phones that give you all the information you want with GPS location and walking tours; then I just had my books and backpack.

OK, enough of me and my fascination with Roman history. I hope the group will like Rome. Sadly, the Forum will be the last of their 'must see' sites. They've voiced more interest in St. Peter's and the Sistene Chapel, the fountains and gelato. So, there shouldn't be any problem to please them all, except Andi—I can never please her. She doesn't appreciate history or art or architecture. She's just like Nino; she mostly likes to eat and drink. It should be an easy and enjoyable job for me. We will spend three nights and four days in Rome. We'll fly out of Rome, heading back to Atlanta and the end of another successful European trip.

I've failed to mention that the most difficult job of all is Nino's. He is the driver, the luggage packer, and the unloader during our entire trip. He is the most patient of spouses. To put up with me and my sister alone is an amazing feat. Now, add to that the drinkers, churchgoers, teenagers, gays and straights and whatever fate brings our way, and he is a saint. Andi and I can roll with the punches; we're pretty open and enjoy most personalities. But Nino, he's pretty straight laced.

"Andi, is everything set for the trip on your end?" I ask. "Everyone has confirmed with me that they have their passports, their driver's license as ID, credit cards, and cash. They have been told to bring warm weather clothes with a light sweater or jacket. The women have been warned that bare, uncovered arms are not allowed in the cathedrals. I have my notebook with all the confirmation information. Our flight leaves Birmingham at 1145, and then departs Atlanta, direct to Milan, arriving at 0800. Is there anything that I've forgotten?"

"Magnus did tell me that to prevent everyone from losing their passports that I should just take them up. But I told him, Hell no, I'll not be charged with human trafficking, though there are a lot of humans that I'd like to traffic right out of here. Was I supposed to be in charge of anything? I haven't done anything and I'm ready, I hope all of them have their selves ready. No, really, the rental van is ready for pickup after our visit with Mr. Brevonni. The hotel reservations along the way are confirmed. Oh, yeah, but didn't you do all that? Yeah, you've pretty much done your job, so we're ready. I've got Nino some sedatives, so we're good."

"Guilia sent me an email last night that Marco will be at the airport with two limousines to bring us up to his place. She insisted that once we touch down, our only concern is to go through customs and gather our luggage. Once we pass through the restricted area, she will be there to meet us and take it from there. Please try not to be crazy, Daphne, everything is fine."

"Andi, I do try not to get uptight but you know how easily things get out of hand. We're meeting everyone at the Delta ticket counter at 8:45. You know Nino insists on being there, checked in three hours ahead of time. Is Magnus ready? Are you going to pick him up? You know how late he always is," says Daphne.

"Not when it comes to men and fashion," chirps Andi. "But he does seem more excited about this trip than any of the others. Daphne, I'm a little worried about him. He's acting crazy. He has this weird fixation about our picture. You know the one that Nino took of us on our first Florence trip. It's the picture with me and you standing on the corner in Florence. I've got it hanging just behind the cash register in our shop. He looks at it all the time, more than looking—he seems to be studying it. Then he touches it and stares some more. Sometimes, he mumbles 'balls' and giggles a bit. I don't know what in the world that he finds so interesting about that picture. It was not even our best look. It was the last day of that trip and we were not good at all, in fact, we looked pretty damn awful. Just me and you in the same clothes we wore for the third time, not even smiling. You know how pissy I get by the end of the trip. Well, anyway, I'm set and I will get Magnus' gay, hung-over ass to the airport. I'm good to go."

"I hope so, Andi. I'm always so uneasy when you and him are together and entrusted with something responsible. Separately, you're bad enough, but together, you're like The Three Stooges and you don't even need the third stooge. Worrying about you two, along with all the thousand other things that I have to do without your help, sometimes makes me want to scream."

Andi says, "Honestly, you kill me with all these details and complaints about me. Why in the world do you carry on with things like you do? Everything's good, don't worry about the details. What you really need to worry about is putting Magnus and Nino together in a van for ten days. Cause you know, the minute Magnus realizes that his affectionate ways bother Nino—he will consider that a challenge. I will try my best to stop it, but I don't know if I can. Now, that's what you need to worry about. I think that Sebastian and Jackson will help keep Magnus in line, you'll see."

"Nino is not Magnus's only problem. He will also be in the van with several other diverging personalities. Bobbie Jo, Roni, Georgette, and Hudson, so please tell him to be nice. I know he could spend endless hours antagonizing them, but hopefully, he will use all his charms to endear them, not torment them, and us in the process of maintaining peace."

"Okay, we can work with that, but I'm pretty sure Ms. Preacher Lady needs to sit up front and Magnus in the back. But no wait, oh hell, I mean, praise God, where are we going to put her? She can't go up there with Nino. He'll go nuts. You know Magnus, they won't know how to take him for the first few days, but by the end of the trip, they'll all love him."

"I hope you are right, Andi. He can be over the top and somewhat annoying, but deep down, I know he is truly good. He would do anything for you. I guess that I shouldn't worry. Everyone has to get along, and it is up to them and their raising to figure out how to do it. I'm sure it will all work out just fine. And three hours is the longest amount of time that we are locked in the van together. "

"Now Daphne, did you clarify luggage weight limits to the two fashionistas that are traveling with us. You know they have to match their shoes and bags with every outfit. Not to mention making sure that we can fit in a van and that we won't require a huge bus for the luggage. I have assigned Sebastian full packing authority for Magnus, because he also tends to overpack. Sebastian is a buyer for one of the most famous menswear stores in Birmingham. He travels extensively all over the world and he knows how to pack light. He's promised he will get Magnus squared away."

"Yes, I sent everyone the flyer on airline restrictions, hoping that will be enough. Our brochure also states that bags are limited to two per person. However, they may realize that they can pay the airlines extra for overweight or additional bags. If they think of that, we may be in trouble, as monetary fines or penalties are not a deterrent for them as they probably have enough money to hire their own plane and bus with chauffer through Europe."

"Do you know what, Andi, I am so excited for Bobbie Jo. She has probably never been out of Alabama. I gather from talking to her that she has experienced more than her share of hard times. She has raised her grandson, and I understand he was probably falsely sentenced to prison. I know how hard that must be. I can't imagine how I would feel if that was one of my grandchildren. Anyway, she is a devout Christian and is looking forward to seeing St. Peter's and bringing her Bible history to life."

"Daphne, there is something that has been on my mind. That friend of Magnus's, Jackson, those two seem to be spending a lot of time together lately. For all the years that I have known Magnus, he has never mentioned him. But since Memorial Day, they visit every other weekend it seems. Jackson inherited his daddy's monument business in whatever little town they went to high school at. I think it is Opp of Arab or something like that. I think Jackson's wife died a few years ago, and they are suddenly like long lost friends. I hope they are behaving. You know how Magnus can get when he's with the wrong crowd, and trouble just seems to find him. I'll be glad to meet him so that I know Magnus is in good hands."

"Sister, you worry about him like he's your son or something. What's up with you two, Andi?"

"Daphne, you know we're soul mates deep down. We are closer than most married couples, but could *never*, ever be married. We have decided that whoever our partners in the future should be, they must understand we are a package deal."

"Well, that explains it, Andi, you two will never find anyone else. No one would be willing to put up with two immature people in a relationship. It's bad enough that you live next door to each other, but to have to accept two individuals in one partnership is asking a bit much. Forget it; you two will grow old together."

"I can't talk anymore about this, just make sure all his friends are well behaved and that they don't act out too badly." Daphne begged. "And don't worry about Jackson, I bet he will be just fine. It's Magnus that I'm worried about. You know what I mean. He doesn't mean no harm, trouble just seems to find him."

"Most everyone else is seasoned travelers and should be fine. Daphne, it will all be fine, just like it always is. You are such a worrier. After the introduction dinner that Magnus is preparing on Tuesday night everyone will meet each other, and we'll have an idea of what to expect and how to plan their interactions."

"I promise that I will keep him with me at all times—well, almost all times. We will plan to tag team him. I won't let him out of my sight until I tag off to another keeper. How's that, Daphne?"

"Sounds good, Andi, that's our plan then."

Chapter Eighteen
PRE-TRIP DINNER

"Magnus, what can I do to help with dinner tonight?" says Andi. "I know that you never want my help to cook, but is there something I could bring or do?"

"Now, Andi, please, please, don't try to help me. I'll just need you to be here to greet our guests as they arrive."

"Well, I've got that, don't you worry, big Kraken. I wonder if they've seen the video. Maybe I can show that for entertainment tonight. That would be fun, huh?"

"Stop it, Andi, you are not funny. And look just how well all that turned out. I got the job as the Brevonni man. We took a great trip to Lake Como, Italy. We got to stay at the home of Riccardo Brevonni. We were his private guests. Not to mention the big honkin check that I got two months ago. I was able to pay off what I owed for my home remodel. We made great friends: Brad, Stefan, Guilia, and don't forget Mr. Brevonni. And, I've got this sensational sofa collection that I never dreamed I'd have. How great it all turned out. Huh?"

"Don't you try to pull that crap on me, Magnus. This is just one of your turds that came out smelling good. Think of all those other situations that didn't turn out so well. A repeat of that kind of stuff has me a bit alarmed about this trip. Something has me uneasy, but I can't put my finger on it. How's that friend of yours, Jackson? Is he going to be good for our trip or will he embarrass us? I get the feeling that you and him are up to something. I'm sure that it is not about our trip, but are you guys planning on robbing a bank or something?"

166

"Andi, you will never meet a more down to earth, likeable guy than Jackson. Just wait until you meet him tonight. You'll see. He's a wonderful guy. Now, I admit, he is probably not well traveled, but that don't mean you can't take him nowhere. You'll like him, I'm sure."

"Well, then, how about Sebastian? Do you think he will fit in with us? You and I both know that he thinks he is better than everybody else. He's upper crust, isn't he? Didn't his daddy do something great? Did he leave him a fortune, or did he have a fortune and disown him? What's his story?"

"Honey chile, he ain't nothing. His daddy didn't have a pot to piss in. He makes everybody think he is all that, but he ain't. He ain't no better 'n me and you! How's that for some southern slang? That was good, wudn't it? No, really, I don't know much about his family. He keeps it secret. He lets everyone assume that his family was big time money from up around Huntsville, but I know a lot of people from there, and no one has ever heard of the Wainwright family. I think there is a story there, and me and you should snoop it out sometime. But, I guess our snooping will have to wait awhile. We don't have time for all that right now. Right now, I need Daphne and Nino to get here and help me."

"I asked if you needed help and you told me to answer the door. So, you need Nino's help in the kitchen, huh? You are big ol' liar; you know I was a lot of help when we cooked for Mr. Brevonni."

"When who cooked for Mr. Brevonni? What is this 'we' stuff? I did all the cooking, and you peeled potatoes and onions. Andi, don't even get me started on you and your ineptitudes. You, little miss, couldn't cook a hot dog. You will never find your way around a kitchen. It's okay though, you've got me to cook for you. You were a lot of help to me then, but now your job is to meet and greet and mingle and tingle. I mean tinkle. Don't spend too much time in my bathroom tonight. Stay out here and help me, okay?"

"Oh, you need my help, do you? Well, only for you Mag, only for you and Daphne will I be playing the hostess with the mostess. I think I hear Nino and Daphne now." I run to the door and yep, it's them. I help them bring in boxes of food and another box of folders. I'm sure that is everyone's personal folder of Daphne's detailed history of every little place we will stop. She should have been a history teacher; she loves this stuff so much. She bores the crap out of the rest of us. I hope they all tolerate her and won't hurt her feelings too much.

"Hey Magnus, what can I do to help?" Nino says as he enters the kitchen. Magnus immediately gives him a hug and tells him to start the bruschetta. He tells him that he has the egg yolks and parmesan ready. He's already chopped up the onions and the parsley. The pasta is boiling. Nino asks, "Tell me you made the tiramisu?"

"Sure I did. It's Italian night. We had to have the tiramisu, and I know you love it. Of course I have it ready. I also have the cappuccino machine ready to go. Let's get this dinner ready and start up this party."

Me and Daphne are in Magnus's living room when everyone starts arriving. Jackson is the first to arrive. He makes a quick greeting and then heads to the bathroom again. Maybe he has an enlarged prostate. While he's in the bathroom, Georgette and Hudson arrive. They seem a little quiet and reserved, but I'll open them up. They don't know what's about to come at 'em. I'm pouring red wine for everyone and passing out glasses. Georgette is taking in Magnus's living room furniture and asking me all about it. She assumed I was Mrs. Mag until I enlightened her. Just wait until he comes out of the kitchen, I tell her, then you'll know that I'm not for him.

At that moment, Magnus walks around the corner, holding a bottle of San Pellegrino water. Georgette's eyes almost pop out of her head. For just a moment, she loses her manners and acts like a commoner. Georgette pulls Hudson close and whispers in his ear. They both grin, and Hudson reaches out to shake his hand. Magnus says, "I can only guess by your reactions to seeing me that you recognize me. Now, that could really be from anywhere. So tell me what you've seen?"

Georgette snickers and responds, "Well, I have a friend that goes to Pensacola every Memorial Day, and he sent me a link to the YouTube video. Until then I didn't know that you were the Pork Man at Tidal Town."

"Well, nice to meet you, I'm Magnus Bruce. And please don't hold that video against me. My friends just find it irresistible to make fun of me. I am a very nice guy, and you'll see that I'm nothing like what they portrayed me to be. Welcome to my home, and I'm happy that you joined us for dinner. I look forward to our trip together next week."

At that time, Roni Abernatha arrives with Sebastian. He has met her as she was getting out of her Jaguar. He had decided to walk over from his house. He lives on the street behind us. He has already introduced himself to her, and as they enter he is introducing her to Magnus and me. We introduce everyone and pass out more wine, and Magnus is asking everyone to come to the table.

Jackson comes out of the bathroom with a measuring tape. What in the hell is he measuring? What kind of competition is that? I know these guys measure some strange things and take a lot of pride in the length of a certain anatomy part, but heck. Really? Coming out of a bathroom and not even putting up your metal tape measure before you enter the dining room. Eewee, what was he doing? Did he wash his hands? I didn't even hear the toilet flush. Everyone goes into the dining room, and I make a quick dash into the bathroom. Against all my better instincts, I allow the toilet lid to lift by motion activation, and then I feel of the seat. It's cool, so he wasn't sitting on the pot. I wash my hands real thoroughly, and then wash them again. The room just feels a little contaminated. What in the world is going on? I run back to the dining room with a plan to find out what Jackson was doing.

As I come down the hall, I notice that they've all moved into the dining room, when I hear the doorbell. I yell that I've got the door. I open the door and, to my surprise, it's a sixty something year old woman that is a little short and squat. She's got about five feet of brownish gray hair twisted and twirled into a huge-ass bun on the top and back of her head. She's wearing a long denim skirt and a T-shirt that has the letters WWJD on the front. She has bobby socks and tennis shoes that are about fifteen years old, and yet not worn out. "Hello, I'm Andi, please come in."

"Hello Ms. Andi, I'm Bobbi Jo. I am goin' on the trip with ya'll to Itlee. I am so sorry that I'm late, but I got lost up here in this big city. It's not like it is at home, so I've been driving around for a little while. Am I at the right place?"

"You sure nuf are, Bobbie Jo, let's join everyone in the dining room. You can meet everybody that's going on the trip. Magnus, he's my friend. He's also a great cook, and he's been making us a great Italian meal. Would you like some wine?"

We enter the dining room and no one even notices. They are chatting and laughing and seem to be getting along just great. "Law naw, I can't drink no wine. I'm not an alcoholic. I follow the teachings of the Bible, and I'll not be partaking in no alcoholic beverages."

Magnus hears her and walks over with a glass of San Pellegrino water. He throws an arm around her and says, "You must be Bobbie Jo. I'm Magnus Bruce, and I can't drink either, so we'll be a team, you and me. Here's some sparkling water that comes from Italy, so we'll drink this and won't be denied the Italian theme of the night. How's that?"

"Well fella, that will be fine, but I ain't no loose woman and I'd appreciate you not slinging that big arm around me. You're being too fresh," says Bobbie Jo.

Magnus then turns on his most gentlemanly southern charm. "Yes ma'am, I respect that. I know what you mean, we particular kind of people don't allow just anyone to be touching our person, do we? No worries, I get it. Would you do me the honor of sitting by me at dinner tonight?"

"Well now, that is certainly better. I sure would, Mr. Bruce."

I work my way over toward Jackson and try to breach the subject of the measuring tape. I can't seem to get his attention because his eyes are glued to Bobbie Jo. I walk around the other side of Bobbie Jo and am facing him and he doesn't even see me; he is too busy making conversation with her. Just when I'm about to butt in, Daphne grabs me by the shoulder and asks me to help hand out the travel packets. Oh hell.

Magnus and Nino have everyone seated, and Magnus is explaining the menu. He and Nino are passing out small salads, and Sebastian is refilling the wine glasses. While Magnus is being the chef introducing his food to all, Bobbie takes the first sip of her San Pellegrino. She immediately spews it into her plate.

"I'm so sorry, but what was you slipping on me, Mr. Bruce? That had to be some kind of alcohol. I've never tasted me no water like that. What did you give me?"

Magnus quickly intercedes, "No, no, I'm sorry, Ms. Bobbi Jo, that is water, it is carbonated and imported from Italy. I'm sorry that you didn't like it, but rest assured, it is just water, no alcohol. I'll get you something else. Would you like sweet tea or tap water?"

Before she can request either tea or tap water, Jackson has jumped up and is in the kitchen awaiting her request.

"Sweet tea, if you have it, sir," she replies.

"Coming right away," Jackson says.

He's back in a flash, and she's happily sippin' her tea and drying out her plate with her napkin. Magnus continues explaining what he has prepared. He goes around the table, formally introducing us and what role we have in the trip. Damn, if he isn't good at this stuff. I'm ashamed of myself, and I'm certain that Daphne is ashamed of me. Nino is making a toast for our shared enjoyment of the upcoming trip next week. Everyone starts eating, and I still haven't gotten to have a word with Jackson.

After the salad, Magnus goes to the kitchen for the pasta. I jump up and offer to help him before anyone else does. Once we are out of earshot from the others, I ask, "Mag, I saw Jackson coming out of your bathroom with a measuring tape. What was he doing? What on God's green earth was he measuring? And you had better tell me the truth."

After he recovered from a snickering fit, he says, "he was measuring my wall, Andi, what did you think he was measuring? You filthy minded little slut! What is wrong with you?"

172

"Sure, what is he measuring your wall for?" I ask.

"It's really none of your business, but if you must know, he's making me a plaque for my wall and he wanted to measure the place that I want to hang it so that he can finish it up next week."

"What kind of plaques does he make? Maybe I want one."

"I don't have time to talk about all that right now. We are hosting a dinner party. Have you forgotten your manners? Just carry the Parmesan and the grater and I'll take the pasta. You grate the cheese for our guests, will you please?"

"Fine, let's go."

Everyone enjoys the next course of the meal. All seems to be going just fine. Sebastian is preparing a little dessert cocktail for everyone except Magnus and Bobbie Jo. Magnus is serving the tiramisu. He tries to assure Bobbie Jo that there is no alcohol in the dessert, just coffee. She tells him that is fine, because the Bible don't have no problem with people drinking coffee. She drinks it all day long. She is rattling on and on. She's talking about her Wal-Mart brand instant coffee as the best coffee in the world. Nino is in the kitchen making cappuccino for all of us. He brings a tray with several cups. He goes back to make some more and asks us all to enjoy our dessert and coffee.

"This is the best tiramisu that I've had in years," whispers Mrs. Roni Abernatha. Georgette and Hudson agree. Magnus is wearing his sweet little boy grin. Daphne and I are enjoying our dessert and cappuccino as again Bobbie Jo starts spewing her coffee onto her plate.

"Whew, Lawdy Mercy, what was that? That felt like a kick by a mule. What did you say that was?"

Sebastian comes to the rescue and explains that it is strong Italian coffee. "Strong ain't the word for it. That stuff is stiff enough to hold a stick. My word, I love coffee, but that don't taste like coffee," Bobbie Jo says.

"Don't worry, ma'am, you don't have to drink it. Let me take it out for you, and I'll get you another plate with a fresh slice of dessert," Magnus begs.

"Thank you son, but I'd like to try it again, just a little sip to see if it goes down a little better. And I sure liked the taste of that dessert and if it is made with this coffee, I should like the coffee too. It just took me by surprise, that's all. I'll go with you in the kitchen and help you with another dish. I'll just take this coffee and sip it by the sink. That way if I need to spew again, I'll just aim it in your sink and run some water."

She pulls through it just fine and as she is finishing her tiramisu, she asks for a second cup of coffee. We might have created a monster. She asks Daphne if all the coffee in Italy is this good. Sebastian jumps in and tells her it certainly is, every day, all day, as much as she wants. She nearly swoons.

Daphne has handed out the folders, and everyone is sitting around the table discussing the trip. Daphne and Nino are answering questions and explaining the details. Bobbie Jo asks to be excused to the 'little ladies room'. Oh God. Jackson shows her the way and returns to the table. Now the conversation has changed to the Bankhead's and Roni's appreciation of Magnus's furnishing and decorating. They are all talking about his love of Italy and the surprise gift of the living room suite from Mr. Brevonni. No one knew that Magnus had modeled for Mr. Brevonni until then. Now, they're all treating him like he's a rock star.

Suddenly, we hear a loud, shrill scream and an exclamation of "What in the hell?" Several of us run toward the sound of the scream from the hallway. Jackson is the first to arrive as Bobbie Jo is running down the hall out of the bathroom, and as she runs she is pulling up her panties. She slips and almost falls as Jackson reaches out for her. His hands are outstretched, going for her shoulders, as she slips again, and now his hands are landing right in that big ass bun. Hair starts to tumble and as she is falling, the hair is now on the floor and is tripping her even further. Hair and more hair and tennis shoes with grannie panties hugging her ankles all combine to make her fall even more problematic. Her dignity is well preserved with that long skirt. Jackson finally gets her on her feet and she is near tears. Daphne thinks she's hurt and pushes Jackson out of the way, directing her into Magnus's bedroom to help her regain her decency. No one knows quite what to think of her misfortune. Only me, Sebastian, and Magnus know what is going on. She has been spooked by the toilet.

Once Daphne helps to get her clothing reorganized, she discovers that Bobbie Jo isn't crying, she's laughing. "Good Lawd", she said, "I've heard of them fancy be-dett toilets, but I ain't never seen me one of 'em. And, it's all automatic. I was surprised when I got positioned in front of it and the lid started raisin' up by itself. But, I had to go so bad that I didn't have time to worry about it too long, I had to hurry and sit down. After I got sat down on a square toilet, I ain't never seen me no square toilet either, but after I sat on it, I noticed that it was nice and warm. So, I took a little longer than necessary, just enjoying the heat, when music started playing and my 'kitty cat' started getting squirted with some nice warm water. I was shocked, but then, a fan started blowing on my 'kitty cat'. I got so tickled and scared at the same time. I didn't know what was happening to me. I hadn't had any of those feelings in a long, long, time; not since my Woodrow died, anyway. I jumped up and the toilet started flushing all by itself and it was more 'n I could take. I started running. I didn't realize that I hadn't pulled up my drawers. By the time I got outta the room, I was tumblin' down. My Lawd, that was an experience. I think it is like that coffee, I'll have to try that fancy toilet again. I think I'll start to like it. And look at that bed! What kind of man has a fancy bed like that? This house is like a palace. I bet this kind of stuff is what Elvis would have in his house. Lawdy Mercy. This is what I get, coming to the big city. I feel like the country mouse."

Daphne and Bobbie Jo come back to the table and we all laugh and enjoy the story. Bobbie Jo doesn't even mind the laugh at her expense. She says that she don't know of anything that ever happened to her that was funnier than that. After the story and Magnus's explanation of his Numi toilet, everyone demands a toilet tour. Sebastian shares stories of other friend's reactions with the toilet as well. Hudson says that he is ordering his as soon as he gets home tonight. Georgette is thrilled with the announcement. Even Roni exclaims that she would like to have one like that. Jackson is the only one not too impressed. He says a toilet is a toilet and that he doesn't require all that fancy stuff. He says he doesn't ask more than that it flushes and everything goes away as it should.

It takes a while, but we all finally gather in the living room. Daphne explains that through Magnus's work for Mr. Brevonni, we have all been invited to spend our time in Milan at his personal villa at Lake Como. Georgette is the one squealing now. Roni smiles and says that this makes the trip invaluable. I know the length that Sebastian has gone to make this trip for that purpose alone. Jackson and Bobbie Jo don't seem impressed at all and just keep looking at each other.

Everyone is thrilled with us as their choice of travel agency. Everyone except Bobbie Joe and Jackson, that is. Maybe they'll be happy in the long run, but for now, they are just content to pretty much ignore us and gaze at each other.

We all agree to meet at the Delta counter at the airport at eight-thirty on the morning of departure. Nino insists that we are there three hours prior to departure; I know he will make sure we are there at seven-thirty. He's always paranoid about that, so all I can do is go along. Everyone assures me that all their documents are in order and will not be forgotten.

As everyone is walking out the door, Jackson and Magnus walk down the hall and go into the bathroom together. They leave the door open, thank God, so I don't have to worry if something is going on there. I can't hear their conversation, as it is low and muffled by the musical toilet. I decide to leave them and see everyone off. All seems to be good, so I hope Daphne is going to settle down now.

Magnus calls to Jackson, "Hey man, come with me to the bathroom. I need to make sure that the plaque is ready to go. Did you check the measurements earlier?"

"I sure did. Everything is perfect. I came in earlier and confirmed the measurements. I've got everything set. Are you good with the plan?"

"Absolutely, it is fool proof. A baby could pull this off. Well, at least a teenager. Just like when we were young. There is nothing to worry about."

"I know. After our rehearsal last week at the shop, everything will work fine, I am sure."

"Okay, then, did you leave it in my room like we planned?" "Yes sir, I've already slipped it under your dresser. All you've got to do is put it in your packed baggage. We're set."

"Okay then, not another word between us until 'go' time."

Daphne and I see everyone out. Jackson finally comes out and leaves in his old pick up. Nino and Daphne offer to help clean up, but Mag and I assure them that we don't need their help. They have a couple of hours drive home and it's already ten at night. Magnus is awfully quiet as we clear the table and load the dishwasher. If I didn't know him better, I'd swear he had something up his sleeve. But I do know him better than anyone, and I'm certain that he has something up his sleeve. I also know him well enough to know that if I were included in the plan he would have told me. Since he hasn't mentioned it, I guess I'm out of this one. And I should probably be very happy about that. In fact, I am. Magnus in trouble in the US is easier than Magnus in trouble in Italy.

Chapter Nineteen

EARLY DEPARTURE

The night before our trip, Magnus tells me that he is going to get up early and make us a good breakfast. He says he thinks it's very important that we begin our trip with a good southern breakfast. He wants me at his house at six in the morning, and he'll have everything ready.

I go ahead and pack. I'm not much for fashion, so it doesn't take me long. I have four pairs of jeans, a pair of khaki pants, some shirts, sweats for sleeping in, and one good pair of shoes. A few toiletries like toothbrush, toothpaste, shampoo, soap, deodorant, and a cologne miniature, and I'm set. Oh yeah, I need my hair gunk or I have curls from hell to fight with every day. That's it, this is all I need. So, one suitcase packed and I'm done. I learned long ago to fly with those cargo type pants with about ten pockets. So my only carry-on is a simple backpack with about thirty little pockets. I need lots of places for my electronic gadgets, pens, paper, snacks, more snacks, mints, tissues, and any other little thing I might need for about eighteen hours of travel. Daphne always makes fun of me for all my pockets of stuff, but whatever little thing you might need, I'll have. I only have one concern at this moment: Magnus.

I plan to get to his house earlier than six so that I can start going through his luggage and removing clothes. He always packs too many clothes and shoes and hair products. I have to remind him that this flight will not be as luxurious as his modeling trip. But he did insist on paying the extra for the exit row seat. So did Nino. We have six exit row seats reserved for Nino, Daphne, and me on one side of the plane and then another row for Jackson,

Bobbie Jo, and Magnus. Sebastian, Roni, Georgette, and Hudson all booked first class, of course.

My sister Daphne has this jetlag all worked out, too. She takes her bottle of low-dose sleeping pills and passes out one to anyone in the group that wishes to sleep. One may also choose melatonin if one wants to take the gamble. Anyway, she is right on this one. Once you arrive at eight in the morning you feel rested and ready to start the arduous tour that she has planned, although you've missed two meals, four snacks, and two movies. For years and years, Nino and I just wanted to check into the hotel and sleep. But, oh, hell naw, she don't allow that. Go, go, go, that is her motto. I'm sure she'll bring a couple of bottles along with her tomorrow, too.

That's it. I'm done. Off to bed for me. I'd better sleep while I can. The suitcase is packed. My clothes are laid out. My pockets are filled with the essentials, and I'm ready. I do like Italy, so I'm actually looking forward to this trip. My sister has dragged me all over this world, and most of the time it is not my preferred style of vacation. As I said, she likes to go, and I like to sit. But what can I do? She is my older sister, therefore she thinks she knows everything.

My alarm goes off, and for once I'm awake and ready for breakfast. I think that is the only reason I'm in a good mood. I jump in my hot shower because I don't know when I might get a modern shower again. You see, my sister likes to pick cheap little hotels or pensions that sometimes turn off the heat and the cold water at designated times. Those times are usually the times that I like to get showers. I lather up the medusa hair and enjoy the hot water. I shave all the essentials. I don't know when I might get around to that again; it could be awhile. I'm finally done and force myself out. I slap on the deodorant and the hair gel. I put on a single pair of small diamond stud earrings. I put on my cargo pants and load up my pockets. I pull on my favorite comfy travel cotton long sleeve T-shirt, and I'm ready to go. I pack my passport and ticket away in one of the inside pockets of my super-duper travel backpack. I throw the backpack over my shoulder and pull my suitcase out the door. I lock everything up and go through my back yard path to Magnus's house.

His lights are on, thank goodness. There have been times in the past when he had these big plans to get up early and make me breakfast and I have had to wake him up after we both overslept. Nope, I can tell by the aroma from outside that his skillets are fired up. I open the door, and the man is all dolled up with his big apron on.

Biscuits are on the table, bacon and sausage are fried to perfection, and he's hard at work with some kind of omelets. He has about five bowls with lots of different ingredients set to the side. He doesn't bother to ask me what I want in my omelet, he is just cooking away. "Good morning, Mr. Sunshine," I tell him as I walk by.

"Hello Tootsie," he greets me. He plants a kiss on the top of my head as I walk by, dragging my suitcase. I head to the front door, dropping my bags in his living room. I don't see his luggage, so I'll have to make a quick dash to his bedroom as soon as I can. I head toward the kitchen.

"Hey Andi, pour us some coffee, will you?" I pour our coffee and take it to the table. He brings in the plates of omelets, and we dig in. I've got my biscuits buttered and have lathered on the homemade blackberry jam that Daphne makes. The bacon and sausage are cooked perfectly. This omelet is great, a little spicier that my stomach normally accepts, but overall it is good. I don't know what all he put in here, but it is tasty. We both clean our plates. We talk awhile about his packing, and then we're done. We quickly clean up the kitchen, wash the dishes, and retrieve our bags.

I make a last pee pee run in his bathroom. He has such a great toilet. I could stay in this bathroom for hours. I hit my favorite playlist on his fancy toilet and get comfortable for a while. He really has this bathroom looking nice. I wonder what his little Mrs. Carmichael thinks of it. I bet she likes it, too. As I attempt some maybe unfinished business, I notice that his wall is blank again. He's never happy with anything for very long. I'm sure he'll find another piece for it soon. All I manage for my time is an empty bladder. I wash up and watch that magical toilet flush itself and smile. I turn out the light and head back into the kitchen.

"Magnus, how many bags do you have?" I ask.

"I only have three, Andi, so don't worry. I didn't over pack. I need everything that I have. One is a carry-on, so don't worry. I've even weighed them, and I am legal."

"I don't believe you, Mag, drag 'em out here for show and tell."

"All right, I'll get them, be prepared for the shock of your life."

Oh this cain't be good!

Magnus goes into his room and returns with two suitcases and a carry-on. He brings his little handheld scales and demonstrates the weight of less than fifty pounds on each bag. His carry-on is within legal size and is amazingly small for what I had expected. This is unbelievable. I ask to go through the bags just to see how he did it. I'm reaching for the larger one and he pulls me away. He flat out refuses my inspection. He tells me that this time he doesn't need his mommy checking on his packing. I nod my head in agreement with just a twinge of concern back deep in my brain. This is not like he normally behaves. But I choose to blow it off, thinking I am being a little like a mommy and not trusting my teenager when I should.

I can't help asking him to show me his passport and ticket, which he quickly pulls out of the inside pocket of his light khaki jacket. That's another thing. He's dressed like a world traveler. Comfort is not his style. Style is his style. And of course, I'm dressed in my usual travel outfit. Standing side by side, we don't look like we could even know each other, much less be perfectly suited friends. He's always trying to dress me, and I'm always resisting his advice.

We start loading our baggage in my car, and I notice my tummy feels a little rumbly. I quickly think back and remember that I did have my regular morning ritual before my shower. So, whatever that was is probably fine. We excitedly load the car and fight over who will drive. Magnus is driving my car to the airport today. I spend five minutes lecturing him on helping me get into the airport. I beg him not to leave me stranded this time. I don't want any mishaps like last time. I don't want to end up under a greasy car. I don't want him to run off and leave me. I expect to walk into the airport with him by my side. He agrees and apologizes for the minor problems at the airport last time and insists that he'll never do that again.

As he is sincerely telling me how sorry he was in abandoning me, I notice my stomach again. It is really rolling like thunder down there. I wonder what he put in those omelets. I saw those bowls of ingredients. I think there were black beans and spinach, jalapenos and onions. Hmm, could that be my problem? About that time, I feel a little slippage. Oh no, was that a gas bubble? I'm not really sure. Maybe it was just rolling, not releasing. Magnus is going on and on with sorrow of my abandonment, when I notice a smell. It is just a little twinge of a smell. Maybe it won't linger.

He turns and looks at me, saying "Do you smell something? Did you see road kill? It kind of smells like something dead, doesn't it?"

"Nope, I don't really smell anything." I think to myself that I'm all right now. I think my stomach has quit turning flips. I pray that it's gone because I sure don't want to get on a jam-packed plane farting up a storm.

We finish our drive to the airport without any other distraction. We head to the long term parking area and find a space without problem. We are way early, so there is no rushing. I'm sure that is because we didn't have to repack Magnus's suitcase. Like a gentleman, he has popped the trunk and is locking up the car. I have the trunk open and am reaching for my bag as he steps up beside me. We both have our heads in the trunk as I quickly lift my suitcase. As soon as I am at maximum force lifting my bag, a tight high-pitched little fart sneaks out. I had no warning with this one. I'm shocked and embarrassed at the same time.

"What in the hell was that, Andi? That was you earlier, wasn't it? I thought you said that you didn't smell anything. You let me blame that stink on some poor dead animal when all along you knew you did it. Honey, what has tore your stomach up so bad? Did anything come out with that fart? If I had known that you were having some stomach issues then I wouldn't have made you that high fiber, gaseous omelet this morning. I would have just made you have some yogurt."

"You asshole! What do you mean gaseous, high fiber omelet? Who the heck ever heard of a high fiber, gaseous omelet? How can you possibly make a simple omelet have a lot of fiber and gas? This is unbelievable. No, my stomach was fine until we started packing the car. It was only then that I felt the rumble and tumble of a gaseous, high fiber omelet shart, well really I don't know that it was a shart, it could have been just a fart with no liquid. I thought omelets were constipating, with all that cheese and just eggs. I still don't know how you could make a high fat, high protein food become fibrous and gassy. What did you put in there?

"And, oh yeah, I'm sorry Mag, I thought it was just one single little fart in the car and I didn't think I'd ever have to own it. I thought if it never happened again, it wouldn't hurt a thing for a non-existent little animal to take the blame. And if I had known a fart was sneaking out, I would have pretended I dropped something and it rolled all the way across the parking lot, and I would have went over there and farted just the way any decent person would do."

"Well, you didn't do that, did you? You just dead-lifted that suitcase and farted in my face. And, I think this one was worse than the first one. And, I was thinking ahead! We needed to start the day with a high protein, high fiber meal. Everyone always gets constipated when they travel because you don't want to poopy anywhere but your own house. So, I was starting us off on the right foot. A lot of thought and planning went into that breakfast. I had to cook the black beans, clean the spinach, and chop the onions. I even threw in a finely chopped apple to add more fiber and give it just a taste of sweet. I would have never dreamed that your stomach didn't know what to do with a little fiber. I tell you over and over again that you need to feed yourself better. How many times have I told you that? You never learn, do you? And, by the way, you cleaned up that omelet. You didn't leave a single bit on your plate, so don't go trying to blame me."

"Well, I didn't expect an innocent omelet to be so volatile. Leave it to you. And I apologize to you; I didn't mean to have gas in front of you. But I'm sure that it's over. My stomach feels fine. That must have just been a lingering strand of gas. Please just let it go and let's not think of it again."

"That is fine with me. I don't want to think about it another minute. Just let me do the rest of the lifting, and you just pull the suitcase on its wheels. I have only one request. Please don't bend over in front of me for the next fifteen hours."

Chapter Twenty
AT THE AIRPORT

We leave the parking deck and find our way to the Delta departure area. It is seven forty-five, and Nino and Daphne are already here. Leisurely they sit, sipping coffee. "Hey there," I say as we roll up. "Is anyone else here yet?"

Daphne answers, quickly on her feet to greet us. "Sebastian is here. He is off getting coffee. And Jackson is at the Top Side Restaurant having breakfast. He asked us to tell Magnus to join him as soon as he arrived."

Magnus tells us they will be back here by eight-thirty, and off he goes to find Jackson. It will be good for Mag to spend some time with his friend. And with Jackson being a widower, I am sure that a trip with an old friend will be good for him, too.

I decide to go for coffee, leaving my luggage with Daphne. And it's a good thing that I do, because no sooner than I walked about hundred feet, I feel my belly fluttering again. What? Oh, no. Please don't let this start up again? What kind of man puts black beans in an omelet? What am I gonna do? I decide that I'd better make a trip to the nearest bathroom and try to eliminate those beans.

Luckily there happens to be a bathroom just before the coffee place. I go to the farthest stall, glad that I don't see any feet under the remaining doors. I start to sit and sure enough, I blow a big one, thank goodness the place is empty. At least I think so, until I hear a five-year-old little girl bust out laughing and ask her momma if she heard that. Of course, she heard that, they probably heard that in the hall. The momma can't seem to stop the little girl from laughing, when I get tickled, too. Oh no, I shouldn't have started laughing. Now there are laughing farts popping out of my ass. Now, I'm laughing, the momma is laughing, and the little girl is hysterically out of control. I finally stop farting, but none of us can stop laughing. This is beyond funny—it is just that kind of crazy uncontrollable laughter that you can't stop, even after the funny moment has passed. The memory of the funny moment keeps you going.

Now, it's a waiting game. I can't come out until they leave, and they can't leave until they can regain some composure. None of us can regain composure. So we all remain behind our closed stall doors laughing so hard and getting sillier by the moment. I hear another person walk in and run to the stall next to me. She barely makes it in time and is peeing like a horse. I think to myself, "is that Daphne?" The little girl starts it up again. Then I start it up again. The momma is trying to fuss her into submission when the momma starts it up again. Oh man, we were almost there, and now we are crazy laughing again.

Surely, I am gas free now. All this laughing would have pushed out any remaining gas, and the little girl and I haven't heard anything else. Now she could very well have missed it if I had, because we are laughing so loudly that we can barely hear the pissing. I can't imagine what that woman must be thinking. But I certainly would have felt it, wouldn't I? I really do feel that I've rid myself of all this gas. I am just so very thankful that it was gas and not diarrhea. Now that would make for a bad trip.

I feel good about my exit, I mean leaving the stall. I haven't heard any giggles for about forty seconds. Maybe they are gone. The pisser is out there washing her hands, and since she didn't hear me farting I don't mind showing my face to her. I quietly reach for the door and make a quick exit from the stall. As soon as I step out, the mom and the little girl exit their stall. She points to me and says to her mom, "she farts just like you mommy," and it all starts up again. We're all three face-to-face, laughing with tears streaming down our faces while we wash our hands.

I feel a camaraderie with these people now. We have been through a sort of minor battle together and come out unscathed. Well, almost unscathed. We exit the bathroom together, still snickering, and wave to each other as we go different directions.

I finally make it to the Roasted Bean and order my Cuban Colada. Everyone says that this is way too strong for one person, but I like it dark, rich, and strong. I'm enjoying my little shot of caffeine while I walk back to my sister. I arrive just as everyone is gathering around. Mag and Jackson are there, huddled up and talking privately. Sebastian is seated next to Nino, and they appear to be in deep conversation. Georgette and Hudson are cute and cuddly, talking to Roni. And Bobbie Jo, traveling like a Holy Roller, bun sportin', tennis shoe and skirt wearing Christian is seated by Daphne, looking way out of her element.

I walk up to Magnus and ask him if he knows where the nearest trashcan is located. He takes one look at my cup and pulls me by the wrist away from Jackson. We're about three feet away from anyone when he quietly but forcefully shouts in my ear, "Did you just drink your famous Cuban coffee? Don't you know that caffeine works as a laxative? Are you crazy? You are about to board a loaded airplane for the next several hours. Your only choice of a bathroom is a port-a-potty on a plane. You are full of gas already, and now you add a stimulating stool softener to your colon. I'm just saying one thing; I'm not sitting beside you. You are to trade seats with someone, anyone; just don't sit (shit) by me." He doesn't even allow me to answer as he walks away and returns to the conversation with Jackson. I guess that must have been a really bad smelling fart for my best friend to disown me like that.

What have I done? Why didn't I know that? Our flight to Atlanta is only an hour. If anything starts to move, I've got to hold it for an hour. That sounds like misery; I could explode. And this time, everyone will know that it is me. Now which pocket did I put that Immodium AD in?

Daphne finally gathers us all around and corrals us to the agent. One by one we get our tickets and start forming our line through security. We are inching along in our long row as I notice that Magnus and Jackson drop back. They do this very subtlety. I look back to ask Magnus his seat location, and I see that he and Jackson appear to be bent over, looking for something. They motion several people in front of them. I don't know what to think. Do I go back for them or continue along? I decide to continue along, and the next time I look back, they are even further away.

We all make it through security, and Mag and Jackson are still back there. They motion for us to go on ahead, so we do. But as we walk away, I turn back and see that they have pulled them to the side and are unpacking their carry-on bags. I see some friendly conversation between them and the security official, so it must be all right. Then they repack their bags and walk on through. They seem to be in deep conversation between themselves. I hang back waiting for them, and when they catch up they are laughing and relaxed. "What happened back there guys?" I ask.

"Nothing," Mag answers, "I started emptying my pockets and dropped a bunch of change so we stopped to find it."

"What was in your bags that they had to search them?" I ask again.

"Nothing," Jackson says, "they just said it was time to search and I drew the lucky number, that it was nothing personal."

"All right, let's get going then. We're down at gate B-37, aren't we?" I wonder out loud. "Where are you sitting?"

Magnus quickly answers, "We're on the economy comfort row, and you're not sitting with us are you?"

I look at him with slightly evil eyes and explain that I am not seated next to him and that I am glad of it. He throws his head back and laughs at me. No, I have the pleasure of sitting with Bobbie Jo. On this short flight to Atlanta I think we are scattered everywhere. Daphne is sitting with Roni, and Nino and Sebastian are together. Of course, Georgette is with Hudson. But we are all over the plane.

Eventually we are all boarded, and it feels good. I'm getting excited about the trip. I'm sitting with Bobbie Jo, and I start to realize how uneasy she is. She says that she has limited traveling experience and that she thinks she will be fine to Atlanta because it is a short little ride. Then she confesses that when she is really nervous she has bouts with gas. As we're preparing to lift off she starts rambling on and on, first about her grandson, then about her church, and finally about her friend Dorothy McKorkle. I realize that she is one of those people who talk a lot when she is nervous, and soon would learn that she farts a lot. We're twenty minutes into the flight, and she hasn't slowed down. I'm not one of those talkative people, and she is just about to drive me nuts. I wonder if it is too early to ask Daphne for one of her little sleeping pills. Just when I don't think I can take any more, I lean over to get a book out of my backpack stowed under the seat, and damn if a little toot doesn't slip out.

Bobbie Jo looks at me and is wearing a grin all across her face. She quickly throws both hands over her mouth and starts laughing her head off. "Lordy Jesus, Andi, did you just fart, too?" she whispers quietly between snickering. Then I laugh at her laughing. What an icebreaker. We enjoy great conversation for the rest of the flight. I guess all the others enjoy their short little flight.

After landing in Atlanta, we have a three-hour lay-over. We all gather without any problems at our Milan flight gate. Everyone is now deciding which restaurant they want to visit, and we all agree to meet back at the gate an hour before our flight. Magnus, Jackson, and Bobbie Jo decide to go to the Brewhouse. I'm a little concerned with Mag and Jackson taking our churchgoer to the Brewhouse. I hope they are bein' hayved. Sebastian, Roni, and Nino chose the airport's swankiest gourmet restaurant. Georgette and Hudson go to the Delta Sky Club. That leaves me and Daphne here with all the carry-on bags. I go to get us a drink and some BarBQue nachos to share.

It is nice to have some quiet time, if I can call time alone with Daphne as quiet. We discuss the tour details. Guilia's email last night told me that as soon as our party exits the airport we are to look for Mr. Brevonni's driver, Marco. He's arranged everything. We will be transported from the airport directly to his villa, where he will be awaiting our arrival. When I share this with Daphne, her eyes light up, and she hugs me like never before. "Sister, *please* tell me that you will not act so star struck. Mr. Brevonni and Guilia and everyone I met that worked for him are very nice and down to earth."

"I know, Andi, I just can't believe that I'm able to stay at a private villa at Lake Como. You know that I've always wanted to go there. I am so thankful that he doesn't know you and Magnus like I do, or else we'd never have got this invite. Thank you so much for being on your best behavior."

"Hey now, that was unnecessary," I say, as I lift my right butt cheek to allow some gas to expel loudly. "Why would you say such a mean thing to me? What kind of grateful sister are you that you would bad mouth me and Magnus like that?"

"Just stop and think about it, and did you really just fart directly at me? I could start telling everything that I *know* about you and Magnus and all of your crazy adventures, and if I didn't stop until I told them all we could fly from here to Australia and back and I wouldn't be finished. I'm not saying that I don't love you, even though you deliberately just farted on me. I'm just saying that you two didn't do something crazy that might have shed a more realistic light on who you really are."

"Again, you just slammed me again. If you don't stop it right now, I'll tell Guilia that you aren't with us and we'll leave your butt at the airport. We'll see Lake Como from a private villa without you. And another thing, *we* don't always get into trouble. It is usually just Magnus, and I'm involved because I'm trying to pull him out of his mess."

"I am sorry then. Maybe I am wrong. Let's agree to use this trip as a test to evaluate whose theory is right. I say you and Magnus are always up to or into or trying to get out of trouble. You say that you never get into anything crazy. Just remember that either way I have always loved your zany, carefree personality. I've always been envious of it, in fact. I was just saying that I'm glad things worked out so well and you and Magnus impressed Mr. Brevonni."

We leave it at that and enjoy the nachos. I do tell her about my gas and how embarrassed I am. She just grins and makes an invisible check mark in the air like she just won a point or something. I tell her that I'm feeling fine and hopefully it is all over. She says she's never heard of black beans in an omelet either, but agrees that his idea of a high fiber meal before a trip did sound reasonable. I knew she would agree with him. And she had the nerve to chastise me for eating BarBQue Nachos on a tore up stomach. My stomach feels fine, it's just south of the stomach that's irregular.

As we are fresh out of insults for each other, Nino, Roni, and Sebastian arrive. They are talking about the great meal they just had. They describe to us, as if we care, their Wood Smoked Skirt Steak with Sicilian Herb Sauce and the Planked Salmon with Maple Glaze and the Chicken Marsala. I hope none of them get airsick and throw up all that expensive food. Too bad that Magnus is not here to truly enjoy and appreciate their delectable meal. All this description and praise is wasted on me and Daphne.

When Georgette and Hudson arrive they just sit and listen quietly to the rest of us. I hope they are going to enjoy their vacation. I have a feeling that we are just background to them. But they are young and newlywed and probably can't muster up a lot of interest in anything we are talking about, planning, or doing. They are very cute off to themselves just cuddled up. It's sweet.

They have been boarding our flight now for ten minutes. Daphne offers her little sleeping pills to Sebastian and Roni before they board for first class and they both decline and laugh, each of them saying that they have their own medications, thank you very much. They tell us that they will see us in Milan, and off they go.

Georgette and Hudson are also boarded for first class. They too decline Daphne's pill pushing. They explain that they are young and well-traveled and will be fine. They insist they know how to deal with jet-lag, and off they go. I close my eyes for a minute and dream about my last first class flight and know in my heart that it will never happen again. Sister and I are just not first class kind of people.

They have already boarded our zone and Magnus, Jackson, and Bobbie Jo still haven't returned. I'm really starting to get concerned. Not so much for Mag and Jackson, but I'm worried that Bobbie Jo has been corrupted by those two.

Daphne and I are the only remaining passengers waiting to board. Nino said he wasn't going to worry about adults boarding a plane. He left us about fifteen minutes ago. Suddenly I notice some commotion down the concourse and I see two men holding a woman off the ground as they run. She is dangling between them with her skirt billowing and tennis shoe feet running as fast as they can, except that her feet are about eighteen inches off the floor. The guys are pulling out tickets, and we run to greet them as they reach the agent.

Bobbie Jo is singing, "He filled my heart with love, wrote my name above…"

Jackson is filling in with bass, "Now let us have a little talk…"

"What in the hell happened? You almost missed the boarding. Is Bobbie Jo alright?" I ask as we assist them in finding Bobbie Jo's ticket.

We finally get all the tickets out and are quickly passed through the gate and head down the jetway to the plane. Magnus is talking to Jackson as they continue to carry Bobbie Jo to their seats. Nino is seated with his headphones on and reading something. He doesn't even act like he was at all concerned that we were not yet boarded. Once he sees us, he gets out of his aisle seat and motions Daphne in. Row 10 in Economy Comfort are roomier seats for an upgraded charge but worth it for an eight hour flight. In the middle are Magnus and Jackson, and me and Bobbie Jo are on the other side. She looks like

195

she might have already gotten into Daphne's little sleepy pills.

I still don't know what happened to her. I put her by the window seat and belt her up. The guys are all whispery and are glancing at Bobbie Jo. As soon as we are all settled, I ask Magnus, "What did you two do to Bobbie Jo?"

Magnus is seated in the aisle seat next to me. He shyly glances at Jackson, and then turns to me, saying, "Long story short, she had a Long Island Iced Tea."

"Why did she drink alcohol? You know that she is holier than us, and they don't drink. Did you guys put her up to that?"

"No, hell no, we tried to stop her, but she wouldn't listen. Jackson ordered the Long Island Iced Tea, I ordered a coke, and she ordered Sweet Tea. When our drinks arrived, she said that she liked Jackson's tea glass because it was so narrow and tall and cute and all. We just let her have a sip thinking that she'd spit it out. But man, were we wrong. She gulped it down before we could stop her. As soon as she took her first breath we told her that we didn't think she should drink that, because there was alcohol in it. She said that she knew better, there wasn't alcohol in it, in fact she said it was the best sweet tea she'd ever had. She said we don't make it this good in LA (lower Alabama). She finished it off and then got mad because we wouldn't let her order another one.

"Jackson had to have a big glass of sweet tea. But it was all right because we were so entertained that we barely had time to eat our burger. Andi, you wouldn't believe all the stuff she was talking about. She may be church-going now, but that wasn't always the case. She has experienced quite a colorful past. After she revealed all of her deep dark secrets then she started preaching to us. Me and Jackson then had to hurry her out of the bar as she

196

was upsetting quite a few fellow drinkers. But as soon as she stood up she went down. And then she went out. Then we had to grab her up and get her out of the bar and to the nearest chair. I was carrying her, but that flappy skirt kept blowing up in my face, exposing Lord knows what to passersby. After we got her to a chair, we had some trials on how best to transport her. We finally figured out that the quickest way was for each of us holding her under the arms and walking / running as fast as we could. She would sing a hymn as she came in and out of consciousness. Could you check a pulse?"

"What did she say, Magnus? You have to tell me, you know that," I say as I reach for her carotid artery. I feel a very slow and relaxed pulse, possibly at sixty or so. This little churchgoer must be in good cardiac shape. I wonder what she does for her workouts. I bet she don't run or do Hello Dolly's; it would be tough with those long skirts on.

"Andi, I'm not going to confide drunk secrets to you, so just hush. After what I just learned about Bobbie Jo, I'll guard her dignity forever. She's a good person who has had a difficult time. I've placed her under my big hen wing and I'm her guardian. I'll just tell you there was something about a tornado and some chickens and her mama and that is all that I'm gonna say. You just sit there and take care of her or else I will."

"Fine, don't have a hissy fit. She's good. This will probably be the best flight that she's ever had. And she won't need sleeping pills either." I have to admire Magnus. He is really a very good man. Once he's on your side, hell or high water is not going to turn him away from you.

After some minor delays, we are taxiing toward the runway. I'm relieved that we're all on board and ready to go. That is quite an accomplishment for this particular group. I still think something is up with Magnus and

Jackson. Even for a gay guy he is more than usually gossipy and secretive with Jackson. That would not be a concern if Jackson was gay, but he's as straight as an arrow. So, what is up with 'em? Something is, I'll guarantee it. I'm gonna keep a sharp eye on them during this trip.

The plane is now second for takeoff. I'm excited. What an unexpectedly great trip this has become. Just wait until they all experience the hospitality of Mr. Brevonni. I was worried about Bobbie Jo, but she is genuine if nothing else, and Mr. Brevonni values that above all the glitter and glamour that you can throw at him. And I know the fashionistas in the group will be in hog heaven. I'll probably have to devise some type of sling or harness for Daphne's chin, because she'll never be able to keep her gaping mouth closed. I bet that for once in her life, she will be stunned silent, just a hanging open mouth every time she turns around. She's going to be in a constant state of 'Ahhhh.'

The takeoff went just fine. We are airborne now and close to our cruising altitude, or so says the pilot over the intercom or whatever they call that form of communication. Bobbie Jo is still out of it. I guess she won't talk my way through this flight. I'll have to find a way to give her some more 'sweet tea' before our flight back. This will be nice, just me and my Netflix. Daphne is way over there, so she can't bother me. Magnus and Jackson are all deep in obvious plotting and planning, I just don't know why. Nino never bothers anyone. He is quiet with his headphones on, watching the airplane's screen. That leaves me all alone for eight hours, lucky me. I've got my meals *and* Bobbie Jo's all for myself. It doesn't get better than this. Everyone can just leave me and my stinky ass alone.

I've got my earphones on and enjoying the music with my eyes closed as I feel a tug on my sleeve. "Andi,

Andi, are you sleeping?" squeaks Daphne with her annoying sisterly tone.

"Well, yes I was, sister. What do you want?" I really wasn't, but I thought maybe she would take the hint and leave me alone. I should have known better.

"I needed to wake you up and give you your little sleeping pill," she says. What is wrong with her? Did she hear what she just said? Wake me up to give me a pill to help me sleep. She is a nut.

"Sister, did you hear the words that just came out of your mouth? I don't think I need it, Daphne, but thanks," I say and quickly close my eyes and lean my head back again, hoping that she will go away, but pretty damn sure that she won't.

"Now, you know you will wake up in an hour or so, as soon as they bring dinner. Then you'll eat, and then you'll start watching some dumb movie, and then you'll try to sleep, but you'll be too awake to go to sleep. So, here, take your little pill and forget about eating and watching movies. Just take it. I want you to sleep so you'll be ready to help me with the group on arrival."

"I know, Daphne, I know. Just give me the pill and go away."

"Now, don't you take that tone with me, little sister. Here, take it."

"I've got it. Now, go."

"No, I mean, let me see you take it. I have good reason not to trust you. Remember the last tour. You took that pill from me and you never took it. You ate your way across the ocean. You watched all the movies in your library. And, when we arrived you slept for the first five hours in the van. You weren't even able to help me with the group. I'll have no more of that. Take the pill, take it now. I want to see you take it."

"Fine, give it here." I take the little Ambien and swallow it down with some water that she insists on me. "How is it, Daphne, that you can coerce me like this? This is probably against the law, being forced to take drugs against one's will. You know how much I like the food and the movies, so why can't you leave me alone? Why do you always get to boss me around? You ain't the boss of me. You don't boss Nemo around, do ya? He doesn't let you. I've got to talk to him about that. I need to learn whatever it is that he uses to shut you up."

"Andi, you just wait one dat-burned minute. You are on the job, and I need you to be coherent tomorrow when we arrive. You are the one who must get us to Riccardo Brevonni's villa. I can't do that detail. Now, hush up and go to sleep. I can't stand here and argue with you as my little pill is starting to take effect. I've got to get back to my seat while I can."

"You just remember this, sister. All my life I've been younger than you, and you have bossed me around. But one day, you'll be way, way old, and I'll get to be the boss of you. And you had better know that I intend to make it h e l l oooonnnn youuuu. "

As I say this, somewhere deep in my brain I think that she has already left me and didn't hear one single bit of my threat. I hooppe she didn'tttt mmmake it anddd mayyybe sheee feelll doownnnn…..

Chapter Twenty-One
IN FLIGHT

"Jackson, the story worked fine for the TSA—they didn't even care that I've got a marble plaque in my carry-on. We did it, at least, half of it. Once we get into Italy, we're set for the job. Nothing can stop us now."

"I know. I know. I've gone over it and over it and this is going to be easy. I'm only concerned about the distraction while I do the job. Thank you so much, Magnus, for including me on an exciting adventure. It's been so long since I've had some good, almost clean fun. My life has been so serious for so long. I'd forgotten how fun life can be. And not to mention that it occurs in Italy. You know that I've never traveled and I always wanted to. I never dreamed that I'd be going to Italy. I really want to spend some time looking at the ruins and the architecture. Thank you for including me, Magnus."

"Including you, hell, I couldn't have done it without you. You are the one with all the knowledge. I just had the idea."

"What you wanted is simple and easy. The fun part is in the doing."

"We've worked a good, strong plan. It really can't fail."

"I'd like to change the subject, Jackson. And if you would rather not talk about it, that is fine, just say it. What do you think of Bobbie Jo? I noticed you two at the dinner talking a lot, and you seem to be watching her all the time. Is anything going on with you?"

"I don't know, really, I don't. I don't know what it is supposed to feel like to have feelings for someone. It's been so long. It was only my wife for me. We were true to each other until the day she died. I've never had feelings for anyone else. But, there is something about Bobbie Jo that draws me to her. Now, I know that she's a little rough and outspoken, but that doesn't bother me none. I've thought a lot about it, and I think I'll use this trip to spend some time with her and see what I feel like later."

"That's a good idea, Jackson. I agree that she is a very nice woman. Now, she is a little strange to the average person, but deep down she is a good person. After her confessions down in the bar, I can assure you that I will watch out for her and enjoy our time together. I'm just not sure what she will think of me once she knows that I'm not straight. I'm sure that her religion doesn't condone that, and I don't know if it will affect her feelings toward me. But, I'll do my best to show her that I'm as good a person as she is and that I shouldn't be judged by others' opinions either. I think she'll understand that, now knowing her past like I do."

"Hey, Magnus, what is happening with Andi over there? Look at her."

Magnus glances over just as Andi is unfastening her seatbelt. She starts to stand, then she falls back into her seat. She attempts to arise again. She has her right hand extended overhead, with her index finger trying to point toward us. "Daphneeeeee. Daphneeeee, youuuu druggggedd meeeee."

With that she falls back into her seat, passing out. Magnus quickly fastens her seat belt again. "Oh my God, she didn't just stand up on a crowded plane and scream out an accusation of her sister drugging her. And look at Daphne, she's passed out herself and doesn't see or hear a thing. Nino has those huge noise reducing headphones on, and he didn't hear it either. That is the funniest thing I've ever seen!"

"Do you think she's okay?" Jackson asks Magnus.

"Sure she is. She just took one of Daphne's Ambiens. She's fine. We'll have to watch her, though. She might start sleepwalking and sleep eating and try to sleep drive or fly. This is hilarious."

"I just want to say that this is the best trip I've ever started with these two crazy sisters. How much better could it be? Only a couple hours into the flight and both Andi and Daphne are sound asleep. Bobbie Jo is passed out with alcohol intoxication. And thanks to the noise reducing headphones, Nino is oblivious to everyone but his movie. I feel like we've got this flight to ourselves. These are great seats without anyone in front of us. I've got plenty of leg room, and I never have enough leg room."

"Hey, tell me about Milan. What will we do there?" asks Jackson.

"This is truly extraordinary. You'll never get this experience again. As soon as we arrive, we will be met by the employees of the greatest Italian menswear fashion designer. They will take us to his private villa north of the city. We get to stay at his estate for our entire time in Milan. I guess the next day or so, we can go into Milan for the tourist stuff. I'm sure that Bobbie Jo will want to see the fresco of daVinci's Last Supper. And I'm sure that Roni and Georgette will want to shop. You may not know it, but Milan is the fashion capital of Europe. I need to pick up some clothes there, too. So you can go with me or hang out with Bobbie Jo if you want."

"Oh, man, you know that I want to spend some time with her. That will be great. I've always been a kinda regular churchgoer too. I want to see that painting myself."

"Then that settles it. We'll get Marco to take us into town and direct us where we need to go. We can meet back up at a specified time and place for a ride back up to the Lake Villa. Wait until you see his place—it is great. It sits on the most beautiful lake in all of Italy. A lot of the movie stars have places there. No one else can afford it. We're lucky to experience it like this."

"I can't believe that I'm going there. This is a once in a lifetime opportunity for me. And who could have known that I would have met a woman like Bobbie Jo? I don't know if anything will ever become of it, but what a chance. Just think of our memories together if something did work out. What about that?"

"I know. I'm happy for you. I had a relationship hopeful with this guy named Conrad, but it has fizzled out over the past several months. But I'm happy, I truly am. I have a great life, I got to model fancy clothes, and I have the greatest friends ever. And I have a great toilet, not to mention Lamborghini furniture. I'm learning as I get older that a relationship isn't the major part of my life. My friends are the best part, and I really do value them and keep them close."

"So, you and Andi are good friends? I haven't been able to tell, really. I think that you are, but it seems as if you are keeping her at a distance today."

"Today, yes. That's because she started the morning with this God-awful gas. She farted on me in the car. She farted on me unloading the luggage in the trunk too. And I know her all too well. She's gonna keep on farting for the next six hours or so, especially when she's sleeping. She's always been a sleep farter. She denies it, but she is. It's not personal, I just don't want her in my personal space for a while. Hey, come to think of it, do you want to change seats? There is only an aisle between me and her stinky ass. I'm just kidding. I wouldn't do that to you."

"Good, because now that I know that stinky fact, I'll keep my distance, too."

"Jackson, look at Nino. What's he doing?" says Magnus.

"I don't know. He's standing up and seems to be looking for something. He's still got those headphones on and is looking at Daphne, then toward the seats behind him. He's looking at that older couple sleeping in the seat behind theirs."

"*MY GOD DAPHNE, WAS THAT YOU?!*" Nino screams.

Magnus laughingly whispers to Jackson, "He's forgotten that he has those headphones on. He is shouting because he can't hear himself. What is he talking about? Oh, Lordy, I smell something. Where is that coming from? Daphne is trying to open her eyes and look at him, but she can't come to. Do you smell that? Nino is sniffing around everywhere. He is looking at us." Magnus nods his head negatively.

Nino unplugs his headphones and is sniffing. He follows his nose past Jackson and Magnus and follows a waft of air toward Andi.

"My God, that was Andi! What in the hell did she eat to make a smell like that?" Nino asks Magnus, more quietly than his last exclamation. "How can you guys sit by her? It must have risen straight up and followed the contour of the plane ceiling and curved its way to my side of the plane. I hope it doesn't linger much longer. I thought it was the two old folks behind me. Then I thought it was one of you guys. Geez, can you believe that that nasty odor went all the way across the plane?"

"I know, Nino," Magnus whispers. She started it early this morning. She's been blowing them all day. I hope it stops soon, but be warned, in my experience we've got a few hours remaining."

"Do we need to wake her and get her to go to the bathroom? Do you think she shit her pants? It sure smells like it! Farting is bad enough. I don't think I can take another four hours smelling her shitty pants all the way to Italy."

"Naw, I'm sure it's just gas. I've smelled it all day. Don't worry, it won't last long. Go back and enjoy your movie. Try to forget it. I know what to do. I'll get her blanket and my blanket and cover her up from the waist down. We'll trap the gas and it can dissipate downward and maybe under the seat and go behind her."

"Fine, that sounds like a good idea," Nino says as he heads back to his seat.

Magnus quickly finds two blankets and covers up the sleepy Andi. "That should do it."

Jackson, Magnus, and Nino eat dinner and watch movies throughout the flight. The lights go down and they all get to nap for a few hours. Just as the plane is filled with soft snores and stretches, the lights are turned on. The attendants pass out warm wet clothes for refreshing your sleepy eyes. Then breakfast is served.

Just on cue, Andi starts to stir. It must have been the smell of strong, hot, coffee and warm food. As she awakens from lala land, she finds herself confined in blankets and wonders how that must have happened. And then she recalls dreaming of gas; she's not sure if gas was passing or gas was being inhaled. Bobbie Jo is also stirring. Once she is awake, she looks up and down and all around and with the biggest eyes you've ever seen. As consciousness returns to Andi, she realizes that perhaps Bobbie Jo might be about to throw up. Her skin tone is slightly greenish. Andi quickly finds the vomit bag and hands it to Bobbie Jo.

Bobbie Jo grasps it and looks at it like she doesn't understand what is about to happen. Andi leans toward

Bobbie Jo, "Honey, just lie back and be still. I know that your tummy isn't feeling so good, but it will get better. Just sit back, and I'll get you some strong coffee. Do you remember what happened?"

"I don't even know what you mean, 'what happened'?" Nothing happened. I went out to eat with the guys, I had a great sweet tea, and then I bet that Daphne slipped me a pill. I told her that I don't do drugs and I didn't want one of those pills. Anyway, she must have, and then I must have fallen asleep on this plane. Funny, those pills must be retroactive. It must have erased my recent past memory. I don't even remember getting on the plane. I'll do like you say and just be still and have coffee. This sleepy grogginess will pass quickly, won't it?"

"I hope so," Andi says as the attendant delivers the breakfast tray. "And if you don't feel like eating, in fact, you probably shouldn't. I'll eat yours if you don't want it."

"No ma'am. I don't want to even look at food. You can have it. Later, I need to ask Jackson to help me figure out the recipe for that sweet tea. That was so good. They must make it different than we do."

After the breakfast is cleared, the pilot announces that we are approaching Milan and should be on the ground within thirty minutes.

"I'm so excited!" Andi exclaims to anyone who will listen. Bobbie Jo just smiles and leans her head back against the window. Magnus and Jackson smile and tell her that they can't wait to get off this plane. Daphne is all chipper and smiling. Nino is Nino, no change there.

The landing is smooth, and we all quickly exit the plane. Fortunately the luggage is retrieved without incident. Georgette, Hudson, Roni, and Sebastian all look great, like they just landed from a first class flight. How nice for them.

With luggage in tow, we all head out to the transportation area. Magnus and I look for anyone holding a paper with their name on it. Suddenly there are shouts of "Andi, Magnus, over here." Sudden recognition occurs, and me and Magnus run to embrace some beautiful Italian people.

"Oh Guilia, I'm so happy that you came to meet us. I didn't expect you to be here," I say as Guilia and I hug. Guilia jumps up and down excitedly while I hang on for dear life. "I'm glad that you're finally here. I've been looking forward to this. I'm made lots of plans for us. I've prepared the villa and planned the most wonderful meals!" Guilia exclaims.

Magnus strolls over and hugs Guilia and shakes Marco's hand. "Wow, what a reception. I've never been met in another county like this. It's wonderful to see you again. You both look great. Let me introduce you to our group."

Magnus and I introduce everyone. Guilia and Marco show them the way out of the airport. There are two limousines with drivers. They assist everyone with their luggage and start loading up. Magnus, Georgette, Hudson and Sebastian head toward a limo with Marco. Roni takes one look at Marco, and she eases her way with them. I lead Daphne, Bobbie Jo, Nino, and Jackson toward the limo with Guilia. Once loaded, the limousines start the ride to Lake Como.

Both Guilia and Marco in separate vehicles tell the riders about the city of Milan and Mr. Brevonni and his villa and Lake Como and on and on. Of course everyone is stunned by the views of the city and countryside. The scenery is breathtaking and everyone is in awe of the reception and transfer from the airport by private limo to a private villa. Even Roni, Sebastian, Georgette, and Hudson have never been treated to this kind of reception.

Just as I expected, Daphne has barely said a word. But, every two minutes, she is tugging on either me or Nino and pointing at a passing scene with her mouth wide open in the 'O' shape. I smile each time, just knowing how appreciative Daphne is at this privilege. Even Nino loves it. He's speaking Italian to Guilia as he points to something and then asks her something in Italian and she answers and points to something else and they converse some more in Italian. Jackson and Bobbie Joe are just looking out the windows without much expression. You'd think they were riding the bus from Rock Holler, Alabama to Talledega. Bobbie Jo seems to have pretty much recovered from her drunken stupor. She's still just a little pale, but the greenish glow is gone now.

Onward north we travel, out of the city and into the countryside. We drive through farm land, orchards and quaint villages. Daphne has yet to complete an entire sentence. And just the opposite, Nino is talking up a storm. Their bodies have become possessed by the other's mouths. In over thirty years, I've never seen this happen before.

As we reach Como and travel up the Via Toma toward Bellagio you could hear a pin drop in this luxurious limo. Even Jackson and Bobbie Jo now recognize an unknown beautiful landscape. Who could have imagined that I would experience the quietest peaceful drive through gorgeous northern Italy with a group of gaggling tourists, not even to mention Daphne? And who would have expected that the only talker in the group would be Nino? Mind boggling, that's what this is. I hope the rest of our stay here is like this. Even with Nino talking so much, I don't have to participate, because I can't understand a word that he's saying. Guilia continues to give me little sly glances, and all I can do is smile.

As we approach the gates to the villa, not a single word escapes all these mouths. Oh yeah, except Nino quietly and appreciatively exclaiming, 'Bellisimo.' The limo pulls up to the long, open vaulted walkway with ivy creeping up the columns. No one can move. They are all glued to their seats, as if they are not allowed to walk on these hallowed grounds, just allowed to peer through windows. No one except Nino, that is. Who is this man? I've never seen this side of him. It is like he drives up to this mansion every day. He is so at ease now. He is out of the limo, smiling and looking all around. He finally comes around and helps me pull the stunned and silent Daphne out of the vehicle.

Guilia runs up to the staff and rapidly directs them on taking the guests to their rooms. Once she's done this, she runs back to me and puts her arm through mine and directs us toward the villa. Now, even Roni and Sebastian, Georgette, and Hudson are in awe. As we near the end of the walkway the landscape opens to the mountains, trees, and lake. We are actually entering the side door into the expansive living room.

Just before we reach the door, dear Mr. Brevonni is coming out to greet us. He calls out for Magnus, and Mag nearly runs over the others to reach him. Magnus gently gathers him up and spins around with him. They kiss cheeks, and Magnus lowers him to the ground. Sebastian's eyes are about to pop out of his head. I don't know if it is because he is standing on the grounds of this fashion giant or if it is because Magnus is so familiar with him. Mr. Brevonni very graciously introduces himself to every single one of them. What a truly wonderful man he is to have brought us all here and personally welcome us to his home.

Guilia then asks the staff to escort each guest to their room. She tells me and Magnus that we have our same rooms and that our luggage will be taken there, but we are invited to join Mr. Brevonni for a coffee in the kitchen. Guilia says she will show the others through the living areas and assure them that they are welcomed guests and may come and go anywhere they desire. She will ask them to meet us in the kitchen for cappuccino or espresso whenever they like.

She's off with the others and me and Magnus are sitting at the nice old table with Mr. Brevonni. It is like time hasn't moved. It feels like yesterday that we were sitting here. Mr. Brevonni is sincerely happy and is talking quite rapidly for him. He's asking about our lives since he's last seen us. He tells Magnus how pleased he is with the photos and the ads that his marketing team has completed. "We've saturated the market with this line and it is more successful than ever. Don't be surprised to see yourself throughout Italy. Frankly, you are everywhere. In Milan, Florence and Rome, they have created large photographs that hang from high-rise buildings. You might find that you will not enjoy the solitude that you once had. You could be recognized everywhere you go. Do not worry, however, as Italians and Europeans in general are not as star struck as you Americans, you should still be able to walk anywhere you like; however, you can expect stares from people who appreciate your appearance."

Magnus seems stunned. I expected this news to overjoy him, but it is just the opposite. If anything, he appears worried. But it quickly passes as Daphne and Nino enter the room. Nino starts the conversation, thanking Guilia for the cappuccino and thanking Mr. Brevonni for his generous accommodations. He is talking in Italian to Mr. Brevonni and they are chuckling and enjoying their coffee. I swear, I don't know this new Nino. I have never seen him like this; he is alive here. And he seems to have brought laughter to Mr. Brevonni. While they continue their private conversation, the others seem to drift into the kitchen.

Guilia and her helper are seating everyone and preparing their coffees. Guilia is offering options for the day. She suggests that everyone relax and walk the grounds while she and Maria prepare lunch. Then, after lunch, we can choose whatever activity we would like to do. We can go boating, riding around the lake, go into some of the local villages, or relax and do nothing. We are to let her know what arrangements she can make to accommodate our needs.

Mr. Brevonni offers a suggestion for tomorrow. "I've arranged for the guys to be taken to our offices in Milan tomorrow. They can tour the factory and choose a wardrobe if they like. Gratis," he says. "It would be my pleasure to offer you what I take most pride in: my clothing. For you ladies, I am sorry that I only design men's clothing, but I have talked to my friends at Valentino and Dolce&Gabbana, and the same offer holds for you there. So, if you like shopping, tomorrow you are welcome to shop at my pleasure. I've arranged for Marco to organize transportation into the city. And, I understand that Miss Bobbie would like to view the Last Supper. I've arranged for that as well. Giovanni will take you on a tour of our sacred sites if you desire. If there is anything else you might wish, please alert Guilia or Marco or myself and it will be accomplished for you. I offer you my home for your pleasure. I must now excuse myself and attend to some business. Welcome and enjoy. I will see you again throughout the day. And, later today, if you could accommodate me Sebastian, I'd like to talk to you about business. Arrivederci."

How does this man know everything that everyone wants? He must have some kind of investigator that knows everything about each of us. I do remember the email from Guilia about a month ago, asking for the names of each person in our group. I thought she must want to alert the local officials or something. That must be the secret of his success. He knows all there is to know about those in his acquaintance. Oh, well, none of us have secrets, except for maybe Magnus and Jackson. I should ask Mr. Brevonni if he knows what they are up to.

Chapter Twenty-Two
VILLA CERVIDI

It seems that our group is scattered everywhere this afternoon. Guilia made a great lunch for us. She and Maria made a delicious caprese salad, a light pesto pasta dish, with mixed vegetables and a small salad. We finished it with espresso. Best of all, it was served outside under the vaulted walkway. They moved a line of tables into the walkway and covered them with multiple square tablecloths placed diagonally throughout the length of tables. They pulled up benches and chairs, and it was splendid. We sipped sparkling water and local wines for hours. We enjoyed lunch, and then everyone slipped away. Guilia explained the custom of napping after the noon meal, and most of our group seems ready for naps, probably because they didn't partake of Daphne's sleepy pills. Everyone is gone except me and Daphne.

We decide to walk around. I show her the grounds and the lake. We wander quietly through the villa. We decide to take the long walk down to the village. It is wonderful. Daphne is being so sweet. Now she is talking up a storm, rambling on and on and on. She's rambling about the beauty of the villa, the grounds, and the lake. She's rambling about the easy relationships with Mr. Brevonni, Guilia and the staff in general. I explain that it is very surprising that they are just like us. They don't seem to know that they are great. I have not seen Daphne this ecstatic since the birth of her grandchildren. We walk along and get gelato. I tell her about Magnus's photo shoot here and how great it was. I tell her about my drive around Lake Como in the Alpha Romeo being driven by Marco.

"Oh, Andi, can we do that? I would love a drive around the lake. Will you go with me? Can we?" Daphne begs.

"Sure, I'd love that, sister. Only, we can't be stopping at every beautiful corner, because if we do, the trip will take two weeks."

"All right, all right, if we can just stop at one place along the way and you pick the place. I'll be content to just sit back and enjoy," Daphne promises.

"OK sister, when we get back I'll tell Guilia, and she will make it happen. I do know where I want to stop. There is a nice little shop in Bellano that has those nice silk scarfs that you like. I'd like to take you there, and you can have whichever one you like. I'm buying. How's that?"

"Let's go, I am ready now. Let's start back up the hill to the villa. Do you think we could go in the Alpha Romeo sportster? I'd love that, but who could drive? Isn't it just a two seater? Can you drive?"

"Sure, I can drive a little antique sports car around a huge lake with high mountain roads. It will be fun, just me and you, sister. But, I think you fired me though, didn't you, for coming here to Italy and not helping you dig for treasures in old chicken houses? What are you going to do about that?"

"Oh, you know that I was just kidding. You know that I didn't mean it."

"But sister, I knew you would love it here. Isn't it amazing? I can't believe he would invite us here out of the goodness of his heart. We are so lucky."

We take the long walk back to the villa. I guess we have been gone for a while, because as we approach the house, we see Marco and Roni leaving in the Alpha Romeo

Spider, and damn if that Roni doesn't have a scarf tied around her hair and is wearing sun glasses. She looks like I wanted Daphne to look. Roni waves to us as they pull out of the drive, and Daphne and I look at each other and say "shit" almost simultaneously.

We go on in and discover that Bobbie Jo and Jackson have gone out in the boat. Sebastian and Mr. Brevonni are talking business in the office. Magnus and Nino are in the kitchen with Guilia cutting and dicing vegetables.

"Where have you gals been?" asks Magnus.

"We took a walk into town. We got some gelato and walked along the lakeside and looked around the town. We decided to come back and drive around the lake this afternoon." Daphne replies.

"Well, Andi, you wouldn't believe it, but little Roni latched onto Marco and asked if he could drive her around. She seemed like she couldn't wait to get out of here. Mr. Brevonni offered the limo for everyone to go together, but we all wanted to wait for you two. It was like she wanted Marco and that little sports car all for herself," says Magnus.

"What about Georgette and Hudson? What are they doing?" asks Daphne.

Magnus leans in and quietly whispers, "Oh, honey, you know they are newlyweds. They told us thank you for everything, but they would see us in the morning and they haven't been out of their room since. They said they didn't even know if they would come down for dinner. Guilia told them about the little intercom button in their room and asked them to call and she would bring them up a tray."

Nino lays an arm along Daphne's shoulders and asks if she wants to be chauffeured around the lake in a

216

limo. He says that he and Magnus would love it and that they want us to go with them.

Guilia insists that we take a couple of bottles of wine and pushes us out the door. She calls the driver and tells him that we're ready. Just that fast and we are loading up in a limo. This really worked out much better. Great weather and a limo and Lake Como in Italy and wine and friends and family; can it get better than this?

Our drive along the lake is heavenly. It is similar to the Amalfi Coast, except in miniature. There are beautiful mountain roads weaving on and off of the shoreline. It is complete with lots of hairpin turns and hills and valleys. The roads wind through the picturesque quaint villages. Needless to say, there is always a breathtaking villa wherever you look. And best of all, we view it from a roomy limousine sipping Italian wine. I am so thankful for this God given opportunity. I am truly blessed. We southerners always say that, and we always mean it. Bless you. Have a blessed day. I am so blessed. The translation is that we are aware that our daily accomplishments are far more than we can achieve alone, and we recognize and are thankful for these Heavenly blessings. Anyway, I'm sure that in years to come this is an adventure that we will never tire of recalling.

Needless to say, it was perfect. The views, the scenery, the wine, the limo and even the frequent stops for Daphne to extoll the incessant beauty make for a perfect day. Of course we had to stop for Daphne to pick out the scarf that I promised. The nap made it possible for Nino and Magnus to enjoy the scenery while I remained awake.

We returned to the villa later than we had planned. The driver phoned and explained to Guilia that we would be late. So, when we did arrive, Guilia had our dinner set aside and was eager to hear about our drive. Our entire group was there, talking around the table, enjoying each other's company. It was nice to see they were all getting along without the two mamas to keep the peace. How grown up they are.

Now, Guilia invites us to sit while she brings our dinner, "Everyone is making their plans for tomorrow. What are you guys going to do?"

"I'll go into Milan and make arrangement for our rental van," replies Nino.

"We've already arranged that, Nino," says Guilia. "Mr. Brevonni instructed me to have it delivered here on the morning of your departure. Everything is set. A driver will deliver it here to the villa."

"Molto gracie," Nino says.

"Bene," says Guilia, waving her hands as if it were nothing.

Nino happily admits, "I guess I'll have to go shopping with the guys. I would love to see the fashion production of the great Brevonni."

"You will never believe it," yells Magnus. "It is like nothing you could imagine. I can't wait to see it again. It is amazing. What about you other guys, do you want to come along?"

"Wait a minute, Magnus," says Sebastian, "I've spent several hours this afternoon talking with Mr. Brevonni. He's agreed to sell to Ward's Limited. I will have exclusive rights to his line. Imagine that, Magnus? Anyway, he wants to go with us tomorrow so he can walk me through the complete process, from initial sketches to ready to ship. I could never have done this without you. Thank you so very much. And from now on anything that you want at the shop is yours, free of charge."

"Wow, are you kidding? What about my current bill from your store? Why are you doing this, and for how long do I have this deal?" begs Magnus.

"Forever—that is, as long as my contract with Mr. Brevonni is current. And you know how much I love you, but that was Mr. Brevonni's requirement. He said that with you as his 'Brevonni Man', anything you want is given by our company at our cost," explains Sebastian.

"I don't know how I can ever thank that man for all he has done for me. It is me that is grateful for him," says Magnus. "So, what better way to see his place than with him as our guide? What about you girls? What will you do?"

Roni is quick to answer, "We are all being driven by Marco to the designer's stores for our own shopping spree. I tried to explain to Mr. Brevonni that we could all easily afford our own purchases and would be grateful for the transportation, but he insisted that as our host, this is his gift. What a generous man! We don't make them like him anymore in the US, do we?"

"This is becoming more and more unbelievable, isn't it?" says Daphne. "I never, ever expected such generosity for plain people that he doesn't even know. I think I love him. I mean really, I love his kindness, his goodness. You guys know that we don't deserve any of this."

"Well, now, that is the wrong way to think, Mrs. Daphne von Hohenfeld!" exclaims Bobbie Jo. "God is good and is always finding ways to bestow his gifts on you. And after spending some time with Mr. Brevonni and all his staff, they are truly the hands and mouths of God. They are so good that God just oozes right out of them."

"Amen to that," says Jackson.

"You can sure say that again, Bobbie Jo," says Roni. "Especially that Marco, he just wants to give and give and give and ohhhh. I'd better stop myself or I've got to get out of here." Her eyes are closed and she's sipping wine, but I don't think she's with us here. I think her mind is somewhere else.

"Why is she smiling like that? What is she talking about? What has that Mr. Marco given her?" asks Bobbie Jo.

Guilia grins and walks to the stove, avoiding our gaze. The guys have quickly turned away from the conversation and are drinking their wine and looking uneasy. What the hell is going on here, I wonder. I walk over to Guilia as Daphne has quickly redirected the conversation and everyone is talking about Lake Como. Bobbie Jo is telling everyone that a driver is taking her and Jackson to see The Last Supper. She is almost talking in tongues, she is so excited. But I wonder, doesn't the rule state that if you talk in tongues, doesn't someone have to be there to interpret? Maybe Roni can do it; not. I quietly start assisting Guilia in doing nothing and look at her with a questioning eye. "What was that about, you know something, don't you?"

"Now Andi, you know that we know everything. Bobbie Jo is right, we are a little like God," responds Guilia.

"Well, what was that? Was Roni about to have an orgasm there or am I on the wrong track?"

"I can't really tell anything. I learned long ago that the first rule of hosting is that you maintain all secrets. I will say nothing. Just believe me, there is no harm done and everyone is happy. What happens in the Alpha Romeo, stays in the Alpha Romeo."

"Well, I know why everyone is so happy, and I think I can figure out why Roni and Marco are extra happy. I agree with you, good for them both. I'm sure that you and Mr. Brevonni know her past too and can appreciate all that she's been through as well. I don't know how you guys do it. You are like genies in a bottle, and we have all rubbed it and have been given whatever we wished for. Thank you, Guilia."

"You are most certainly welcome, Andi. Now get to that table and you four start eating. When you are finished, we will get you all to bed so you can prepare for your day tomorrow. And let me say that it is so good to have you and Magnus back again. Mr. Brevonni has really looked forward to your return. You two have brought more joy to that man than I've seen in years."

Everyone sits and talks with us while we eat when I realize that Georgette and Hudson are not here. Roni explains that Guilia took them up some trays and they asked her to tell us that they will join us tomorrow. We all enjoy our time together. Dinner is great, as if that were ever a concern. We all find the way to our rooms around midnight and are asked to be downstairs by nine tomorrow morning for our quick breakfast and coffee.

Once Magnus and I are in our adjoining rooms again, we sit and talk some more. Again we are shocked that we are being treated like royalty when we know that we are just good ol' country folks. We acknowledge our gratitude to Mr. Brevonni and Guilia and again wonder how we can express our appreciation. We say our goodnights and sleep like babies.

Chapter Twenty-Three

MILAN, ITALY

Me and Magnus awake just as before, to the smell of strong Italian coffee. We each hurry into the shower and get dressed. I think I will probably dress for sightseeing with Bobbie Jo and Jackson, as I'm not much of a designer clothes wearer. I don't even think that designers make clothes in my size. I'll be much happier with the churches and history than with the fancy clothes. So, I throw on some jeans and a t-shirt and put on my tiny diamond stud earrings. I squirt some hair gunk on my palm and give it a good rubbin'. Then I spread it out all over my crazy curls. I'm ready to go—oh yeah, I almost forgot the deodorant. Swipe it here and here, and now I'm ready.

I knock on Mag's door, and he steps into my room looking like the model that he is. How do people do that? I just wasn't born with that capability. He gives me one glance and hangs his head in shame for me. While his eyes are closed and he's nodding his head back and forth, I whack him on the arm with my fist and tell him to come on. We know our way directly to the kitchen through our small secret passage.

As we enter the kitchen, Mr. Brevonni and Guilia are sitting at the huge rugged table in quiet conversation. When they see us, Guilia jumps up to get our breakfast, and Mr. Brevonni smiles and beckons us over to join him at the table. We resume our casual conversation as if we were next door neighbors with back door privileges. Guilia rejoins us, and we all laugh and talk on and on. Mr. Brevonni is all excited about his planned day with us. He seems so young at heart today, like he's taking all his children to town. I love him, truly I do.

While Mr. Brevonni and Magnus start a conversation about clothes and photos and ads and such, I insist on helping Guilia prepare breakfast for the others. We are at the stove and the sink and the coffee machine doing all kinds of stuff. I'm just following her instructions, and she's working me silly. I'm preparing fruits and grains and creams and yogurts. I've been put in charge of spooning marmalades into pretty little crystal containers. I've even got to remove honey from a perfectly good container and put it in fancy crystally bowl.

We are interrupted with the group seemingly to appear en masse. Everyone is talking and scooting chairs across the floor. Guilia seems to be flying all around while I am spinning in circles, literally not moving an inch. She has got everyone served, and they are asking for condiments, and I am still holding the honey. I gather my composure and start delivering my marmalades and croissants to the table. I've got a bowl of boiled eggs that I bring to the table too. Of course me and Magnus have already eaten, and he finally breaks away from the conversation and sees me working up a tizzy. He excuses himself from the table, offering his seat to Jackson, and insists that I have no business in a kitchen. I wonder where he's been for the past fifteen minutes while I was working up a storm.

He is heading toward me as I turn around, returning my huge jar of local honey to the pantry area. He is being charming, still talking to Roni, as he slams right into me. "Whoa, Magnus, watch out," I yell. It is then that I realize I'm losing my balance. I am tilting backwards as his big ass arms reach to grab me and only succeed in pushing me further backwards. I know that I am not going to recover from this, I just know it, I'm going down. As I fall, I lose the honey as I grasp at thin air to stay upright. The honey falls before I do. The jar breaks and honey is slowly creeping across the old tiled floor. Of course my foot finds it, and I go down faster than I fall when I try to ice skate. My left foot flies up and hits Magnus in his you-know-where. It's just a glancing blow, not a full force kick in the nuts, but it's enough to send him crumpling, too. By now I am on my back as I see this huge man falling toward me. The looming shadow closes in as I defend my face with honey covered hands after they landed in the honey flow as I fell. My head is lying in a pile of honey, as I am trying to protect myself from a Magnus squash.

Magnus is now muttering, "Andalusia Eufala on me again. Well, kinda, I fell on you, but it was because of you."

I might have failed to notice how beautiful Mag's long, black, curly hair looked this morning, which is just as well. As I wrap my honey hands around his head to protect it from slamming in my face, my honey fingers are tangled in his mane. Now he is screaming like a girl as I unsuccessfully try to get my hands out of his hair. He has landed just to my right with both of his hands at his groin area, as if there is any protection left to him. At least during my entanglement in his hair, I braced his face and head so he didn't bust it open on the floor or my face. Now he lies crumbled up in the fetal position to my right as my arms appear at abnormal positions. I scoot back to allow my arms to normalize their extension and decrease the force which is about to break both my forearms and wrists. Now I have to untangle my hands from his head. Just as all this is coming to realization, I hear Daphne squealing, and I feel the vibrations in my back and side of thunderous footfall.

"Oh no, Andi, are you okay? Did he land on you? Can you breathe?" she is stammering.

That's all she has time to say before her right foot hits a spot of honey and here she comes. "AAHHHH, help!" I hear my mouth scream. At that moment I see

Magnus's eyes as huge as saucers as he is seeing what is heading at us with the speed and weight of a rhinoceros. I thank God that she doesn't have a horn, or we'd be goners.

Simultaneously we both expel all the air remaining in our lungs. She lands on us equally which, due to some physics formula of energy that I don't understand, causes our bodies to separate, with Daphne landing flat on the floor between us. This force is still not strong enough to separate my honey hands from Magnus's curls. But I do hear him yelling as my gooey hands have stretched his curls to their fullest capability before separating from his head. I feel the tautness against my fingers as he scoots closer to my hands to release the pressure. With that he has caught Daphne in the squeeze. Now she is groaning a guttural type sound. I think maybe her breath is gone, too. She raises herself up just enough to ease the vise-like squeeze we have on her. Now she is resting up atop us like a stack of dominos or some cheerleader stunt she might have done in high school.

We all lie perfectly still, regaining our breath and thinking about how best to unstack our pile of sticky, slippery selves. As we quiet down, I realize that there is laughter all around. Not just giggles, but I mean tear-rolling laughter. And it's coming from *everyone*. I even hear Mr. Brevonni laugh. Now that we can breathe again, we are laughing too. Daphne is hysterically laughing, and that seems to be jarring against the rhythm of my laugh, so it's almost like an earthquake on my side. Magnus's big ol' chest has no trouble getting his laughs out, but with every exhale he is pushing Daphne more over to my side. Within two minutes she is lying right on top of me and Magnus is free. We still can't think of how to get up because every attempt creates a new hysterically funny reposition of our pyramid. We must look like the Chinese acrobats from hell. Oh yeah, and my hands are still glued to Magnus's hair.

Finally, Jackson regains some composure. He approaches with the practicality that I expect from a man from Arab, Alabama. With hands on hips, he looks down on us from every angle. He walks around the giant mess that we've made. He encourages no one to move until he has fully assessed the situation. As if we can move without repositioning our acrobat act. After making two rounds of assessment, snickering all the while, he has Guilia bring some dry towels, about four, he says.

While Guilia gets the towels, we just lie and giggle. Only Magnus stops giggling when I accidently manage to pull too tightly on his hair. I think I hear phone camera clicking and endless laughing. I'm not blaming them, I'm laughing my butt off too. As we are sure that cameras are clicking amidst the laughter, I hear Magnus grunt, "Shit, not again; I hate YouTube." This makes me and Jackson and Guilia and Sebastian laugh even harder because we all recall Magnus's YouTube fame.

Guilia hands off the towels to Jackson. He places two of them on the floor onto the honey mess at our feet. He instructs Daphne to roll onto her hands and knees in between us. Once she achieves this, he ties an end of the towel to the refrigerator handle and gives Daphne the other end. She slowly and luckily without slippage gets herself upright on another dry towel that he has placed between us. "Now, Daphne, slowly take off your shoes and socks and toss them out of your honey wrestling ring," he says. She does this and, using the towel for leverage and balance, slowly steps above our heads onto the clean floor in her bare feet and walks away unscathed.

"Now for you two," he ponders. "You are going to have to get up as one and walk to the sink together. Once at the sink, we'll rinse your hands out of Magnus's hair. This will be hard for you Magnus, because of your height. Can you two try to get on your knees and inch your way back to the towels at your feet?"

"Sure, we can do that, just sit back and watch," I say with a little attitude. After three failed attempts and an almost black eye for Magnus, Guilia approaches with a large container of warm water. She pours it slowly onto Magnus's head. My hands are coming free, and Magnus is gurgling something about water boarding. As he is gasping, my hands slip free from his hair and he lurches backward, free at last.

"Son of a bitch, Andi, what the hell have you done to us again?" he asks me quietly. As we continue to laugh and yell, we work our way onto our hands and knees and remove our shoes and socks. We crawl out much like Daphne did. Once we are free, we are laughing so hard that we can barely stand up. Everyone starts laughing again with us, giving us a play by play of how it looked from their view. On and on for several minutes everyone is laughing. We finally gather up our shoes and socks and go to the shower and redress.

We gather back in the living room and match up with drivers. My goodness, that Roni is standing awfully close to Marco. Her back is against his chest and there are some subtle hand movements going on. *Good for you, Roni girl, go for it*. I'd just bet that Marco is taking the girls shopping. There will be another driver for the guys' fashion trip and still another for us churchgoers.

"Daphne, what are your plans?" I ask. "Are you going shopping or are you going to church with us?"

"I think I'll go with you all to see the painting. Designer clothes will be a waste on me in Rock Holler, Alabama. Can you see me in those clothes digging through old chicken houses and barns looking for forgotten treasures? Even when I dress up to go to Lucy's coffee shop, I'll not be needing fancy clothes like that. Anyway, I think I'm too big to matter to a designer. And besides, I would enjoy the time on the streets, strolling and drinking cappuccino. Is it all right if I join you?"

"Absolutely, we'll have a good time, just like the old days," I tell her. "I'm sure that Bobbie Jo and Jackson would enjoy us hanging with them. Guilia said that our driver has been instructed to take us to see several cathedrals in the city. We do have an appointment for The Last Supper, as it is seen by a ticketed schedule. Mr. Brevonni has even arranged for a church historian to meet us for the day. She will accompany us to all the churches. It's me you should worry about because you know my thoughts on big cathedrals; if you've seen one then you've seen them all."

Chapter Twenty-Four

THE LAST SUPPER, MILAN, ITALY

An hour later and everyone is off their separate ways. All the shoppers are more excited than if they were meeting the Pope. Even the guys! I expect it from the ladies; most women love shopping. Throw in designers and free and you've just as well have given them the moon. I hope they don't live this for the rest of the trip. I can just hear it in the van travelling throughout the country. If it gets too bad, I'll have to tell them to shut up, and the most annoying one will probably be Magnus.

We are loaded up with our driver, Marcello. He says that we are to meet at a restaurant in Milan around one for lunch with the entire group. That's good. I'm glad someone was thinking of my stomach, because it would have reminded me, and I would have bugged the crap out of our churchy group wanting to eat instead of looking at churches.

Our driver takes us directly to Santa Maria delle Grazie Church for our viewing of The Last Supper. We approach the entrance to a large, red brick church with beige brick trim around all the windows and doors. This is not an impressive church, not for Italy anyway. It was completed in 1490 by the Duke of Milan Sforza. The Last Supper was completed by Leonardo da Vinci in 1498.

That is why we are here. Not for the great architecture or the famous dome. We are here because Bobbie Jo has cross-stitched The Last Supper and framed it, and it hangs in a place of pride above her kitchen table. I asked her about the questionable figure next to Jesus being Mary Magdalene, his wife, and she was none too happy about that. She told me to shut up that blasphemous talk or I would go you know where. So, I shut it up because I don't want to go you know where.

We enter a light and airy central nave with side aisles. It is much larger than it appears from outside. The arches are lifted and are magnificently painted. As I walk down the nave, I whisper quietly to Daphne. I take a few more steps and turn to look at her, wondering why she hasn't answered me. I see Daphne, Bobbie Joe, and Jackson still standing right where they entered. Each of them has an open mouth and they look as if someone has glued their feet to the floor. I have to go back and take their hands and pull them forward. Their eyes are looking up and slowly around, mouths still agape. "The historian is waiting on us in the refectory, rectory, whatever it is. We only have fifteen minutes to see The Last Supper. If you don't move it we will miss our appointed time. We can come back and look at this with the historian explaining everything. Come on!"

I feel like I'm pulling a mule, not that I've ever pulled a mule, but I remember my grandma talking about that difficulty. They are slowly following my tugging pull, eyes still wide and mouths still open. Marcello introduces us to our guide. Ms. Sabina quickly escorts us into the small room. Covering the back wall is the now restored Last Supper. We are alone in the room with this famous painting. I could hear a pin drop—everyone is speechless. And then, I hear a human drop with a thud. With all eyes looking forward at the painting, no one notices that Bobbie Jo isn't slowly approaching the masterpiece. She must have been so overcome with emotion or the spirit, whatever it was, she fell flat back. Now the silence is broken, big time. First with the 'thud', then with expletives that shouldn't be said in a holy building such as 'shit' and 'damn' and 'oh my God'. Thank goodness we didn't have any young adults or the 'f' word would have been flying.

When I reach her, Jackson is seated behind her and has her resting in his lap. Ms. Sabina is running into the office to get ice or water or something that might help. Daphne is sitting in the floor in front of her, gently saying, "Bobbie Jo, Bobbie Jo, can you hear me?" She says this about three times. Now she ain't so gentle. She is slapping her and shouting, "Bobbie Jo, Bobbie Jo, can you hear me now?" Well she's not a telephone, but she still ain't hearing her now. Jackson is gently rubbing her face and whispering in ear. I pull Daphne off of her and go to find Ms. Sabina.

As soon as I come back into the room, Bobbie Jo has roused up. Jackson is checking the back of her head. "No blood," he says, "but she's got a big goose egg." She is coming around as a stretcher appears out of nowhere. In Italian these medics are talking fast and working efficiently. They load her up and are rolling out of the room and back down the nave and out the door. By the time they get her in the ambulance she is having a damn fit.

"Let me out of here! Who are you and why have you tied me up? Let me the f**k outta here!" Bobbie Jo is screaming.

"Whoa, who is that?" I ask Daphne. "Can you become possessed by a demon while fainting in a holy place?"

"No, I don't think so. I think it was the head injury. That's all that can explain it," replies Daphne.

"I don't know. Back in Atlanta, Magnus told me she has had a rough, hard life, not all that innocent at all. Maybe it's coming back to her. Or else, maybe you slapping the shit out of her caused a contralateral type head injury."

"Just shut up and let's help Jackson," insists Daphne.

231

We run up to the ambulance and Ms. Sabina is trying to translate for everyone. She explains what happened to the paramedics, and they explain their assessment of her injuries. She then tells us, "They say she is feisty and they think she should be all right. They say she may have a concussion and need a hospital." More Italian is flying back and forth, peppered with Bobbie Jo's expletives. "They think since she is against going to the hospital, if you agree to monitor her for signs of concussion you can take her home. If she were to start vomiting or having neurological symptoms, we should get her to a hospital. It is most important that she not receive another head injury or there might be permanent brain damage."

We agree, and they happily cut Bobbie Jo loose. Jackson is great at calming her and getting her to the limo. We apologize to Ms. Sabina and rejoin Jackson and Bobbie Jo in the vehicle. Bobbie Jo is less combative and seems to be herself again. Except for the language; how does she know how to cuss like a sailor—make that a teenager— these days? Where is that coming from? She knows her name, where she is, and what she was doing. I am slowly realizing that she is mad as a hornet because she never got to see The Last Supper. She is mad because she didn't get to see the church. She is mad because we won't let her get out and go back in. She is mad at us for stopping her day of church goin' as she calls it.

As the driver is taking us back to Mr. Brevonni's villa, I whisper to Daphne. "She's mad at us? Are you kidding? She's the one who kept us from seeing The Last Supper. I'm a little thankful to her for saving me from a whole day of church seeing, but I only took two steps toward that painting when I heard her go down."

"I know. That's about all I got out of it too; but none of that matters, you selfish thing. What matters is that she is OK. I hope she is anyway. Surely she doesn't have a serious brain injury. Oh, Lord, what will we do? I'll never forgive myself for her disability," says Daphne.

"Stop it!" I tell her. "She don't have no brain injury. She just hit her head, and she'll be fine. You'll see. Gosh, you worry too much. You're just like mama. Settle down and enjoy the show. She's fine, I promise. But, one thing for sure, when she goes in any other of these cathedrals, we'd better circle around her like a wagon train. That way, when the spirit overtakes her again, she won't hit her head."

"Yeah, and maybe we should stop in one of them pharmacies and get some smelling salts."

Guilia is awaiting our arrival and has a doctor there to assess Bobbie Jo. They all take her up to her room. Jackson isn't leaving her side. Me and Daphne go to the kitchen and sit at the table. How crazy. I wonder if anyone has ever fainted while looking at a painting before. This could only happen on one of our tours.

Guilia joins us and says that the doctor said she should be fine. "It is just a mild concussion which doesn't require further work up at this time. He instructed me and Jackson on how to check her throughout the night. I told him that I would do it, but he refuses to leave her side. I'll have another bed placed in her room for him. Oh, yeah, I called Marco and asked him to inform the others when they have lunch. I told them not to change their plans; I just wanted them to know that your group would not be joining them, so I'll make our lunch. You and Daphne go for a walk. When you return, we'll eat and Jackson and Bobbie Jo should be able to join us."

I wonder what kind of day all the others are having. Hmm, lots of shopping and eating. I sure wish I was sitting at Mr. Brevonni's favorite restaurant in Milan, sipping some wine, dipping some bread in fresh local olive oil and awaiting my order of Spaghetti alla Bolognese.

Chapter Twenty-Five
LUNCHEON IN MILAN

Everyone is seated at Carbonara, enjoying some wine and bread after ordering our meals. Mr. Brevonni is expressing his gratitude for a most enjoyable day spent with friends. All present are chattering about the wonder of seeing the Brevonni line brought to life in his factory. More and more chatter about the shopping adventures. It's as if the entire table is on a communal shopping high. Each person is sincerely happy and enjoying their time together. There is not enough time for each to express their favorite stories of the day.

Magnus interrupts the table, asking, "Hey guys, I want to look into that little chapel next door real quick. I read somewhere that they have this miniature stone crucifix that was the first thing Michelangelo ever sculpted. I think he did it when he was thirteen or something. I had actually forgotten all about it until we passed by just now. It took me a while to remember why that church name was stuck in my head. Does anyone want to join me? It will only take a minute. We should be back before our lunch is served."

"I'll come," says Roni, "I'm too excited to sit still." She scoots her chair back and looks for her large Gucci handbag. "Is anyone else joining us?"

"I guess I will," says Sebastian. "I'm kind of antsy too. This is the best day of my life. It is hard to sit quietly after our exciting morning."

The three of us excitedly walk out the door and turn right. Two doors down as we try to enter the little church, two men and a woman almost knock us down running out of the chapel. "Must be exciting in there."

"Or else, it's very convicting. Maybe as you lay eyes on it and you've just sinned, you can't get out of there fast enough," says Sebastian.

Roni laughs, "I thought they just wanted my new gorgeous bag. I was holding on as tight as I could. I know I'm a genteel southern belle, but I would have fought over that bag. At least I would have started a fight, knowing that I had you big guys to reclaim my honor." She continues to snicker, as if her honor were in question.

We make our way into the chapel, which is empty. We look all over the walls and the niches and do not see a little stone crucifix anywhere. Because it is rather dark, without any source of natural light we take a closer look. Still we can't find the relic. "Maybe I was wrong," I tell them, "it must have been some other little church in the city."

"Oh well, that is fine with me. I'm hungry and was just coming with you to keep from sitting still," says Sebastian.

We make our way back into the restaurant just as our food is being delivered. We are enjoying a terrific lunch with true friends as we notice a gathering of people in front of the restaurant. Then carabinieri join them. There seems to have been some sort of confusion that might be illegal or criminal. The carabinieri are talking to everyone and searching through people's bags. We notice a small priest talking to them and pointing into the restaurant.

Our table continues to eat and watch the commotion outside. Just as our tiramisu is served, the carabinieri enter the restaurant with the priest. They whisper, and the priest points to our table. As they approach, Mr. Brevonni speaks to them quietly in Italian. They seem to be scrutinizing me, Sebastian, and Roni. Mr.

Brevonni is talking again, and there is a lot of back and forth conversation which none of us understand. Georgette is telling us that she is fluent in Spanish, and from what she can glean of the conversation, a relic is missing from that little church, and the priest says he saw two men and a woman leaving the church.

At that time, Mr. Brevonni asks if Sebastian, Roni, and I will come to the back of the restaurant and for Roni to bring her bag. We leave the table and are followed by the police to the back of the room. Mr. Brevonni asks me to tell them of my actions after we left the restaurant. He tells us that the carabinieri do speak some English and will understand what they are saying.

I nervously respond, "I had read somewhere about the tiny carved crucifix from Michelangelo being at this little church. So, when we walked by it, I recalled that fact and wanted to see it. After we ordered I asked if anyone wanted to join me. Sebastian and Roni said yes, so we walked out the door and turned right. At the entrance to the church, we were almost trampled by two men and a woman running out of the church. We all joked about it and then went inside. The church was empty and quite dark. We looked on all the walls and niches and didn't see the small crucifix, so we left. I thought that I must have been wrong and this wasn't the church at all. I apologized to them and we went back to the restaurant. That's it."

The police talk back and forth and with Mr. Brevonni. They ask that the two men return to the table and ask to speak to Ms. Veronica 'Roni' Abernatha alone. Roni later told us that they asked her to tell them what happened. Her story was in agreement with mine, and then they searched her bag.

The older officer pulls Roni aside and questions her further. He is an attractive early sixtyish tall, dark, and handsome guy. Before the end of the interview, they are laughing and enjoying each other. There is an exchange of cell numbers, and a planned dinner for later that evening is confirmed.

"I'd love to have dinner with you, that sounds lovely. I'll shop the rest of the afternoon and meet you here at the Cathedral at six this evening," says Roni. With that settled she returns to the table and finishes her meal. Everyone plans to return to the villa, except Roni. She explains that she has plans and will return later and if not she will call me or Daphne.

"Yeah, honey, just call me. I've half a mind to stay and shop with you some more. You've got good taste and style. We shop well together. Thanks for helping me pick out my girly gear. I really couldn't have done it without your advice," I tell her.

"No, no, no, I'm sorry dear, but I have other plans after shopping that don't include you. Me and Mr. Hot Italian Officer have made some dinner and maybe after dinner plans. So another time maybe," explains Roni.

"Yes ma'am, I understand. Good for you girl, and have a good time. I'll take care of explanations for you. And you know where we will be in Florence if you can't make our departure tomorrow morning. I'm sure Mr. Hottie will make arrangements for you to meet us there if necessary," I say with a grin.

"Thanks, sweetie. You're a gem," says Roni, with a wink.

The villa group loads up and tells Roni goodbye. Georgette and Hudson are talking more than they have the entire trip. They tell Mr. Brevonni that they are overwhelmed at his generosity and beg him to come to Birmingham to visit them. He laughs and promises that he might just do that the next time he is in Atlanta. "I only go to Atlanta every couple of years, and I was there last year, but I will remember your invitation, along with that of

Andi and Magnus. If I ever get to Birmingham, I think I will stay with Magnus, but I am sure that we will arrange a dinner or two. You are all so nice and remind me so much of my people in Sicily," says Mr. Brevonni.

"Damn right you are staying with me and don't even think of staying anywhere else. Oh, that reminds me; let me show you the pictures of my new furniture, it's great! That's how Sebastian got on this trip. He was so tickled with my furniture and when he heard all about it, he had to meet you. The girls had their tour full and so many friends wanted to book with them. So we decided to have a party and auction off a single space. Daphne agreed to only charge the expenses, and all the profit went to the local children's hospital. It was a win-win for everyone. Sebastian was determined, and his winning bid was nine thousand and seven hundred dollars. He rounded it up and donated ten thousand dollars to the hospital," I explain.

"That is wonderful. You people talk about my generosity. Thank you, Sebastian. What you did was generous, and just to meet me—I am astounded. I'll tell you what; I will match your donation for the children. I'll send the check back with you guys, and you can deliver it to the hospital for me. You can't get ahead of God with giving, he'll always out give you," says Mr. Brevonni. The conversation continues during the drive back to the villa.

I go running in all excited to show Andi my new clothes. I run up to our room and start pulling clothes out of bags. I go on and on about the clothes and the caribineri and blah, blah, blah. "How about all of the churches and The Last Supper? Was it great, or what?" I ask.

"Or what," Andi blandly replies.

"What?" I ask.

"There were no churches, and there were no cathedrals, and there were about three seconds of The Last Supper," Andi says with disgust.

"Well, what in the hell did ya'll do all day?"

"We nursed Bobbie Jo. Our first stop was the Santa Maria delle Grazie. We met our historian/guide. She walked us into the room where The Last Supper is painted. We entered in the back of the room, everyone said 'ahhh,' and then we took about three steps toward the painting. At that exact moment, when we were still thirty feet from it, the Spirit overtook Bobbie Jo, and she hit the floor like a brick. She was out for about five minutes, while Jackson held her and tried to talk her awake, and Daphne tried to slap her conscious. From that point the guide went to call an ambulance. The ambulance arrived and they strapped Bobbie Jo down and she started cussing them like crazy. She let the 'f' word fly like an eagle. It was crazy! We brought her home before she assaulted the paramedics. And then Mr. Brevonni's doctor checked her out here and instructed us to watch her. We can't get Jackson to leave her side. So, we didn't see nothing. We were thirty feet from The Last Supper and didn't see a thing. All we saw was Bobbie Jo drop like a rock. That was our day," Andi explains.

"Sorry about that, honey. Maybe you should have come with us, we had excitement too. We were questioned by the caribineri because three people had just stolen a relic from a little chapel that me and Sebastian and Roni went into. In fact, the thieves ran over us coming out of the church as we went in. I don't really know if the police believed us; they didn't act like it. They even went through Roni's new Gucci bag. Oh yeah, I almost forgot. Just after the officer went through her bag, he asked her out. There must have been some extracurricular searching going on, because she didn't even come back here with us. She said if she didn't meet up with us tomorrow morning, she'd find us in Florence. Can you believe that? What a quick pick up for her. She might be all uppity, but the lady knows how to enjoy herself."

"Girrrlll. How about her? That is pretty great. She needs to live it up while on vacation. I hope she is safe. We might shoulda had a talk with her about sex these days. Do you think she knows about protection from STDs?" Andi asks.

"And there is something else I forgot to tell you. We were talking to Mr. Brevonni about how Sebastian got on our tour, with our little auction and donating ten thousand dollars to The Children's Hospital. And he thought that was so nice, he wants to match it. He's going to send us a check to donate for him, once we get back home. Does the goodness of that man ever stop? He is the most considerate, giving person that I've ever known. We are lucky to have ever met such a man. I've learned a lot of valuable lessons from him. He is very impressive," I say.

"He sure is. I've never met anyone like him before. You're right, we've learned a lot from him," replies Andi.

We all meet in the kitchen for dinner. It has been a long unproductive day. At least the shoppers had fun and got some new stuff. I sneak Daphne aside and tell her about Roni. We both smile and shake our heads. No matter how much you plan, you can just never predict how these trips will go.

Dinner is great, as usual. The night is wonderfully spent with old and new friends. We stay up late sipping wine and telling stories. Bobbie Jo and Jackson come down for a little while. Bobbie Jo is quiet but seems fine. I like her better like this. Cussin' Bobbie Jo is hard to take. She'll probably be herself tomorrow after a good night's sleep. That girl is going to have a long row to hoe in Italy if she falls out every time she goes into a magnificent church. She will be a holy roller literally rolling in a lot of Holy places.

We might better check into getting her a helmet to wear. We could match it up to her tennis shoes or skirts. She wouldn't look too cool, but it is important to protect her from a consecutive concussion.

Me and Magnus finish up the night with a moment alone with Mr. Brevonni. We again express our gratitude for his kindness to us and our friends. He tells us that we bring him joy and laughter and that his relationship with us is not going to end. He has further plans for Magnus to wear his clothes, and he considers me and Magnus a package deal. He sends us to bed and says that he will see us off in the morning. We haven't heard from Roni yet, so I guess she's having a good time with Officer Guido or Reynoldo or whatever his name is.

Sleep tonight is easy. I'm all comfy in my soft bed and Magnus is in his room sawing some logs. Our door between us is open, so I can hear it all. It doesn't bother me; in fact, it is comforting as I smile and fall asleep.

Just as Mr. Brevonni promised, our large van awaits us in the drive. Everyone brings their luggage down, and Marco and Nino load it up. I can see that Guilia has already packed us three goodie bags of snacks. Once the van is ready, we meet in the kitchen for one last breakfast. It is a bittersweet meal. I'm sad to be leaving this place, but hopefully I'll have the chance to return. After breakfast, we solemnly leave the villa and climb up in the van. Magnus and I are the last to reach the vehicle. We have said our goodbyes to Guilia and Mr. Brevonni. They look as sad for us to leave as I feel leaving. Kiss, kiss, kiss. And we are off.

Chapter Twenty-Six
FLORENCE VIA PISA

We set out on our trek to Firenze, we say Florence, but Fear In Zaa, sounds prettier. We've got several hours in this van. Roni never called us, so I guess the big girl can take care of herself. Magnus said she would call him. So, let me think about this seating arrangement. Georgette and Hudsey are cuddled up in the back. What a sweet little snooty couple. Bless their hearts, give them some years of life and let's see what happens. I can pretty much guess, but I'll keep it quiet.

Sebastian is back there with them, too. He's says that he planning on sleeping all the way, because he and Mr. Brevonni were up most of the night talking business. "We've worked out all the details for our store to be a direct buyer. We'll have his new lines as soon as they're released. He and I think we need to bring in the local 'Brevonni Man' connection with an area wide billboard blitz featuring Magnus Bruce."

"Whoa, man, I didn't know anything about that and I don't know what I think about it. There are times, aren't there Jackson, when I don't want to be recognized. But then again there are times that it would be *so* cool. I'll have to think on that for a while. It could mean good things for the shop, huh, Andi?" says Magnus.

Magnus, Jackson, and Bobbie Jo are sitting in the middle seat. "It would work out well for us. Maybe we could put a picture of you lifting some heavy piece of antique furniture on the billboard just below your fine clothing ad," I reply.

I'm sitting up front by the passenger door. You never know when my sister will drive me crazy and I'll want to jump my ass out. Daphne is in the middle serving as navigator, she likes that title. Nino is driving and cussing Daphne's navigating. How many more miles do we have to go? Maybe I should have hooked up with Roni and traveled with her and left these bunch of crazies. I could have met them in Florence too. I hear the trains are nice here, I might have to keep that in mind.

Bobbie Jo is looking good this morning. No more foul language. I'm glad she's not brain damaged as Daphne feared, but that was some funny shit. I am tempted to bring that up when we get bored on this drive. Daphne would slap me if she thought I would say anything. But sometimes, you need some distracting conversation. And Bobbie Jo seems to be loosening up with every mile we travel. Let's see, so far she has passed out drunk at the airport in Atlanta. She made the entire TransAtlantic flight comatose. She might have fallen in love with Jackson; at least I think he's falling for her. She was again comatose in one of the most famous churches in Italy. She cussed out the Italian paramedics, quite fluently I might add. Now she's asleep on the shoulder of a handsome man with his arm around her like she is his little pet. I hope that she's not a stripper by the end of our trip.

"Where the hell have you taken us, Daphne? I don't think this is right. We should not be seeing the damn ocean between Milan and Florence. You have one responsibility. I should have brought your grandson instead of you!" Nino is yelling.

"I don't know. I told you the way it said to go. You must have messed it up. Nino, just eat shit!" growls Daphne between clinched teeth.

"And die," I say quietly, reaching for the door handle. Then she snickers a little.

"What are you talking about Andi?" says Daphne, teeth still clinched.

"She said 'and die', you don't even know how to insult people without it becoming a joke," says Nino, as he erupts into laughter.

Now, Magnus and Jackson and even little Georgette and Hudsey Dudsey are laughing. The entire van load of us are laughing hysterically. Magnus says, "I got your back, Nino. I've fired up my GPS Navigator on my phone, and we're fine. I'll get us back on track."

"Thanks Magnus, and I'm sorry but there's not room up here for you to be the navigator, but one thing is for damn sure, Daphne, *YOU'RE FIRED!*"

"Well, since we're here along the coast, we might as well swing by Pisa," suggests Nino.

"Oh, that would be great," little Georgette squeaks, "I've always wanted to see that. Is it open? Can we climb to the top?"

"Yeah, terrific idea," adds Magnus, "I've always wanted to get a picture of myself holding up the tower. You know how they do that, Andi? Isn't that cool?. Maybe I'll actually hold you on my shoulders and you can be pushing the tower upright. What do you think, honey?"

"Oh yeah, great, like Daphne hasn't made me take that picture three times already," I complain.

"But, don't forget, Andi, there's that great restaurant on the street around the corner from the cathedral area. Remember the last meal there?" asks Nino.

"Oh my God, yeah, I'd forgotten about that. Hell yeah, I want to go to Pisa. I'll be in the restaurant with you, Nino," I answer.

"Oh no you won't, little honey child, you'll be with me for our picture. You have to Andi; it will be great. We'll blow it up and frame it for the shop. Maybe a black and white or sepia and I'll put it in one of our antique frames. You have to, Andi, *please*. For me," begs Magnus.

"Fine, and then I'm eating," I state.

We travel along, our little gang of rednecks. Suddenly, I sit bolt upright. I whisper to Daphne, "What about Bobbie Jo and the cathedral at Pisa, and her falling out? When we get there, I'll tell Jackson and Magnus that we will have to encircle her as soon as we get out of the car. The sight of it alone will overcome her, I'm sure."

"Oh goodness, you're right. So much for your getting to the restaurant early. I'll need you to help me with her throughout the Pisa detour. Thanks sister," says Daphne.

So much for that, I think. I have to be holding the hand of a tennis shoe and sock wearing, long skirt flowing, bun headed church lady that is so spiritual she can't withstand the glory of a beautiful church. Maybe I'll take her to the side and pray with her for God to give her strength to enjoy his Holy sites.

Magnus has done a fine job navigating from the middle row of seats. Of course he doesn't need to sit up front. Poor Daphne and Nino do not understand electronics. Silly things with their paper maps all over the front seat area. I've actually tried to trample up all the ones that have landed under my feet. Smooth move, Magnus.

Approaching Pisa, Bobbie Jo, Jackson, and Magnus seem surprised that there is actually a city here. I was like that the first time I saw it. I thought there was just a tower in the middle of nowhere. I sure didn't expect an entire religious complex with a famous Cathedral, Baptistry, and Tower. There are also some famous Italian sculptures here. Knowing Daphne, this is not a slight diversion; this will be a full day of sightseeing. I'm glad that Nino is here. I can always count on him to find great restaurants and fine dining. It is seldom fancy, but he has some kind of internal radar that magnetically pulls him to the best foods. That makes me think of Rome. I know we will go back to that hole in the wall restaurant where we ate all night long. Four of us eating and we spend a hundred and fifty euros on food. That was a memory, forget the forum.

There is excitement in the van as we drive past the complex and Nino lets us out. I volunteer to ride with him to park the vehicle. Daphne and all the others get out and will meet us at the lawn area at the cathedral. Daphne says she will talk to Jackson and Magnus, and they will keep Bobbie Jo within reach.

Me and Nino ride around for a few blocks before we can find a parking space big enough for this tourist van. As we are walking back to join them, Nino is orienting himself to walk by our favorite Pisa restaurant. He says he just wants to make sure that the same little old man is inside, which means that his little old wife will be in the back cooking. Yep, there it is. Damn, if he isn't good.

We walk in, and Nino starts speaking Italian to the old gentleman. After a few minutes, they both laugh and shake hands. As we head back to join the others, he tells me that the man was flattered that we wanted to eat with them again. He will have several tables reserved for us in about three hours. Nino asked him to have a lot of spaghetti with pomodoro sauce.

As we arrive, Magnus, Jackson, and Bobbie Jo are frolicking in the grass between the tower and the baptistry. Bobbie Jo looks and acts fine, so far. Daphne has gone in to purchase our tickets. Georgette, Hudson, and Sebastian are studying the exterior of the Cathedral. They all see us and walk our way. Yes, the Tower is open for the three hundred or so spiraling steps to the top. I complain, but it is well worth it. How many people can say they have climbed the Leaning Tower of Pisa?

We walk toward the Tower as I see Daphne running toward us, waving some papers, probably tickets. But I have a very uneasy feeling as I see her running. I pat Nino on the shoulder and tell him to look at her. Before I can think it, he says it, "Oh shit, she shouldn't be running; she's gonna bust her ass. She can't even walk and think at the same time, and she never could run. This is a sure accident waiting to happen. Get your phone camera ready, I know it's coming."

"I know, I know. Do you remember the one time in Germany when she fell off that curb?" I ask him.

"I remember every damn time she fell. And do you remember how mad she gets because we laugh at her. We'd better try to reach her so she can stop running," Nino says.

"How can you not laugh, it's too damn funny not to laugh. I mean, I know I shouldn't because one day she is actually gonna hurt herself, but when that happens, she better fall so that it looks bad, not where it looks funny. I promise, Nino, I can't stop myself. Let's go."

We make our way toward her. She is running at her top speed, which is really like one of those slow motion segments in a movie. I swear her long, grey, flat, ugly hair is bouncing slowly up and down with every two inches her knees lift as she runs. Now that I see it from a distance in slow motion like I do, I can understand why she falls all the time. She don't pick her feet up. I bet you couldn't slip a piece of flat potato chip between her uplifted foot and the ground. Nino is about to reach her, because I had to stop and just study her stupid running technique. But as he closes in I can see her mouth fly open.

"Neeenooo!" she yells as tickets fly in the air and her hands fly out in front of her to attempt to brace the fall of a short, fat, old woman. She always does that, too. She will call the nearest name to her as she falls. I've hear it all, 'Aaandeee,' 'Neeenooo,' 'Sissssterrr,' as if we have fifteen foot long arms and can catch her before she embarrasses herself and me or Nino.

As I am making my way toward my sister, Nino turns the other way and starts walking as if he doesn't know her. Of course I can't reach her in time. The slow motion movie repeats itself once again. Downward she starts; it's funny how muscles and bones react to the flow of gravity and impact. The initial impact is absorbed by her palms. This throws her head back just a little, and the long, nasty gray hair is slung skyward as the neck and chin bounce backwards. Next to hit the ground is her knees. It's a good thing she has on jeans. The knees and hands skid about eighteen inches, as four plugs of grass are symmetrically removed from the earth. Equaling this momentum is the reverse movement of her crazy-ass chain handled purse going upward around her neck and with the purse flying behind her. Then, once it is caught by the chain, it lands heavily on her back. I don't know if it is the blow of the purse on her back or the law of gravity and physics of the object in motion, but now her boobs are plowing up two little—no, maybe they are big—trenches of grass. I can't wait to see what this multiple crater impact to the ground looks like once I haul her big ass up.

As I arrive, she is face down on the ground. "Sister, are you all right? Is anything hurt? Give me your hand," I ask her. I happen to be looking down at the back of her head. As she lifts her face, she smiles up at me, and I can't help but notice the dirt in her teeth. She begins to laugh as dirt snorts out of her nose. She takes my hand, and I assist her to her knees. Unable to completely stand, she rises on her knees and sits back on her heels while she attempts to gain some composure. We are both laughing, as I turn and look around shouting to everyone in sight, "Did anybody get that on video?"

At that moment, a fellow American tourist approaches us laughing uncontrollably. "Hell yeah, I got it," says a large six foot two guy. I didn't want to say anything, but once I saw you both laughing I couldn't contain myself. I was recording my friend walking to me with our tickets when this old lady starts running past him. I got it all. Hollywood couldn't have directed a better fall scene."

"You know I've got to have that. Will you forward that clip to me?" I ask him.

"Sure, we'll do it as soon as we get her up," he says.

We are all still laughing like crazy as the both of us help her up. Once she is standing, it gets even funnier. Her new white shirt now has two green skid marks corresponding to where those heavy low hung breasts droop. Her jeans bare the same markings on her knees. Then I look at her face, with all joking aside, I ask, "Are you really okay?" She nods yes, as she laughs hysterically. "I needed to know you were not hurt because you seriously have dirty, grassy snot running down your face, and there's some blood around that grass in your teeth."

As I back off to gather up our tickets, I notice that Bubba has got his camera on again. As I collect the tickets, I have to take a knee because I'm laughing so hard I can't stand. I know her cue, so I can't look at her at this point, because if I do, Daphne will start pissing all over herself again. It's happened for years every time we start laughing. That's why Nino always leaves us. He knows it will never end with just a fall. It always escalates to a full-blown theatrical production and always ends with the purchase of clean underwear and pants.

I collect myself and go back to help Daphne. I get her upright, thankful that she is wearing dark jeans. We are still laughing, but we've thus far avoided her bladder release. I resist looking at her directly, as history has taught me that mutual recognition of whatever hilarious moment we find ourselves in is the trigger for insuppressible laughter and thus bladder relaxation. Once this moment occurs, there is no holding it back. I've figured out that her laughing muscles cause sphincter release. And I have seldom seen her just release a dab of peepee. Hell naw, we get caught up in our laughter, and it doesn't stop until her bladder is completely empty. More than once, she was left standing in a small puddle around her wet shoes.

I am trying so hard to avoid this, but now our cameraman friend is busting a gut as he has resumed filming of her skidded up shirt, pants, and face. He's laughing, and then we look at each other and it's on. No stopping this train now. Any minute she is going to yell the code word that we have developed for the unavoidable moment. I don't know how I feel about 'Bubba' recording an incontinent episode. That may be a little too personal even for me, but then again, I doubt it.

"Code Yellow!" she yells, as our eyes meet. Then laughing tears start flowing down her dirty little face leaving tracks of clean, untainted skin. Suddenly we both erupt in hysterical laughter again as she slinks downward to the ground. Even though we know what is happening, it cannot be stopped. On the ground we sit and laugh and laugh until her bladder is empty and a slight urine odor is drifting with the wind. 'Bubba' approaches us and we exchange numbers. He says he has to go now and will send me the clip as soon as he gets in line for the tower. Maybe he doesn't know about the peepee part.

While we sit and laugh, I call Nino with my phone because he has got the hell out of dodge I suppose. He is nowhere in sight. I tell him that it happened again and that he has to come and get the tickets because we have to buy some pants at the nearest shop. We can't walk back to the van, because it is a mile away and her fat little thighs will be chafed sore by the time she walks all that way. He shows right up and smiles, looking down at us as he gets the tickets. He asks Daphne if she is okay, and she grinningly nods that she is.

As we get her up we are still snickering, but we've pretty much got past it. We walk towards the shops across the street just as my phone alerts to a new notification. Before we cross the street, we sit on the nearest bench as I open my message from 'Bubba'. Without even looking at it, I forward it to Magnus. Hm, do I show this to Daphne now, or do I wait until she gets some new clothes and then we have to buy her some more new clothes? I know she cannot get through the video without peeing again. But then again, from the look of her today, I think she has squeezed the last drop of urine from her urethra. We might just sit here a minute and let her air dry.

At this moment, a loud familiar thundering voice yells, "Daphne, are you all right?" laughing and yelling at the same time. Magnus has reached our bench now. "Oh my God, Daphne; now that I know you are okay, that is some funny shit." He sits with us on the bench.

Suddenly two phones start dinging nonstop. While both me and Magnus are looking at our phones, Daphne gives me a look like, 'You bitch, I know what you've done'. I look at Magnus, and he grins and shrugs his shoulders and says, "There are a lot of sad people out there and they need laughter, too."

At that moment my 'Baby Girl' ringtone notifies me that my momma is calling. The only words out of her mouth are "Is your sister okay?" and I lose it again.

"I don't know mom, why don't you talk to her and find out?". I hand Daphne the phone as I press speaker.

"Momma, is Daddy okay? What's wrong? Why are you calling us now? Has something happened to the grandkids? Has the house burned down? Has there been a tornado?" I hear Daphne ask.

"No, honey, everything is fine here. You know I love that Magnus and I follow his website. I just happened to check his latest post and saw you fall and was worried about you. Are you hurt? I was worried about that blood in your teeth? Did you break your nose? Honey, I told you that you needed to get you one of those bras that help you lift and separate. You know that I've always worried about you girls falling on your breasts from way back when ya'll was diving on the softball field. I just needed to make sure that you were okay."

Daphne assures her that she is fine and disconnects the line. Then, she looks at me and Magnus with dagger eyes. "Oh, Magnus, if looks could kill, we'd be lying here dead, cut to pieces with those eyes," I tell him.

"Well, Daphne, you've just got to see this and you'll understand that I couldn't help myself. I think that Magnus knows what good can come from the whole world seeing your most hilarious moments. He got a modeling contract and new living room furniture out of it."

Daphne cuttingly remarks, "What do you think I'm gonna get out of this, a new bra commercial for the heavily endowed grandma crowd? How dare you two! Just show it to me."

We show her the clip. Not a word is muttered. Just three people sitting on a bench. There is snickering, then laughing which erupts into full blown hysteria. Once this quiets down, I hear a faint, drip, drip, drip.

After the giggling and dripping finally subside, we all cross the street and go into the first women's dress shop we can find. The little noises of the scritch, scritch, scritch of Daphne's wet denim at her thighs rubbing together have just about grated my last nerve. Magnus has directed us across the street, between traffic with cars and Vespas blowing their horns and yelling probably rude Italian phrases at us.

The three of us enter the store, and immediately two sales girls start to yell. "The Brevonni Man, it's the Brevonni Man in our shop!" the youngest one shouts. All the customers and those out on the street that recognized him (that's what all the horns and yelling were about) run toward him. Displays are being bumped, and women are hanging all over Magnus. He smiles and starts talking to the ladies. I ask him to tell them we need some clothes. They either do not realize that we walked in with him or they are choosing to ignore us. He finally communicates our needs, and they simply point us to the far corner of the room.

We go to our designated corner as Magnus tries to satisfy his female admirers. We look for some jeans and a shirt—oh yeah, and panties and a bra that aren't grass stained. "What the heck do these numbers mean?" asks Daphne. "I'm just choosing the biggest number. I've got some jeans, and isn't this a pretty little pink top? Now do you see the lingerie?" she asks.

"Oh, I found it all right. But this isn't what we would really call panties. All I see here are fancy thongs; I'll get you the biggest number size. And these bras, I just don't know, only a little bit of black silky and mesh fabric, and I don't care how big the number is, these little cups aren't going to lift and separate those melons of yours. You might better hope that your bra ain't stained. Here, take these panties with you and go try on these clothes. I see a little closet door there, try it, maybe it's a dressing room." I hand her the clothes, and off she goes.

I go back and try to rescue Magnus, but I can't get close to him. The crowd has now grown, and he's thronged by a mass of people. At least he's two feet taller than petite Italians, so I can see him and he sees me. I motion that Daphne is trying on her clothes. I turn and walk back to Daphne, just as a well-dressed man is coming out of an apparent office upstairs. And then three other men enter the door from the street. As if that wasn't enough of a spectacle, it doesn't come close to what Daphne springs on me.

She is walking out of that little room looking like an oversized, aging, slut poured into some skinny jeans. She is wearing a skintight top in fuschia pink with ruffles that don't quite sway because they are pulled too tightly. The neck is cut very low to draw one's vision to a beautiful décolletage, which she does not quite have. Instead, she is showing two large pendulous breasts just about to pour out of what a size four female would claim to be a beautiful flattering designer blouse. Not so beautifully designed for Daphne.

"Look at these great clothes, Andi. Aren't they gorgeous? Don't they make me look elegantly sexy? No wonder Italians always look so good, it's the clothes. I love them. Nino will be so excited. And you were right, thank goodness that I didn't need that bra; I couldn't have got one boob in that bra, much less two. And these panties, whew, they make me feel full of frisky. Is that why those young girls wear them? Let's go pay and start climbing that tower. I'll just bet that my legs can climb, climb, and climb in these little panties and pants. Wow, look at me."

"Yeah, I'm looking, and I'm not so sure that you want to walk outside looking like that. Those clothes are a bit tight on you. You know they wear their clothes a little tight here in Italy, but we don't really have the bodies that these young girls have. So no, just because most Italian are sexy, doesn't mean just anyone squeezing their plus size body into tiny Italian clothes becomes sexy. I don't think a fifty-something year old woman is best flattered with these type clothes. Have you noticed the little Italian grannies walking around? They all dress more appropriately for their ages. They are made more like us, short and dumpy. And they dress with dresses that fall between their knees and ankles. They wear their little black shoes and their little knee highs that tend to roll downward as their day progresses. Sometimes you notice the little stocking rolls around their ankles. That's more like us, Daphne."

"You are kidding me, sister. You are just jealous. Come on, we'll get you some. Then you can walk around loud and proud like me. And, for your information, Nino will love this outfit."

"Oh, you are loud but you sure shouldn't be proud. And no, thanks, I prefer my own clothes. Let's go then. And you'd better know that I love you, sister, or I wouldn't walk within ten feet of you. Let's pay and get out. We've got to rescue Magnus, he's trapped at the front of the store with enthralling fans."

"Mangus—I mean Magnus, I always think of Mangos and Fungus, so it's sometimes hard for me to get Magnus out of my mouth when I'm excited. Anyway, look at my new clothes," says Daphne, as they approach the group near the door. All heads turn and all mouths drop open.

"Sweet little Daphne, what a doll you are!" says Magnus. He turns to the manager, "How much do we owe you for these, sir?"

The manager replies, after looking Daphne from head to toe and turning up his Romanesque nose. "Is she with you, Mr. Bruce?"'

"Yes, sir, she is. Your clothes look great on her, don't they? What do we owe you?" Magnus asks.

"For you, Mr. Magnus, they are complimentary. But I would request that you sign a few of our posters. You are our own Brevonni Man here in Italy. When you get into the larger cities, you will see the large three story posters hanging from the high-rise buildings. You will soon realize that you are a star here," the manager replies.

"Thank you sir, I'd be happy to sign anything for you. Just know that I am not a star. I'm not sure what a star is, I just know that I am an ordinary guy from Birmingham, Alabama. I appreciate your gift for my friend. I'll tell everyone that her clothing is complements of Giardini in Pisa."

"Oh no, no, please, Mr. Magnus, don't do that. Please let that fact remain anonymous if you will. We don't need to advertise our shop in that manner. Let's just keep this between us."

"Certainly, if that is your wish, you got it. And I think that I understand your valid concern here. Now, we are off to climb the Tower. Thank you again."

Well, how about that. We make our way out of the shop and cross the street. We find the others waiting just outside of Tower. As they see us approach, they look at us as if we've picked up a new friend. They keep staring at Daphne like she's a stranger or maybe someone to proposition.

"What in the hell are you wearing?" asks Nino, none too quietly.

Proudly, Daphne claims, "I know, isn't it lovely? Doesn't it make me look so much younger? These Italians really do know how to make clothes. Maybe I should have went designer shopping with you guys yesterday. Oh yeah, Magnus, tell them about your fame."

Magnus quickly tries to change the subject. "Let's get up the Tower, guys. Jackson, hold back, I need to talk to you."

We all start the three hundred step climb. What a line of misfits we are, huffing and puffing our out of shape way up these stairs. It's tough with Jackson and Magnus in the back, pushing us faster that we old farts can move.

Magnus pulls Jackson back. "We've got a huge problem, man. When I went into the shop with the girls, everybody recognized me from the Brevonni ads. We're gonna have to change our plans. I really can't do my part as we planned, because a lot of people recognize me now. I've got an idea, if you are comfortable with it. I'm just glad that I was able to go shopping with Roni. I've got some great girlie clothes. I can pull it off in drag. What do you think of that? Do you think it could work?"

"It's perfect. Why didn't we think of that before? If suspicion ever turns to us, we are clear because they will be looking for an ugly woman," replies Jackson.

"Hey, I'm not ugly, you just wait and see. And yeah, it might not be a bad plan after all. As soon as we get into the room tonight, we will check out the site. We need to look at it from every angle and make a detailed reconnaissance of the surrounding area. And then we can talk through the plan, polishing up the details as we need to. Early tomorrow morning we will walk through it, using the stopwatch to establish our timing. Now let's push those girls on up these stairs."

Around and around and around and around we climb. Stone walls with stone stairs winding up to the top of this bell tower. Not only is it dizzying, it is exhausting. And damn that Magnus, he keeps pushing us from the rear. Doesn't he understand that my legs are less than twenty-nine inches? That makes each step double effort for me. If I had a thirty-eight or forty inch inseam, it would only take me one hundred and fifty steps to reach the top. It is a very tight space in this tower as well. And each little step has two areas worn down by thousands and thousands of feet for hundreds of years. It is amazing to consider all the people throughout the centuries that have climbed these steps before me.

Once we finally reach the top, we are rewarded with the most astonishing view. The size of the Cathedral and the Baptistry are evident from this height. The views of the old town and the winding streets remind me of the deep history of this town. The red tiled roofs are perfectly Italian. It is breathtaking. I could spend hours here feeling an electric connection with the past. After about ten minutes, Nino is herding everyone back down the stairs.

Going down is almost worse than climbing up; it's very hard on the old knees. And most of us have old knees. Once we are down, we decide to go to the Cathedral and then the Baptistery. Me and Nino just want to go to lunch. He's told us that we have two hours, that's it. Then it's time to head to the restaurant.

Daphne and I have instructed Jackson and Magnus to stay with us to protect Bobbie Jo from the Holy Spirit taking her over and throwing her to the floor. Daphne is intent on hauling us to every sculpture in these two Holy Sites. She has talked and talked about the artists who have works here. She tells us about how ancient this site is, and blah, blah, blah.

So, off we go to the Baptistry. Our little group of Southerners, one of us dressed like a slender, young, Italian wannabe, even though she's a hefty country hick from Alabama. We walk in a line toward the tall, round structure. I don't even know what a Baptistry is. I know that it is old. I know that it is the tallest Baptistry in Italy, again, whatever that is. I think it is called Baptistry after John the Baptist, but what is its function? Did they dunk their babies and children and wayward adults in there? The only thing I learned from Daphne's rattling off boring facts was that it is an acoustic masterpiece.

She said that "The Leaning Tower of Pisa" website explains that one person could sing their own blend of chords by simple hitting a note, pause for one to two seconds and sing another chord and on and on, and the echoing acoustics of the building will make their voice sound superb. I hope that she doesn't try it; no building in the world could make her voice sound superb. Oh my God, I just had the worst thought. What if she stood in the middle and started whispering her rote endless string of facts and history? They say that these buildings could fall at a time far, far away. Well, if Daphne started her history lesson in that acoustic miracle building, they would all tumble within the hour.

As we enter the Baptistry, I really am impressed, it is so large and open. It's pretty empty; I again wonder about the purpose here. There is a large octagonal altar type thing in the middle. There are huge columns that maybe hold up this leaning building. All the buildings on this piazza lean, not just the tower. There is a man whispering a little opera song, I guess. He's singing in Italian. I approach Jackson near the center and start quietly singing my favorite newly written country song, "What is the Wind Doing?" As I'm into the chorus about the funnel cloud, twirling, twirling, twirling, I realize that I am sounding pretty damn good. The building is silent except for my song. Everyone is looking at me and smiling and starting to clap me a beat. I can see Bubba across the room with his girlfriend, and they quickly move to my side of the altar and start slow dancing. Then Jackson takes Bobbie Jo's hand and starts spinning her around. I swear there are even some Europeans forming a line dance on the other side of the altar. As I conclude the last verse about 'the three legged cat' and 'the tree limb in the old tater cellar,' the crowd is applauding me as they finish their dance with the repeat chorus. I can't believe I sang my new song in the Pisa Baptistery. I do hope somebody puts that on YouTube. Where's Magnus? Maybe this is the function of the building—concerts.

Once everyone has shaken my hand as they leave the Baptistry, we walk toward the door. I felt a little bit like the Baptist minister after altar call as everyone leaves church. The last one to leave was the Italian Opera singer. He didn't shake my hand, he just gestured some Italian hand motions toward me, and I'm thinking they weren't too nice, either. He don't know it, but he should just be glad that I didn't have my guitar with me. My next song may just be about him. I'd better Google what it means when Italians extend one arm straight out and appear to chop it in the middle with the other arm. Hm, maybe he just liked it but was embarrassed by the tornado lyrics or line dancing.

Bobbie Jo seemed to do fine in there, probably because my song sucked all the Holy Spirit right out of the place. Sorry God. I didn't mean to have a country concert in the building that I don't know the sacredness of. Anyway, Daphne herds us up for her lecture on the historic facts of the Cathedral as we walk toward it. I just look at her and imagine that I am deaf. Maybe I am becoming deaf after my beautifully performed song, because I don't hear a word she is saying. I see her mouth moving, but I don't hear a thing, thank goodness.

I think she must be finished or else she finally realized that nobody gives a shit, except maybe for Bobbie Jo. She was looking into Daphne's mouth like she was expecting a worm from her mama bird. She hangs on every word of this history crap. Daphne walks back to me and gives me a little hug and tells me how I sang really good. She says that she is again sorry that when we were little she didn't take my singing seriously. Then she reminds me that we are about to enter a grand cathedral, and we have to watch Bobbie Jo closely. She expects me to stick right with her and Bobbie Jo throughout the cathedral tour.

"Damn it, Daphne," I tell her. "You don't know what you are asking of me. I don't mind the cathedral. But all the architecture and art history facts that are about to spew out of your mouth for the next few hours are more that I can take. I've heard it all before, over and over, and over; same words, different place. I don't need all the facts. I'm good just looking at it and not knowing all that other stuff. Don't make me do it, please."

"There is something wrong with you, sister," she responds. "All the work that I put into learning things, and you don't care. Do you know that you're the only one who doesn't appreciate knowledge?"

"Oh no, I am not! Just ask Sophie or Andrew, or Nino, or Magnus, or anybody. Are you telling me that for the past thirty years, you thought all of us were thrilled at the facts that rattle around in your head and fall out of your mouth? Sorry that we failed you."

"I simply don't believe you, but fortunately, we don't have the time to debate this right now. You will stand next to Bobbie Jo and assist me in protecting her from the Holy Ghost," she demands.

"Fine, but again, I must tell you that you are not the boss of me. I will do it, but please just suffer us with every other fact, not every fact."

I dropped back and told Magnus and Jackson to stay near us for the swooning. Georgette, Hudson, and Sebastian have all moved ahead and are now entering the cathedral. Smart people, two days into this trip and they know to avoid Daphne's guidance and lectures. At least Bobbie Jo has enjoyed all the useless 'Jeopardy' knowledge.

As we near the Western front of the cathedral, Bobbie Jo slows her pace. Soft little praises are coming out of her mouth, "Lordy Jesus," "My Sweet Jesus." She has that stone-like look again. As she is admiring the huge bronze door carvings, her eyes slowly moving up and down and side to side, I grab her by the hand and lead her through the door.

Benches are arranged from front to back along each side of the nave. There are two aisles on each side. A white marble floor and long white columns guide the eye to the front as it takes in the ethereal arches and windows. It appears to be open to the sun; it is so light and airy with a hint of golden color misting from the ceiling. We all are standing just inside the door in awe.

I start to feel Bobbie Jo's hand loosen its grip, and she is muttering over and over, "Glory, Glory, Hallelujah." Her eyes are wide open, and there is a peaceful smile on her face. I take the chance to follow her gaze and look up. The lower columns are flowing into arches, which serve as bases for another layer of columns that are layered with white and dark marble. The front of the cathedral is crowned with pointed white marble arches. Light is flowing in from an unseen source, so much that you have to blink out the above light and lower your gaze again.

Now Bobbie Jo appears to be safely 'in the Spirit.' She drops our hands and starts walking to the front as if she is actually being led by the Spirit. Daphne and I quickly glance at each other and move into position surrounding her. She is still muttering. "Lord, I've never seen anything so beautiful." "My Heavenly Lord, Rock of Ages." She is moving faster now. She is almost running to the transept and chancel. I only know these words because I've heard Daphne repeat them so many times.

Once she reaches the little altar at the transept, her gaze is affixed to the view of Christ at the dome. It is a gold mosaic background with Christ in the center. Upon seeing this she drops to her knees. I guess she's forgotten that this is marble and not the carpeted altar at her Holy Rock Church in Rock Holler, complete with the crushed velvet cushion. I hear a crack at the impact. I can only 'pray' that she didn't dislocate a patella. I don't have long to pray as she is now starting to praise God even louder. "Sweeet Jesus, Sweeet Jesus, Sweeet Jesus." She is looking up at the gigantic sweet Jesus and praising and praising. She is starting to talk in tongue again, and her arms are extended in front of her with her palms open receiving God's mercy. Daphne and I crouch beside her with Magnus and Jackson standing with their knees supporting her back.

I can't focus on our Sweet Jesus, because I'm so concerned with the look on Bobbie Jo's face. She's turned a grayish, greenish, pale color, and her eyes are rolling upward. I try to figure out if she is looking up at our Lord or if her eyes are rolling back to see who is touching her back. They keep rolling and the tongue talking continues until she starts to crumble. I'm glad the guys are behind her, because she can't fall backward, which means her head will be fine.

Or so I thought. My relief suddenly turns to helpless panic as I see her tilt forward. She's definitely out and leaning forward faster than I can grab her. I realize that I wish there was a velvety plush cushion in front of her instead of stone cold marble. I see it happening and can't stop it. It's the slow motion thing again. "BAM!" Her forehead has hit the marble. At least she was kneeling and not standing. I never thought to protect her from the front.

She has crumpled over to a right-faced fetal position with her knees still under her. Magnus is fighting with his jacket pocket and quickly removes a little vial. He hops over our heap and waves it under Bobbie Jo's nose.

Quickly, she snaps to attention, continuing her Holy conversation with God, as if nothing happened at all. She rises up, sitting back on bended knees and resumes her outstretched hand position. I lean around her to look at her forehead. There is no bleeding, no laceration, no bump—it is not even red. Good Lord, this is a miracle. Our miracle has occurred at the Piazza dei Miracoli, inside the Duomo. Bobbie Jo's countenance is serene. She looks like those videos you see of those three little girls in the early nineteen hundreds or whenever it was. Those three little village girls in some far off country that was visited by Mother Mary, I think. Where are Daphne's facts when I need a few?

Anyway, now we are all transfixed, just looking at Bobbie Jo, as she is apparently looking at God, or Jesus or Mary or some saint with whom she is speaking in their unknown language. Slowly, she blinks a few times, then rises and says, "Praise the Trinity!" Then she looks around at all of us, "Just when I thought you people were a bunch of heathens, I see that you are here worshipping with me. I apologize to you all. Now, Daphne, could you show me those famous sculptures that you were talking about?"

We are all staring at her with open mouths. We stand and follow her and Daphne. Now is the part that I can barely handle. And, on an empty stomach, it may be too much. Daphne and Bobbie Jo lead our little group to the Tomb of Emperor Henry VII, blah, blah, designed by Tino de somebody. Then we ever so slowly move on to the pair of angels by Ghirlandaio, blah, blah. Where is Nino? I've got to hang with him. He has experienced years and years of torture and found a way to suspiciously remain far away from any haphazard chance of another history lesson.

I am unable to make my escape because our cluster has arrived at the 'Masterpiece,' as I hear Daphne call it. The Pulpit is from Giovanni Pisano in the thirteen hundreds, blah, blah. This is enough for me. I grab Magnus by the arm and pull him back as they are now searching for some bronze angels that are supposed to be in here somewhere, shaped by somebody, sometime, blah, blah, vomit. Daphne, Bobbie Jo, and Jackson walk toward the choir. I do know a lot of good words, though.

We find Nino at the back of the cathedral, texting. Just then my phone beeps. I glance at Nino. "I could see you suffering from back here and decided to give you an excuse to break away from the Daphne tour. Don't worry, I'm only giving them fifteen more minutes, and we're leaving. I'm here for the food, and my little treasure of pasta is awaiting."

We sit on a bench and begin our wait. In a few minutes, Sebastian joins us on the bench. This is the best part to me, sitting on these pews, just looking at it all. I don't need all of Daphne's explanations; I just like admiring it in silence. Five more minutes of supreme quiet and beauty and Nino says, "I'm getting them. Can you guys find the lovebirds and meet me at the gate? Then we can all walk to the restaurant and eat." And he's off.

In about ten minutes we are at the gate and here they come. We have the lovebirds, and Nino has the saint and the historian, accompanied by poor Jackson. That guy may also be a saint. He's had to endure the entire tour, worrying about Bobbie Jo and tolerating Daphne's incessant mouth.

Nino walks us to the restaurant faster than I've ever seen him walk. He's at the front with Daphne and Bobbie Jo in the back and the rest of our pack in the middle. We are constantly interrupted with people recognizing Magnus. Jackson and Magnus talk quietly most of the way to the restaurant. They look a bit concerned by the fanfare.

We make it to the restaurant and are seated next to a small group of local young men. Nino is in heaven, ordering all kinds of food. Magnus has joined the small group of guys next to us. They are talking Brevonni fashion stuff. We start drinking wine, and our group quickly absorbs most of the other customers in the restaurant as the gossip of Magnus being here has circulated. The locals have texted and phoned friends, and the restaurant customers are pouring in. All the tables are full and there is a relaxed, comfortable atmosphere. The owners are all smiles, taking orders left and right.

We eat and drink for hours. It looks like Magnus has had some wine—I see him slumping in the chair. I run over and smoothly take his wine and tell him that we need him back at our table. He's only had half a glass, so I think I've saved him and the Brevonni campaign from an embarrassing setback. I get some more food in him along with some sparkling water. He's fine, along with everyone else. I have to find Sebastian as we gather our group to leave. He's at the table with the same guys as Magnus. They must be family. Oh, well, some harmless flirting never hurt anyone.

Nino pays the bill, and we leave with hugs and kisses from the owners. This time they make sure that Daphne and Nino have their phone number for future arrangements. We make our way back to the van and load up.

Nino instructs Daphne that she can follow along on the maps, but tells her that Magnus is in charge of directions. Mag puts in the address of our hotel. We've booked a quaint little B&B just across from the Duomo in Florence. It's a great location: we can wake up, open the curtains, and see the Cathedral. It's only a one hour drive, maybe another hour to unload and park the van. I know one thing, I'm sticking with Nino.

It's a quiet ride; most of them are drowsy after their late lunch with wine. Bobbie Jo is wide awake but quietly taking in every detail of our drive. She is quite a unique person. I'm beginning to like her. I hope that Florence and the Duomo are ready for her.

Chapter Twenty-Seven
ANOTHER HOTEL, ANOTHER CITY

We quickly arrive in Florence without mishap, thanks to Magnus and his failsafe navigation app. It does, however, tour us all around the city through the quaint small streets to reach our hotel. It is a small hotel on one of the side streets near the Duomo.

As usual the streets are abuzz with Vespas and pedestrians going every which way. The stone walls endlessly line ancient streets. All the buildings with terra cotta tiles impress you with an ancient sense of grandeur. If you can ignore the hustle and bustle for just long enough, you can imagine aged societies with their own daily lives seen just out of reach of reality.

Here is a return to my reality. Daphne and Nino are arguing over the best way to park and unload. Thank goodness, the hotel representative runs out to direct us just around the corner. He asks us to unload, and he will take our vehicle for parking.

Everyone is unloading and walking toward the hotel. Daphne pulls me by my arm and along we go to check everyone in. Nino and Magnus start unloading luggage. The curb is already looking like a foreclosure cleanout. They've stacked suitcases and make up bags and Wal-Mart bags and shoes and sweatshirts and baseball caps onto the curb. I shake my head as me and Daphne enter the building.

Checking in is easy; they had all the details right. That rarely happens with my sister. It is usually chaos and craziness from start to finish. Daphne and I are given eight room keys. The attractive young Italian girl (do they come any other way here in Italy?) is explaining floors and bathrooms and beds while we try to understand what all the hurry is. Why can't she slow down and speak where we can understand her? I knew we should have gone to Sicily, where the pace and conversation is slower, like we are. Oh, what the heck. We just take the keys and nod and walk away.

We developed the strategy of room selection early on in our travels. After a few crap shoots of passing out keys to unknown rooms to outreached hands with us ending up with the ugliest rooms, we learned us a better way. Once, I received the key to this little cubicle of a room on the fourth floor of a hotel that didn't have a fourth floor. In the far corner of the third floor were some narrow stairs, about eighteen inches wide, which led up to an attic cubbyhole. The bed was in the opposite wall, which was the width of the tiny little bunk. When I sat on the bed, I swear I could feel the floor move beneath me. I didn't think much of it until we left the hotel later and I glanced up where I thought my room must be and the bed nook was a sixteenth century add-on that was hanging out extended from the wall into oblivion. I slept as carefully as possible, with a giant bell startling me awake every hour. As if that wasn't bad enough, the little village bell tower was about twenty feet from my overhang. And, just like the sixteenth century, it rang every hour, on the hour, counting out the hours all night long with its huge-ass bell.

Daphne had a similarly crappy room once when she, Nino, and my mama got the crapshoot key grab to a room in an old building built in 1572. There were more mazes in this building than a habitrail. Their room was through about ten tiny corridors, without rooms lining the corridors, just long narrow spaces into the guts of an old building, which finally ended at a doorway. Upon opening the door, you had to quickly step down three tall, narrow steps into a cold dark room where three tiny single size travel beds lined the walls of the coldest, darkest, room in the city. The ceiling was about twenty feet high and in the middle, dangling from about four feet of old electrical wire, was a single 40 watt light bulb. My mother was sure that this must have been the potato cellar way back when. Needless to say, none of us ever went to their room.

To make matters worse, a pair of our guests won the round with their key selection. Their room on the second floor overlooked the main street in this walled town of wonder. Looking out their window was a picturesque winter wonderland with horse-drawn carriages in a postcard setting.

Well, we wudn't born yesterday. We knew from that moment on that we leave everyone to gather their things while we speedily break away from the pack and check in privately. We take all the keys and make a mad dash, inspecting each room and putting the favorite room keys in our pockets. Alas, even this method has flaws, at least for us it does. There have been times when all the rooms looked great and we don't remember which room we wanted and have to run back through them, only to be caught by our guests as they have found us, because we were taking so long. After these experiences, we have honed our skills a bit. Now we know that timely room assessment is essential.

We look at the keys and look at the elevator. Oh, yeah, my sister's too cheap to find a real hotel with a real size elevator. This elevator is the size of a suitcase, *a* suitcase, not several suitcases. We look at each other, then the stairs, then the elevator. We both rush it at once, each trying to beat the other because we are pretty sure only one of us will fit.

We reach it simultaneously with the combined power of an elephant herd. Crash! Our force pushes us both through this tiny little door, and we are now stuck inside an elevator that is about two square feet. This is an old elevator where you have to pull the door closed, then another door, and then push the button. We are trying not to make a further scene, so we silently assess our situation. Daphne decides that she can just reach the sliding doors with her left hand that is pinned to her side. Thus pinned, she can only use her wrist to slide the heavy iron door. She whimpers and whines and finally does it. My right arm is in an upstretched position, but my elbow can reach the number button.

After she gets the door closed, I elbow the button. The elevator motor moans and groans. I hope that it makes this noise every time it lifts and not just this time, because it is carrying about three hundred and twenty pounds of two hefty American tourists. I am also glad that the lobby room is empty, because we are quite a scene in this little lift. Not to mention that it may be unable to lift our fat asses to the second floor. It is now grinding some gears as it finally moves an inch upward before it starts screeching again. But, with the screech, there is true lift-off and we begin our ascent to the second floor.

As soon as we are out of earshot, we start our giggling—the same giggling that always gets us in trouble, from the time when we were six and nine years old at our Grandma's kitchen table, to a few hours ago when my sister peed her pants in Pisa. I ask her if her bladder is empty, concerned now that if there is another mishap, there could be some back splash my way from which I cannot escape in this tiny space. We laugh even harder at that thought, when suddenly the elevator falls from its upward motion about three inches and stops at the second floor.

My sister reaches for the door to slide it open when she realizes that her wrist doesn't have enough room to rotate a half-circle to the left so that her fingers can grasp the slide. She begs for more room, so I try to fling my numb, tingling, upstretched right arm back so that my shoulder can lean to the rear. This works as I realize the doors are open and we are tumbling out into the hall onto the second floor. Once our two rolly-polly asses are flopping around on the floor, we vow to take the stairs down.

We stand up, only to realize that what we thought was the hall is the balcony overlooking the first floor lobby. Our group is gathered in the lobby observing the entire scene. "Damn it." We have lost our chance at the select rooms, because here they all come up the stairs.

They reach us before we can gather up all the fallen keys. Everyone, in fits of laughter, is grappling for keys. Everyone except Georgette and Hudson—they are not the grappling type, I guess. Once the crowd clears, there are four keys on the floor. Georgette extends her hand, expecting us to hand her a key, and of course, we do. That leaves three. The crapshoot is on again. I look at Daphne, she looks at me, and we both look at the keys. As we are weighing our options, trying to arrange the hotel rooms in our minds and correlate that with the remaining key numbers, Nino's big hand reaches into the pile and pulls out a key tag. So, that leaves me and an extra key. This must be Roni's. Aha, since Roni is not here, I get to choose between two rooms. Great, I take both keys.

As I rise up with a smile on my face, holding two keys, Daphne, giving me the evil eye, grabs my hand and pulls me to the side. Everyone else has scattered, going to their rooms, happy as can be. Me and Daphne and Nino realize that we have some choices. I'm not so happy, because I know Nino trumps me in the hierarchy of selection. But at least we can rule out the ugliest room, giving it to Roni.

Just as we are heading toward the nearest room in our selection, I hear hoity-toity giggling and Roni and her policeman/loverboy approaching us on the balcony. "Just in time for check in," she says as she reaches into Daphne's hand and removes a key. "Vitorio decided to join me on this leg of our tour. We'll meet you all for dinner. Toot-a-loo." And they are off. Hell, right back where we started from.

We three look at the two rooms for which we hold keys. Both are great, both have views of the Duomo, both have adequate bathrooms. Nino makes his choice, and I am left with the other.

We have decided to meet downstairs at seven o'clock for dinner. Nino has already been reconnoitering for his favorite little Florence eatery. It's six now, and I've got an hour to myself. I don't even know where the others' rooms are. In the melee of key grabs, everyone is scattered. I wish I knew where Magnus is. And little Bobbie Jo, I know what Mag meant by the urge to protect her. She is sweet and so far out of her league here. She must be wide-eyed and scared, somewhere in this hotel. And Roni! What about her, showing up here with lover number two in three days? I wonder if we will see her and lover boy at all. They'll probably be like Georgette and Hudson, mysterious lovers amuck on our tour. Oh, well, that means less people that my sister will make me baby-sit.

I throw my suitcase down and look out the window for a while. That cathedral really is magnificent. I kinda hope that Bobbi Jo doesn't have a view like this; she'll be weak with wonder every time she goes to her window. Hopefully her window faces a quaint alley.

I think I'll spend the next hour walking around the hotel, trying to find everyone's room. As I am locking my room door, I notice some singing coming from the room opposite mine. Pretty good voice, but I can't make out the tune, so I lean my ear against the door. I can hear water running and the faint "shall we gather at the river" vocals from Bobbie Jo. So, I've found Bobbie Jo's room without any serious snooping. Thank goodness her room is opposite the Duomo. She should be safe on her own.

I follow the long hallway, feeling like Dorothy following the yellow brick road. It is an expansive rolling burgundy rug with bright yellow, pink, and white intertwining florals weaving down the center. The quiet of the hall fades as I know I am nearing Nino and Daphne's room. Alongside their door, I hear Daphne saying, "I know it, Nino, I said…" With this, I busy myself on down the hall before she knows I am on the prowl. If she knew, she'd be right by side, not giving me a moment's peace.

At the end of the hall, I take the spiral stairs up to the next floor. At the top of the stairs, I follow the long carpet back down the hall. At the first door on my right, I hear the rhythmic thumping of a bed. Hmmm— either Georgette and Hudson, or Roni and Vittorio, or some other romantic couple in that room. Three doors down and on the left, I can hear two male voices. It's English, I decide as I get closer. I again lean my little ear into the door, as I quickly hear footsteps and southern style cussing. Just as I realize that it is Jackson talking to Magnus, I reach up to knock.

But suddenly my fist pauses, as I hear Jackson tell Magnus, "How are we going to do it then, with everyone recognizing you? We can't even walk over there together and look at the heist site. How can we plan it if we can't look at it together? And, I've got to get all the materials together and start mixing the chemicals."

I realize that I'm cold and starting to shiver, my mind busy with what they could possibly be planning. As I start to back away, I bump into Vitorrio. I scream in panic, scared mostly by Magnus and Jackson, yet alarmed that Vittorio was stalking either me or Magnus. I know that he heard everything, too. In a flash I consider that he's a policeman and for some reason, he was sneaking up on Magnus and Jackson. As the scream starts to evolve into a noise, his big old hand covers my mouth. First of all, I wonder where has his big old hand been before it landed on my mouth, and then, why is he shushing me when it was him that scared me?

"Shhhh. It's okay, Andi, I didn't mean to startle you, and I didn't want your scream to scare everyone. I am on my way outside to find a pharmacia for Roni," as he smiles and elbows my shoulder. "You've got to be safe, if you know what I mean. Why are you sneaking around here listening to the doors of strangers? Are you hiding anything?"

"Aren't you going the wrong way? Outside is the other way down the hall. Are you sneaking around?"

"No, of course not, I was going the other way, until I saw you. Then I just thought that I would ask if you needed anything from the pharmacia."

"What would I need from a pharmacy?" I ask in dismay.

"Well, one never knows what fun mischief one needs to be prepared for, do we?" A heavy snickering escapes from his mouth.

"Oh, gross. Hush that up, Mr. Policeman Vittorio. I would never....well, maybe I might. No, no, I wouldn't. You're nuts."

"You shouldn't be so firm in your response, Ms. Andi. We Italians are handsome, charming, and we are very persuasive. Maybe you should just relax and enjoy yourself. I'll see you at dinner. Ciao."

With that, he turns and walks down the hall. I just have an eerie feeling that he is following me. Why would he do that? And how long had he been standing there? Did he hear everything that I did? I don't know what Jackson and Magnus were talking about, but they are my friends, and Vittorio had better stay away from them. I know they were probably just planning a fun evening. They are harmless. But, they sure picked a fine time to throw around words like 'heist' and 'plan'.

Just as I'm considering walking quietly away, their door opens, and I almost scream again. I jump back as I grab for my chest. My heart is beating faster than a thumping rabbit. Magnus, with a concerned look on his face, grabs my shoulders and says, "Andi, are you all right? You are as pale as a ghost, and you look like you might faint. Have you been to the Duomo? Has the Holy Spirit visited you in this very hallway?"

I do go limp as he picks me up and carries me in his room. He lays me on his bed and says that he's going to get a damp cloth for my face. I start to get up and try to assure him that I'm fine. "Magnus, really, I'm just fine. You scared me, that's all. I didn't expect to see anyone in the hallway, and when you threw that door open, I was just startled. Leave me alone and put that washrag back. What are you guys doing here? What's all that stuff in the floor?"

Jackson quickly starts gathering up stuff. It looks like stone stuff, but I really can't tell. Oh, I don't know and don't care. This is just crazy boy stuff. There is no telling with Magnus, but I do know that it can't be criminal or dangerous. I'll try to keep my eyes on these boys and keep them out of trouble. But, was Vittorio spying on them? Lord, no, why would he do that? I'm paranoid, that's all; it's just the fright in the hall when I was sneaking around that has got me all worked up.

"It's nothing," says Jackson. Me and Magnus was sorting through our stuff. We got our things mixed up back in Milan. That's all. How's Bobbie Jo? Do you know where her room is? I'd like to spend some time with her before dinner."

I tell him her room number, just across the hall from mine. He takes an armload of things and walks out, telling us that he'll see us downstairs. I turn to Magnus and give him a good look-over. He is grinning that mischievous grin that he knows melts anyone. I open my mouth to ask him what is really going on here. He recognizes my questioning eyes and waves me off with his hand. "Let's walk around a while before we are expected downstairs. Come on."

I give in, as usual. I show him around the hotel that I've acquainted myself with. When we get to my room, we hear laughter coming from Bobbie Jo's room. We both smile as I show him my room. We appreciate my view of the Duomo and then head downstairs.

Sebastian and Nino are already seated on the sofa in the lobby. They seem to be in deep conversation. Probably discussing the merits of Italian food verses the pretentiousness of French cuisine. Who am I kidding? I don't know one cuisine from another. I just know when food is good or it isn't. Roni and Vittorio are hugged up in the corner, all giggly and intertwined. Georgette is sitting on Hudson's lap in the chair adjacent to the sofa. She whispers sweetly in his ear with her arms around his neck. Bobbie Jo and Jackson are talking animatedly and looking out the window. Daphne is in the corner, texting on her phone. Seeing that everyone is gathered, Nino directs us to follow him to the restaurant.

Daphne, laughing hysterically, is running up to me with her extended arm holding the phone. Let me just say this. We Americans laugh out loud way too much for the comfort of most Europeans. My sister has caused us more stares and turned up noses looking down on us than I care to explain. Every country is the same; nothing makes you stand out more as an American as laughing out loud. Europeans walk arm in arm, quietly, even somewhat shyly, whispering to each other. Now and then you may hear a snicker, but never belly laughs like we do. So, I'm a bit concerned that whatever she is about to show me will once again boldly draw attention to us.

Daphne and I fall back as the group moves ahead of us. She is laughing so hard that she can't even tell me what is so funny. She's started the story twice, then waves her hands away and starts that crazy laughing. Finally, she forces the phone into my hands. I begin to read the text.

"Hey Mom, latest saga. We took the kids fishing, 4 kids, 4 sets of gear, including Barbie fishing pole for you-know-who. Stopped at the bait shop for crickets. All the kids wanted to hold 'em. All's well, until Chase gets a turn. I hear 'UhOh', then high-pitched girl screams, boys laughing like crazy and a cacophony of crickets. He dropped the box right next to his sister. Pulled over and recovered about 20, probably 30 are still in my van. Fished 2 hours without a catch. 2 days later and I hear them and occasionally see them jump as I drive down I-20. Nothing changes here."

Now, me and Daphne are arm in arm, trying to look like locals, but our laughter is *way* too loud, and people are looking at us. We pass the phone around so our group can make sense of our behavior. Damn, those kids are funny. I can't imagine a car full of crickets. I would freak out if one jumped on me while I was driving. My niece is superwoman, that's all I can say.

We exit the hotel onto a wide pedestrian road. People are everywhere. Walking arm in arm, men and women, and women and women, they are in quiet conversation; all these fashionable people with cell phones to their ears hurrying along to private rendezvous. We turn left, away from the Duomo, and walk about fifty feet.

We pass storefronts and ancient ruins. Bobbie Jo and Jackson are just ahead of me and Magnus. They keep slowing us down, gawking at everything. We are barely able to keep up with the rest of them when we notice that they have turned right onto a smaller alleyway. We go another twenty feet and arrive at our restaurant.

It is a very small, local establishment, crowded and noisy. We are directed to several small tables at the back. Nino is hugging the proprietor as they speak Italian and laugh and seem genuinely glad to see each other. We sort ourselves out to the many scattered tables. Sebastian, Roni, Vitorrio, Georgette, and Hudson are in the far corner. Nino, Daphne, Bobbie Jo, and I are at another table. Somehow Magnus and Jackson have a small little table to themselves against the wall to my right.

Another highlight to Nino's tour begins anew. Again, at every restaurant, he lights up with all the joy of a child at their birthday party. He offers to help everyone order, if they need translation. After everyone has ordered and the wine has been poured, a calming relaxation starts to ooze from all of us. Lighthearted conversation abounds. We've had enough days on our trip that we can all share experiences with one another. I'm sure the other tables are enjoying their conversations, but at our table, no one can talk except Bobbie Jo. Her Holy enthusiasm flies out of her like a Nascar 400 race. As Daphne or I try to interject a word here or there, we are cut off just like the racecar drivers. On and on it goes. I'd feel sorry for Nino, but he isn't listening anyway. He is eating and appears quite oblivious to any external stimuli. No one can interfere while he's enjoying his dinner tour.

As early evening becomes late evening, Nino pays the bill, and we make our way outside, bidding farewell to our hosts and paying our compliments to the chef. Another dinner has surpassed the others. They are really all equally good, but the memory fades from one dinner to the next, thereby fooling the brain to think that each is the best, until you have the next 'best' dinner.

Once outside the restaurant, Daphne starts it up again. "Everyone, pay attention, I have important information. Our tour of the Duomo will begin promptly at 0900. I expect all to be ready in the lobby at nine. No delays. I'm anxious to see that beauty again."

She and Nino start their way back to the hotel. Bobbie Jo runs after them, eager to rest before her big day tomorrow. I can hear her and Daphne talking excitedly. Good for Daphne, she finally has someone eager to hear all that historic nonsense in her head. Everyone chats for a few minutes and then seems to drift off in different conversations. I stand here alone in this crowd. What happened? It's as if they all have plans that don't include me. What's wrong with me? I don't have cooties, do I?

As Roni, Sebastian, Georgette, and Hudson wave off, they follow their navigation app to a local club; Vittorio excuses himself back to the hotel. He complains that he is exhausted and needs some extra rest. He smooches all over Roni and abruptly leaves. I run up to Magnus and Jackson, asking what they have planned and can I come along.

"Oh, sorry Andi, we're off to do guy things. You really wouldn't enjoy it. Catch up with the others and go on back to the hotel. Get some rest. You know that tomorrow will be busy, and you need your beauty sleep," Magnus says as he kisses the top of my head.

"What is that crap, Magnus? You know that me and you do more guy things than you and Jackson. Why can't I go?"

Magnus pulls me aside and whispers, "You know that Jackson needs me now. He wants to talk about his feelings with Bobbie Jo. We just need some time to talk.

You know that I'd love you to come along, I really would, but just allow me this time for my old friend."

"Sure, you guys have a good time. Ya'll go on and I'll see you in the morning."

They turn and go all quiet and whispery-like. I walk back toward the hotel, thankful that sweet little Jackson has a friend like Magnus. Magnus will help him sort through his emotions about Bobbie Jo. I've been so busy inside my own head that I start to realize that I don't recognize any of the buildings that I'm passing. I must have missed my turn somewhere, so I turn around and backtrack. At every little alley intersection I look around, trying to recall any buildings or signs or anything familiar. I look left, nope. I look right, nope. I walk another stretch of road and look left and am almost knocked down by Vittorio. He catches me and asks if I am okay.

I explain that I'm fine but that I'm lost and trying to find the hotel. He tells me to follow this alley to the end and turn right. The hotel will be on my right. I ask him where he is going. "I thought you were tired. Why are you running the opposite way from the hotel? You didn't have time to go back to the hotel, did you?"

"Yeah, but I realized that I may have dropped my phone at the restaurant, so I've come back for it," he quickly replies as he is brushing past me and leaving me alone.

Well, that was a little weird, I think, as I walk back to the hotel. This is the second time in a few hours that this man has bumped into me. He's starting to creep me out. Both instances were explained away, but still, why me? Has he been bumping into anyone else? Weird, that's all. I make my way back to the hotel and go right to my room. I may as well put all the wine to good use and sleep.

Chapter Twenty-Eight

MAGNUS AND JACKSON ON THE PROWL

Finally rid of Andi and out of her sight, I pull out my phone to quickly find our way to Piazza del Giglio. "I can't wait to finally see it in person, Jackson. I've been living this dream for almost six months. This is so exciting. But, all the same, I feel like a criminal. I'm taking something that is not mine. But, I've got to have it. I really do. We've made a replacement, so I'm putting back a newer, improved version. And another concern is that once I have it at home, I have to deal with the ghost of Ms. Carmichael. I hope it's okay with her, or we'll be bringing it right back and criminally returning the thing. Tell me it's all right, Jacks. I don't want to bring this back."

"Oh Lord, Magnus, of course it's fine. It's like a street sign. I'm sure they don't even care. I'm anxious to see it too. I need to check the wall to which it is mounted and purchase the epoxies. And then we need to talk through our plan and walk through our timing."

We continue our walk toward the Piazza. I can see the approaching Duomo when people start looking and pointing at us. Jackson explains that he felt odd that people were watching them. I tell him that he is being paranoid. "These Italians don't mean anything. They just know how to appreciate two fine male specimens."

As we reach Via Dei Calzaiuoli, pedestrians seem to be out in full force. Everyone is window shopping at this time of the night. After strolling about a hundred feet, I'm oblivious to the stares as I window shop myself. Jackson pauses and elbows me several times before I turn to him. "Look at that," Jackson says as he points down the street. At the next intersection, hanging from the top story of the corner building is a huge picture of me, wearing the top selling Brevonni suit, along with my crazy grin that Andi loves. Floodlights do as they intend, bringing every eye to gaze upon this huge ad.

I look up. "What in the hell is that? Oh, shit. People are looking at me because they've just looked at a giant me. Quick, give me your baseball cap, Jackson." I hurriedly slam the cap on my head and pull it down over my eyes. I look down at my feet and start walking double-time.

As we quickly walk toward the Piazza, people continue to whisper and stare. We manage to maintain the pace, hoping to avoid direct contact. We're almost there when some hot little Italian cutie bumps into me and begs a camera picture with her. I agree, and Jackson gets the shot. At that, the girl runs away giddily.

Once into the Piazza, we both pause at the center and look around. Jackson finds the plaque and we gradually drift toward it. As we near it, Jackson sees a man float back into the alley. "Did you see that, Magnus? It looked like a man that didn't want us to see him. Do you think we are being followed? Oh, probably because of your ad and he is just too embarrassed to approach you. Now, let's get to work."

I seem to come to life as I finally gaze upon the actual plaque. While I'm as excited as a little kid, Jackson studies it with the eye of a skilled master. He is critiquing while I just smile. A man's shadow remains at the corner, watching.

After studying the plaque for about twenty minutes, we walk around the Piazza for another thirty minutes. We thoroughly examine it from every angle in the square. We study the buildings and the lighting, walking around all the side streets. The access to the area is assessed. Finally we walk down each alley for about fifty feet, then turn and walk back to the square. All along, I have the uncanny feeling that we're being watched, that a shadow is tailing us just out of sight. It's probably just nervousness. I'm being paranoid.

"Hey Magnus, did you say that the plaque translates loosely to 'don't play with balls in the street?'"

"Yep, that is how it was translated to me by an Italian customer at the antique store."

"Look at this place, Magnus, I can see it. I can see the young boys kicking their balls all around this square. I see the ball landing in the tomatoes at the vegetable stand. I can see them landing too close to the blacksmith area. I can see the artists walking nonchalantly along and getting hit in the torso by the ball. I see their mommas chasing them, yelling at them to stop kicking that ball out here. I can even imagine the town council bombarded with complaints by the citizens, voting to make this a 'ball free' zone. Isn't it amazing? I wonder where the poor kids had to go to play ball. The plaque says 1742. I can see this square so busy with the daily activity and kids running through here, disturbing all the busy, important adults. I just kinda wish that the sign read 'no conducting business in this place, this place is for playing ball.'"

On the way back to the hotel, I keep my head low and hurry along, avoiding eye contact with anyone. I still can't shake the feeling that we're *not* going unnoticed, and I won't feel like we're in the clear until we're behind closed doors again. We get into my room and lock the door. Jackson pulls out the plaque and lays it on the table. "OK, Magnus, I'm excited now. This is do-able. I can be ready within twelve hours. My part is good. Now, let's go over your plan for diversion."

"Well, originally, I was going to have you pick a fight with Andi, down the street and around the corner. That would draw all the attention away while I get the plaque. Then in Milan, when I thought I was going to be recognized, like apparently I am, I would be the distraction, creating a scene and having everyone flock to me, giving you the opportunity to do the job. But I hate for you to do it yourself, so I came up with my final plan. Tell me what you think.

All that shopping in Milan was not just for the male me. I also bought some very chic but very large clothes for the female me. I will dress in drag, and we will go out together and do it. It's a good thing you are tall. We'll make a mighty attractive pair."

"Magnus, I don't mind you being on my arm. But I don't know about how attractive you can be in a dress and heels. And, I'm just a little worried that Bobbie Jo will find out and get jealous."

"Well, jealousy is often good for a relationship. And you are dead wrong. I will be gorgeous in those pink pumps and narrow skirt. And wait until you see that blouse that Roni helped me pick out. And all the accessories; wow! You won't believe that it is me. Not to mention, with all my make-up, breathtaking is what I will be. *And*, I got a Brevonni suit for you. I think it will fit, because I gave the alteration guy your measurements. That way, if anyone were to see us and report us, they will report a well-dressed couple, not some rednecks, which would be a sure give-away. Since no one has ever seen you in a suit and no one here has ever seen me in drag, it's the best distraction. We just can't get caught."

"Shit, man that is perfect. And, Bobbie Jo will never know, so she won't have to be jealous. That is a great plan. What time do we do this? And how do we get away from everyone?"

"Easy. Tomorrow, we hang out with everyone all day. After all, we still have to protect Bobbie Jo from the Holy Spirit. At dinner, I'll pretend to drink a couple of glasses of wine. You may not know, but when I have alcohol, even in small amounts, I tend to pass out. So, I'll pretend to come back to my room and sleep it off. We'll tell everyone that you just need some sleep. We will get dressed up and leave separately. We can meet at a restaurant sidewalk café and then leave together. I'll bring my new red bag that just happens to be big enough to carry the plaque. We're set! We can do this."

"That sounds good. And since we will be working together, I think we can do it in about ten minutes. We only have to have contact with the plaque site for about sixty seconds. As soon as we arrive, I'll spray it with the chemical release formula. I brought a direct nozzle with a small six foot transparent hose. We let it sit for about ten minutes. Then we reach up and give it a tug. I will then apply another glue set, which I spray with another nozzle. We let that wait for one minute and then put up the replica. You're so tall, you can just lean on it for a few minutes and that's it."

"Jackson, I can't thank you enough for this. It does feel like a sneaky high school prank, doesn't it? I'm not really a mean person, but this isn't harmful and I really, really, want it. I will be the envy of all my gay friends. You know, you might want to make several plaques in English and put an ad in the gay magazines. There could be a great demand for these plaques."

"No way, we can't tell anyone what we did. I don't know if I want Bobbie Jo to know I was involved in a theft. Now, what time do you think we should do it, Magnus?"

"I'm thinking that it should be pretty deserted about one o'clock. Is that good with you?"

"That sounds good. Let's leave here at midnight and meet at that little bar restaurant at twelve-thirty. We'll have a drink and then make our way to the Piazza."

"Good. That's it then. You make your store run in the morning and purchase your supplies. We'll be ready. Now, Jackson, let's go on to bed. We won't get much sleep tomorrow night. Thanks a lot man, I appreciate it."

Chapter Twenty-Nine
SISTERLY WAKE-UP CALLS

I hear banging at my door. I open my eyes and look around. Oh, yeah, I'm on a trip. Where? Oh, yeah, Florence. Whew, I was out. "Andi, Andi. Get up and open this door. Let me in."

Shit. Is everyone cursed with a sister like mine? Or do most people have sisters that are normal, sisters that let them sleep when they want to sleep? Sisters that don't wake up every morning ready to go and insist that everyone else be just as enthusiastic. Sisters that are not bossy. Sisters that . . . "knock, knock, knock, knock."

"Daphne, stop it. I'm coming. Quit banging on the door."

I open the door and let in this perfectly touristy dressed maniac. "Daphne, what is wrong with you? Why can't you let me sleep?"

"Because it is eight-thirty and everyone will be downstairs ready to tour the city in thirty minutes. I knew you wouldn't be ready. I knew I should have made you stay in my room. I'm telling Nino that you have to stay with us from now on, so that I can keep you on track. Now, get up, get your clothes on."

"Well, I'm safe from that threat. Nino is not going to let me stay in his room, so ha!"

"You may be right, but he'd sure as heck let me stay in your room."

"Shit, you're right. He'd be all for that idea. He'd like nothing better than to be rid of both of us. All right, all right, I'm up. I'll meet you downstairs in thirty minutes. Now, go."

Off she goes, grumbling every breath. Damn, she's a pain in the ass. Poor Nino, but he sure as hell would make her stay with me. I'll set my alarm for the rest of the trip.

I throw on some clothes and prepare myself for baby-sitting tourists and protecting Bobbie Jo from herself. She had better get used to all these churches and Holy places and do it fast. I'll say a little prayer for her. Maybe God will listen to me, because Daphne sure won't. I brush my teeth and gel up this hair. I grab my phone, and I'm out the door.

I get downstairs and there sits Daphne, all alone. Damn her. Nobody is up and ready. Or else, they all have realized that they don't need Daphne's useless knowledge to enjoy the sights. Only three days into this trip and they have her figured her out. I bet all of them feel sorry for me that she is my sister and I can't get away from her.

"Alright, Daphne, where are they? It's just me and you to go see sights that we've already seen a hundred times. Where is your crowd of tourists?"

"Oh, just sit down and be quiet. They are coming. But get over here, you have to see this text that I just got from Andrew. Little sweet Caroline just said her first cuss word. Look at this text."

I reach for the phone and she pulls it back. "Let me explain this for you," she says, as if I need an explanation. I'm better at background than she is. I get nuances that you have to hit her with a brick to get. Here she goes, anyway, as always, doing what she always does, boss.

"You know how Andrew is. Since he's been in Boston, he's developed a little road rage language." What does she know? He's always had some road rage, and Boston may have intensified it, but not developed it. "For twelve years, poor Alise had to listen to it all, and now with kids, sometimes, my dear sweet little boy lets it slip. Well, little Caroline is buckled up in her car seat in the back while Andrew is driving. Suddenly she shouts out to her daddy, 'Daddy, did you see that damn car?' Isn't that hilarious? Here, look at the text." She passes me the phone.

"No, that's okay, why do I need to see it? You've already told me everything. As usual, you've ruined the punch line. Forget it. But that is pretty funny. Maybe that will teach Drew to watch his mouth while driving. Hey, I'm going to the dining room for my coffee and Danish or whatever crap they have. Breakfast is when I miss Germany the most. Come and get me when everyone is ready."

Off I go to the dining room. Surprise, everyone is in here. Great! I don't have to worry about Daphne. She can sit out there and wait, and we'll stay in here and eat and enjoy our coffee. I grab my coffee and rolls and join them at a vacant seat. For thirty minutes or so, we just eat and drink merrily.

Soon, Daphne comes sulking in. I go to her and take her to our table. I get her coffee and allow her time to sulk. I tell her that everyone thought she meant for them to convene in the dining room at nine. She takes that well and quickly gets over it.

We finish up our breakfast and Daphne starts directing the tour. First stop is the Duomo.

Chapter Thirty

SISTERLY TOURS

The exterior of the Duomo is a wonder of architecture. My eyes cannot consume it slowly enough. That's what I feel when I look at the Duomo. No matter what I'm looking at, I see too much. I miss the fine details.

There's just so much that I want to appreciate. My eyes strain to avoid the overall and zoom into the individual statues, the lacy scrolls dripping on each piece of trim, the little florettes, the curves and sharp angles and the arches. I want to be aware of all it separately, and then step back and see it all as one. But my eyes are just too ADHD to slow it down. I wish I could slow my eyes and my brain to give this structure the full appreciation that it deserves. But, alas, my sister calls. I run forward as everyone is waiting on me to join them as we enter the door.

Once inside, the décor is a little plain and unimpressive. The marble floors are nice, but the walls look modern somehow, like drywall. There are some beautiful circular stained glass windows here and there. And big, that is what I notice most. I swear the kids could play football in here, it is so big. And quiet. It seems that most of the early crowd is respectful of the silence sign today.

We start wandering. Everyone is drifting in different directions. I see that Jackson and Magnus are staying close to Bobbie Jo. And Daphne is right there with her, too. I think I've seen enough already. I should have stayed outside at the piazza with Nino drinking a cappuccino and eating some pastries from the bakery that I know he is walking to. I don't think anyone would miss me if I were to just sneak toward the door and back out of here. Damn it, here comes Daphne.

"Sister, why are you back here? Bobbie Jo is chomping at the bit, wanting to stand under the dome and look at that painting. You know how dangerous it is in here for her. I need you with us, come on."

"Sure, I was just going to find you, I knew you'd be wanting me. But, do you know what I want? I want a pastry and coffee with Nino. But, oh no, I will sacrifice and come with you and protect little BJ from her own holiness. No really, I'm sorry, I like Bobbie Jo a lot and I don't want to risk another head injury for her. I think she might be OK in here, there's not too much gold and glitz and statuary in here, not enough to hurt her anyway."

We walk up to the front and find them seated on a bench with their necks hyperextended, staring straight up. I'm glad that Magnus and Jackson sat her down for that. We join them and sit on the pew just in front of them. Magnus is to her left, and Jackson is to her right. Magnus has his right arm on the bench in front of them, and it is to the center of Bobbie Jo, and Jackson has his left hand outstretched on the bench to the center of Bobbie Jo. It looks like they have her penned in and safe from a forehead slap on the forward bench. Since she is seated with her neck back, staring straight up, she can't fall backwards. She looks perfectly secure this time, so I throw back my head and stare upwards, too.

Maybe I'm too far away, or maybe my fifty-something-year-old eyes need more assistance than my contacts are giving them, but all I see is a sea of gold, with a bunch of human and angelic body parts swimming around. And the way the dome is shaped, with the wide part closest to me and the narrow pointy part farthest away, it appears as if God has hit the handle on the toilet and they are swirling around toward the center, about to go right down the drain. The more I look, the faster and faster they are flushing away. Whew, I don't think I should continue trying to look so hard to appreciate what I am sure is fine art. I'm feeling a little drifty, maybe just a might dizzy. *Shit*, I think I'm about to—yeah, I feel weak and warm and slummpy.

I come to with Daphne slapping me and Bobbie Jo holding my head, praying and praising with her left hand on my forehead and her right hand in the air. *Shh*, I'm thinking, *will someone tell her to tone it down?* It feels like she is screaming in my ear. I open my eyes with my neck still back, resting on the pew back, and see the same blurry gold swimming bodies of old. Oh, no, I think, and close my eyes again. Man, I think I might be sick. I feel somewhat nauseous. I start to smile, thinking of that word, my mama used to say it so funny. With my eyes closed again, I'm feeling a little better, less nauseous. I've got to think about that word when I'm at my full wits again. Nauseous. Gaseous. What funny words. As my mind is returning to the surface, I feel another slap from Daphne. With that, I try to leap up and take her down.

"Sister, if you slap me again, I'm going to tackle you right here in this cathedral, in front of God and everybody. I'm alright now. You guys move back and give me some air."

Everyone sits back down, except Bobbie Jo. She is now holding my face in both of her hands, telling me how happy she is to have me in the fold. She's mumbling about the excitement of being saved under this magnificent dome in this Holy place. "Bobbie Jo, I wasn't saved, I just cut off the oxygen to my brain with my head back like that, then I couldn't see because of these old eyes, and the more I studied that stupid painting the more dizzy I got, until my brain couldn't take another second without some air and it knocked me over so I could breathe again. I'm not saved, I'm the same old sinner I ever was. That's not what

I mean; I'm saved, I was saved the day I was born. I'm a believer and all, but what just happened to me was pure science and biochemistry. My brain needed some oxygen, that's all. And it's better now; did you not just hear me say big words like science and biochemistry? I'm not spouting off 'Holy Fathers,' I'm just talking super brainy words. Now, that's definitely not like me, maybe you're right. Maybe I did receive some kind of Holy powers sitting right here under this toilet bowl scene. Maybe God has just now, at age fifty-something, given me the gift of a super brain."

Just then, I realize that I'm talking a little too loud as people are looking at us. Or, maybe they are looking at us, astounded by my sudden thunderbolt of scientific wisdom. Or, maybe, I still am oxygen deprived. I'm hallucinating. I need more air. Is this the spell that Bobbie Jo is under? That's it; they all probably just hold their breath with the intent of passing themselves out. And then, when they come to, they call that their religious awakening. While I sit pondering all of this I realize that they have left me alone. They are walking around, studying the place and forgot that I could have just had my first symptom of a brain tumor. Or, maybe I scared them away with my miraculous sudden understanding of biochemistry. Oh, what the hell. I want to find the spot where Savonarola preached. I bet little Bobbie Jo would have been a follower of that fanatic.

I must say, even though I told them all to leave me alone, I'm a little hurt that they did. Did I not take care of Bobbie Jo and have I not intended to keep her from hurling her body to and fro, overcome by her own lack of oxygen? Oh, nevermind. Where did that book say Savonarola preached here? I know he preached from San Marco, but I think he did preach here a time or two. Not that I really care, I can't respect a man that, with his Bonfire of the Vanities, burned so many irreplaceable works of art.

Whoa, did I just think of all of that, and have a profound opinion of it? Maybe holding your breath and passing out does make you smarter. Or, though I'll never admit it, maybe God did just touch me with some wisdom that I was lacking. Darn, I even think that when I think now, I'm thinking with gooder grammar. Where is tour guide Daphne when I need her? Maybe I hurt her feelings, but she was slapping me really hard. I'd better go find them.

After slowly walking and fully recovering, losing some of my brilliance in the fifteen minutes since my religious high, I see Magnus, Jackson, Bobbie Jo, and Daphne looking at a plaque on the floor. They all hug me in as I approach. I look down and see what looks like a common concrete plaque. Daphne whispers that it is Brunelleschi. Who the heck is he, I wonder. I shrug my shoulders and walk off as all of them continue to stand and gawk.

I walk toward the back door and see Roni and her police boyfriend Vittorio, looking at me and pointing at Magnus, Jackson, Bobbie Jo, and Daphne. I walk over to join them and they immediately turn and walk toward something else. I shrug again and keep heading to the door.

The bright sunshine is a welcome change from that dark interior. I briskly walk to the side of the door and bask in the warmth. I find a bench and just sit quietly, quite thankful to be alone for a moment. I consider our plans for the rest of the day. Within thirty minutes, those of us who choose to do so will be climbing the Duomo Tower, hopefully all four hundred and sixty three steps. If Bobbie Jo decides to try it, we'd really better hang on to her once we get to the top. It is such a beautiful view. It's a once in a lifetime opportunity to appreciate the terra cotta rooftops as their curves and sways follow the little roads and smaller pedestrian pathways that snake out from the

Duomo. This is really the Medieval Florence that has remained relatively unchanged since that time.

Nino approaches, interrupting my daydreams of carts pulled by roughly dressed smelly men and women. "Here, Andi, I bought you a pastry. I knew you'd be out here, but you're later than I expected. I didn't think you would stay in there as long as you did. You surprised me. Did Daphne finally say something interesting that kept you at her side for fifteen minutes?"

"Naw, you know that when she's touring, she goes crazy. I've heard it all before, she's got nothing new to interest me. I just sat a while, looking at that dome painting. I felt a little sick and came outside. I bet this pastry is all I need to perk me up. Are you going to climb the tower today?"

"You know that I don't usually climb the tower of every city we go to, but I think I will today. I want to see the reaction of Jackson and Bobbie Jo. They are interesting people, and I enjoy the look of wonder on their faces. It's like when we travel with the grandkids, except they're adults and are better able to verbalize their feelings, and they go to their own rooms at night."

So, we both just sit and snack, content with our solitude. After another fifteen minutes, our little group trickles out and congregates with me and Nino. Of course Daphne is the last one out. She and Bobbie Jo are linked arm in arm, talking animatedly about who knows what. Thank God that she's got someone to impress with her bucketful of useless facts. She's not bad really, and they're not altogether useless, just exhausting.

Roni really doesn't want to climb the tower, but Vittorio insists that it will be romantic and persuades her to accompany him. He still creeps me out. It's like he's watching us all the time. I bet he isn't as interested in romantic interludes as he is watching us. Am I the only one who has noticed his strangeness? Georgette and Hudson make their excuses and leave us for the day. What do those sweet young lovebirds need with us and our tour? We will probably not see them again until tomorrow morning. Sebastian also wants to bow out of our plans for the day. He says he has work to do. He reminds us that he is on assignment here in Italy, working for his menswear store. Since he got the contract with Brevonni, his company has him working their contacts in Florence and Rome. He hopes to see us later for dinner. He has quickly learned that Nino is the best food guide to Italy.

Being the astute tour guide that she is, Daphne deftly forms our little group and directs us to the entrance of the Duomo Tower. I notice that she doesn't bother to tell anyone just how many steps there are. Hell no, it's like a damn rite of passage with her ass. She didn't tell me either, because if you knew, you wouldn't go. I remember the first time I went up there. After about step two hundred and fifty I was ready to kick her ass back to Sunday. And by step three hundred and fifty I thought I was gonna die. And off we go; another trail of repeat tourists from America attempting to reach back and touch a distant history that we never get to experience in our country as our Native Americans left little that we can touch or see. Because we've eaten it, killed it, blown it up, diseased it, and downright ruined the pristine country we took from them.

Our brisk start quickly slows to a sluggish, lethargic pace. A string of us spiral around and around and around. Each hundred steps or so creates multiple expressions of oxygen deprivation. As I look back behind me, I kinda feel the flushing motion again. What's with my brain and the connection with a toilet? Most of us are grunting with each breath and step. Daphne seems to hiss and howl with every step. The need of her legs to consume most of her energy has left her mouth slack and quiet, a fact that the others can't appreciate for worry of their own exhaustion. I bet by the end of this trip they will realize just how much nicer it is when she wears herself out. Everyone is quietly ascending, anxious to see a light at the end of this upward tunnel. Everyone except Magnus, that is. He insisted on being in the front of the line this time because he said he was tired of pushing us upward.

So, with his big lungs and long legs, he led our way, and by halfway he just gave up and left us. He was able to talk to us most of the way up, and then he got quiet. The others thought he was too tired to talk, but I knew that he just gave up and left us. I was right.

We finally do see the light, literally, but not in the religious way that Bobbie Jo wanted for us. I crawl my way onto the platform and reach back to help Bobbie Jo. Jackson helps from behind, and we get her onto the deck. Magnus is waiting for us, ready to share his discoveries with us, as he has been looking around up here for several minutes already. Jackson expresses his wonder while Bobbie Jo expresses fear and is hugging the dome, not even approaching the rail. It takes us a while, but we finally succeed in urging her to slowly look from the rail. After five minutes or so, she is on the rail, working her way around the dome, observing the city's roof.

Vittorio has pulled Roni up the stairs, hurrying her more than she liked. I hear them arguing over to my left. Well, Roni is arguing while Vittorio appears to watch Magnus while half-heartedly conversing with her. Magnus doesn't act like he suspects anything. There is probably nothing to suspect; I am just a corny old mystery sleuth.

Daphne and Nino are looking toward the Arno area with Nino, talking and pointing. I bet Daphne can't breathe enough to talk yet. Nino isn't impressed with this picturesque view—he is probably just trying to identify the most direct path to our appointed dinner restaurant. I hear him telling her that he has booked us for dinner at Il Latini. I've heard of it before, but we've never been there. I should have known that Nino would have planned it as soon as he knew we were going to Florence. After another several minutes, Nino gathers everyone and suggests that we go down. He tells us that others need the viewing space, and we've taken enough time. But, I know he really wants to eat some lunch at a street pizzeria/trattoria.

We descend as slowly as we went up. It seems that going down steps is as stressful on old knees as climbing is on old quadriceps. Once we're down, Nino tells everyone that he's going for a pizza snack and invites those interested to join him. He says that after that, he is done for the day, and everyone is to be in the lobby at eight tonight if they want to go to dinner with him.

With this, we seem to break into small groups. I'm with Nino until he shows me the food. Daphne and I will take a group to the Uffizi Gallery after lunch. Magnus, Jackson, and Bobbie Jo want to see the galleries. I would have thought that little Georgette, being the art history graduate, would have wanted to see it, but I suppose a young attractive husband outranks a museum filled with paintings and sculptures. Roni isn't interested, but Vittorio seems to want to do anything that Magnus wants to do. Oh, maybe, that's it, Vittorio likes Magnus. Hmm, so it seems that minus Nino, everyone that climbed the tower will see the arts.

We follow Nino down little alleys out from the Duomo. We turn onto the large pedestrian street of Via dei Calzaiuoli. He tells us we are going to the best little Trattoria in Florence. He says along this road we will turn onto another little alley, Via delle Oche, and there it will be. But, just before we reach it, we are met with a huge hanging billboard of 'The Brevonni Man'.

"Is that Magnus?" Roni exclaims. "Oh, you look so good, honey. I sure wished you played on my team. Look at you."

Magnus replies, "Oh, Roni, you know how to tempt a man, don't you?"

"Well, I'm old enough to know that people can't change and be what they are not. And in fact, I like you just the way you are. Who else can I go shopping with that understands the passion women have for fashion and accessories, not to mention shoes? I'll keep you a dear friend. I can always show you off to my contacts in Mountain Brook, can't I? I didn't know that you are so famous. I'm going to be calling you a lot, if you're game."

"Oh, yes, Roni, I could use some time running in your circles. You just let me know when, and I can be your official escort for your social events. And, thanks to Mr. Brevonni, I've got all the clothes for any occasion."

She leaves Vittorio's arm and allows Magnus to escort her down the street. They look like a high society couple for sure. Vittorio looks a little peeved. I don't think he likes the idea that Magnus can attract women—and men—so easily. Vittorio hangs back and follows quietly.

As I'm walking beside Bobbie Jo, I see her slow down and start to think. "What did Roni mean when she said that?"

"Said what?" I ask her.

"That Magnus doesn't play on her team. Is Magnus a homosexual?"

"Well, yes he is, Bobbie Jo. You didn't know that? You couldn't tell?"

"Lord have mercy on his soul. I know what he needs. He needs some religion and to beg God's forgiveness. Why hasn't he done that? He seems so nice, and I really did like him. He's funny and kind, and he picked me up and carried me when I went to sleep at the airport. Oh my Lord, he touched me."

"Hold on a minute, girl. You just hold on one minute. Now, I like you, I like you a lot. But don't you go judging Magnus and others based on what you think is right. And, how dare you, Magnus is crazy about you. He doesn't judge you, even though others may think that you are strange. And you just don't have any idea how valuable a friend like Magnus is. He is truly a good person, and maybe you had better go talk to God and ask Him how he would expect you to act."

"What I think is right? It's not me thinking it. It is the good Lord himself, telling us in his Holy Bible that homosexuality is a sin and that he will burn in hell unless he changes his ways and begs forgiveness."

"Bobbie Jo, you should just think about this before you say anything more. Talk it over with Jackson and think about your own life and make sure that you are clean enough to go casting stones. And until you come to a conclusion about that, might I suggest you remain quiet and don't hurt Magnus with your opinions. Can we agree on that?"

"Yes, Andi, I do agree, that's the best strategy. I should think about my own life. I know you think I'm perfect, but I've had a past to answer for myself. I will not say anything to anyone else."

"Just try to love and appreciate Magnus for who he is, OK? If you do that, you will be content in your soul."

I leave her and run up to Jackson, telling him that Bobbie Jo has just discovered that Magnus is gay. I explained that she is set against that type of sinner and ask him if he can talk to her.

"Sure, I will talk to her," says Jackson. "Don't worry, she will understand. I know that deep down she is much more open and accepting than she appears. She will be fine with Magnus, just give her some time. By the way, wasn't that an amazing ad with Magnus? I've never known anyone famous like that. Who woulda thought that our friend is a model? And in Europe? I wonder if there will be ads back home like that. Well, it couldn't happen to a better person. And he's the one man that I know will never be changed by all this hoopla."

"You're right, Jackson. He will always be the same. Ever since I've known him, he has never changed. Ups and downs, good and bad, he's always the same. It looks like we are here. Let's eat pizza."

We all enjoy the informal street food of the city. 'Yum' is not a good enough word. This pizza is great. Leave it to Nino. He'll never steer you wrong when it comes to food. We eat and eat and eat some more. This is just good food. After we all finish, Nino takes us along to a wine shop, where we sample wine. All of us sample, except Bobbie Jo, of course.

Nino then takes us along to a gelateria. It takes a lot of sampling for each of us to make our choices. Only Bobbie Jo and Jackson have not experienced Italian ice cream. Big, sweet Magnus is helping them with the flavors. Once we all have our cups, we go outside and walk through the streets. This is perfect. What a nice interlude between some serious architecture and art.

After the gelato, Nino heads back to the hotel while we continue to the Uffizi. I'm not much into art, but this place is full of famous stuff that even I recognize. Daphne gives us the facts, and facts, and more facts than we want. As usual, the only one listening is Bobbie Jo and, out of kindness, Jackson. Daphne leaves us outside while she collects the tickets. Roni is back on Vittorio's arm, as cuddly as ever.

Magnus is talking to some people in line for the museum. They recognized him immediately. They tell him that they love his accent and his clothes. It's funny—they are not thronging, like we would in America. They are using the opportunity to talk to someone that they have seen wearing smart men's clothing. If there's one thing that Italians appreciate, it is fashion. They do not want autographs, but he is posing with some of them for selfies. He is so likeable, he really is. He is agreeing to all suggestions of poses. Most are funny, some are romantic.

Daphne comes back with the tickets, and we are admitted entrance. It's a good thing that she purchased tickets in advance, because there is such a long line today. This is the most famous art museum in Europe, with over one and half million visitors a year, so you don't want to wait in that line. The building was started in 1581 by one of the Medici's, but I can't remember which.

This place is way too big to visit in a few hours, but that's what we have. Tomorrow is our free day, so some may want to come back then to finish it up. There are forty-seven rooms filled with the most famous Florentine paintings, as well as work by other Italian artists spanning from the 14th to the 18th century. There are also masterpieces from other countries such as Germany, Holland, and Spain. Ancient Roman and 16th century sculptures can also be seen here.

The most famous paintings housed here are Botticelli's *Birth of Venice* and *Primavera*. Fillipino Lippi's *Madonna and Child with Two Angels* can be found in Room 8. If you are into art, you will not be able to sleep, thinking about all the art that is in this museum. Old masters like Cimabue and Giotto, along with some of the most famous Renaissance painters like Carravagio, Rembrandt, Fra Angelico, and Masaccio are represented here. I can't believe I know these things Goes to show how easy it is to learn things. Even if you're not listening and you hear something about fifty times, it seems to stick. Thanks, Daphne.

We agree to go our separate ways since everyone wants to see different paintings. We plan to meet back at the hotel at seven-thirty. Daphne is with Bobbie Jo and Jackson. I'm staying with Magnus, hoping to keep him out of trouble. I know he will be looking at all those nudes, and I don't want him acting up and making a scene. I have known him to get out of hand.

We're having fun, looking at art through the eyes of art deprived rednecks. We try to be serious, yet sometimes we can't. He makes wise-cracks here and there, and I make fun of the old fashions and funny looking people before painters thought it wise to paint anatomically correct instead of caricatures. I've pointed out to Magnus that Vittorio is watching every move we make. He is sly and certainly acting like a detective, but I don't know why. Magnus says he hasn't even noticed him and thinks I'm overreacting. Maybe he is following me, not Magnus. Shit, what if he has a thing for me? I don't think so. He is not my type, either. I have to quit thinking crazy things; he probably looks like a detective because he is a detective, that's all.

We finish up and head back to the hotel, and, not that I think anything, but Vittorio and Roni are following about fifty feet behind us. We stop along the way and have another gelato. I choose Nocciola, a yummy hazelnut. Magnus can't decide on one so he chooses Pistachio and Zabaione, which is a custard flavor made with Marsala wine. I take a big lick, and it's good. I think I'll get it next time.

After our gelato and some more walking, we start looking for coffee. We meander down several out of the way roads. He takes me to several piazzas where we sit and watch people. He first took me to Piazza Santa Croce and Piazza del Giglio. We passed through the Santa Croce area quickly, but when we got to the little Piazza del Giglio, we went to the first open bench and sat and sat and sat and sat. I had two double espressos. Needless to say, this is not the most exciting place in Florence. It's *boring*. I can't get Magnus to leave. I can't even get him to talk to me. He just sits and looks, and then he will walk around looking at the walls. This feels so funny. It seems like I've been here before. I've had lots of time to look at this place, sitting alone, while Magnus walks and thinks.

I hope he isn't worrying about Bobbie Jo or Vittorio. Speaking of Vittorio, I've become a pretty good detective, too. Vittorio and Roni are here. I don't think Roni knows that we are here, because if she did, she would come and sit with me. The longer Magnus leaves me here, the longer that I feel I know this place. Suddenly, my mind locates a little, tiny memory of years ago when Daphne, Nino, and I came here for the first time. That was before we started our tour business. We ate at a little trattoria over there by the corner. When we came out, we were acting crazy, as usual, and Nino took a picture of us. I didn't even remember it until he gave me the framed picture for Christmas that year.

Finally, he's worked himself through whatever it is that has him so withdrawn. He comes to the bench and asks me if I'm ready to go. Certainly, I'm ready—my butt hurts, and I want to get moving again. We walk rather quickly back to the hotel. It's like we are in a race, complete with stop-watch. I want to run into a grocery market to buy some espresso, but he won't let me. He just hurries me all the way to the hotel. We don't stop until we get to his room, when I notice he does look at his watch. He's acting strange all right.

I leave him and go to my room. Needing some relaxation, I take a warm shower and lie down on the bed. With an open window, the breezes and foreign chatter ride the light wind from the Duomo into my room. So soothing. Rest comes easy as I recall the activities of the day. I giggle to myself, thinking about how Bobbie Jo must be suffering through the realization of personally knowing a gay man. Certainly, she will come around.

I awake with banging at my door. It's Magnus telling me to open the door. It's time to meet downstairs. It's a good thing I took Chase's advice about dressing before going to bed. He says that when he wakes up for school, he just needs to wake up and go—he's already dressed. Having checked my hair, I probably look like Chase going off to school with bed hair. I open the door and find Magnus waiting on me.

The restaurant is only a short walk from the hotel. It is so charming. It used to be a palace kitchen, and the wife would cook for the household. Over the centuries, it has continued to provide the best Tuscan dishes to the locals. Inside are half wood paneled rooms with hams hanging from the ceilings. Pressed white tablecloths cover small square tables lining the walls. Bottles of wine are standing around the room on narrow little boards.

We started our experience with wine, then more wine. Everyone enjoyed it except Bobbie Jo. Somewhere along the way, we convinced her that she had drunk alcohol and become intoxicated while at the airport in Birmingham. And Magnus didn't notice that I saw him have two glasses of wine. I hope he can make it back to the room. But, something's funny, he isn't even acting sleepy yet. This is some of the best wine that we've had while in Italy, so why doesn't it knock him out? I guess good wine works different in him than cheap wine.

There may be a menu, but I didn't see it and we weren't offered one. There seemed to be just a set menu for the evening. The ambience is enchanting and the evening wonderful. Nino really outdid himself with this one. He's already mentioning coming back tomorrow night and canceling the other restaurant he had reserved. Well, I trust him completely. I've never eaten bad food with that man. We are there for two hours and want to stay longer. The time goes by so quickly. Everyone really, really enjoys it.

Once back at the hotel, I expect Magnus to go out with me. We always do that. Every time we go on vacation or even on business to a new city, we seek out the local club culture. We didn't talk on the walk back, so when I knock on his room door, he tried to shoo me away. Insisting that he let me in, I find that he is already in the bed. "Honey, I'm just too tired to go out tonight. I shouldn't have drank that wine, but it so much better than the stuff we usually have. I can't stay awake. I'm lucky that I was able to walk back here. I think I'll be asleep in ten minutes, if you'll just leave me alone. Love you, night, night."

Fine, I go back to my room. After fifteen minutes, I'm roaming the halls trying to find someone to go out with me. I don't want to stay late; I'm old and want to get back to bed by midnight. I knock on Daphne's door, and she starts talking and talking, and before I even ask her I decide that I'd rather go back to bed than go out with her and listen to her mouth for two hours. I try Jackson, and he says he's going to bed early tonight, too. Lastly, I resort to Bobbie Jo. I cross the hall and knock. She doesn't answer. I knock again and she opens the door, already in her pajamas and her hair down. Damn, she looks like Rapunzel's grandma. She offers to go with me, but she would need about thirty minutes to up-do her hair and get dressed again. After considering it for about two seconds, I decline her offer and go back to my room. That's it.

Chapter Thirty-One
SLEEPLESS IN FLORENCE

Quickly realizing that flopping around in a bed can be dangerous and a waste of time if you are not tired, I jump up and look out the window. For an hour, I've tried to be still and relax and finally gave up. The Duomo is ethereal at night. Lighting is strategically placed to accentuate its great size against the old dark city. Thoughts flood my mind of ancient days when the great minds of the Renaissance walked these streets. Torches aflame light just small segments of the street where ill kept, black, brown, and gray dressed peasants huddle and converse with smiling smudged faces pondering their day's successes and failures. I can just imagine their conversations and how different they must have been from the huddled groups I now see. How fleeting and circular time really is.

Suddenly an odd couple leaves our hotel below my window, walking toward the Duomo. They are really quite elegant and breathtaking. Where could they be going at midnight, dressed so fancy like that? The man is dressed so smartly in what seems to be a custom made Italian suit. I can't quite get the color from here, damn these old eyes; but it's a dark smoky blue or gray, almost black, but not. He's even wearing a hat. Wow, almost American 1940ish gangster style. He really looks nice, even if I do just see him from behind.

And the woman, wow, she is an Amazon. I wish I could see her clothes from the front. She equals if not surpasses her gentleman friend's elegance. Her dark suit is well fitted. The jacket also appears to be custom made. Her skirt is tight and straight with a single back vent so that she can walk. She has dark hose and heels that most women would kill for. I can't see the details from this distance, but I bet that ensemble cost a small fortune. Her hair is long and dark, with cascading curls hugging her back. And the most striking detail is her fluttering scarf. It is a swirl of pale, pastel colors; pink, yellow, peach, sage, and lavender. It is truly gorgeous. I wish that Daphne could have found one that pretty in Milan. We should have shopped more thoroughly, because I bet you could only find that gorgeously expensive scarf in Milan. The tall lady is also carrying a large thin bag. I don't know what the fancy word for expensive, business bag is, but that's what she's got. The bag really catches my eye, because it is thin, but large. What can she have in there? It's probably just meant to carry folders and business papers. Maybe a skinny cell phone, that's it. Maybe a mini-pad. I think a maxi-pad would cause a bulge. Why do I think of these stupid things when appreciating a handsome couple out on the town? I'm crazy, just like my sister has always said.

Oh, yeah, back to the couple. As I watch them walk away, I notice how tall they are. The man is several inches shorter than the woman. I bet he wishes that she'd wear flats. Who knows, maybe some men like tall women. What do I know? Suddenly, they hold hands and trot across the little road. Damn, if that woman doesn't have some calves on her. She looks like she does the elliptical machine in those stilettos. I've never seen such muscular legs on a lady before. And tall, she is so tall. Most of these Italian women seem so tiny and petite to me. If you stacked one on top of the others shoulder's they might equal the height of this lady. Wow, the interesting people you notice once you are bored out of your mind on vacation in a great foreign city while the rest of your acquaintances would rather sleep than go out. I'm starting to feel like my sister, because that's what she does.

That's it. I'm going out for a drink or two. I don't even care if I have to go out by myself; I can't stay in this room a moment longer. I grab my ID and some money and make another bathroom visit. You quickly learn that Europe is not equipped for all of the pee-peeing tourists that wander their streets, so you'd better make yourself go every time you are within fifty feet of a toilet. While washing my hands, I notice the hair. It's a good thing I looked at it before I went out. My dangerous tossing and turning sure created a Medusa Masterpiece this time, this hair has to be touched up. I half wet and half gel it up and I'm good to go.

As I reach the lobby, I notice Vittorio sitting alone with a glass of wine. He's chosen a seat that faces the stairway and teensy, weensy, elevator. That's odd. Why isn't he facing the street like most people? Why sit, looking at the stairs, he's more boring than I thought. I guess if these small, winding streets of intrigue are your daily life, you've seen it all by the time you are as old and boring as he is.

"Hey, Vittorio, what's up? You look as bored as I feel. I'm going out for a drink, you want to go?" I ask him, hoping he will say no.

"No thanks, Andi. Roni is waiting for me upstairs. I had to make some business calls, and I'm just finishing off my wine. Have a good night."

Leaving the hotel, I turn back for a quick glance, and I notice him get up and put his wine glass, half full on the table and look my direction. I give him a halfhearted wave and walk across the street. I don't really know where I'm going, so I just wander for a while. I find a bench at the Duomo piazza and sit and admire the light effects on the old cathedral. Realizing that I'd like a coffee, I leave my little piece of heaven and choose a narrow, winding side street. Halfway down, I feel like someone is following me, but when I look back there is no one there. What, now I'm scared of imaginary shadows?

At the end of the street, I'm nearing the large Piazza della Republica. There is a lot happening here. Lots of people, lots of cafes, and I can smell lots of coffee. I find a little café and sit at an outside table, watching the people on the square. Into my second cup of coffee, I notice the couple from my hotel window. They are having coffee at another café across the piazza. They are so sophisticated; I could never pull off dressing and going out for coffee looking like that. Damn, that's a big girl. I finish my coffee and pay my bill. As I drift out into the piazza, I notice that they've left. And I notice something else, something disturbing.

I see Vittorio leaning against the wall of a nearby alley. He's smoking a cigarette and looking very noir detectivish. I'm right, he is following me. Why on earth is he following me? I haven't done anything, have I? Nope, I haven't broken a single law on this trip, not yet anyway. I'll test this. I slowly meander down every little street I can find, back to our hotel and check my shadow. Yes, every time that I sneak a peek, he is there. What the hell? Do I approach him or continue to watch him, watching me? I'm going to ask Magnus tomorrow. I'm telling him all about this. No, maybe I shouldn't tell anyone. If Daphne knew, she would go nuts. She is crazier than me.

I make a big entrance into the hotel. I stop and talk with the receptionist a while, and then take the stairs slowly to my floor. Just as I thought, I see him sneak into the hotel behind me. As I walk down my hall, I hear him climbing the stairs. I quickly unlock my room door and jump inside, locking the door behind me. I can hear his footsteps outside my door. I sure wish that I had a little peephole. Who am I kidding; I know that it is him. I listen and hear him walk away, back to the stairs.

Now I am tired and a bit concerned. It's not that he scares me, it's just that I feel like he's watching me for some reason, only for the life of me I don't know why. I change clothes and jump in the bed. It's late, almost 1:30, and I don't think I will have any trouble sleeping.

Chapter Thirty-Two

MAGNUS AND JACKSON - IT'S TIME

"Jackson, I think we're ready. We've made our appearance at the local cafes and walking hand in hand as a couple. It's almost 2 AM, the streets are now quiet. Let's do it," I whisper.

"I'm ready. You've got everything in the bag, don't you?" asks Jackson.

"Yep, within the hour, it's done and we're back in the room. It's just here around the corner," I tell him.

As we approach the Piazza del Giglio, I'm happy to see that it's dark and deserted. "Take my hand again and let's mingle lovingly over to the corner near the plaque," I tell Jackson.

"There's not much light, but that's good." Jackson says as he removes his solutions from the bag. He expertly mixes and attaches the long narrow nozzle. While pretending to reach towards me as he is leaning against the wall, he guides the nozzle around the rectangle plaque and squirts it lavishly. He then drops the solution bottle back into the bag.

"We only need to give it two or three minutes. I'll prop my hand on the plaque, holding it steady as it releases. Magnus, will you bend your knees a bit, and slink on down into the bag and grab the replica? Once this releases, we need to be ready to throw the other one up real quickly."

"Got it. Is it releasing yet? I'm ready when you say. I will go ahead and take it out. I need to lay it down flat and squirt the adhesive on it so that it is ready when you give me the OK."

"Magnus quick, I need help. This thing is heavy. It's loosening, and one hand is not enough to secure it. Leave that one now that you've got it prepared and stand straight up. Pop your head between my hands and it will look like we're getting very romantic, but what I really need is your strong back leaning hard against it. With your back and my hands, it shouldn't fall."

"This is good, Jackson, I think we do look like two giant love birds. I'm about to be ravished against the wall. Just like in those old movies. If I had a big voluminous skirt, you'd just pull it up and have me right here against the wall. And then you would just walk off."

"Hush, Magnus that is disgusting. You're not my type."

"Nor are you mine, dear friend."

"It's ready Magnus. Let's make the transition. I'm going to grip my fingers around this one and let's drop down together while you pick up the replacement."

"Now that really will look romantic. Ready, set, go."

"Magnus, quickly take this and give me the fake. Thanks. Put the original in the bag, and I'll go up with this one and you crawl back between my arms and lean firmly against it. Ready, set, here I go."

"This is so exciting. Doesn't this feel good, Jackson? We're doing it. Well, we're not doing *it*, but we've just about done it. How long do we need to hold it? And, there's no one in sight. I only dreamed it would really be mine, but in a few minutes our mission will be complete. I can't thank you enough."

"Don't thank me until we're out of Italy with it. But this is a mighty good prank for two aging friends. We need about five minutes, so just shoot the breeze some more and we should be able to walk away."

"Well, Jacks, what do you think of Italy so far? And, are you still thinking of Bobbie Jo?"

"Italy is fantastic. I never dreamed that it would be this exciting. And, I am really liking Bobbie Jo. I think by the time we're in Rome, I'll ask her on some private outings and see if she's interested in me. We live quite a distance from each other back home, but if there's something there, I've decided that I'll make the road trips and see how this plays out. She's mentioned a grandson that she's raised; he's in prison right now. She talks like he was set up, but it sounds to me like he's a meth head. I can empathize with her, not wanting to face the truth. But who knows, maybe I can help make it all less painful."

"That all sounds good, Jackson, but I'm getting a cramp. These heels just don't give me the platform to sustain this pose for too long. Do you think we can test it?"

"I think it's been long enough. Release some of the pressure. Yeah, that feels secure. Why don't you gather everything in the bag and I'll pretend to lean against the wall propped with one hand. Yeah, with just one hand I don't feel any slippage. Once you get everything ready to go stand back up and just lean your shoulder on that side. Make sure that you've got everything in the bag. Don't leave any evidence."

"I've got it, my friend. I'll lean here as you remove your hand and I'll slide to the center. Double check after me when you're sure it's been long enough. We'll depart arm in arm with my bag."

"Magnus, I think we are good here. I'll hold the bag while you pull away. That looks fine. Act like you're distractingly touching it and move your hand firmly all around the edges. That's it. We're ready. Let's go."

Arm in arm we walk away. We've done it, I think to myself. I've never felt so exhilarated. Just as we round the corner of the piazza onto Via delle Oche, we hear a crash. Then silence. We quickly make our way back to the hotel. No one is in the lobby and we walk in with our heads bowed, like we're lost in our quiet conversation. We take the stairs rather rapidly and go to my room.

Once inside, we fall on the bed and start giggling like little girls. I jump up and throw off my shoes and jacket. I tell Jackson that I can't stay in this skirt a minute longer. He already has his jeans and plaid shirt in a bag in my room. I go to the bathroom and start removing all this get up. It's got to be tough on women, all this stuff, layers and layers of restricting clothes. Jackson yells that he's decent and I come out, of the bathroom that is. He's got the suit all stored in his bag to take back to his room.

"Thanks for the suit, man, I don't know when I will ever wear it back home, but I'm sure there will be funerals here and there," Jackson says.

"Or, maybe a wedding," I add. "Hey, do you think anyone will notice a fallen to pieces plaque in the piazza? I guess we didn't hold it long enough."

"I guess not. But, I don't think they will notice that it's a replica. I bet they will think that it's the original that for some unknown reason has crashed to the ground. They'll make another and replace it and that will be the end of it. And you, dear Mag, will have the bathroom décor of the century. Or do you say four centuries?"

"I know. I know. It's so great; I can't wait to put it up. I'll put all of our solutions into this plastic bag and throw them in a dumpster tomorrow. I'll wrap up my little prize and stow it away out of sight. Now, go on up to your room and let's get some sleep. I just hope that I can disguise my glow for the rest of the trip. I could never have done this without you, my friend, you just name it and I owe you."

I tidy up my room, putting away my 'Maggie' disguise. I wrap the plaque, the glorious plaque, in some sweatshirts that I brought and sandwich it between lots of layers in my hard body suitcase. I've got to protect this baby.
I put the solutions into a plastic shopping bag that I got from the fruit market in Milan. Once I'm sure that everything is secure and out of sight, I flip off the light and jump in the bed. I fall asleep with a smile on my face.

Chapter Thirty-Three
THE MORNING AFTER

Whew, all my intrigue last night has left me a bit groggy this morning. What time is it anyway? I promised Daphne that I would be downstairs at eight o'clock. Fine, seven-thirty, plenty of time for a shower and a hair fix. Same routine, different day; today's agenda is a city tour of Michelangelo's art. My sister and Bobbie Jo are excited about it; me and Nino could care less. I'm not sure what the others think.

I find my way downstairs and am surprised that everyone is gathered around the tables. All discussion is about what a good night sleep everyone had. I glance at Vittorio and he looks a little pissed about something. I will be glad when we go to Rome and hopefully he takes himself back to Milan. I say it's time for Roni to find herself another boy toy. I'll have to be on the lookout and maybe I can spot her one. Georgette and Hudson say they are seeing the city on their own today. Sebastian says he might tag along a while before working this afternoon. He confirms dinner plans with Nino. Nino agrees to text him with the time and place. He's even suggesting a gastronomy tour with Nino as the guide. A European trip of eating, now that is something that I bet even has Nino excited.

Jackson, Magnus, and Bobbie Jo want to see the Masterpiece tour with Daphne today. Me and Nino will follow at a leisurely distance, just doing window shopping and eating shopping. We'll be in charge of coffees and gelatos. Once all the plans are settled, Vittorio decides that he should see these sites too. Roni agrees, citing her art benefits back home for the Children's Hospital as inspiration for seeing the originals. Great, copycat cop noir on my trail again.

As we're finishing up our coffee, our hostess, Bianca, comes in and turns on the television to the local morning news. There seems to be some kind of hype about stealing a plaque or destruction of a plaque or something. I'm glad I don't speak Italian, as they are blabbering back and forth and using all kinds of hand gestures. Whatever it is, they seem to be really upset about it. Suddenly, Vittorio jumps up and excuses himself, saying he may not see us today after all. He is almost running out of the breakfast area. Magnus and Jackson are glued to the television, asking Nino what they are saying.

"It's something about an old plaque in one of the Piazzas. It seems to be pretty historic, and they are discussing what would have made it just fall off the wall. See, they are showing it lying in pieces on the cobblestones. But, wait; now they are saying that it is a fake as there are English markings on the back. There are some numbers written in inches on the back and since they've always used metric here, they are investigating it as a possible theft gone wrong."

"Well, that is just stupid, who would want a plaque that they can't even read? Americans and British people wouldn't want something like that. What did it say anyway?" I ask.

"Shhh, I can't hear them. The expert there says that it says, loosely translated, 'Playing with balls and other games are not permitted in this place,'" Nino translates.

"Stupid. They'd better not go blaming that on Americans, too. Everyone already hates us for God only knows," I continue to complain.

"Andi, what did I tell you about using God's name in vain like that? You'll go to hell, girl. Now just stop it and pray forgiveness. I pray for you every night. I know you try to be good, but you've got to try harder. You know being a good person is not enough; you've got to be saved. You know what John 3:16 says, 'for God so loved the world, that he gave his only begotten Son, that whosoever believeth in him should not perish, but have everlasting life,'" Bobbie Jo preaches.

"Good God, Jackson, you think there's something there; you'd better put on your HolyRollin Pants," I tell him.

We talk about God and theft and crazy Italians and plaques and balls for another hour. Georgette and Hudson take their leave— straight to the room I think. Sebastian says he'll make some early business calls and leaves us.

Upon that, Vittorio rushes back in, accompanied by the local Carabinieri. "Wait one minute, no one leaves this room. Daphne, please ask Georgette and Hudson to return immediately. The police have questions for all of you."

"What?" Roni exclaims. "What do you mean, questions? Are you working here or are you with me?"

Smiling, he whispers to her, "Honey, you know I am here with you. I just went down to ask about this, and when they knew I was with Americans they asked me to assist them with some questions."

"Fine, but I don't appreciate being implicated in some juvenile mischief of taking a sign. This is ridiculous. Just order a new sign for goodness sake, it is not a big deal," Roni complains.

"I agree, amore mio, this will be quick and we can go on with our day," he encourages her.

We are all questioned about our whereabouts last night. There is talk about a couple being seen prior to the plaque removal. They explain that they intend to question every known British or American tourist and that we will not be bothered unless necessary after the questioning.

Well, our only couples are Daphne and Nino and Georgette and Hudson. Maybe, it is Georgette and Hudson as they are highly educated in the arts. Not that this is art, it's not like they stole a famous artwork, this is a sign for heaven's sake. Or maybe, it's Roni and Vitorrio. Maybe I should tell the Carabinieri about his snooping around and strange behavior.

That's it. He's following us and watching us. Or he's following just me. No, it can't be just me. What connects him to us? When did he come in contact with us? With Roni? Oh yeah, in Milan. Everyone was with Mr. Brevonni except me, Daphne, Bobbie Jo, and Jackson. Yeah, and that's when that crucifix was stolen from the little chapel next to the restaurant where they had lunch. They suspected Roni, Sebastian and Magnus. Then he hooked up with Roni. She was his ticket to follow us. Well, that is just fine, we didn't do anything. Let him work his teeny Italian butt off trying to catch us doing wrong.

We are each questioned and our whereabouts confirmed. It is explained that Magnus drank wine and passed out for the night. This explanation included some YouTube views that prove his inability to hold his liquor. And since Vittorio himself was witness to his drinking, he was cleared. Only I left the hotel, and thank goodness that Vittorio followed me around, so he knows that I wasn't involved. The Carabinieri leave, and Vittorio explains to Roni that he must assist with the investigation and will meet with us again at dinner. That low-life, piece of scum, dirt-bag, son of a gun, I hope he finds the real culprits.

Daphne promptly resumes her role as tour guide and hands us tickets for a local tour of Michelangelo. We will learn about his famous David and see the original. The tour includes his Bacchus and the Tondo Pitti. Our guide will give us the history of Santa Croce, where he is buried. We will conclude with the Gallery of the Academy. I expect this tour might even interest me and Nino because there will be a certified expert tour guide giving us details that surely Daphne doesn't even know. This tour is expected to last for at least three hours.

We lunch at another pizzeria across the Arno on Via Maggio. It is superb. I eat a whole pizza by myself. After lunch we take the famous Ponte Vecchio crossing. It is the oldest bridge in Florence, last rebuilt in 1345 and it has housed businesses since the 13th century. The Medici built a private bridge atop of the goldsmith's shops to allow passage of the river to their new palace without exposing themselves to contact with the commonfolk. It is the only bridge that the Germans did not destroy as they retreated from the city during World War II.

Our little troupe continues to walk the streets, stopping at interesting sites along the way. I like this freestyle touring. This is much better, in my opinion, than all that planned stuff. Daphne has always overplanned everything. We wile away the afternoon like this, stopping for gelato twice. Exhausted, we arrive back at the hotel around four. Nino asks everyone to be in the lobby at eight for our dinner gathering. He promises another enchanting evening.

Me, Magnus, Bobbie Jo and Jackson meet in my room. Bobbie Jo is still frightened that Magnus's gender preference will put her in a bad light with God, but she is trying, I have to give her that. We all find a slouching spot and talk about everything. The guys seem to be preoccupied with the plaque theft. I suddenly remember the other night when we sat in the square for over an hour while Magnus kept looking at that plaque and all the other strange things that Magnus has been doing for the past six months. No, it couldn't be. I will not even ask him. It is all coincidence, isn't it? It must be. He'd tell me about something like this. I know he would. We've shared everything for years.

It's soon time for dinner and we all agree to freshen up and meet downstairs. I don't really know what freshen up means. Most girls will redo their hair and maybe change clothes. Not me. If I'm stinky, I will take a bath, but otherwise, the face and hair that I have at eight PM are the same face and hair that I had at eight AM. I'm ready.

Wine in hand, it seems that most of our group have met at the lobby bar early and are having a pre-dinner drink. I'm sure there's a fancy Italian word for that, but I don't know it. Nino tells everyone to finish up and that if we're late, we will lose our reservation. We walk out of the hotel and across the street to Piazza di San Giovanni. Our restaurant is right there.

Wow! That's all I can say. Another small, historic restaurant, complete with vaulted ceilings and tiled floor. Beautiful stairways flow into the brick vaulted rooms with terra cotta tiles. The walls are faded beige with half wood paneling. There are dark heavy wood furnishings and finely dressed tables with white linens. Pictures of famous people cover the walls. We're quickly seated, and the wine is poured.

The menu is endless, though there appears to be a *menu degustazione*, which is what I want. It is the chef's sampling of five courses. I'm taking that. Everyone orders something different. The wine starts to flow more freely and the first courses are brought to our table. We work our way through all the courses, flushing it with lots of wine.

"Hey sister, remember the time at that BarBQue place up in Decatur, was it? Remember, I ate so much that I had to unzip my pants. Lord, have mercy, do you think they have a vomitorium here? I don't know about y'all, but I'm going to take my newly looking Buddha Belly to my room and go to bed," I tell them.

Bobbie Jo looks at me with concern and says, "Now Andi, I've been witnessing to you before about these far

Eastern religions. You know my heart is burdened for you. If you don't get your heart right with the Lord, you're gonna spend your eternity in hell. You know there's only one path to salvation, and that's through the blood of Jesus Christ, not through Buddha."

"Just as they had wine at the last supper, and I think I ate all of the last supper. Here, you have some wine Bobbie Jo. I can't hold another swalla. Jesus drank it, so it's ok. And I only said Buddha because he had a fat belly and of all the Jesus art that I've seen today, he looked pretty skinny," I tell her as I turn sideways to exhibit the aforesaid belly.

At this point Magnus has a shit-eating grin on his face, and I look at him and curl my lip and say, "Bobbie Jo, do you know that Magnus has not met your Christ Jesus, or Jesus Christ, now which is it? I can't remember which it is."

With Magnus giving me the 'we're both going to hell' look, I get up and waddle back to my own hell of indigestion and TUMS.

The group settles up and follows me back to the hotel. I hear Bobbie Jo telling Jackson that she is going to see my soul saved if it's the last thing she ever does.

Great. Dammit to hell. Hell's Bells. Shit fire, Son of a Bitch, why does she have to do this? I'm not a bad person, I'm not. I believe in God, I just don't believe that he's going to send me to hell for not believing what Bobbie Jo is telling my ass.

So, filled with venomous rage at being called out for being less than the perfect Christian, I spew out my frustration at all of them, including my sister with this last word of advice. "I hope y'all studied your history packets, because I'm here to tell you that tomorrow is a Vatican kind of day. And Daphne will have more useless information for you all, and you'll be expected to be enthusiastic about it. And I swear to you, Bobbie Jo, if you say a word to me about God I'm gonna bitch-slap you, because I'm not in the mood. I have seen 'The Borgias,' I've seen 'DaVinci,' I've seen all the cable series of how the church dominates information. That's why all you blind Bible believers don't know stuff, because all the hidden knowledge is locked up in the Vatican basement, so y'all's minds can be brainwashed into believing only what they want you to believe. And you, Vittorio, I'm sick to hell of you following me around. I don't give a rat's ass that I'm part of this company and I shouldn't be cussing you out, but I know you been following me and I don't know what your problem is. And, furthermore, Roni, you need to find you another boytoy, because this one ain't about you, there's something fishy about him. I've caught him following me and Magnus and Jackson and I wish to God that he'd start following Bobbie Jo, so that when she faints her Holy Ass self, and busts her Holy Ass head, then he can pick her up, because she damn sure don't appreciate me protecting her Holy Ass self. And sister, let me just tell you a few things while I'm at it. Shut yo damn mouth. I know what you're thinking, but she crossed the line. I know that I've crossed the line, but I can only handle so much God in a day. I know that you're disappointed that I'm going off on our customers……"

I see Daphne with her mouth agape and her hand holding her chest, as I clear the foam from my mouth. She may really just about be having herself a serious heart attack.

"And you, Nino von Hohenfeld—er upper. I've got a few damn things for you, too. You want to rumble, come on. You want a piece of this? And Georgette and Hudsey, I can't say nothing bad about y'all because you've kept your horny little asses in the room, not bothering nobody."

I can see Magnus out of the corner of my eye, with his big-ass left hand about to clamp over my mouth. And then I feel his big-ass right arm against the back of my knees, and all the world seems to spin as I am tossed up with my Buddha belly landing against his shoulder. "Magnus, I swear to God that if you don't put me down, I'm going to throw up the entire contents of this big ass Buddha belly all over the back of this fine red silk Italian shirt…"

Before I finish my threat, I am heaved onto the pavement. As my ass hits the pavement, I let out the biggest fart of my life. Me and Magnus and all the crowd bust out with laughter. Magnus leans over and quietly says, "Now look here, my little soulmate, you know that I love you no matter what, but you need to calm your little ass down. While everybody knows that everything you said was accurate, did you really have to say it? Did you really have to go off? And if I hurt you when I threw you down, it's your own damn fault, because you don't threaten my silk. You did quite a bit of preachin' yourself there. You don't have anymore right to be judging others than they do to be judging you."

Magnus turns to the group and explains, "Please accept my apology for my friend. But she's had a little too much to drink and a little too much to eat and not only is she tired, which makes her cranky, but she's awfully gaseous, which always makes her combustible. It will all be better tomorrow, and she'll feel guilty and apologize to everyone. Actually, this usually occurs on day three, so she's made it longer than normal. I should have been watching her a little more closely. And Daphne, up in your room, why don't you find you a little 'sedative' and get you some rest. You really need it. It's been a busier trip than normal, and I know how stressed y'all get. It will all be better tomorrow. Now off to bed with all of you."

Chapter Thirty-Four

Roaming the Ruins

We are slow to awaken on the morning of our departure for Rome. Nino has asked us all to have our bags ready for loading at eight. Once loaded, we meet downstairs for coffee and a light breakfast. Everyone seems in a good mood. Maybe Bobbie Jo is preached out and Vittorio is copped out and Sebastian is businessed out and the newlywed love birds are you-know-what out and I'm bitched out. It's a quiet, subdued group that we are this morning.

We check out and load up. Roni and Vittorio plan to meet us in Rome. They are driving down in Vittorio's Alpha Romeo Spider. Vittorio didn't want to ride with us. So, here we are again. Georgette and Hudson are cuddled up in the back. I run to the back with them as fast as I could. I plan to sleep all the way. I just hope that Daphne thinks she left me at the hotel and doesn't bother with thinking of talking to me. Magnus, Bobbie Jo, and Jackson are on the middle row. Daphne and Nino are alone up front. This is liable to be the most boring drive of our trip.

It's been thirty minutes now, and we haven't found our way out of Florence yet. Nino is cussing, and Daphne is fussing. The middle row is conversing about everything under the sun. Our back row is sleeping or pretending to sleep. I just want us to get on the Autostrada. I'll just close my eyes again and hope for the best. Maybe I'll do as Bobbie Jo always says and pray that Nino happens on the correct little tangled road that leads him out of here. And this is Florence traffic. Rome is way worse, so I'm dreading that for sure.

I wake up and am glad to see that we are on the Autostrada. I'm not sure where we are, but I'll quietly check the GPS on my phone and not say a word back here. Yeah, I feel a little bad about not helping Nino get out of Florence with my GPS, but getting lost and wasting a few hours was better than listening to them argue about directions. I sure didn't want to get caught in the middle of that.

Everyone is laughing and talking about Erich. Erich is my great-nephew. He is Daphne's grandson, Sophie's third son. He's in kindergarten now. Daphne must have got another text or phone call. "Daphne, what are you saying about Erich?"

Daphne laughingly replies, "Well, I just got a call from Sophie. She said that Erich had to go to the principal's office yesterday because he got in trouble for talking and not sitting down. The principal asked him why he didn't sit down and stay quiet. He told her that God was on the phone talking and must have been too busy to tell him to sit down and be quiet."

"Well now, Bobbie Jo, why are you keeping God tied up on the phone all the time, trying to save my soul?" I ask, with a smirk on my face.

"Now Andi, I'm prayed up and ready for you today. I am not going to get into it with you. I'm going to be happy and drown you with love. That's all you'll get out of me."

"Well now, praise God for that," I tell her.

"You took you a good long nap, Andi," said Daphne. "We're almost to Rome. Do you have a road finder thingie on your phone? Can you crawl up here and help us get to the hotel?"

Well, shit. Why did I ever even open my damn mouth? "Sure, sister. Here I come."

I climb over two seats and find myself sitting between Nino and Daphne. I recognize immediately that this is a precarious position for me, but what can I do? I'll just get us there as quickly as possible. Our hotel is on the Via dei Serpenti, a road leading right into the Colosseum. You can see it right from our hotel door. GPS is wonderful. Even in Rome traffic, we got here without a single wrong turn. There is no parking though, as usual. Nino pulls up on the curb like all Italian drivers do, while me and Daphne go and check in. We're again given a handful of keys, and the receptionist goes out to direct Nino on where to park. Everyone unloads and brings their luggage in. Nino and Magnus leave to park the van.

In a flash, everyone is inside with us and the handful of keys. Hands are flying everywhere, grabbing and reaching. In less than thirty seconds, me and Daphne are left holding three keys again. It's a little late to run now. Everyone has their luggage and is gone. We drag our luggage over to an elevator, which is equal to the tiny one at our Florence hotel. I'm beginning to understand why Nino prefers to stay in Hiltons and other Western Hotels. The amenities there are the same as in the States. An elevator is an elevator. A bathroom is a bathroom. There are no surprises. But no, Daphne insists on the 'real' foreign experience, elevators and bathrooms and all. Anyway, we load up the elevator and send up our luggage. Daphne awaits our luggage on the third floor. After I press the elevator button, I take the stairs and am able to beat the elevator, even at my age and weight; I'm faster than that tiny old little elevator.

Me and Daphne unload the luggage and leave it in the hall while we investigate the rooms. Damn luck. One room has a small full size bed and overlooks an alley filled with trashcans and garbage. Another room has another small full size bed and overlooks a narrow little road with apartments with laundry hanging on the balcony. The last room has a single bed and is smaller than most closets. There are a toilet and sink in the room, and a showerhead without a curtain or enclosed area. And guess whose room this one will be? I guess I can sit on the toilet and pee and poop at the same time that I shower. Daphne and Magnus can fight between the other two prime rooms. I hope the other rooms are better than this or there is going to be some mad folks.

We drag our suitcases into our rooms, all on the third floor. I don't hear anyone else, so I suppose they are all on other floors. That's good, because they won't see just how bad our rooms are. Nino and Mag arrive just after we finish the hard labor. Nino is pissed that we've got crappy rooms. Mag is easy and doesn't even care, he just wants a bed. Nino tells us that they found a family run trattoria just around the corner and are ready to eat. Yeah! Let's eat.

I run down to the second floor and find everyone coming out of their rooms. I ask them all what they think about the rooms. Everyone agrees that they are perfect. Each room apparently has a view of the Colosseum. Each room is apparently large with a nice bathroom. Each room has a large bed. Yep, that is the way it goes. How is it that this happens to me so often? Maybe the next trip, I make the reservations and talk to the people and book my room separately from the tour. I tell them all that we're meeting downstairs to follow Nino to a restaurant if anyone is interested. I remind them that today is a free day, so they are on their own until tomorrow morning, or they can hang out with us.

Georgette and Hudson want to join us. The lovebirds must be hungry for something other than love, because even they want to hang with us now. So, we all proceed down to the lobby, and off we go. When we step outside, we turn left and see the Colosseum. Amazing! I can't imagine how it would feel to live here, looking at that every day. Nino quickly turns us around and we walk to the right and hang the first right. The little restaurant is on the right.

There are probably less than ten tables in the narrow little restaurant. They don't have a menu either. They just start bringing large bowls of salad and pasta and artichokes and eggplant. They offer water or wine, and the wine's cheaper. Within ten minutes we are digging into the best plain food that I've ever eaten. A few people start talking about how good this is, but I notice that Nino doesn't say a word, just eats and eats. After thirty minutes of eating, we sit back, and that must be some kind of signal, because three girls run in and clear our plates. Another girl comes out with a large sheet cake size pan of Tiramisu. The other girls bring out coffee and sugar and cream.

We then eat the best Tiramisu that I've ever had in my life. After another fifteen minutes, a little old Italian grandma figure emerges from the kitchen. She is maybe five feet tall, with a dark dress that reaches down to near her ankles, where I notice rolled knee high stockings. She wears an apron on which she is drying her hands. She asks us if we were pleased with dinner and we all sing her praises. When she gives us the bill we are shocked. All that food, all that delicious food for eight people for only eighty Euros; we gladly pay her a hundred. We walk away well fed and content.

Now the lovebirds want to go back to the room. Jackson and Bobbie Jo want to go walking toward the Colosseum and Forum. Me and Magnus agree to go as well. Nino and Daphne even want to go. We leave the restaurant and go left, take the next left and walk directly to the Colosseum. We walk for about fifteen minutes and cross a large four lane road and walk right up to the Colosseum.

Bobbie Jo and Jackson are unbelievable. They are holding hands and running toward the Colosseum. They look like young kids. They are walking around and we follow them. The Roman gladiator actors are out front talking to them and posing for pictures. Before I know it they are buying tickets and running inside. I guess they forgot about us. It's all right, I'd rather her be bothering Jackson than me. She needs to be practicing on saving Jackson's soul. They need the time alone. We stroll outside for a while and then get tickets to go inside.

Several people stop Magnus and talk about the Brevonni Man. We proceed through the Colosseum Tour and start walking through the Forum. Daphne pulls out her damn little book again and starts spewing off more blah, blah, blah bullshit. Where is the gelato? I'm out of this tour. Maybe gelato won't even work anymore. I need bread, olive oil and garlic, that's all. "Y'all continue on and enjoy every bit of this unique history lesson that only my sister can bring to life. I'm going over to that little market and bring us back some snacks. Oh, yeah, and by the way, I'm very sorry if I hurt anyone's feelings last night." I turn to walk away before anyone has the chance to speak. But I quietly mumble to myself, *'but if the foo shits....'*

I return with bread, cheese, salami, and two large bottles of water, one with gas and one without because I don't figure that I need any more gas. I've been gone for almost two hours, because I always say I'll be right back, but I never mean it. I've cruised several streets and I found the FedEx store for Magnus. I don't even know why he wanted to find FedEx, but he did. I found a fine leather shop where I bought a Bible cover for Bobbie Jo. I even found a tourist stand with a new history book that Daphne doesn't have, and I bought it for her.

When I arrive back, I see that my sister hasn't moved ten feet through history. They are standing at the very next monument from where I left them. "Daphne, now either you've managed by some miracle to surround yourself with four people who love history as much as you do, or else, you just need to move on," I tell her with all the kindness I can muster and nothing but love in my heart.

"And Nino, am I to believe that you've stayed with Daphne all this time?" I ask.

"Oh no, I had to find a toilet, so I left right after you and looked and looked, finally having to go back to the room. I got back just as you were walking up," he replies with an eat shit grin on his face.

"Well, I've brought back some things that I thought you would all like. Daphne, would you be so kind as to direct us to the House of the Vestal Virgins so we can eat our little snacks and I can show you what I've found?" I remember her story of Nino doing this before and it being the best thing that ever happened to her.

"Oh certainly," she says, and takes us down the hill and to some poles sticking up out of the ground.

And on the way, I know I heard at least five, *thank you, Andi*s; well, yeah, that was the least I could do. We all gather round, and Nino helps me pass out the bread and cheese and salami. I give Daphne the new little history book that I found. Bobbi Jo is thrilled with her little Bible cover. I tell Magnus that I found the FedEx office and I will only show him where it is if he promises not to mail me home. Magnus just smiles at me and winks. Jackson just eats.

Nino quietly adds, "Yeah, Magnus said she'd feel guilty. What else can you get us, Andi? I need some Italian hand-made gloves." He grins and says "Thanks."

We finish up our little picnic and decide to walk around until dinner time. Jackson wants to see the Spanish Steps. Magnus wants to go mail his dirty clothes home. I ask him if I can add some, that I've overpacked as usual and could benefit with the decreased baggage weight on our return flight. He says sure, and I'm about to walk back to the hotel to give them to him. Then I tell him to forget it, that I'm on my best behavior today and will not leave the group. I think it's odd, him mailing home a package to himself. He's never done that before. But, I guess with all the new Brevonni clothes, he does have too much stuff. He sure seems in a hurry to mail that package, though. I would have thought he would wait until tomorrow. He makes me tell him where the FedEx store is, and he flies out of here.

We all wander around town for hours. We've walked and found all the things we want to see tomorrow. Nino even got so tired of walking that he figured out how to ride the city bus. We also took a little tourist bus showing us the highlights of this ancient city.

Back at the hotel at seven, everyone is waiting for us. Nino again has found us an old historic restaurant in the Trastevere part of town. The interior is vaulted and heavy timbered and wears that old and worn appearance. We eat well and drink well and return to our hotel.

Daphne explains that tomorrow morning, after breakfast, we will tour the Vatican. She's arranged lunch this time at an old convent near the Vatican. The little café is in the room where the sisters held their morning and evening prayers. I bet that Bobbie Jo will like that. Daphne hands out flyers with options for tomorrow afternoon for different tours. Everyone is instructed to check their preference, if any, and she will make arrangements.

I ask Magnus if he wants to walk around town with me and have a coffee or something. We intentionally don't invite anyone else and, frankly, don't care what anyone else is doing. Sebastian has arrived late and goes straight to his room. Roni and Vittorio had dinner with us and Vittorio seemed to be giving me the eye. I am kinda sorry that I went off on him, but he still worries me.

We walk along, arm in arm, content to be alone at last during this vacation. I ask if he found the FedEx place, and he says that his package is by now safely in flight back home. He says he mailed it to the shop so that there will be someone there to receive it. He seems relieved, and I feel perplexed. How can dirty laundry be that stressful?

Sitting at a small outdoor café table, we watch the locals for an hour or so and then stroll to the Trevi Fountain and throw in our coins, finally meandering back to the hotel. He walks me to my room, and we plan to meet for breakfast at eight. I know Daphne will have the day packed full. I crawl into bed just thankful for family and friends, even if they are Daphne and Bobbie Jo.

Chapter Thirty-Five
ARGUMENTATIVE BREAKFAST

The breakfast room is filled with foreign conversations. I can hear German, English, French, Japanese, and even some Scottish accents which I should be able to understand but can't. Our group has occupied the tables at the back wall. Roni and Vittorrio are in the back with their noses in a newspaper. As Magnus and I approach, Vittorio asks that we sit across from him.

We grab our coffee and sit down. He shows us the newspaper from Rome with the article about the plaque theft. We see in the paper there is an artist sketch of the suspicious couple seen in the vicinity of the crime but as yet remain unidentified. Magnus looks at the picture and laughs, saying, "Whew, she looks tough. If I'd seen her, I would have went in the opposite direction. Hmm, that's a big hunk o' woman."

"Magnus, be nice," I say, thinking to myself that they look oddly familiar.

"So there are no leads? They don't know anything?" Magnus asks.

"No, they have nothing, and since it is not considered art theft, they have listed it as unsolved and filed it away. They do not have the resources to devote to this minor incident," explains Vittorio.

"Yeah," I say, "back home we have traffic cams. Don't y'all have any of those? What about YouTube, any hits on that? We put everything on YouTube. Anyway, what's the big deal? Isn't it just a street sign? It's not valuable, is it?"

336

"Cafone," Vittorio replies quietly, "No, we don't have traffic cameras, and we're not obsessed with seeing ourselves on the computer like you Americans. No, no, no, cafone, it is so much more than that. It is a piece of our history. This plaque was there for over two hundred years, and it represents our past in a way that we cherish and hold dear. Our city is ancient, and through time we have learned how to maintain order. That plaque, in that piazza, was an order from the city rulers that the area was not to be used as a ball field. Other business and activities were performed there. Ball play was permitted in another area. It was posted to maintain safety and organization in the city."

While he's rambling, I'm Googling 'cafone' and am appalled that he just called me 'trailer trash'. "First of all, Vittorio, I might be from the South, and I might have grown up in a trailer, but I ain't no trailer trash. Magnus and I both graduated from the University of Alabama, and thieving ain't my style, and it sure as hell ain't something that Magnus would do. Now, I admit, when I was young, I might have found that a challenge, but we're both in our fifties and we don't need to be stealing signs like some sixteen year olds."

"I know, I know, I know, that is why I asked you both to sit here. I wanted to have an honest conversation you. I've already explained everything to Roni with all this. And after your fit the other night, I would like to clear the air. I've been following you since Milan and I am thoroughly convinced that you people had nothing to do with it. I've cleared you as well from the art theft in Milan, I'm happy to say. What it would take to pull this off requires more intelligenza and cervelli than all of you have demonstrated."

"Magnus, why do I feel like we've been insulted?" I ask him.

"Andi, let it go, the man is trying to talk."

"Now, if you will all pardon me, I wish to spend time with Roni. I am off duty and very happy that she has allowed me to share her last day here in Italy. Again, Andi, I just wanted to apologize for following you and to let you know that you were correct in all of your ranting and ravings. I wish you two a very happy day." With that, Vittorio and Roni smile and leave the hotel for a day of their own planning.

"Magnus, wait until I tell you all the times I caught him following us. I caught him outside your bedroom door once. I caught him following you and Jackson two different times. I caught him following me twice. He was really creeping me out. I'm glad he's gone, but I'm a little pissed that he thinks we're not smart enough to take a sign if we wanted to. In fact, now that I give it some thought, I guess I'm twice-pissed. I'm also pissed that he ever thought we would have stolen a sign. I have a good mind to go steal a damn sign."

"Andi, let it go."

"Well, Magnus, what makes you act like you do? You don't seemed offended at all that we were more or less called stupid, ignorant, thieves, and trailer trash in the same sentence."

"Andi, it's over. Why can't you just let it go away? Don't get yourself all worked up; it's our last day. All the weirdness and pissitivity is gone, almost like it's packed up and over with."

"Damn it Magnus, I know that you're trying to pick me up and make it all better and I was receptive to that, but look who's coming. It's Daphne and her damned excited, happy self ready to drag me up some more stupid stairs today."

"Forget it, Andi," Daphne says. "I didn't deserve that. I'm tired of your bitchin' and your snapiness. You

338

don't have to go anywhere with me today. You can stay right here in this hotel by yourself all day. In fact, that's probably best. We all might have the best day yet, without your whiny ass with us."

"You're right, Daphne, I'm sorry, you didn't deserve that. I apologize and would you like me to go get you some coffee while I tell you this stupid ass conversation that we just had with Vittorio?"

"Andi, you can tell me anything you want as long as you don't use that bitchy tone that you picked up in Milan and have carried all over Italy and haven't yet laid down."

Jackson and Bobbie Jo arrive to witness me and Daphne having a little kitty-cat fight. "And, how is everyone doing this beautiful God-given morning? I'm so excited to be going to the Vatican today. I'm going to see the Sistine Chapel. Never in my life did I imagine that little ol' me from a little town in Alabama would get to see the Vatican. I read about it all night, and I'm planning to be there all day. I'm going to see St. Peter's Tomb, St Peter's Square and Basilica, the Swiss Guards, the Gardens, and all the artwork inside," Bobbie Jo rambles.

"Please y'all, in the name of Jesus, please just sit down. I have something very important to tell you," I beg. Everyone sits and huddles into our little corner. I revisit the whole story, justifying that I was right all along and that Vittorio was following us and thought we were thieves until he decided that we are a bunch of simpletons from Alabama and could not have possibly been smart enough to pull off a sophisticated heist. As I explain, I keep noticing Jackson and Magnus sharing glances and nods and I even thought I saw Jackson wink at Magnus.

This whole story doesn't seem to infuriate anyone other than me. I don't know what the hell is wrong. Maybe my hormone patch isn't working and needs some dosing adjustment or maybe I just have a hard time letting insults go, as Magnus says. Because, by God, I still feel insulted. He had a lot of damn nerve, accusing my soul-mate Magnus of such an immoral, unethical thing. But, why am I mad? Magnus doesn't seem to care and Jackson don't seem to give a shit. OK, that's it; I'm letting it go right now, dammit.

Daphne jumps right into my pondering and heads us outside, explaining to everyone their arrangements for the day. Our little Vatican group includes everyone, so she's scheduled a pick up and return ride for us with private transportation. We load up and are delivered just outside St. Peter's Square.

The immediate awe from everyone that hasn't seen this spectacular site is emotional. It's all we can do to pull them up the long square and into one of the largest and most renowned churches in the world. Bobbie Jo startles me, as she is the first one anxiously urging us into the building. However, once inside, she again freezes. Even Jackson is frozen in admiration. And for once I can see why. We are all moved over to the side by an usher that realizes that we are blocking the way. Magnus, Nino, Daphne, Jackson, Bobbie Jo, and me are each reverently captured by the scene in front of us.

It's a large open expanse of the most Holy place that I've ever seen, and I've seen a lot of them, and I've seen this place several times, but it's never looked like this. There is light marble everywhere, floor to ceiling, reflecting the most subtle gold that I've ever seen descending like a soft fog lazily floating to the floor, reflected by the white tiles. It's glorious, nothing short of glorious.

After twenty minutes of reverent appreciation, we all sluggishly drift in several different directions. Bobbie Jo and Jackson seem to have solidified their coupleship.

Daphne has wandered off alone, which is probably best. Nino, Magnus, and I just roam without a destination. We agreed before we entered that should we become separated we would meet at the Obelisk at one o'clock for our lunch appointment at one-thirty. Needless to say, the Basilica keeps us inside until the last minute.

As Magnus, Nino and I near the door at one o'clock, Daphne reaches us, out of breath, telling us to come with her, that Bobbie Jo needs us. Crap, I forgot about Bobbie Jo. If she is hurt, I will never forgive myself. We follow Daphne over to a side altar, where Bobbie Jo is in tears on her knees. Jackson is smiling, with a few tears on his cheeks. I run to her and holding up her face, check her forehead. No bruises, no cuts, no blood, so why the tears and why the smiles.

She reaches for my hands and looks in my eyes, as Jackson kneels down beside her and wraps his arms around her. She starts a long, soft discourse of what she has just experienced. "Andi, I am so sorry to have judged you and Magnus and the entire world like I have. I had convinced myself that what I thought I had was religion. Things you said the other night convicted me and have weighed heavy on my mind. Once I got here, I was truly touched by a God that I did not have a relationship with. I have been in this little chapel for an hour. God has revealed my flawed, quite unholy, behaviors. I have been so wrong. It is not my place to judge and enforce his rules. It is my mission to love in an unjudgmental way. That is all, love. God has the job of the hard stuff. I feel so light and at peace. I love you. I love Magnus. I love you all, accepting flaws without judgment, which is what I have learned here."

As we help her up, we are all crying. We exchange hugs and I love yous and tears and slowly make our way outside. We meet the others at the Obelisk and silently walk to "Sorella's Cucina." Once inside, we are seated at a very plain table in a very plain room. The essence here is anything but plain—it is simple and serene.

We order from a farm fresh menu and enjoy a light little lunch. Bobbie Jo shares her new birth experience with everyone, and the atmosphere becomes joyous and light. We spend an hour with the 'sisters' and ask for our bill. They bring us separate checks and as I'm sitting beside Bobbie Jo, I am shocked that her bill is 30 Euros. She can't afford 30 Euros. I stop the waitress and ask about her bill, saying that is way too much, is she sure that it is right. Bobbie Jo, grabs my hand and tells me, "Andi, I appreciate your help and 30 Euros is a lot of money, but right here, right now, in this Holy place, it is really worth more than that, and I'll happily pay that bill."

Wow, I really, really, love this new Bobbie Jo. We make our way back to the Basilica and find our way to the line for the Sistine Chapel. Our entry ticket is for two-thirty, and we are ready. I've never been with a happier, better group than this. As we are led by our knowledgeable tour guide through the history of the papal buildings, we are again touched by the spiritualism of this place.

The art of the Sistine Chapel is magnificent. Thousands of words can't adequately describe it. Breathtaking, of course, since I don't think that any of us have spoken or breathed since we entered the room. We spend our allotted fifteen or twenty minutes with our necks bent backwards and eyes never leaving the ceiling.

We are then ushered on into other areas of the palace. Our tour guide does a great job, providing lots of detail that we would never have known. Another hour passes and we finally leave the palace and exit outside, finding our way to the Obelisk meeting point again.

We meet our transportation at five o'clock, and it's a melancholy ride back to the hotel. For the first time, we are quiet. Nino has left everyone's dinner plans to themselves. We plan to go upstairs and pack up for our early morning flight. Once packed, I'll see who wants to go with me for a last night out.

It only takes me thirty minutes and I'm done. I go to Daphne's room and Nino has it all organized and nearly complete. "Do you guys want to meet me downstairs in an hour and we'll grab a bite?" I ask them.

"Sure," Nino says. I'm hungry and ready for my last Italian meal.

I knock on Mag's door, and he comes out asking if I'm ready to stroll around the town on our last night. I tell him sure, give me thirty minutes to check with the others. He agrees to come with me, and we go to Bobbie Jo and Jackson's rooms. They both agree and will meet us downstairs. Georgette and Hudson say they want to join us as well. Vittorio opens Roni's door and says that he would enjoy some time with us all. Lastly, we find Sebastian's room and knock. Sebastian peeks out of his door and says that he is entertaining and will see us tomorrow morning for the shuttle to the airport.

My, what a conclusion to a week with strangers; we have somehow formed a cohesive group of friends. What an adventure. I'm so happy. My bitchy bitch is gone. We go downstairs and await the gang.

Once our group is complete, we leave the hotel, and Nino takes a right and another right and goes to the little family restaurant on the right. The little grannie comes out to meet and seat us, pleased that we have chosen to dine with her again tonight. It is simple and great and relaxed. What a perfect last meal in this great country. Everyone is cordial and laughs and toasts and laughs some more. We spend two hours here, content in each other's company.

After we finally wander outside, we decide as a group, to walk to the Pantheon and then to the Trevi Fountain. It couldn't be better. The dusk, then the nightfall, the lights, the sights, the friends; it has never been better than this.

Exhausted, we sadly make our way back to the hotel, aware that after this night the magic that we've just discovered will likely fade. This discovery is nothing new to me. After a week, a group of strangers become friends. But never before do I recall the closeness that has developed here with these people. I am pretty confident that when we return home, the relationships will continue.

We all return to our rooms, quiet and yet content. It's an early morning call tomorrow. The shuttle arrives at seven, and we're to be at the airport by eight for our ten-thirty flight.

The flight is eventless. We are all exhausted and seemed to have accepted that we must pass into the last phase of this trip, separation and resumption of our lives. We are all so different and travel in differing circles. It will require effort to stay in touch, but we will I am sure.

Chapter Thirty-Six
BACK HOME

"Andi, did you mail all the invitations?" Magnus asks me.

"Of course, I did, what do you take me for, a slacker?" I ask. Dammit, I'd better make an excuse to get out of this shop before the mail runs and drop those off at the post office.

"My heart, you are the biggest slacker that I know. Where are they, in your car? We've been home for two weeks, and it is important for me to let the group know that I consider them friends and want to cook a meal for them. And, guess what I'm cooking? Oh, I'll just tell you: Wienerschnitzel and Pommes Frites and Cucumber Salad and Black Forest Cake. Do you think they will get the theme?"

"How did you know that? Are you psychic? Yes, they're in my car. But since you know, I'll leave right now and take them to the post office. Why couldn't you have used the computer like everyone else and just sent an email? And yeah, I get it; German food must mean a Germany trip. What have you and Daphne got planned? Why doesn't my sister tell me about our trips? I'm her travel partner."

"Me and Nino have talked, not Daphne. We want to go to the Christmas Markets again and drink Gluhwein, strolling the medieval streets in winter. So this time, it's me and him planning a trip. And maybe, if you and Daphne promise to behave, we'll consider letting you go with us. And to answer your first question, I wanted to host a formal dinner for the best travel group that I've known and offer them first dibs on this trip. And because this is a formal event, I want it done right. I want everyone to know that I thought them special enough to receive a handwritten invitation to my home next week. They should have been mailed three days ago. I should have known that I couldn't entrust you with this important task. Now go, get down there and get them in the mail. People need time to sort out their calendar and make their plans."

"Fine, I'm out of here. And maybe I'll accept your invitation, or maybe I'll be busy that night. And maybe I'll go to Germany this Christmas without you. How about that?"

"Andi, we both know that you are coming with me, now go."

A few days later, I call Daphne and ask her if she's heard about the trip. She said yeah, that's all that Nino is talking about. He's planning the cities and the sites and the restaurants already. We laugh and decide that this time, we'll let the boys be in charge, and we'll go along for the ride and not have any responsibilities.

The day before the dinner, Nino calls me from Rock Holler and asks if I can go by our local liquor store and pick up the German wines and beers that he's ordered. I agree and ask if there is anything else I can do. He tells me to go to the costume store and get a dirndl costume for our little Octoberfest and pull out all of our German beer steins and mugs. He adds that I might need to buy two outfits and some push-up bras for me and Daphne so we can be servers that night. LOL, right.

I pick up the booze and take it home. I'm glad this thing is not at my house. I should check with Magnus and ask if he needs my help to cook, but I'm sure that he will refuse. I'll call him anyway.

"Oh, naw, Andi, don't come in my kitchen. You'll create a disaster, I just know it. And guess what? Everyone is coming, except Vittorio, thank God. Even Sebastian is coming. And, speaking of Sebastian, he tells me that he's received the first shipment of the Brevonni line and asks if I can come down for their 'Brevonni Opening Night'. Isn't that a hoot? I told him sure, if I could wear my flannel lumberjack shirt and overalls. I was kidding but he starts referencing the contract with Brevonni, which states that all my appearances will be in Brevonni clothes. He's nuts, I don't even have a flannel shirt or overalls. Very funny, huh?"

"That is funny, Mag. Well, if there is nothing that I can do to help, then I'll see you tomorrow night. Daphne and Nino and Bobbie Jo are driving to my house, so once they are here, we'll walk over."

Chapter Thirty-Seven
DINNER WITH MAGNUS AGAIN

It's cool and crisp on this late October night. I'm anxious to see everyone. Sister and Nino and Bobbie Jo should arrive any minute. I've already opened up Nino's German wine and am on my second glass. The doorbell rings and in walks Daphne and the others. Hugs and kisses abound, and I pour everyone some wine. Even Bobbie Jo asks for a small glass. Nino pulls out a box of printed travel brochures for a Christmas Market trip to Germany. They look great. Damn, he did a good job. If I didn't know that I wanted to go, I would want to go. These are high gloss, color, enchanting brochures. He may put me and Daphne out of business. We gather up our things and head over to Magnus's.

Magnus is busy in his kitchen, laying out dishes and setting the table. He has everything ready, and it looks fabulous. Gosh, he is really talented. And the smell, it's like I just walked into the Weinstube and can smell the battered pork frying and sizzling in the kitchen. A polka oozes from a swaying accordion somewhere in my mind. Yeah, I'm ready to go back to Germany. I'm sold.

Magnus refuses wine, preferring to be on his best, awake behavior while selling his trip to his new friends. A doorbell ring disturbs my mental wandering. I tell Magnus that I will get it, and I open the door to Jackson. Bobbie Jo runs to greet him, falling into his arms, and there is some serious kissing going on. Wow, Bobbie Jo, smooching it up, and she's wearing a nice blouse and sweater with some khaki pants and has a new hairstyle. She has undergone a radical change.

Before I move the lovers inside and off the street, another car arrives, and it's Roni. The three of us run out to the car to meet her. We all hug and exchange sincere greetings. Before we know it, Sebastian has crossed the street and has joined our team hug. This is really so very nice and comforting. It feels like a true reunion. I encourage them all inside. Magnus greets us with a serving tray of good German wine and beer assortments. At that very moment, Georgette and Hudson pull up in their SUV.

We're led by our noses to the table. Comfortably seated, we all chat and catch up while Nino and Magnus work the kitchen and then serve up the meal, without dirndl wear. It feels like a year since we've been together. We catch up on each other. Roni's been working her volunteer events and is mentioning wanting Magnus to join her for their Halloween fundraiser at Children's Hospital. Sebastian beams with pride in his advancement in the menswear world having secured the Brevonni Line in Alabama. Georgette and Hudson announce that they've just discovered that they're expecting a little one. Jackson and Bobby Jo, say they've got an announcement.

I hold my breath, not sure how much more shock that I can take. Jackson says that he and Bobbi Jo discussed this last weekend, but tonight they want to make it official. Jackson reaches into his pocket and drops to his knee beside her chair. He pulls out a radiant, sparkling, diamond solitaire the size of an M&M. Damn!

"Bobbie Jo, I know this is sudden, but I've never been more certain of anything in my life. I didn't realize that my life before two months ago was only an existence. I thought I was happy. I had my children and my business, but I didn't have a life. Once you wandered into my life, by mere chance, I now have fulfillment. You've brought me joy, love, and smiles, and returned to me a world of emotions that I had lost so gradually that I didn't even know to miss them. Now, I realize that I cannot live without this any longer. Will you honor me with the privilege of making sure your life is as joyous as I can make it? I promise you love, joy, and happiness for the rest of your life."

A tear of joy trickles down her sweet little cheek and she hugs him close and accepts his proposal with a mere, choked up sob.

We hoot and holler and carry on for ten minutes. Magnus finally insists that we sit and eat before our dinner gets cold. We eat with gusto, praising our cook and talking about the engagement.

Georgette excitedly tells them that she knows the perfect place for a wedding, and she believes it's close to where Bobbie Jo lives. She explains a beautiful botanical garden at the mountain's edge there at Rock Holler. I look at Daphne and our grin quickly erupts into obnoxious laughter. Everyone looks at us like we are crazy, and we are laughing so hard that we are in tears. We fail at several attempts to slow down enough to explain. Nino finally, without any fanfare at all, explains that the gardens border their property in Rock Holler and that during Georgette's wedding, Daphne and Andi drove themselves nuts using floppy white trash bags to pick up trash and toys and bicycle ramps and twirly things that were flying all over the yard to deter moles., and three old toilets were quickly hauled to the other side of the yard. He then dismisses it all and asks for second helpings on the schnitzel.

Georgette looks as us and busts out laughing too. "I always thought you two looked familiar but could never place you. That is hilarious! I had my binoculars and saw you two running around. I thought you people were crazy, and now I know that you are. I even realize that I'm crazy now. You guys must be contagious. Did you know that me and Hudson were signed up for your trip?"

"Yes, and we were worried to death that you'd find out that the redneck yard next to your wedding belonged to your travel agent," explains Daphne.

"Enough of that," announces Magnus. I'd like to take this opportunity to invite you all to join us for another trip." He passes out the brochures and they all express interest.

I have an idea, so I ask, "Bobbie Jo, when are you and Jackson planning your wedding? Maybe the trip could be your honeymoon. How about that? And by the way, I promise to help Daphne clean up her yard before the wedding if you want to get married in 'The Gardens'."

"Well, we have talked about it some and think that we'd like to marry during the Thanksgiving holiday. We are so thankful to have found each other and that would be an appropriate holiday for it," Bobbie Jo says.

"That sounds perfect. The trip would be a perfect honeymoon," I add.

"Yeah, except, honeymoons with this group certainly have permanent consequences," laughs Georgette.

I'm laughing so hard that my bladder is about to rupture. I excuse myself and run to the bathroom. I barely make it to the toilet and get my pants down in time. Thank goodness that this toilet has been kind enough to raise its lid for me. I get all comfortable and warm and listen to the music. Once past the initial relief, I relax into it and look around the room. I'm suddenly shocked right off of that toilet. 'What in the hell?' Right there in front of me on the wall opposite this toilet is *the plaque*. The damn stolen plaque from Florence is right in front of me. *Right in front of me!* I pull my pants up and leave the toilet to flush itself.

I run into the dining room and meet Magnus's grin. I can't contain myself as I scream, "You did it. You son of a bitch, you did it, didn't you? I defended you all through

Italy. I called Vittorio all kinds of names. You dog!"
Magnus continues to grin as everyone else runs to the
bathroom.

Dena Eskridge:

I love to go. I always have. My daddy always encouraged my going and my momma always tried to slow me down. My going won out and I've never stopped. I grew up in Alabama and have lived throughout the United States and Europe. I served as an Army nurse in Europe where I traveled every other week. Having completed a Masters in Nursing and furthering my appreciation of history, I continued to work so that I could travel even more. With an off-kilter sense of humor, I now write about funny but historically correct places to go.

Cindy A. Eskridge, LTC (R), US Army:

I am a retired US Army Lieutenant Colonel with over 22 years of military service. I served as a Battalion Commander in Afghanistan in support of Operation Enduring Freedom. My Bachelor's Degree is in Management of Human Resources and I am a graduate of Command and General Staff College. After retirement I was employed as a Project Manager working in Force Protection at various locations throughout Iraq. I am currently an Army JROTC Instructor in Alabama. Now I enjoy the simple pleasures in life like spending time with my family and friends and writing silly southern humor books with my sister.

Made in the USA
San Bernardino, CA
01 May 2014